brenda

Brenda
who lik

"Brend
with

"I will not be surprised when I see the name
Brenda Novak on the bestseller lists!"
—Detra Fitch, Huntress Book Reviews

"Brenda Novak skillfully blends richly developed
characters and emotionally intense issues
to create a powerful romance."
—Pamela Cohen, *Romantic Times*

Brenda Novak's books are "must-reads
for the hopeless romantics among us who
crave sweeping adventure, pulse-pounding reunions
and gloriously satisfying endings."
—bestselling author Merline Lovelace

Brenda Novak's "powerful storytelling voice"
provides "the novel with depth
seldom matched in this genre."
—Cindy Penn, WordWeaving

"One thing is for sure: I know I never,
ever want to miss a book by Brenda Novak."
—Suzanne Coleman, *The Belles and Beaux of Romance*

Dear Reader,

The research for this novel took me to the small desert town of Florence, Arizona, a unique place where seven prisons (including the juvenile detention center) dot the arid landscape. Atmospheric and intriguing, Florence still has the feel of the Old West, without the gimmicks and tourists that clog so many towns with similar roots. The Old Territorial Prison is there, as authentic and captivating as the town, from the Pauper's Graveyard behind the complex to the original cell blocks.

But this isn't a story about the town or the prison. Not really. It's about an innocent man stripped of everything he holds dear, a man left only with his character and his courage, and the woman who sees him for what he is. It's a story about a woman who is torn between justice and mercy, and ultimately follows her heart. I hope you enjoy their journey.

I'd love to hear from you. Please feel free to contact me at P.O. Box 3781, Citrus Heights, CA 95611. Or simply log on to my Web site at www.brendanovak.com to leave me an e-mail, check out my news and appearances page, or learn about my upcoming releases.

Best wishes,

Brenda Novak

TAKING
THE
HEAT

brenda novak

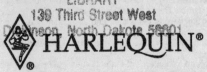

HARLEQUIN®

TORONTO • NEW YORK • LONDON
AMSTERDAM • PARIS • SYDNEY • HAMBURG
STOCKHOLM • ATHENS • TOKYO • MILAN • MADRID
PRAGUE • WARSAW • BUDAPEST • AUCKLAND

ISBN 0-373-83570-1

TAKING THE HEAT

This edition published by arrangement with Harlequin Books S.A.

® and TM are trademarks of the publisher. Trademarks indicated with
® are registered in the United States Patent and Trademark Office, the
Canadian Trade Marks Office and in other countries.

Visit us at www.eHarlequin.com

Printed in U.S.A.

To my third daughter, Alexa,
for possessing the purest heart I've ever known.
Alexa, you're always loving and remarkably kind,
quick to smile even when things don't go your way
and the first to sacrifice for others. I truly admire
your generosity. In short, you're a rare jewel
and a blessing to all who know you, especially your
mother. If you forget everything I've ever taught you,
remember this: my love is everlasting.

ACKNOWLEDGMENT

I owe special thanks to the state of Arizona's
Department of Corrections for their willingness to
provide me with a tour of the Arizona State Prison,
Florence. Rhonda Cole, Public Information Officer, and
Blaine Marshall, Deputy Warden, ASPC-Eyman/SMU II
were both more than kind and provided me with a
wealth of information. I would especially like to thank
Officer James A. Robideau, CO II, for the time he spent
reading this story when it was only in manuscript form
and double-checking my prison facts. Meeting these
wonderful people was truly a pleasure. They made
my trip to Arizona well worth the time.

I would also like to thank my husband, Ted, for his
support of my career. He's read every book I've written
and always gives me plenty of love and encouragement.

This is a work of fiction. I saw nothing at the prison
that would indicate corruption of any kind.

"The truth which is certain
is known by means of intuition,
the probable truth
by means of proofs."

James Beattie,
Scottish professor of moral philosophy

PROLOGUE

"DON'T WORRY, Mr. Tucker, it's almost over now."

Randall Tucker sat next to his attorney in the courtroom, feeling utterly alone, even though the gallery behind him was packed to overflowing. He prayed to God she was right. In all his thirty-two years he'd never experienced anything so confusing, so terrifying or so painful.

"They can't convict you without a body," she said, repeating what she'd told him the moment he hired her. "When the jury gets back, you'll see."

When the jury gets back...

They were sure taking a long time. They'd been deliberating all day, and every minute seemed like an eternity.

Regardless, it'll end well. They won't put an innocent man away. Truth and justice will prevail.

"I never touched her," he said, but he'd been saying that ever since his wife had gone missing, and it hadn't made any difference before.

His attorney smiled confidently. "You'll be home with your son in a few hours."

He might go home, but their lives would never be the same. Andrea wouldn't be there. They'd lost his wife, Landon's mother, and there'd be big adjustments to make—

The door opened and fear clutched at Tucker's throat

as the jury filed into the courtroom and resumed their seats. Their foreman, a tall, balding man with a dark mustache, remained standing.

"Have you reached a verdict?" the judge asked.

"Yes, Your Honor."

"Will you read the verdict, please?"

The man glanced nervously around the room, then looked down at the paper in his hand. "We the jury find the defendant, Randall C. Tucker—" he cleared his throat and peered at the judge, who nodded for him to continue "—guilty of the crime of murder in the first degree."

Guilty? The word hit Tucker like a crowbar to the gut, momentarily stunning him. Numbly, he tried to raise his hand to rub away the pain, but it was no good. His chest had constricted so tightly he couldn't breathe, couldn't move.

"But I'm innocent," he said, or maybe he only thought it. Someone was screaming inside his head, drowning out the chaos that erupted around him, drowning out his lawyer's soft, concerned words, blocking everything but the memory of his promise to Landon. *I'm not going anywhere, buddy. I won't leave you, I promise.*

And then the judge, his voice mere background noise until that moment, said something about reconvening for sentencing. Randall was pushed and prodded from the room. He spent the next few days in numb incredulity, caught in a nightmare he couldn't escape.

When he faced the white-haired Judge Forester again, the subtle contempt Tucker had sensed during the actual trial was more apparent. Forester said it was a sad commentary on the state of society that such a successful man as Randall would murder his wife in cold blood. He asked Randall to tell authorities where he'd hidden the body so Andrea's friends and family could receive some sense of closure. And he added his regret that the death penalty wasn't an option in this particular case. Then he said the words that echoed through Randall's soul.

"I hereby sentence the defendant, Randall C. Tucker, to prison for the rest of his natural life."

CHAPTER ONE

OH, GOD, a fight!

Gabrielle Hadley quickly turned off the bathroom faucet and sought a paper towel to dry her soapy hands as hoots and hollers resounded outside. What had started as a few distinct shouts was quickly growing into a loud roar that bounced off the prison's cinder-block walls. It was a sound she knew, a sound she feared.

"Not again," she moaned. "This is only my third day!"

Her heart in her throat, she tossed the wadded paper into the wastebasket and left the small corner rest room in the guards' station. Lunch break or no, she had to get out there and back up the other officers. And she'd probably have to wield her baton, as well, even though the thought of actually cracking it against someone's skull still turned her stomach.

"Have you radioed for the Designated Armed Response Team?" she asked Eckland as she dashed by him. The only other officer in the small caged station outside the bathroom, he didn't answer. But she was in such a hurry to get inside the cell block, she scarcely noticed. "Open the door."

He cocked an eyebrow at her. "I don't think—"

"What are you waiting for?" she cried. Through the metals bars that separated her from the inmates and their cells, she could see a small group of jumpsuit-clad men circling something or someone in the cement-floored common area. Feverish cries rang out from those who watched, along with a chorus of support from the men still locked in three stories of old-style cells above. Yet she could hear the thud of fist on bone, a grunt of pain and a few muttered curses.

"Eckland!"

Finally the gears began to turn. The door slid to the left. She slipped inside the cell block and began looking for the other officers as the door closed immediately behind her.

She caught a glimpse of brown and khaki, a uniform like her own, and realized Hansen and Roddy were already in the middle of the fight. Swallowing hard, she started after them, hoping the Designated Armed Response Team would arrive soon, their shotguns filled with birdshot.

"Back off. Go to your cells now, or we'll lock you down for three days!" she shouted, hoping to sound far more forceful than she felt.

Someone showed her just how much he respected her authority by grabbing her ass. Brandishing her stick, she whirled to face at least five inmates who could have done it. They grinned, their eyes alight with insolent challenge. But a particularly filthy string of curses called everyone's attention back to the blows being leveled only a few feet away and they forgot her in their effort to gain a better view.

Forging on, Gabrielle broke through the ranks to find four men ganging up on one.

"That's enough! Break it up," she said. She half expected one of the brawling men to punch her in the jaw, but Sergeant Hansen was the only one who touched her. He took her by the shoulder and yanked her back, motioning for her to wait. Then he spread his arms wide to keep the onlookers from crowding too close. Roddy was doing the same.

What was this? Gabrielle gaped in surprise at the look of rapt attention on Hansen's and Roddy's faces. They weren't trying to break up the fight; they were only keeping things from getting out of hand. And they were enjoying the spectacle as much as the inmates, maybe more.

"They could *kill* him!" she cried, hoping to bring them to their senses.

"They're not gonna kill him." Hansen's terse words barely reached her ears for the noise.

"They're just teachin' the cocky sonuvabitch a lesson," Roddy muttered, closer to her. "It's about time somebody did."

But it wasn't up to the prisoners to teach anyone a lesson. And it certainly wasn't up to Roddy, or Hansen for that matter, to decide whether or not an inmate deserved a beating!

Fortunately the lone prisoner knew how to fight, or he wouldn't have lasted this long. He was lighter and more thinly built than his assailants, but as Gabrielle watched with wide eyes he whirled and knocked one of them to the ground with a karate-style kick. He deflected a fist aimed at his face and smashed a third man's nose with a rapid jab, but he couldn't possibly recover quickly enough to prepare for the man coming up from behind. A blow to the back of his head sent him face-first to the ground, and the others instantly swarmed and started kicking him.

Blood spatter brought another round of raucous cheering. The crunch of each blow caused bile to rise in Gabrielle's throat. The victim was curling up, trying to protect himself as best he could, but she was afraid they were going to kill him. Someone had to do something.

Her heart pounding so hard every beat vibrated out to her fingertips, she raised her baton, jumped into the fracas and clubbed one of the four attackers. Adrenaline must have lent her strength because all two hundred and fifty pounds of him dropped to the floor like a stone, giving her the chance to hit another before the rest knew what was happening.

"Get off him," she cried. "Get off him or I'll club you senseless." She glared at the remaining two, who paused to look at her with hatred contorting their sweat- and blood-streaked faces. They shuffled a few steps away, but their eyes flicked repeatedly to her baton, and she knew they were only waiting for an opportunity to disarm her.

The two on the ground stirred and shoved themselves up, but before anyone could make a move, Roddy and Hansen finally rallied and began to break up the fight.

"That's enough now. You've had your fun," Hansen said. "That's enough for today."

Roddy grinned with satisfaction. "You finally took him, Manuel. You finally took him."

With a little help from his friends, Gabrielle wanted to add as she stared, shaking, at the man on the floor. Eyes closed, lip and forehead bleeding, orange jumpsuit torn, he was lying perfectly still. Was he unconscious? Seriously hurt?

The violence sickened her. Fighting the urge to throw up, she bent to feel for a pulse at his neck and found herself staring into a pair of the bluest eyes she'd ever seen. Framed by long, thick lashes that matched the black of his hair, they were also, by far, the prettiest.

"Are you okay?" she asked.

He didn't answer. He tried to sit up, but she gently pushed him back. "Wait. Let me check a few things first." Quickly she threaded her fingers through his hair and felt his skull, searching for cuts or lumps, anything that might indicate a concussion. She knew he'd been hit in the back of the head. He could have been kicked there, as well. But she didn't find anything indicative of serious injury, other than the knot she'd expected, the obvious busted lip and the gash above his left eye.

"I'm fine," he insisted, batting her hands away as though impatient to escape her probing. He staggered to his feet but favored his left side so badly, Gabrielle was sure he had some damaged ribs. He held his hand at an odd angle, too.

"I'm afraid you've got a few broken bones," she said. "And your forehead probably needs stitches." She glanced at his blood on her hands and knew touching him had been foolish. He could have AIDS. Prisons were full of HIV. In training, they'd warned her about that. She even carried a pair of gloves on her belt. But she hadn't been at the job long enough to have established any kind of habit and in the heat of the moment her natural impulse had won out.

"Why don't you sit until I can bring a doctor in here?" she asked.

"He doesn't need a doctor. He'll be fine. Get him back where he belongs." It was Sergeant Hansen, her supervisor. He'd overseen the herding of the men back to their cells, but now he hovered over her, frowning at the injured convict, who stood half a foot taller than both of them. "Afterward I want to speak to you at my desk," he told her.

Maybe she'd been stupid to break rank with the others; maybe it was going to cost her her job. But Gabrielle had acted according to her conscience and wasn't prepared to back off yet. "He needs a doctor," she insisted. "I'm pretty sure he's got a couple of—"

"Save your breath," the inmate interrupted. "I'm not going to get a doctor because, according to your boss and his henchmen, this little incident never happened. Too many fights in one cell block might lead to the truth—that they're being staged. And staging fights could cost your buddy Hansen, here, his cushy job."

His voice held a distinctly challenging edge, but even his anger couldn't fully eclipse the smooth, cultured tones underneath. After seeing him fight like a man born to the streets and witnessing firsthand the power of his muscular body, the fact that he sounded more like a business executive than a maximum security prisoner came as a surprise to Gabrielle—but no more so than his accusation.

"Of course it'll be reported," she said. "The response team is probably on its way right now." She looked to Hansen for confirmation, but the narrowing of the sergeant's cool gray eyes and Eckland's strange reluctance when she'd demanded to be let into the cell block shook her faith.

"I was thinkin' of doin' you a favor, scumbag," Hansen said. "I figured you wouldn't be too eager for me to report another fight, seein' as how you could lose your privileges again. But maybe you don't know when a guy's tryin' to be nice. So I'll report it if you say so. Is that what you want?"

The inmate didn't answer, but a muscle flexed in his jaw and his eyes turned hard and glittery.

Hansen grinned. "That's what I thought. Now get your ass back where it belongs before I change my mind."

"WHAT DO YOU THINK you were doing out there?" Sergeant Hansen shouted once Gabrielle had composed herself enough to appear at his desk.

"I was trying to stop a convict from sustaining physical injury," she said. "I thought I was doing my job."

"You were risking your fool life, that's what you were doing. I had things under control."

Gabrielle had promised herself she'd be diplomatic. She needed her job. The small desert town of Florence, Arizona, revolved around seven prisons, including the juvenile detention center. There wasn't anything else that would pay her enough to survive, at least not anything she could get. After running away from home at least a dozen times in her teen years, she'd barely graduated high school. College had been out of the question. But she was too honest to suck up to Hansen and pretend she agreed with his actions, so she folded her arms and kept her mouth shut.

"Randall Tucker killed his own wife, Officer Hadley," Hansen announced as though he were playing some kind of trump card. "I'll get his jacket so you can read it if you don't believe me."

Gabrielle didn't want to read his jacket or anyone else's. The inmates's wrap sheets were sometimes available to the officers, but she purposely avoided anything she didn't need to know for fear she'd lose the nerve to do her job. Working for the state provided good medical and dental benefits, an excellent retirement plan and favorable hours. Arizona needed corrections officers in Florence so badly, they'd even offered her bonus money to work in this particular prison, and they'd given her days even though most rookies had to take the night shift.

"That's his name, Randall Tucker?" she asked. "I think I read about him in the paper when I was living in Phoenix."

He nodded. "Then you know he suspected his wife of having an affair, got insanely jealous and hired a private detective to follow her around. When he found out she *was* cheating on him, he flipped out and beat her to a bloody pulp with that karate shit of his. No one's ever found the body."

"If they've never found the body, how do we know what happened? Did he confess?" she asked in surprise, wishing she could remember more about the story. She was new at corrections, but she'd seen enough court TV to know the rarity of such a conviction.

"Hell, no. Tucker's too smart for that. He's still trying to get out of here. But a whole roomful of people watched him drag her away from an aerobics class the night she disappeared, and he was the last person to see her. He didn't even report her missing for three days. By then her friends were getting suspicious, but all the police could find was blood spatter in the garage consistent with a blow to the head. The kind made with a fist."

Shying away from the mental picture Hansen was purposely creating in an attempt to intimidate her, Gabrielle went back to the name—Randall Tucker. For a moment his deep, angry, fathomless blue eyes flashed into her mind. She recalled his face. A rugged, very interesting face. The face of a man who'd killed his wife in his own garage.

Gabrielle stifled a shudder. "I don't care what he's done," she said, remembering her ideals. "It's not up to me to punish him."

"I'm not punishing him. I'm just letting him pick on someone his own size."

"Four to one is hardly a fair fight."

The muscles of Hansen's arm flexed as he rubbed the top of his blond flattop, studying her. What he lacked in height he tried to compensate for in the weight room, which made him appear almost square. "You think his wife would want him to have a pleasant stay here?"

"I don't have to answer that. The government dictates what his stay is like, not me. Or you," she added.

He chuckled bitterly, finally seeming to accept that he wasn't going to convince her. "Damn bleeding heart liberal, that's what you are. It's a shame what people like you have done to this country. Prisoners are treated like guests at the taxpayer hotel while we work like slaves to keep food on the table."

"What good does it do to behave like them?" she asked. "Just because we work with depraved men doesn't mean we have to lose our humanity."

"You think I've lost my humanity, Officer Hadley?"

Gabrielle hesitated but, in the end, her natural frankness won out. "I don't think what you did back there was right. And I sure as hell don't think you should have denied Randall Tucker a doctor. He's obviously hurt. We should send him to the health center."

"Let me tell you something, little *lady*. Randall Tucker is fine. He can take two men easily, and I've seen him take three. Far as I know, today's the first time he's ever been beat. He's been fighting since he came here and he'll continue to fight until he dies, or his appeal is finally heard and the judge overturns his sentence. But he's already been denied twice, so I wouldn't hold my breath waiting for that. He's tougher than nails and stronger than a bull. He's a survivor."

Hansen put his elbows on the table and leaned forward. "And you know what? So am I. I've been workin' here since college, nearly fifteen years, and I'll be workin' here in fifteen more. It's only the weak who have to worry, the young, the old—" he cocked an eyebrow at her "—the fairer sex. At least those who don't mind their own business and keep to their place."

Indignant, Gabrielle shot out of her chair. "I don't appreciate the implication, Sergeant Hansen."

He sat back, laced thick fingers behind his head and smiled. "The implication? I'm not implying anything. I'm just reminding you of some basic facts, *Officer Hadley.* You lack the upper-body strength of a good prison officer. You lack a killer's instinct. I don't think you got it in you to do this job. Bottom line, you might need a lot of support from your fellow corrections officers, so you'd better be careful not to piss them off."

Or? The word hung in the air, but Gabrielle refused to say it. She was afraid she'd pushed Hansen too far already. The tentative relationship that had developed between them over her first two days had degenerated into open hostility, and she needed her job. She pictured herself trying to break up a fight like the one this afternoon and having him and his henchmen, as Randall Tucker had referred to them, hold back, stalling several minutes before coming to her aid. She could be seriously injured.

She could be seriously killed.

She hadn't come to Florence to wage any wars against the powers that be. She'd come for other reasons, personal reasons. Her job was just that—a job, nothing more, nothing less.

"So, no doctor for Tucker?" she asked.

He shook his head in obvious disgust. "You don't give up easily, do you?"

Gabrielle returned his cold stare without speaking.

"No doctor," he said at last.

"Then can I take a first-aid kit and see if he's okay? There's a cut above his eye that looks like it needs stitches. It should be cleaned, at least. And I'm pretty sure he's broken a bone or two in his hand."

"If you want to nurse Mr. Wife-Killer, you can do it on your own time, once your shift ends," Hansen growled. "But if he attacks you, don't expect me—or anyone else—to come running."

CHAPTER TWO

GABRIELLE CLUTCHED the first-aid kit in one sweaty hand and moved purposefully down the aisle toward Randall Tucker's cell. Roddy and Brinkman, another officer, flanked her, walking a few steps behind. Worried about the possible repercussions should something happen to her while she was visiting Tucker, Hansen had finally relented and told the two officers to accompany her. But it was time to go home, and Roddy and Brinkman weren't any happier about her errand than Hansen had been.

Could she count on them? The fear that she couldn't kept her eyes focused straight ahead and her chin held high while, inside, her heart thumped louder with each step.

Randall Tucker killed his own wife. Hansen's words seemed to echo through the cavernous cell block, and with them, his promise. *If he attacks you, don't expect me—or anyone else—to come running...come running...come running.*

Locked down because of the fight and with an hour still to wait before dinner, many of the convicts were listless and bored. They lingered near the front of their cells, tattooed arms dangling through the bars as they hollered back and forth to each other or simply stared at nothing, sullen and withdrawn.

Unfortunately, Gabrielle's passing seemed to be just the thing to relieve the tedium.

"Hey, fine-lookin' mama, let's get it on!" someone called after her as small plastic mirrors began to spring up so the men could see her.

"Shut up, ho, she's lookin' fo' a real man, a man like me," came a shout two cells further down. "Come on, baby, lemme take you for the ride of your life."

"Look at those tits," a third man groaned. "What I wouldn't give for five minutes with those—"

Previously, Roddy and Brinkman and the other officers had put an end to the taunts and catcalls the prisoners flung her way by threatening them with no recreation and only a sack lunch for meals. The fact that they said nothing now, did nothing, told Gabrielle they were as angry as she'd thought. They didn't like her interfering and wanted her to know it. But now that she'd taken a stand, she needed to see it through—or Randall Tucker would receive no help, and she would have ruined her relationship with Sergeant Hansen for nothing.

In five minutes she'd be done with Tucker, she told herself. Then she'd be on her way home to Allie.

"Come back and give me some love. I got nothin' but love for you, baby, nothin' but love."

Smooching sounds followed her on the rest of her walk to Tucker's cell. When she reached it, she found him shirtless, hunched over the small stainless-steel sink in the back corner, trying to rinse the dried blood from his hair. Fortunately, all inmates in central unit lived alone.

Singularly intent on cleaning up, Tucker didn't seem to notice her. Or maybe he did and just didn't care that she was there. He continued his efforts until the moisture glistening on his hair dripped onto his broad shoulders and ran in thin rivulets down his chest and back—a chest and back devoid of tattoos and any ounce of fat. Then he toweled himself off, straightened and turned.

"Looks like I have a visitor," he said, leaving his jumpsuit dangling around his hips.

Unless Gabrielle missed her guess, he regarded her with the same scorn Roddy and Brinkman reserved for him. Hatred or enmity she could understand. She'd seen plenty of both since starting at the prison. Officers and inmates were never meant to be friends. But disdain? Disdain implied superiority. Who did Tucker think he was? He reminded her more of a doctor or a lawyer than a murderer.

That didn't mean he wasn't dangerous.

Please, God, let this day end well, she prayed, telling herself that if there was trouble, Roddy and Brinkman would help. They might hesitate long enough to teach her a lesson, but they'd ultimately intervene.

Problem was, a lot could happen in a mere sixty seconds. And there were any number of excuses for delay....

Suddenly seven weeks of job-training didn't seem like nearly enough.

In and out. Five minutes, that's all. Hauling in a deep breath, Gabrielle removed the pin in the door and motioned to Eckland, down in the officer's booth, to unlock Tucker's cell.

Metal screeched on metal as the door rolled to the right. "I've brought something to clean your cuts, Mr. Tucker," she said.

"*Mr.* Tucker?" He eyed Roddy and Brinkman, who

stood with their batons drawn, as though eager for trouble.

"Isn't that your name?" she asked.

"I think you're the first person to use it since I came to this hellhole." Still favoring his left side, he moved forward, and it was all Gabrielle could do to keep from dashing out and running for safety.

Evidently he read her fear because he stopped, giving her some space, and his voice took on a mocking note. "It's going to be mighty hard to dress a wound from back there. Or are you planning to leave that stuff here with me?" A nod indicated the first-aid kit she held in her hands.

Inmates made weapons out of the most innocuous substances. Gabrielle could easily imagine Tucker honing a knife out of the plastic lid and stabbing someone with it.

"I'm not stupid," she said, waving him toward the bed. "Will you sit down, please?"

"Please?" His lip curled into a bitter smile. "At least you're polite."

"Are you going to sit down or not?"

Holding his injured hand like an unwieldy club, he brushed against her shoulder as he sank onto the lower bunk. She suspected he did it on purpose, to test her, so she stood her ground and refused to back away. If she was going to do this job, she couldn't act like she was about to run screaming in the opposite direction every time she came into contact with a prisoner. Besides, she'd noticed the lines of pain and fatigue in his face and was starting to lose some of her fear. He was hurting far more than he let on.

"This is probably a waste of the courage you screwed up to come here," he said. "Unless you brought an X-ray machine and some plaster, I doubt there's anything you can do for me.''

''Sorry, no plaster.'' She set the kit on the bed beside him. ''Some antiseptic and Band-Aids, though.''

''I'd settle for a couple of Tylenol.''

''It's against the rules for me to dispense any medication. You can buy aspirin from the store.''

''Aspirin doesn't work for me.''

''Well, it's against the rules for me to give you anything else.''

The look on his face told her what he thought of her response. ''It's against the rules for you to be here now, but Hansen makes his own rules. What's a couple of Tylenol? Think about it, Officer—'' his eyes flicked to the name sewn on her shirt ''—Hadley. Two capsules of extra-strength Tylenol and you can consider your mission here complete. Then you won't have to dirty your hands by touching a monster like me.''

A monster like him? If he was a monster, it certainly didn't show on the outside. Despite the injuries that marred his face, he was one of the most attractive men Gabrielle had ever seen. He practically exuded virility, from the comfortable way he fit his body to the aristocratic features of his face—the aquiline nose, the thin upper lip, the prominent jaw and those incomparable eyes.

''What makes you think I have a problem with that?'' she asked, snapping open the kit and rummaging inside.

''You mean, besides the revulsion on your face? It doesn't take a crystal ball to see you'd sooner touch a leper.''

Gabrielle kept her focus on what she was doing and didn't answer. He was right. He'd murdered his wife, and she didn't want to come anywhere near him. But he could definitely use what little first aid she could give. Although the blood on his split lip had congealed, his hand had swollen considerably. The cut on his forehead was bleeding again, if it had ever stopped, and he had to keep wiping away the blood to stop it from rolling into his eyes.

"Can you blame me? Your record doesn't do much to recommend you," she said, pulling on the latex gloves she carried on her belt.

"You can't believe everything you read."

She folded a piece of gauze and doused it with antiseptic. "Oh, yeah? I suppose you're innocent, just like everyone else in here."

He sucked air between his teeth as she cleaned the gash above his eye. "I don't think you give a shit whether I'm innocent or not. No one else does."

She fumbled with one of the butterfly bandages from the kit, trying to figure out how to use it. The wound on his head needed stitches. She'd never seen one quite so deep. But the gloves made it difficult to feel what she was doing, and the darn bandage wouldn't stick.

She looked back at Roddy and Brinkman, hoping they would finally see how unethical it was to deny Tucker the medical help he so obviously needed. But they stared straight ahead, stone-faced, and Gabrielle couldn't decide whom she disliked more. Tucker, for being the murderer he was, the very scum of society. Or Hansen, Roddy and Brinkman for their refusal to do the right thing.

She studied the wound some more, knew it was too deep to leave as it was, and finally stripped off her gloves so she'd have a chance of making the bandage stick.

Tucker glanced at the discarded gloves. "Aren't you taking quite a risk?"

"It's a bit late for that, don't you think? I already got your blood all over me earlier."

"And now you think you're going to die of AIDS."

"Am I?"

He shrugged. "Depends on who you're sleeping with. You won't get it from me."

Ignoring his allusion to her love life, she concentrated on what she was doing so she wouldn't ruin another bandage. *Come on…come on. Once this is on, I've handled the worst of it,* she thought, but his next question made her pause.

"Why did you do it?"

She met his gaze, then looked quickly away. There was something so clear and beautiful about his eyes, they could almost make her forget she was confronting a murderer.

"Do what?" she asked. She'd finally got the bandage to close the cut and was nearly limp with relief.

"Jump into that fight. If you don't have a death wish, you're either incredibly stupid or incredibly brave. I can't decide which."

"Fortunately you don't have to. I was just doing my job."

"If you were doing your job, what was Roddy doing?" He indicated Roddy with a slight nod.

"I'll show you what I'll do if you don't shut your freakin' mouth," Roddy warned, slapping his baton against the palm of his hand.

Gabrielle shifted to block the officers's view of Tucker. "You're probably going to have a scar above your eyebrow," she said to distract him from their hostility—and to distract herself from the odd sense of intimacy she experienced at standing between Tucker's spread legs, only inches from his bare chest.

She tilted his chin up so she could clean the cut on his lip and was moderately surprised to find she felt none of the repugnance she'd expected to feel at touching him. He might be a convict, but he was a man of flesh and bone, and the more honest part of her had to admit that his flesh felt better than most. The rough jaw she cupped in one hand and the soft lip she pressed down with her thumb to reach the cut in the very corner sparked a response someplace deep inside her—someplace that didn't seem nearly as concerned with character as it should have been.

She hurried to finish before he could read her grudging admiration of his physical attributes as easily as he'd read her earlier fear and reluctance. "How are your ribs?"

He didn't answer, but he winced as she ran her fingers over his injured side. She was searching for something obvious, something that could possibly puncture a lung, but if his ribs were broken, she couldn't tell. So long as Tucker was still breathing, she doubted she could get Hansen do anything about it, anyway.

"Maybe they're only cracked," she said at last, refusing to acknowledge how smooth and warm his skin was. His wife had probably enjoyed the same sensation…once.

A heartening amount of distaste finally came with that thought. Gabrielle put some space between them and started packing up. "At least your cuts are cleaned and bandaged. Hopefully time will take care of the rest."

He said nothing. Now that she was finished, he looked even more exhausted and wrung out from the pain, which made Gabrielle do something she hadn't intended to do at all.

"Let me see your hand before I go," she said.

Tucker hesitated, as though his first inclination was to deny her, but then Roddy piped up. "Come on, you ain't gonna to be able to do anything for his hand."

"You're done playing nursemaid to this lowlife," Brinkman added.

Their intervention was enough to convince him. Defiance etched in every line of his face, he held out his injured hand.

Shifting to block Roddy's and Brinkman's view one more time, she rummaged through the first aid kit, came up with two Tylenol tablets and dropped them into his palm.

So much for rules. They'd all broken their share today.

"Now get some rest," she said softly and left.

"TELL ME Allie had a good day," Gabrielle said, stepping inside her single-wide trailer and letting the door slam behind her.

"She did great," Felicia said. The eighteen-year-old girl she'd hired to watch Allie was sitting on the couch painting her toenails blue, while Gabrielle's thirteen-month-old daughter toddled around the living room, using the furniture to help her walk. When she saw her mother, Allie gave a huge smile that revealed two new teeth.

"Hi, baby girl," Gabrielle said, sweeping the child into her arms. "Boy, has Mommy missed you."

"Are you okay?" Felicia asked, putting the fingernail polish away.

"Yeah, fine," Gabrielle told her.

"You seem a little…I don't know, flustered."

"I feel bad for being late, that's all. I was rushing, in case you have somewhere else you need to be."

"No, I'm good. You're not *that* late, anyway. It's only a little after four. And you know Allie's okay here with me." She grinned at Allie, who grinned back, and Gabrielle noticed that Felicia had painted her child's fingernails the same color as her own.

"She sure loves you," Gabrielle said. "I can't tell you how grateful I am that you take such good care of her."

The girl shrugged. "We're buds."

Gabrielle dodged Allie's chubby fingers, which were reaching for the earrings she'd put in as soon as she left the prison—sometimes she needed just a little something to remind her that she was still a woman and still living in the world she'd always known. "I wish I could afford to pay you more—"

"You pay me enough. A few more weeks with Allie and I'd probably be willing to do it for free. She's such a good baby, aren't you, Allie?"

Allie gurgled in response, and Felicia stood. "Sorry I don't have dinner waiting. We've been playing. Want me to help you cook?"

Gabrielle stowed her purse on an end table. "Don't worry about it. Dinner isn't your job. Just keep me company for a minute. Tell me about your day." Carrying Allie on her hip, she headed into the kitchen.

Felicia followed her and started washing out an empty bottle she'd left on the counter as Gabrielle checked the cupboards. "We went for a walk this morning, before it got too hot. Allie played in her little swimming pool for a while after that. She loves it when

I dribble water on her. You should hear her giggle."
She shook her head. "Crazy kid."

Gabrielle considered chicken noodle soup, thinking
a salad sounded much better. But she was low on fresh
vegetables, so soup would have to do. "Swimming is
always a favorite," she said. "Allie should've been
born a fish. Did she nap?"

"She slept for an hour in the morning and an hour
and a half this afternoon."

"Good girl!" Gabrielle kissed her baby's soft forehead as she delved into the freezer for something to
add to their meal.

"I was going to take her for another walk, but it was
too hot," Felicia said.

Gabrielle noted the chugging of her air conditioner,
knowing it had probably been on all day, and shuddered at the thought of opening her next utility bill.
"August in the Arizona desert. We don't get much of
a break from the heat."

"Yeah. My folks are sick of it. They're talking about
moving to Idaho," she said, setting the bottle in the
drainer.

Gabrielle felt a stab of worry and paused in her digging. "The winters here more than make up for the
summer heat. We have months and months of beautiful, perfect weather."

"I know. After living here most of their lives,
they're not thrilled about encountering snow. But
they're convinced they want to live where it's green
for a change."

Though Gabrielle had spent the first seven years of
her life in the Phoenix area, she'd moved with her
adoptive family to the Oregon coast and knew all about
green. She'd met Allie's father while waiting tables in

Portland. But a few years after she and David were married, she'd begged him to take her to the hot dry place she remembered from her childhood, trading the rolling, misty hills, forests and picturesque valleys of Oregon for the rugged, harsher beauty of the desert. Because his parents were already living in Phoenix during the winters, he was familiar with the area and agreed easily enough. Phoenix was growing; the economy was good. He'd felt confident that he'd be able to start his own mortgage company here, and his business had flourished almost immediately. Five years ago, his only brother had moved to Arizona, as well. So for most of the year his entire family lived in the valley.

Gabrielle had no family. Though her adoptive parents and their two daughters remained in Oregon, she didn't miss them. They stayed in loose contact, but they'd always treated her more like a guest than a part of the family. She certainly wasn't close to them.

"Would you go with your parents?" she asked Felicia, tensing as she waited for the girl's answer. Gabrielle was finally establishing her independence. She'd moved far enough from David that she couldn't lean on him too much. She had a steady job, a healthy baby-sitting situation for Allie and was just starting to find herself, to decide who and what she wanted to be. She couldn't lose Felicia now.

Felicia folded her arms and leaned against the counter as Gabrielle discovered some frozen peas that Allie, at least, would enjoy.

"No, I'd stay. All my friends are here," she said. "I'm going to live with my cousin and save up for school. But I doubt my parents will really move, anyway. They say they're going to Idaho every time we have a monsoon."

Gabrielle breathed a sigh of relief as she put the peas on the counter and pulled two pans out of the cupboard. Dust storms hit Arizona every August, usually out of nowhere, often accompanied by thunder and rain. Once, a monsoon broke several large branches off the old olive tree she and David had in their backyard in Phoenix and swept the limbs and a bunch of dirt and leaves into the pool. But the storms were so dramatic and such a startling change from the constant heat that she actually liked them. "The last one we had was pretty bad," she said.

"That's what got them talking about moving again," Felicia responded.

"I hope that's all it is, talk. In any case, I'm glad you'll be staying." Gabrielle gestured at the neat kitchen. "Thanks for cleaning up, by the way."

Felicia glanced around and smiled as though proud of the job she'd done. "You bet. I opened the bottom drawer, the one with all the plastic icebox dishes and measuring cups, and let Allie toss them out while I cleaned. She played for at least thirty minutes without a whimper." She checked her watch and shoved off from the counter. "But I guess I'd better go. I've got a date tonight. You want me at four-thirty again tomorrow morning?"

"Yeah. I have to be to work by five." In a little more than twelve hours. Gabrielle couldn't face the thought of returning to the prison so soon.

Telling herself she'd let tomorrow take care of itself, she trailed Felicia into the living room and watched as the girl slipped on her sandals and gathered her purse.

"See ya tomorrow." Felicia gave Allie a quick kiss on the cheek and hurried out.

"Have fun tonight," Gabrielle called as the door

banged shut. Then she and Allie were alone, with the whole night ahead of them and nothing much to do.

"Are you hungry, babe?" she asked.

Allie made another grab for her earring, and Gabrielle caught her hand just in time.

"I hope that's a yes," she said, but before she could return to their dinner prospects, the telephone rang.

"Gabby? It's me, David."

Her ex-husband. Gabrielle smiled. She and David didn't work as marriage partners—she didn't love him in the right way—but they made great friends. "You always seem to know when I need to hear from you. How are you?"

"Fine. Busy. Is something wrong? Did you have a bad day?"

Gabrielle hesitated. David had never liked the idea of her leaving Phoenix to move to Florence, an hour and a half to the southeast. He'd liked the idea of her becoming a prison officer even less. It wasn't exactly most men's number-one job choice for the mother of their children. But then, he didn't understand what was driving her, didn't understand why she needed to support herself, why this strange, rather barren place somehow felt like home to her.

"Come on," he coaxed. "I'm not going to say anything. You've already heard all my arguments against what you're doing."

Gabrielle handed Allie a toy and set her in the middle of the floor, then sank onto the couch. She generally told David everything. Holding out now was only delaying the inevitable. But when she finished relating the day's events, he didn't react as she'd expected. He was completely quiet at the other end of the line.

"David? You said you weren't going to say anything but I didn't think you meant it quite so literally."

"I'm thinking," he said, "and I'm fighting my natural tendency to beg you to get the hell out of there and come back to Phoenix."

"You know I can't do that. I came here for a reason."

"And have you done anything about that reason? Have you spoken to your mother, at least?"

Gabrielle closed her eyes. She didn't want to have this conversation. "No, not yet."

"Gabby, the investigator found her weeks ago. How long is it going to take to summon the nerve to let her know you're there?"

"I'm not sure. I'll do it someday. It's not that easy, David. She abandoned me when I was three."

"I know that was rough, but it isn't as if you weren't adopted within months by a good family."

Gabrielle had no concrete complaints about the Pattersons. Her adoptive parents, Phil and Bev, owned a successful sandwich shop by the wharf in Newport, Oregon, and had, for the most part, provided for her physical needs. They'd never been abusive or overtly neglectful. They'd just never really embraced her as their own. They doted on their twin girls, who were only eighteen months older than Gabrielle. And the natural affinity between Tiffany and Cher had always made Gabrielle feel like an unwanted tag-along. She felt as though the whole family tolerated her presence, but didn't really *want* her. Especially when she'd reached her teens and begun to rebel. Then she could definitely sense a limit to the Pattersons's acceptance. They'd taken her in to do a good deed and had felt it highly unfair that she'd give them any trouble at all.

But she hadn't been trying to give anyone trouble. She'd only been searching for a place where she would truly belong.

"It wasn't the same," she said, knowing from past experience how hard it was to describe the subtle difference in the way the Pattersons had treated her compared to their own children. David had met them a few times and couldn't see anything wrong with them. The Pattersons had come to their wedding and been polite, grateful she was "settling down." But Gabrielle and David had paid for everything, and David hadn't really had a chance to get to know them. Since then, Gabrielle had gone back for Tiffany's wedding, but David had been too busy with work, so she went alone and returned the next day.

"It's in the past, Gabby," he said. "You've got to let it all go at some point."

"I will when I'm ready."

"Then introduce yourself to your birth mother, if that's what it's going to take."

"I will eventually. I'm just hesitant, okay? I've never known my father. He wasn't around when I was little, so she's all I've got. And she obviously didn't want me to disrupt her life twenty-five years ago. She probably doesn't want me to disrupt it now."

"I don't want to sound hard-hearted, but if she's not interested in getting to know you, that's her loss. Face it and get over it. Then you can leave Florence and that damn prison and come back to Phoenix where—"

"David, I'm not coming back," Gabrielle interrupted. "You know that. I want to be here, at least for now. I want to build my life on my own, see where I can go with it. Besides, I could have sisters, aunts, uncles, a whole family here in Florence. You don't know how much that means to someone who's never felt connected.''

He sighed. ''I'm sorry. I don't want to get into an argument. I grew up with both my parents, so I can't pretend to know what being adopted means to you. I only know that I don't like having you and Allie so far away. I don't like you working such a dangerous job. I—''

''We're less than two hours away. That's not far. And it's not as if what I do is anything unusual. Thousands of people have the same job. Someone's got to do it. Besides, I thought you didn't want to argue.''

''I don't.''

''So ease up, okay?''

Silence, then, ''What do you plan to do? About the problem at the prison, I mean?''

Gabrielle let her hair down from its ponytail and ran a hand through it. ''I'm thinking I have to report it to the warden.''

''That's what I was afraid you'd say. Why don't you file a complaint with Hansen's boss?''

''Working my way up the ladder could take months. Tucker needs help now. Besides, Warden Crumb has an open-door policy, and I feel he should know what's going on. There's more at risk than Tucker. Someday Crumb might be facing allegations of major corruption. I'd want a chance to deal with the situation before I was hit with something like that, wouldn't you?''

''I don't care about the warden. I care about you, and I don't want you to go to him even if he'll see you. What if this Hansen guy denies what happened? Won't the other officers back him up because they're guilty, too? It's you against the rest. Not even Randall Tucker can substantiate what you say. A murderer sentenced to life doesn't exactly possess a lot of credibility.''

"I can't let this kind of thing go on. It's not right. Randall Tucker was seriously injured. He could've been killed."

"I doubt Hansen would've let it go that far."

"So that makes it okay? Tucker accused him of staging fights. The only thing missing is the bookie."

"I understand that. But you're new there, Gabby. You don't know how everything works yet. Why not lie low for a while and see what happens? Maybe it was a personal thing between Hansen and Tucker. Now that Tucker's had his beating, it might be over. For all you know, Tucker deserved what happened to him."

"That's not for us to decide."

"So don't. Just wait a week or two, that's all I'm asking. See what happens," he said again. "If you won't do it for me, do it for Allie."

"You and Allie are the only reasons I didn't go to the warden today."

"Thank heaven for small favors," he muttered. "You don't want to alienate everyone your first week, Gabby. Did you get my child support?"

"I did, but you sent more than we agreed."

"I don't want you eating noodles every day."

"I'm not your responsibility."

"You'd send it to me if you thought I needed it."

That, at least, was true. "I'm working now. What makes you think I need money?"

"I helped you move into that piece of junk you call a trailer, remember?"

David was right about the trailer. Nearly eighteen years old, it had brown shag carpet, fake wood paneling and pieces of tattered, mismatched furniture. A small awning covered Gabrielle's white Honda Accord, and various cacti dressed up the desert landscape that predominated in the park, but the place didn't have much to recommend it. Except that it was cheap and clean and she could call it her own.

"I remember. But this is only until I can afford something better."

"I'm sorry I haven't been around very much since the move," he said.

"That's okay. You can't exactly schedule the deaths in your family. I feel bad about Grandma Larsen. I know she meant a lot to you."

"She was quite the old dame. I never dreamed taking care of her estate could take so long, though. I feel like I've been out of circulation for months instead of weeks."

"How's your work now that you're back from Michigan? You doing plenty of loans?"

"Things have fallen off, but I have a new gal on the phones, drumming up refinances."

"I hope interest rates stay down."

"I pray to the interest-rate gods every day. How's Allie?"

"She's happy and chubby and sometimes I look at her and think I could never love anyone quite so much."

He fell silent and, for a moment, Gabrielle feared she'd hurt him. "I didn't mean—"

"Forget it," he said. "We've already been through all that. You love me, but you don't *love* me, as if I'm supposed to be able to tell the difference."

"David, you're my best friend. I never wanted to cause you pain."

"I know." He cleared his throat. "Is Allie walking yet?"

"Almost. She gets around by hanging on to the furniture. When are you going to come see us again?" David's visitation rights included weekends and holidays, but Allie was still so little, he rarely took her to his place. Even when she and David had first separated and Gabrielle was living in an apartment in Mesa, he typically spent the weekends at her place, where they could all be together.

"I've got a lot to do here at the office, and I was planning to get caught up this week. I could come down next Monday. Can you wait that long?"

Five days sounded like an eternity. Gabrielle was tempted to say no. Her life was much easier when David was around. But she wouldn't let herself use him. He needed to let go of her and to meet someone else, someone capable of being the kind of wife and lover he deserved. "Monday's fine, except I have to work."

"Don't you get off at three? I'll come down late Sunday and spend the night so I can watch Allie while you work on Monday, then I'll take the two of you out to dinner."

Allie started to fuss, wanting to be held, and Gabrielle gladly obliged. "Sounds great."

"You be good till then. Let Hansen and the others take the lead. Don't risk yourself for an inmate again, you hear?"

Gabrielle pulled the phone cord out of her daughter's mouth, but Allie shoved it right back in. "I hear," she said.

"That doesn't sound like a real commitment."

Gabrielle thought of Randall Tucker and his broken hand and knew she couldn't make David any promises.

She wanted Tucker's hand X-rayed and set. She wanted him to have stitches so the cut above his eye would heal properly. And she feared the only way to make that happen was by going over Hansen's head.

But would Warden Crumb listen? Or would all hell break lose?

"I'll give it another day or so," she said. "Maybe Hansen will change his mind."

"Yeah, maybe he will," David agreed, but he didn't sound any more convinced than she was. "I'll call you tomorrow."

Gabrielle said goodbye and hung up, but her thoughts didn't linger on David. Instead she pictured Randall Tucker. Intelligent, articulate, handsome, he was so unusual for a convict.

Was jealousy enough to drive a man like that to murder?

CHAPTER THREE

NIGHTS WERE THE WORST. Especially this night, Tucker thought. He lay on his bed trying to tolerate the throbbing of his hand and the snoring of the man in the next cell so he could get to sleep, but he couldn't manage it. He'd waited until ten o'clock to take the Tylenol that Officer Hadley had given him, hoping that might help, but it wasn't enough. Rodriguez and his gang had fixed him up good this time. He needed something stronger.

Still, it wasn't the physical pain that bothered him half as much as the images in his mind—images of Landon taking his first step, Landon playing T-ball, Landon learning to ride a bike.

If a man could die of missing someone, Tucker had one foot in the grave. He'd sell his soul to see his son again, even for only a few minutes. At six years old, the boy had lost both parents. Death had taken one, prison the other. Now the poor kid was being raised by strangers in a foster home in Phoenix, strangers who, in the six months Tucker had been imprisoned at Florence, had never once brought him to see his father. Tucker's own parents had brought Landon down a few times, but it was a bittersweet experience to see him sitting in a booth on the other side of a piece of thick glass.

The guy next door rattled into a wheeze, then guttered out, giving Tucker a moment's reprieve from the racket. Wishing he could ease the pain as well, he shifted, but he was in a world of hurt from which there was no escape, at least until his injuries healed.

Perhaps he'd been stupid to let Rodriguez provoke him. He'd known from the beginning that the Border Brothers wouldn't fight fair. There was no such thing as "fair" in prison. Most inmates did anything and everything they could to hurt and maim. His best defense against the Border Brothers would be to join a rival gang such as the white supremacist Aryan Brotherhood, but he refused to align himself with that group or any other, refused to espouse their twisted ideals. So he had to fight to survive.

Those who didn't join a gang and wouldn't or couldn't fight got shoved so far down the ladder they couldn't take a piss without permission from someone. And Tucker wasn't about to ask a fellow inmate's leave to do anything. Too many things had happened to him that he couldn't control—the disappearance of his wife, the accusations that followed, the single-minded determination of the district attorney to see him behind bars. At least he could defend himself with his fists. At least he could retain control of that.

His neighbor started to snore again. "Shut up, man," Tucker hollered. "I can't sleep."

His outburst brought no change, except a few curses from those he'd disturbed.

God, he wanted it to be morning. Then, if he was still able to function with his injuries, he could focus on his job making thirty cents an hour as a "skilled laborer"—an electrician. It was a trade he'd basically taught himself since coming to prison. His other alternatives, come daybreak, were to take a walk in the yard, lift weights, read—anything to distract himself from the same subjects he dwelled on every night. Landon. His freedom. His dead wife.

He and Andrea certainly hadn't been the happiest of couples. They'd split several times, talked about divorce. They'd been going through a rough period right before the police had found her blood spattered on the cement floor of the garage. But Tucker had cared about her and he'd been trying to hold their marriage together for Landon's sake. They might not have been as much in love as they were at first, but a lot of couples drifted apart during a marriage. The fact that he wasn't a particularly doting husband certainly didn't make him a killer. He couldn't prove his innocence, though, because he'd never dreamed he'd need an alibi.

His thoughts strayed to the strange way his wife had been acting before the night that had changed everything. He was sure she'd been seeing someone else— again. She wouldn't admit it, of course. But Tucker had known *something* was different. He'd felt it. The private investigator had proved that she'd cheated on him more than once. But even that evidence had worked against him. The more suspicious of Andrea he appeared, the stronger his motive to kill her. The police hadn't even considered that one of the men she was sleeping with might have done it. Or they hadn't cared. They'd had their scapegoat.

He sifted through Andrea's friends and acquaintances but, as always, drew a blank. He didn't know anyone who'd want to kill her. She was beautiful, successful, admired by all. If she was also a little selfish, overly ambitious and egotistical, most people didn't know that. She had no real enemies. Even *his* friends quickly became her friends.

His eyelids were finally growing heavy, his thoughts slowing. Closing his eyes, Tucker released the tension in his body and started to relax. The pain in his hand ebbed and his neighbor's snores seemed to fade, along with the other background noise that never ceased in prison. Blessed sleep approached, promising oblivion at last—

Wood clattered on the bars of his cell, jolting Tucker into wakefulness. He opened his eyes to see a guard walking down the corridor, his baton scraping against the cages for no apparent reason. For a moment Tucker wished for five minutes alone with that guard and his baton. But the fact that he'd even think such a thing told him he'd been locked up too long already. Violence was becoming more and more natural to him. The guards were sometimes worse than the inmates, or at least no better. Many of them were cruel, small-minded and shortsighted. It was little wonder Tucker had no respect for them—although Officer Hadley didn't fit that mold.

Only five feet six or so, maybe one hundred and twenty pounds, she'd jumped into the middle of the fight and started clubbing people. The memory of it made Tucker smile, despite everything. It was quite a sight—something he certainly hadn't expected to see. The other female guards stood behind their male counterparts, happy, even grateful, to be somewhat removed and protected.

Hadley had more spunk in her than that. She'd stuck to her principles even though she stood alone. Which didn't mean she wasn't frightened, Tucker thought. She'd been terrified when she came to his cell. But she hadn't let her fear, or him, get the best of her. She'd cleaned his cuts and checked his injuries, then bent the rules just enough to let him know that some people still understood the meaning of compassion.

Tucker knew he was stupid to let himself dwell on a woman, on a guard, no less. He'd ultimately only frustrate himself that much more. But he was so sick of the mystery surrounding Andrea's death and the unfairness of it all, so tired of hating and being angry. What he wanted was to feel a woman smooth the hair off his forehead or to throw her arms around his neck. More than anything he longed to be in love with someone, to be loved in return, and to hear her soft breathing as she slept curled up next to him. Such simple things…things he'd probably never know again. Except in his dreams. When he finally drifted off to sleep, Officer Hadley smiled at him, pressed her lips to his forehead and told him everything was going to be all right.

HE *WASN'T* GOING TO LOOK at her.

Tucker kept his eyes on his Scrabble tiles and away from Officer Hadley, who was slowly circling the common area. She'd come on duty two hours and eighteen minutes ago, and he'd spent the whole of that time trying to ignore her. But certain things filtered through. Such as her perfume. Or maybe it was her shampoo or even her deodorant. He only knew that she smelled like heaven. After being imprisoned with a bunch of crude, sweaty men for more than two years, including the months he'd spent in the county jail throughout his trial, the scent of Officer Hadley drove him almost as crazy as the memory of her cool fingers on his face.

At least Rodriguez and his gang were still in their cells. He wouldn't have to defend himself today.

Using his left hand because he couldn't move his

right, he formed the word "parley" on the game board and started counting up his points. *Double letter score for the* p *makes eight—*

"Parley! What the hell is that?" his opponent demanded. "That's no word! You think you're so damn smart, but I bet half the shit you come up with isn't even real."

Tucker shrugged. If he got upset every time Zinger accused him of cheating he would've choked the man long ago. And he couldn't do that. Zinger was the only one who could challenge him at Scrabble or chess, and he knew he'd go stark raving mad without something to distract him. He worked thirty hours a week and spent a couple of hours each day lifting weights, but he had to fill the rest of his time somehow. Fortunately the warden had recently started a pilot program that rewarded inmates who worked hard and demonstrated good behavior with two hours a week to play games. Since prisoners came up for review only once every six months and Hansen hadn't reported many of the fights in which Tucker had been involved, Tucker still qualified.

"You're missing the *s,*" Zinger insisted. "You were thinking of 'parsley.'"

Maybe he *would* choke Zinger, Tucker thought. At least then he'd deserve to be locked up in this godforsaken place.

"No, I was thinking of *parley.* Check the dictionary," Tucker responded, knowing Zinger would, anyway. The five-foot-two, dark-eyed Chilean took nothing on faith. He looked up every word, even if it had only three or four letters.

"It's a word." Officer Hadley had come to stand over Zinger's shoulder and was studying the board. "If

I remember right, it has something to do with meeting one's enemy, doesn't it?'' She directed her question to him, but Tucker refused to glance up at her. He was afraid he wouldn't be able to look away.

"I don't know what it means. I just know it's a word," he mumbled, hoping his answer would suffice and she'd move on.

Instead she came a step closer. "How's your hand?"

Tucker scowled and studied the tiles he'd drawn, hoping his silence would encourage her to leave. After his fantasies last night, he was even more convinced that a woman like Officer Hadley had no business in a prison. She was too soft, too friendly, too temptingly beautiful. What did she want, anyway—to be every convict's wet dream? To have them close their eyes at night and see only her?

Well, he'd been to that party once already, and it hadn't made his life any easier. He wasn't going back.

At last assured that he wasn't being cheated, Zinger set the dictionary aside and began trying to come up with his own word. Tucker wasn't worried. He had him beat. They were getting down to the last few tiles, and he was fifty points ahead.

"Aren't you going to answer me?" Hadley asked.

Tucker ran his left thumb over the smooth finish of a blank tile. "My hand's broken. What do you want me to say? That it hurts like hell? Well, it does. Happy?"

Ignoring their conversation, Zinger muttered to himself as he rearranged his tiles again and again.

"Come on, you're taking too long," Tucker snapped.

"'Thanks for asking' would've been nice," Hadley said.

Zinger cursed, a frown of concentration on his face.

"Shit, man, I can't do anything. I'm going to have to pass."

Tucker leaned back in his chair, finally giving Officer Hadley his full attention. "You don't want to hear what I have to say. Because if I said what I think, I'd tell you to find another job. You don't belong here."

She blinked in surprise. "I guess you were pretty glad I worked here yesterday when I stopped those thugs from killing you."

"I thought you were just doing your job." He purposely lowered his lids halfway, feigning indifference, and looked at Zinger. "So you pass? It's over?"

"There's nothing else I can do," Zinger said. "I've got a *z,* a *t,* a *q,* a *g,* two *a*'s and a *u.* What can be made with that?"

"Quagga," Hadley supplied. "It doesn't use the *z,* but you can play it off this *g* here." She pointed to the word "grab" on the board.

"*Quagga?*" Tucker repeated.

She raised the finely arched brows above her green eyes and nodded toward the dictionary. "Check it out if you don't believe me. I used to play Scrabble by the hour."

Tucker wasn't about to rise to the bait, but Zinger eagerly seized the tattered paperback and fanned the pages until he found *q.* "Quadrennial...quaester... quaff...quagga." He glanced quickly at Officer Hadley before continuing. "'An extinct mammal of southern Africa related to the zebra.'" He started placing his tiles. "Now, how the hell would she know that?"

Hadley folded her arms across her chest. "Double letter score on the *q.* Double word score on the whole thing. That makes fifty-four points. I'm afraid you lose this game, Mr. Tucker," she said and walked away.

Tucker watched her go, telling himself he didn't care if he'd offended her. At least he'd win the only game that really mattered—survival. She wouldn't be smiling at him or asking after him or offering him any more kindness. And without her to remind him of what he was missing, he could remain strong and endure his sentence as he had in the past. He'd survived by not letting himself feel anything, least of all the kind of want that could harrow a man's soul as nothing else.

The kind of want he'd known last night for the first time since Andrea was killed—all because Officer Hadley had been compassionate enough to give him some Tylenol.

"I HEARD we had a little excitement here yesterday."

Gabrielle put her sandwich down and swallowed so she could answer Officer Bell, who'd just entered the yard office, ending her precious solitude. Normally part of her shift, Bell had been off yesterday, so she'd missed the Tucker beating. But Gabrielle was sure the other guards had already shared every detail, including her role in it.

"Four members of the Border Brothers ganged up on Randall Tucker. It wasn't pretty," she said, taking a drink from her water bottle.

Bell dropped some change into the soda machine, pressed the Pepsi button and retrieved the can that clunked into the small opening. Then she threw a furtive glance over her shoulder toward the gray steel door that stood open to the hallway beyond. "That kind of thing's been happening a lot lately," she murmured.

Gabrielle watched as Bell took a seat across from her. "Why do you suppose that is?"

She popped the top of her soda and lowered her voice. "Hansen's out of control, if you ask me. Thinks he can get away with anything."

"You're saying he's responsible for what's going on?"

Bell didn't answer immediately. "Well, it's not something in the water. You know what I'm saying?"

"But if he's staging fights, all we have to do is go to the warden and—"

Bell interrupted her with a disbelieving look. "Oh, yeah? Good luck. Hansen's the warden's nephew."

Gabrielle let her breath seep out. No wonder Hansen felt so comfortable in his job. She remembered the "survivor" speech he'd given her in his office after the fight yesterday and did a mental eye roll. *I've been workin' here since college, nearly fifteen years, and I'll be workin' here in fifteen more. It's only the weak who have to worry, the young, the old, the fairer sex...* As though being related to the warden had nothing to do with his longevity!

"So the warden knows Hansen is abusing his power?" she asked.

Bell took a drink of her Pepsi, then played with the condensation on the outside of the can. "Abusing his power? That's subject to interpretation. So far, no one's been killed or seriously injured."

"So far? 'So far' acknowledges that it could happen in the future," Gabrielle said, finishing her tuna sandwich. "Randall Tucker's injuries might not be life-threatening, but I'd call them serious. And they could've been much worse."

Bell grimaced, took another drink of her Pepsi and

adjusted the ponytail that held her long dark hair off a rather plain face. "He's an inmate. Life on the inside isn't supposed to be pleasant. You want pleasant, work at a day care, that's Hansen's philosophy."

"Is it the warden's?"

"I don't know. I haven't asked him. We have a chain of command here."

"Will it do any good to go to the lieutenant?"

"Are you kidding? Whitehead and Hansen spend their weekends together barbecuing and drinking beer. You could try one of the captains, but I doubt you'll get anywhere with them, either. Or the assistant deputy warden, for that matter."

"Then the warden is our only option."

"Believe me, he's no option."

"So you don't want to do *anything*?"

"What *can* we do?" Bell demanded. "Our jobs are tough enough as it is. You know what it's like being a woman in a place like this. We make waves, and we won't be around long."

"But what Hansen's doing is serious and you know it. Tucker could've been killed! I could have been killed trying to stop something that never should have happened in the first place. Next time, it might be you or someone else—unless we do something."

"Listen, I'm not involved in what Hansen's doing," she said, growing angry. "I just put in my time and collect my paycheck so I can feed my little boy. There's nothing wrong with that."

"We can't close our eyes just because we're women," Gabrielle replied, finally understanding why Bell had opened up to her in the first place. She'd thought they could commiserate because they were both women and therefore fighting the same battles.

But she'd wanted Gabrielle to come to the same conclusion she had—that she was justified in ignoring the guards' abuses—so she'd feel better about avoiding responsibility. Bell wanted her to say, "Yep, it's not our problem, nothing we can do."

But Gabrielle didn't agree. Someone had to stop what was going on, and she sure as hell knew it wouldn't be Brinkman, Roddy or Eckland. "We could see the warden together," she suggested. "I'm not excited about going over Hansen's head anymore than you are, but if we—"

"No." Bell shoved away from the table and stood, glaring down at her. "I'm not a whistle-blower."

"Do you realize what could happen if we don't?"

"I don't care. I need this job."

"But—"

"Forget it. I'm sorry I said anything. I think the others are right. You're nothing but trouble." She threw her can in the trash and stalked out.

Gabrielle sat with her lunch wrappers spread out on the table in front of her, staring after the other woman. She felt more alone than she ever had in her life—and she was used to feeling alone. No matter how many people surrounded her growing up, she'd always remained detached, a guest in her adoptive parents' home, an outsider looking in. She'd married David to escape the emptiness, but even that hadn't worked. When she'd left him, she did it believing there had to be one place in life where she'd fit, in a down-to-the-soul kind of way, but she was beginning to think she'd never find it.

At least she wasn't going to find it here, at the prison. Especially if she ratted on Hansen.

She pictured Randall Tucker's face when he'd finally

looked up at her while playing Scrabble. He was a hard, unfeeling man. He hadn't been very receptive to her help. And he probably *was* getting exactly what he deserved. Why risk anything for him?

Dropping her head in her hands, Gabrielle pressed her palms to her eyes. Why? Because it was the right thing to do.

GABRIELLE LET HER CAR IDLE, hoping the air-conditioning in her late-model Honda Accord would stave off the incredible heat that shimmered up from the asphalt. The magnificent Arizona sun was melting into the horizon like butter, creating streaks of red and gold far more vivid than anything she'd ever seen in Oregon. But Gabrielle hadn't come to watch the sunset. She was parked across from a Spanish-style stucco house on the other side of town, waiting for Naomi Cutter, her birth mother, and hoping for something else: the courage to approach her.

Sitting in her car seat in the back, Allie clapped her hands and kicked her feet. They'd taken this drive several times already; Allie loved the movement of the car, loved seeing everything fly past her window. But it wasn't as joyful a ride for Gabrielle. Watching her birth mother arrive home from wherever she worked during the day, gather her things from her silver Toyota Camry and enter her small, neat house at 1058 Robin Way was a bit like pressing on a bruise—it hurt, but Gabrielle just couldn't leave it alone.

Today she'd knock on the door and demand to know why her mother had given her up, she decided. David was right. She needed to get it over with. Her adoptive parents had told her that Naomi had been having financial difficulties, but she'd also been twenty-four at the time, old enough to figure out some way to keep them together.

As a child, Gabrielle had made up plenty of excuses for her mother. Naomi had cancer and was going to die. She'd placed Gabrielle in a good home so she wouldn't be sent to an orphanage, or some variation along those lines. But Naomi was only in her early fifties and looked alive and well. Other than the somber expression she wore, and a certain weariness in the way she moved, she seemed perfectly healthy and capable.

Gabrielle noticed the sound of a motor and checked her rearview mirror. Sure enough, her mother's silver Camry was coming up from behind.

Without so much as a glance at the Honda waiting just past her house, Naomi turned onto her drive and pulled into the garage. A moment later she appeared carrying her purse and a bag of groceries, which explained why she was a little later today than usual, and walked out to the mailbox.

Now, Gabrielle told herself. There wasn't any point in waiting. It had already been far too long.

She paused, trying to visualize approaching the woman in the black pants and short-sleeved button-up blouse and telling her who she was, then shuddered at what her mother's reaction would probably be. A blank look, followed by recognition, horror and finally repugnance. Gabrielle had imagined the scene at least a million times, hoping her mother would smile or show some hint of regret for what they'd lost. But if Naomi felt any of the emotions Gabrielle did, they wouldn't have spent twenty-five years apart. Her mother wanted nothing to do with her, never had, and in Gabrielle's imagined confrontation, the question Naomi always asked first was "How did you find me?"—as though being found was the single worst thing in the world.

Gabrielle didn't think she could bear the rejection. It was easier to live with not knowing, wasn't it?

No, she'd come this far. She *had* to know. It was time to deal with the past and to put it behind her.

Bracing for whatever would follow, she shut off the ignition, got out and started to unbuckle Allie when another car pulled up and parked in the drive.

"Mom! Hey!" a tall blonde called from the shiny red convertible.

Naomi turned and the weariness that had existed in her demeanor immediately fell away. "Hi, honey," she said, smiling in obvious pleasure. "What a nice surprise. I thought you had too much work to make it today."

"Are you kidding? You said you made me a German chocolate cake. I couldn't miss that."

Gabrielle realized she wasn't breathing. She stood in midmotion, transfixed, watching as this beautiful woman stepped out of her car and embraced her mother—*their* mother. Gabrielle had been right. She had more family than just Naomi. She had a sister, and there could be more....

Longing made her knees weak, and she put a hand on the car to steady herself. What would it be like, she wondered, to someday walk up to this person and smile that easy smile—the smile that denoted familiarity beyond friendship—and say, "Hi, sis, how was work?"

"Was traffic bad getting here?" Naomi asked.

The blonde shrugged. "I was visiting a client in Chandler, so I didn't have that far to come. And traffic's never bad this late, unless there's an accident or something. How was the Historical Society today?"

"Oh, you know I like working at the museum. They need volunteers so badly. Today someone donated some dental instruments that date back to the 1880s. Should go well with the chair we already have."

"Great. Here, let me get that for you." She took the bag of groceries Naomi carried and began to follow her to the house.

Gabrielle knew she should say something, catch their attention. But she felt like such an outsider, as though she was watching them through the front window with her nose pressed to the glass. She had no idea whether she'd be welcomed. Whether they'd invite her to come any closer.

Allie whimpered, frustrated that she hadn't been set free after the promising motions Gabrielle had already made, but Gabrielle couldn't move. Approaching her mother would be difficult enough when they were alone, she decided. She couldn't do it with her sister there and the two of them laughing and talking. Unless…unless one of them looked up. She'd do it if they noticed her, she promised herself.

She stared after them, willing them to give the slightest indication that they'd seen her. But neither of them even glanced in her direction. They were too caught up in each other. Their voices dimmed as they neared the house, the door opened and shut, and they were gone.

A truck rattled past on the street, windows down, its single occupant visibly sweating. Gabrielle let her breath go and closed her eyes. It was over. It was too late.

Allie started to cry, letting her know she wasn't happy about this strange neglect, but Gabrielle felt too numb to comfort her. She tugged mechanically on the car seat to make sure she hadn't loosened the strap, then slid behind the wheel, still hesitant to go anywhere when what she wanted was inside. If she could only witness whatever her mother and her sister did when they were together, see the house, gain a sense of who these people were so she could know more about herself...

Her mother was married, or at least she lived with a man; that much Gabrielle knew. She'd seen him pass in front of the windows before, wearing a plain white T-shirt and holding a can of beer or soda. She guessed he was retired, spent most of his time doing yard work and watching television. But today she could see nothing. The blinds were down to keep out the sun.

Gabrielle started the car, adjusted the air-conditioning vents and gazed off to the other side of the road, where sand-colored desert spread in front of her as far as the eye could see. It gave her the impression that her mother lived on the edge of the civilized world. Paloverde trees, palm yuccas, mesquites, cacti, brown parched earth, it went on for miles and miles....

Go home, she told herself. *You have plenty of other things to worry about for one night.* And it was true. The warden's secretary had responded to her phone call, informing her that he'd agreed to see her. They had an appointment first thing in the morning.

"I'm sorry, babe," she said to Allie, "I'm as disappointed as you are. But we'll do it someday. Someday soon, I promise. Now let's go home and give you a bath." Shifting into Drive, she made a U-turn and headed back to her trailer.

WARDEN CRUMB reminded Gabrielle of Jack LaLane. Five feet ten, or so, he was nearly sixty but took great pride in his appearance. Even though he wore a suit, Gabrielle could tell he had the body of a much younger man and, while his hair was gray, he'd managed to retain most of it.

"How's our new corrections officer?" he asked, flashing her a poster smile as soon as his secretary showed her into his office. Their appointment had been scheduled for seven o'clock, but he'd kept her waiting almost an hour.

"I'm fine," she said as the secretary withdrew and closed the door.

Crumb didn't get up, but he waved to a seat across from his desk. "Would you like to sit down?"

Gabrielle perched on the edge of an upholstered chair and took a deep breath to ease the tension in her stiff muscles. She might become a pariah among her peers, but she was doing the right thing—wasn't she?

She knew David wouldn't think so. He'd asked her to lie low, and she'd lasted only two days. But someone had to take a stand, even if Hansen *was* the warden's nephew.

Crumb rested his elbows on the arms of his high-backed leather chair and laced his fingers together. "What can I do for you?" he asked, his blue eyes sharp and focused on her face.

Gabrielle swallowed against the dryness of her throat and told him what had happened in Cell Block 2. She mentioned Hansen and the others allowing the fight to continue, Tucker's injuries and Hansen's refusal to call the doctor. As she spoke, she expected a look of surprise or dismay to cross the warden's face, but his pleasant expression never wavered.

"I can understand how you might be concerned by what you saw," he said when she finished. "But fights break out in prison all the time. It might be easy to blame the other guards for not paying more attention to who doesn't like whom, but those kinds of things change, depending on which way the wind blows. Today two men might get along perfectly, tomorrow one might slit the other's throat with a homemade knife. We're dealing with hardened criminals here—rapists and murderers. That's just how things are on the inside.''

"But Hansen and the others did nothing to break up the fight,'' Gabrielle repeated. "They didn't even report it.''

He chuckled softly. "There probably wasn't any need. Prison life isn't always as…straightforward as they paint it in training, you know. Give yourself some time to learn your way around before you panic and cry wolf.'' His smile widened until his teeth glinted in the sun streaming in through the window that over-looked the prison yard, but his eyes had grown cool, and Gabrielle was no longer fooled by his friendly manner. He'd been prepped by someone—probably Nephew Hansen—before she arrived. He hadn't shown one iota of surprise at her story. He'd taken it in stride, as though he'd heard it all before, then he'd dismissed it.

"I've spent nearly forty-eight hours thinking about what I should do regarding this incident, Warden Crumb,'' she said, refusing to let him invalidate her feelings or her opinion. "I'd call that concern, not panic. I'm concerned that Hansen and the others would allow a man to be injured. And I'm concerned that they'd deny Tucker medical treatment for those injuries, injuries that should still be looked at, by the way.''

The warden's smile finally faded at her persistence,

and he leaned forward. "Are you a doctor, Officer Hadley?"

"No, and that's why—"

"Then perhaps you should keep your medical opinions to yourself. I don't appreciate you going around trying to stir up trouble in my prison. You've been here less than a week, which is why I've been willing to give you the benefit of the doubt. But one week hardly qualifies you as an expert on anything. I'm not going to let you tell Hansen how he should be doing his job, and I'm sure as hell not going to let you tell me how to do mine. So I'll reiterate what I tried to say before. Let it go."

Gabrielle stared at him for several seconds. "That's it?"

"More or less. Tucker's a troublemaker. Even if Hansen was at fault, it would be difficult to blame him or anyone else when Tucker gets into so many fights."

Gabrielle remembered the grudging admiration in Hansen's voice when he'd said that Tucker could take two or three men at a time and seriously doubted Tucker deserved full blame for all the fighting. Entertainment value, possibly even gambling, played at least some role in those incidents, she felt sure. But she had no proof. "So you're not going to do anything about it?"

He began to straighten his desk. "The only thing I'm going to do is transfer Tucker to Alta Vista and let them worry about him there."

Gabrielle's spine stiffened at this announcement. Alta Vista was a private prison that housed some of the most violent criminals in the country. For Tucker, it was definitely a step down, and she got the distinct impression it was all in the name of sweeping Hansen's actions under the rug. Better to transfer Tucker, claiming he was a behavioral problem, than to risk a scandal. "Alta Vista?"

"It's near Yuma, not far from the California border."

"I know where it is," she said. "When's he going?"

"Monday." He smiled. "And you and Eckland are driving him."

CHAPTER FOUR

WHAT THE HELL was going on?

Tucker stood straight, jaw clenched, as he tried to keep the pain shooting up his arm from showing in his face. Eckland had barged into his cell at six-thirty, half an hour before he usually had to get up, and strip-searched him. Then he'd put him in handcuffs, leg irons and a belly chain and he'd cuffed his broken hand so tight the bracelet was cutting into his swollen wrist.

"Move it," Eckland said, prodding him forward and out into the corridor. "We need to get an early start."

"Where we goin'?" Tucker asked, breaking his rigid silence. Wherever it was, he seemed to be the only inmate making the trip. The others were still in their beds, though a few craned their necks to peer out at him when they heard the jangle of his leg irons.

"You're going to get some new digs, man," Eckland told him. "You're being transferred. Say goodbye to all the boys."

Tucker halted his chain-clattering stride. "Transferred where?"

"Alta Vista," Eckland told him with a smile. "Just your kinda place."

The only place on earth worse than here, Tucker thought as the despair that had been edging around his consciousness crept a little closer. He'd just received word from his lawyer that his appeal had been denied—again. And now this.

He'd never get out, never get his life back. At times he felt so powerless, he was tempted to pound and kick and rail at everyone and everything until they simply killed him. Then the quest to survive would finally be over. Forever.

But he couldn't give up, wouldn't allow himself to be such a coward…at least not until there was absolutely no hope he'd ever see his son again. The thought of how lonely Landon must be, how confused, cut Tucker to the quick; it was the only thing powerful enough to lend him the strength to keep fighting.

Tightening his jaw against the nausea caused by the throbbing in his hand, he moved on. Eckland had been poking and prodding him in the back for several seconds, but Tucker hadn't paid him any mind. He responded only to his own internal drive. Whether or not the guards understood that, Tucker didn't care.

"We're gonna miss the excitement 'round here," Eckland was saying as they made their way down the stairs. "You always put on a fine show, Tucker. Sometimes I wish I could fight like you. But I figure, why hit somebody when you can shoot 'im, eh? That's the beauty of being a corrections officer."

Eckland wielded nothing more than a baton most of the time and, when he acted as a member of the emergency response team, his shotgun held only birdshot, but he enjoyed the power his job afforded him. He liked baiting Tucker and some of the other inmates, but Tucker generally didn't bother to respond. None of the guards could compare to his real demons, the ones that taunted him from inside his own head.

"Good morning." Officer Hadley came out of the

guards' station just as they reached the outer door, but she was the last person Tucker wanted to see. She symbolized everything he'd lost—love, respectability, his wife, his child. And he couldn't help but remember the way she'd touched him in his dreams, the kindness of her smile, the feel of her lips on his face, her hands on his chest....

"I've got the paperwork," she told Eckland. Her eyes settled on Tucker and her pleasant expression immediately turned into a glower. "You've got him in full restraint," she said, accusation in her voice.

"He's dangerous," Eckland snapped. "'Course I've got him in full restraint. It's standard procedure."

"But he can't wear handcuffs. His hand is broken." She took Tucker's elbow to turn him slightly, probably to check the tightness of the bracelets, but Tucker shook her off.

"It's fine," he growled, because he was too vulnerable to receive any kindness right now, especially from her. The pain lent him strength, fueled his anger, and he needed that. It was all he had. "Tell me you're not going with us."

Her jaw dropped. "Does it matter whether I go or someone else does?"

He shrugged as though he didn't really care, but he did. He didn't want Officer Hadley anywhere near him. Her decency weakened him, made him yearn for the past, for a better future....

A slight frown tugged at the corners of her full mouth as she told Roddy, in the booth, to let them out. Then they were in the yard, beneath a sun so bright it nearly blinded Tucker.

A patrol car waited outside the front gate. Because he couldn't use his hands, Tucker thought Hadley might try to help him into the back seat, but she didn't. She stood aside while he climbed in. Eckland got behind the wheel, and she took the passenger seat. "I can see this is going to be a pleasant drive," she muttered.

Eckland didn't respond. Neither did Tucker. Hansen had just come out of another cell block to give him a final, mocking salute.

"We're gonna miss ya, Tucker. Have fun in hell!" He laughed as Eckland started the car.

Tucker kept his focus straight ahead until they began to move. Then he turned to catch a final glimpse of the hundred-year-old structure where he'd spent the past six months. Painted gray with blue trim, the words Arizona State Prison emblazoned above the central arch, it looked like something out of an old Western. Never had he thought he'd call such a place home.

They went slowly down the drive, stopped for a car inspection, then continued through two fifteen-foot, chain-link fences topped with barbed wire and beyond, into a stretch of dry, packed earth. When they reached the perimeter gate, Eckland paused to speak to the guard stationed there, then turned left onto Butte Avenue, where palm trees towered on their left side and a trailer park sprawled on their right.

The fifth oldest town in the state—or so Tucker had read somewhere—the city of Florence lay in front of them. It had once been a booming silver-mining town and was later known for growing cotton, but now its economy depended on prisons. Florence boasted a pair of state prisons, three private prisons, a juvenile center and a U.S. Immigration and Naturalization Service center, which meant it had to house at least twice as many inmates as the town claimed in citizens.

An unusual place, Tucker decided, one he doubted

had changed much in over a century. He remembered its dusty, sun-bleached buildings from the day they'd carted him there on a bus packed with other inmates, remembered thinking that it looked more like a ghost town.

For him it *was* a ghost town, haunted by his own shattered hopes and dreams.

"Who's watchin' the baby today?" Eckland asked Hadley, breaking the silence.

"Her father."

So Officer Hadley had a child. And a man, too, from the sounds of it. Of course she would. A woman with a smile like Hadley's would never lack for male attention. So what was she doing working as a prison guard? What kind of husband would go along with her pursuing such a profession when she had a baby at home?

Tucker leaned forward to see if she wore a wedding ring, but his cuffed and swollen hand protested any movement, and it was difficult to see such details through the metal screen that separated the front seat from the back. He shifted to ease what he could of the throbbing just as Eckland threw Hadley a disgruntled glance.

"Are you happy now?" he asked once they were headed toward Coolidge.

Hadley didn't look at him. "Happy about what?"

"Your little visit to the warden."

"He tell you about that himself? Or did Hansen?"

"It's no secret, if that's what you mean. And it was foolish as hell."

"I did what I thought I had to do. I don't have to explain myself to any of you."

"Oh, yeah? You've been here a week. Not long enough to know the death house from the health center, yet you've already been to see the warden. What you did sure didn't help Tucker any. You like where you're going, Tucker?" he asked. "You glad Officer Hadley here came to your rescue?"

Tucker said nothing. He'd wondered what this transfer business was all about. Now he knew. He had Hadley to thank, because she was green and idealistic enough to think she could make a difference.

He glowered at the back of her head, but he couldn't really hold it against her. Not after she'd risked herself more than once to help him. Going to the warden had probably been the gutsiest move of all. Didn't she know that?

"Tattling doesn't go over very well with the boys, I gotta tell ya," Eckland was saying.

"If you're going to give me Hansen's survivor speech, don't bother," Hadley responded. "He's already done the honors. 'It's only the weak who have to worry, the young, the old, the fairer sex,'" she said sarcastically. "Frankly, I think his material's a little dated."

"You should listen to him. Your life might depend on it sometime."

Tucker heard the subtle threat in Eckland's voice and wondered if Hadley had picked up on it. If so, she didn't say anything. She sat staring pensively out her window while Tucker considered the very real possibility that the guards might somehow punish her for trying to help him. The thought made something in his gut tighten, something strangely possessive and faintly reminiscent of emotions he hadn't experienced in a long time.

GABRIELLE COULD HARDLY keep her eyes open. They'd been driving through the monotonous desert for nearly three hours and the motion of the car, as well as the hum of its tires, was lulling her to sleep. It didn't help that Allie had woken her several times during the night. Gabrielle had been so stressed about making this trip, she couldn't sleep well to begin with.

She took a deep breath and let it out slowly. She just had to survive the day. Then she'd be home with David. He'd arrived late Sunday afternoon as promised and was with Allie now, which was a comfort. She knew he'd take excellent care of their daughter.

Glancing at her window, she fought the pull of sleep by studying Randall Tucker's reflection, a habit she'd established almost from the moment they'd left the prison. She told herself she was checking to make sure he wasn't trying to get loose, but deep down she knew she was worried about his hand. At Eckland's insistence, Tucker still wore cuffs as well as chains. His hand had to be hurting terribly.

If so, he gave no indication. He hadn't spoken since they'd left.

"How's your hand?" she asked at last, turning to face him through the metal screen. Because of the way he'd acted, she'd promised herself she wouldn't ask about his injuries again, but she couldn't resist. "You okay, Mr. Tucker?"

He was gazing out the window, a hard, impenetrable expression on his face. After a moment the full intensity of his blue eyes shifted to hers. "Would it make any difference if I said no?"

Eckland chuckled, the coarse sound saying it wouldn't, but Gabrielle ignored him.

"It might," she said.

"You saying you'd take them off?"

"I'm saying I could loosen them."

For a moment Tucker simply looked at her. From his tough, belligerent attitude, she doubted he'd admit to needing anything, but he surprised her with a slight nod.

"Are you in a lot of pain?" she asked.

"What do you think?" He scowled and turned back to the window.

"Pull over," she told Eckland.

Eckland ignored her. Signaling, he switched into the fast lane to pass a slow-moving U-Haul.

"Did you hear me?" she pressed.

"I heard ya," he answered. "Doesn't mean I'm gonna listen."

"We should check his hand. He hasn't been out of this car in three hours. Even an unbroken hand would hurt at this point."

"Then let it hurt. He made his bed, and he can lie in it. That's what I say."

Gabrielle had expected this kind of response, but she refused to settle for it. A man was in pain because of Eckland's petty meanness, and she planned to do something about it. "What are you going to tell them at Alta Vista when we show up with an inmate whose hand is swollen to twice its normal size?" she asked.

"I'm gonna to tell 'em he's a mean sonuvabitch who won't quit fightin', that's what. That broken hand has nothing to do with me."

"Except for the fact that it was you who cuffed him. I'm sure it's not going to reflect well on you when I mention that, along with the fact that there wasn't anything wrong with his hand this morning."

Taking his eyes from the road, Eckland gaped at her. "You know his hand was already broken!"

"I do? Too bad there isn't a medical report to prove it."

Eckland's pupils narrowed into small pinpoints of black. "Are you threatening me, Officer Hadley?"

"Threatening you?" She forced a cool smile despite the tension wreaking havoc in her stomach. How had she gotten herself into this power struggle? She'd never wanted to get personally involved with the men she policed, never planned to get caught up in the kind of moral dilemma she'd been facing ever since Tucker's fight. Like Officer Bell, she longed for nothing more than to do eight hours of work for eight hours' pay. She had her own problems. But she couldn't sit still any longer knowing how badly Tucker had to be hurting.

"I'm not threatening anyone," she said. "I'm merely suggesting we pull over and loosen the prisoner's cuffs so the staff at Alta Vista won't be overly concerned. We wouldn't want them to start an investigation, would we? If they find out what happened last week, a few heads are going to roll."

"Yours will be one of 'em," Eckland snarled.

"Mine might be the first, but I guarantee it won't be the last," she said softly, and she meant it. If she lost her job at the prison, there'd be nothing to stop her from going to the press with the story of Hansen's behavior.

"I liked you when you started last week," Eckland said, "but you haven't done much to impress me since then. You're treading on very thin ice, Officer Hadley. I suggest you watch your step."

Gabrielle squared her shoulders and gave him a withering glare. "I suggest you pull over and let me loosen the prisoner's cuffs."

"Fine!" Nostrils flaring, Eckland slammed on the brakes and jerked the steering wheel to the right. The sudden deceleration threw Gabrielle against her shoulder harness. She glanced sideways at him to ask why he was driving so recklessly, but before she could say anything, they nearly clipped the front of a car in the other lane. Eckland overcorrected and hit the opposite shoulder, which spun them like a carnival ride and left them facing an oncoming pickup.

Brakes squealing, the truck swerved, skidded and smashed into them. The hood of their car crumpled like an accordion. Gabrielle heard Eckland scream amid the crunch of folding metal. Tucker cursed and his weight hit the back of her seat as the impact tossed the car into a nearby gully.

For a stunned moment Gabrielle sat there, breathing hard. They'd crashed. Thanks to Eckland and his giant ego, they'd nearly died. Gabrielle knew she was alive, but she wasn't sure she was still in one piece. She did a mental checklist of her body parts, searching for pain or injury, wondering if the absence of feeling meant something worse than the presence of it. Was she in shock? Had she been paralyzed?

She wiggled her toes and fingers and found them all in working order, but her knees had hit her chest. It soon felt as if someone had flung an anvil at it.

Still, she was going to be okay, she decided. What about Eckland—and Tucker?

Eckland was groaning and complaining about his leg. Gabrielle fumbled with her seat belt, trying to free herself so she could help him when she heard Tucker's voice behind her.

"Hadley, get these damn cuffs off."

His hand. His poor hand. She was shaking so badly

she could barely unlatch her seat belt. "Are you okay?" she asked, twisting to peer through the metal screen.

Tucker's door was smashed in and he was doubled over. She couldn't see anything except the thick black hair on the back of his head. "Tucker? Are you hurt?"

He groaned. "Just get these damn cuffs off."

"No, don't do it," Eckland said between clenched teeth. "Just sit tight. I'll radio for help." He shifted, reaching for the radio, and Hadley cringed as she caught a glimpse of his torn pants and the leg beneath, which was obviously broken. She imagined she saw the bone jutting through the skin and nearly threw up. The only way they were going to get out of here was in an ambulance, she realized. They already had one broken leg. Then there was Tucker's arm. Had he sustained further injury? Was there anything she could do to help?

"What's wrong?" she asked Tucker again as Eckland, panting through his pain, placed their distress call. "Do you have new injuries?"

He didn't answer.

"Leave him be! Help's on the way," Eckland grunted when he got off the radio.

She ignored him. Help could take an hour or more. Wrenching her door open, she rushed around the car. At least Eckland was free. At least he could move, to some extent. Tucker was still chained, couldn't use his hands or his legs.

The back door required all her strength to open and creaked loudly as she pulled it back. Hunched over, his wrists still locked in his lap, Tucker barely moved but she could see his hand. It was black and blue and so swollen she couldn't see the metal of the cuff anymore.

And his face, when he finally looked at her, showed glassy eyes.

"I'm sorry," she whispered, fumbling with the ring on her belt for the key that would release him.

"Hadley, don't you dare, dammit," Eckland said, but he was in too much pain to do more than curse.

A thin sheen of sweat was popping out on Tucker's forehead and he'd closed his eyes as though he didn't have the strength to speak.

"I have to. I can't stand to leave him like this," she told Eckland, unlocking the cuffs and kicking herself for not loosening them sooner.

Tucker cradled his hand in his lap and sucked in an audible breath. For a moment, the gray tinge to his skin grew worse. Gabrielle thought he was going to pass out, but he surprised her by grabbing her forearm and pinning her beneath him.

"What are you doing? Don't make things any worse for yourself," she cautioned, the terror of what he could do finally dispelling the dazed confusion caused by the accident. "You heard Eckland call for help. They'll be here soon. Just sit back and relax."

Eckland growled Tucker's name, threatening and swearing at him, but Tucker didn't answer. Suddenly alert and quick-witted as a cat—and seemingly oblivious to any kind of pain—he used his left hand to search through her keys and unlock his belly chain and leg irons. Rolling over her, he held her down with one knee while he recovered the handcuffs, locked her right hand to the screen between the seats and got out of the car. Then he scanned the horizon—and started running.

CHAPTER FIVE

HE WAS ESCAPING. Gabrielle couldn't believe it. She used what little room the cuffs allowed to stand outside the open door of the car, where she could watch Tucker cross the deserted highway. Once he reached the other side, he started jogging into the desert as blithely as though he'd planned the whole thing. Jogging! He was jogging!

"Damn you, Tucker," Gabrielle muttered, even angrier with herself because she'd let him fool her. This was what her compassion had brought her. An escaped convict, an injured guard, another disabled vehicle with God only knows how many people inside—and the burning desire to bring Tucker back, regardless of anything else.

Eckland managed to meet her hand with his keys, and she unlocked herself. It took some doing and by the time she was free, Tucker was well on his way.

Should she go after him? She glanced at Eckland, then the other car, and decided she'd better attend to the injured.

Eckland was swearing a blue streak, but his condition hadn't worsened. The truck, which had rolled at least once, was still partially on the highway. The windshield hadn't shattered, but it was cracked into a spiderweb Gabrielle couldn't see through. A peek in the side window, which was still intact, revealed two occupants—a middle-aged woman driver and a man who looked to be in his early twenties. The driver had hit her face on the steering wheel and cut her lip. She was bleeding, though not profusely, and the man was rubbing a knot on his forehead where he'd banged into the windshield or dash. They were both luckier than Eckland.

Gabrielle helped them out and away from the truck, got a first-aid kit out of the patrol car for their use, and lit some flares to warn other motorists to slow down. Then she stood off to the side to wait for the ambulance.

But the sight of Tucker's retreating figure, growing smaller and smaller as he made his way up the mountain closest to the road, taunted her. If she let him get very far into the desert, they might never find him. The Mexican border was only fifty miles or so to the south. He could slip across and easily disappear....

If he made it to the border. Chances were better that he'd die of dehydration long before he reached Mexico. He was injured, had no water, and they were in the middle of the Sonoran Desert, one of the hottest, driest places in all of North America. Temperatures this time of year often reached one hundred and twenty degrees. Though Gabrielle wasn't sure exactly how that would translate into surface heat, she knew the ground would be a whole heck of a lot hotter than the air, probably one seventy or one eighty degrees.

What was Tucker thinking? That he'd rather die than go to Alta Vista?

Evidently.

Telling herself she'd worry about Tucker later, she walked back to see if there was anything she could do for Eckland, but he didn't want her company.

"Stay the hell away," he growled. "You've done enough."

"Are you bleeding anywhere?" she persisted.

"My leg's broke. That's it. Nothing we can do but wait."

"You don't seem to have a back or neck injury. If it would make you more comfortable, I could probably help you out of the car."

"I don't want your help. I don't want to be touched."

"Okay." Gabrielle took a deep breath. At least she'd tried.

When she rejoined the people from the truck, the man was using some gauze to help the woman stanch the bleeding on her lip. Gabrielle could tell from their exchange that they were mother and son, but they weren't particularly interested in speaking to her. She didn't have much to say, anyway. Other drivers were stopping to see if they could help, creating a diversion. And she was too busy flogging herself for letting Tucker escape in the first place.

Raising a hand to shade her eyes from the bright morning sun—which promised to raise temperatures even more by midafternoon—she watched Tucker's progress through the haze of heat that shimmered all around him, making him look more like a mirage than a flesh-and-blood man. Though he was moving slowly now that he had to climb, he was nearly halfway up the first rocky mountain, which was probably a mile and a half away. Every step he took made Gabrielle grind her teeth in frustration. Soon he'd be out of sight, and then…and then there was no telling what would happen to him.

She remembered the pain in his eyes, knew he

couldn't have faked that as easily as he might have exaggerated his moans and grunts, and made the only decision she could live with. She might be responsible for Randall Tucker's escape, but she wasn't going to be responsible for his death.

Hurrying back to the car, she found Eckland, ashen-faced, head back, eyes closed. But the moment she ducked into the open passenger-side door and started rummaging around, he sat up and glared at her.

"What are you doing now?" he asked.

"I'm going after him."

His brows knitted and anger flashed in his eyes. "You're *what?* Are you nuts? It's got to be over a hundred degrees already. You'll get heatstroke inside an hour."

"Exactly."

"Exactly what, damn you?"

"He can't survive."

"You're still worried about *Tucker?*" He winced and stared down at his leg.

"He could die if I don't bring him back."

"And you could die going after him. You could get lost, run out of water, get bit by a rattlesnake or—"

"I'm taking the gallon of water I brought and leaving you with yours," she said, cutting him off because now that she was heading into the desert, there wasn't any point in giving Tucker more of a lead. "I'll have someone come and sit with you to answer the radio, in case—" she licked her lips "—in case you pass out or something. Help will be here soon. Try to hang on to that."

She checked the magazine in her semiautomatic Glock 9 mm, then slid the warm metal nozzle back into her hip holster. She was trying to save Randall Tucker's life, not take it, but if he attacked her...

She swallowed hard and chose not to think about what might happen if he got the better of her. The vast desert, the scorching sun, the scorpions and snakes would probably get her first. But that thought wasn't much of an improvement over the last. Not with Allie waiting for her at home.

Thank God, David was there.

"I'd stay here with you if there was anything I could do," she told Eckland as she gathered what food and water she had, "but there's nothing. You said it yourself."

He'd closed his eyes again while she was talking, and this time when he spoke, he didn't open them. "Don't do it."

Trying to think of a way to carry the cumbersome water jug, which would prove heavy after a while, she grabbed her giant black leather purse that often doubled as a diaper bag. "I have to."

"Why?" he rasped. "What's one Randall Tucker, more or less? Our prisons are full of filthy murderers like him."

Gabrielle remained silent long enough that he finally opened his eyes. "He's out there because of me. And respect for human life might be the only thing that separates us from them."

"Then you'll be dead."

"Maybe," she said, and slipped the strap of her purse across her body so she could carry the water on her back. "But I've got the gun and food and water. He's hurt, and he has no water, nothing. Why not show a little confidence and have a car waiting for me just in case I manage to bring him back?"

"Right," Eckland said with a hoarse chuckle. "I'll have a hearse parked right by the side of the road."

TUCKER COULDN'T BELIEVE his eyes. He'd known the police would come looking for him eventually. But he'd never imagined Officer Hadley would strike out after him *on her own*. Evidently she wasn't only an idealist. She was a reckless fool. He had good reason to risk his miserable life; she did not.

Pausing in the shade of a rock overhang—the only shade for miles, it seemed—he watched her approach, and felt his mood darken. The initial surge of exhilaration he'd felt at obtaining his freedom had staved off some of the pain in his hand, but now the throbbing surged up his arm and through his whole right side until he thought he might pass out. Battling the dizziness, he mentally pulled himself away from that void, and started climbing again. He had to reach Landon. He couldn't care about what happened to Hadley.

Climb. He wasn't going to let her drag him back to prison under any circumstances.

Climb. Her welfare wasn't his problem.

Climb. Breathe. It was steeper now. His foot, shod only in thin-soled, prison-issue tennis shoes, slipped, and he nearly went down. He barely managed to keep his balance, but even the concentration required to make the ascent couldn't banish Hadley from his mind.

Stop it! Eckland and the other guards can worry about her. There's the ridge. That's it. One foot in front of the other.

After all, she was one of *them*.

Focus. Shove the pain away. Ignore the heat. One more step…

He imagined Landon calling to him, just at the top

of the next rise, and then the next, and that made the going easier. "I'm coming," he promised. "I'm coming for you, buddy. You can depend on me. I won't let you down. I won't ever give up. I won't...ever..."

He had to stop to catch his breath. Though some mountains in the desert rose eight thousand feet, this wasn't one of them—thank God. Still, it was difficult climbing with the use of only one hand, the sun robbing him of all moisture.

At least the pain was starting to ease now that the cuffs had been off long enough to allow his blood flow to return to normal. But the figure following undauntedly in his footsteps, slowly closing the distance between them, dragged at him like a lead weight.

Why didn't Hadley turn back? What did she think she could do, even if she caught up with him? Especially now that they were so far from the highway? He didn't even know where he was going, just somewhere, anywhere, the first small town, outpost or ranch where he could call his brother or Robert, his old business partner, for help. He could wind up lost or dead before he made contact with the outside world, and so could she. Nothing but sun-baked earth and low shrubs—creosote bush and white bursage, the two most drought-tolerant plants on the whole continent, with a few cholla and columnar cacti thrown in—surrounded them on all sides and certainly didn't provide much to navigate by.

"You're crazy, you know that, lady?" he said into air so dense with heat he could scarcely breathe. "What's one more felon mean to you? Go back to the thousands waiting for you at the prison. Go back to the riots and the homemade-knife fights and the gangs, and leave me the hell alone."

He forged on, determined to forget the slight figure trudging through the barren valley below him. She wasn't going catch him. She'd live or she'd die. It made no difference to him. He wasn't expected to care one way or the other—and he wouldn't. He *didn't* care. She was a guard, the enemy, almost a stranger to him.

She is also a woman, with a child at home, his conscience answered. A woman who wouldn't be where she was if not for him. And she was one of the only people who'd shown him any compassion since the day he was accused of murdering Andrea.

The memory of Hadley wiping the blood from his lip flashed through Tucker's mind, and he imagined her standing over him again, her hands on his face. Only this time she was tilting up his chin to give him a drink of water....

Thirst so powerful it nearly brought him to his knees swept through him. The dryness of his throat made it difficult to swallow, and he feared it wouldn't be long before he dropped like a stone. Then what good would he be to Landon?

He had to get some water—and there was only one place to find it. Maybe he was fortunate Officer Hadley had followed him, after all. She might prove his salvation once again.

Reaching the top of the mountain he'd been scaling, he hid behind a rock outcropping that rose like a spire into the broad cloudless sky and leaned against its solid mass to wait.

The minutes ticked by, slowly. He felt her coming close, knew she'd pass the same way he'd come. She hadn't deviated a step from his path so far. He doubted she'd change now. She felt too confident, toting that pistol that was about to do her no good.

The thought that he'd be taking something she needed just as badly as he did sent a flicker of guilt through Tucker, but he knew it was only a shadow of what he would've felt before prison had turned him into the man he was. He ignored it. Landon needed him. And without her precious jug of water, Hadley would be forced to go back.

WHERE WAS HE?

Gabrielle paused to take another sip of water as she squinted at the dirt, rocks and thorny shrubs farther up the mountain. Tucker wasn't hard to follow through the wide, flat valleys—there she could see for miles, and he was the only thing moving—but he'd disappeared over the crest of the mountain, which was still a hundred yards or so away, and she hadn't seen him for ten minutes or more.

He knew she was following him. He'd looked back at her several times already and increased his speed. Was he hurrying down the other side, still trying to leave her in his dust? Or had he settled on a more intelligent plan?

She listened carefully, hoping for some indication of where he was. But she couldn't hear any movement, just the hushed quiet of a desert in midafternoon, when even lizards knew enough to stay out of the sun. Maybe she was still too far away to hear him. Or maybe he'd changed direction and was slipping among the rocks of the mountain peak. In that case, she might never find him.

Telling herself she'd definitely be smarter to imitate the tortoise than the hare, she resisted the urge to start jogging. Instead, she capped the water jug and resumed moving at the same measured pace. At first the oppressive heat had made her curse the warmth of her uniform. But now she was grateful for her long sleeves and pants. She had sunblock in her purse—she always carried it for Allie—but it was the small "glue stick" kind meant for faces and wouldn't have gone far. The fabric of her uniform saved much of her skin from the sun, protected her legs from cacti and other spiney plants, and gave her some hope of withstanding a rattlesnake strike should one occur.

The thought of surprising a rattler made Gabrielle shudder, but rattlers weren't the only creatures she had to worry about. Though not nearly as common, the western coral snake, with its red, yellow and black bands, had a bite just as toxic. Then there were Gila monsters, the large poisonous lizards so common to the Sonoran Desert, and bark scorpions and brown recluse spiders. Even the Sonoran Desert toad was poisonous, although there was little chance of running into one of those.

Checking behind a piece of fallen cactus before stepping over it, Gabrielle thought about picking up a stick—if she could find one of any consequence in this barren place—to use in case she happened upon any threatening wildlife. The small coral snake might not be a common sight, but enough snakes had similar markings to make her nervous about being able to tell the difference.

Sweat trickled down the sides of her face. She wiped it away with one arm as she neared the top of the mountain, hurrying now despite the heat because she was beginning to feel so alone in the vastness. Tucker couldn't be far. As soon as she saw him, she'd relax…a little. He might be more dangerous than any snake, but he *was* human, and knowing someone else was within earshot brought her a degree of comfort. Besides, the closer he was, the sooner she'd capture him. Then they could both turn back and by the end of the day, it would all be over. He'd be where he was supposed to be. She'd be safe. No more worrying about snakes or—

Suddenly, Gabrielle stopped. From where she stood she could see part of the valley below. Tucker wasn't there, but a giant rock stood between her and a full panorama. He could be hurrying down the mountain beyond her sight, in which case she was losing valuable time. Or he could be standing behind the rock that obscured her view, in which case caution could save her life.

She carefully scanned the area, but nothing—no movement, sight or sound—gave him away. Pressing herself to the outcropping that could just as easily be providing *him* with cover, she pulled out her gun. "Tucker? Are you there?"

No answer. She inched forward, craning her neck to see farther than a couple of feet at a time. "Tucker? I'm not here to hurt you. You know I'll be as fair as possible. But what you're doing isn't right, and it isn't safe."

She stopped, listened. Nothing. Was he even there? She was probably making a fool of herself. "Come on, Tucker. We both know I have to take you in."

She heard the sound of small rocks being dislodged farther down the mountain, and let her breath go in relief. She was jittery, that was all. He'd hurried on.

Shoving her Glock into her holster, she abandoned caution in favor of catching a glimpse of him before he could disappear again. But her forward motion was halted midstride when he tackled her, bringing her down hard on her left side.

The jolt of pain that accompanied her fall stole her breath as Randall Tucker landed on top of her. Blinking to clear the sudden spots from her eyes, she felt panic surge through her body like an electric current as he loomed over her.

"I'm afraid I'm going to have to object to a return trip," he said, keeping her pinned beneath him while he took her gun.

Every muscle in Gabrielle's body tensed as she waited to see what he'd do with the weapon. She stared into his eyes, hoping to read his intent so she could formulate some type of defense. But his face remained hard and resolute, his eyes empty. And that scared her more than anything. Until that moment of complete vulnerability, she'd never really believed something this terrible could happen to her.

"What are you going to do?" She gasped because his weight made it difficult to speak. It would be all too easy for him to shoot her and walk away. Or maybe he'd rape her first. She understood how it was with the inmates, how they looked at her, what they said. He was already sentenced to life without parole. A man in that situation didn't have a lot to lose.

Only he wasn't acting as though he had any interest in raping her. He didn't even seem particularly interested in shooting her. He looked as though he was going directly for...the water!

Tossing the gun almost carelessly out of reach, he eased himself up and began to slip the strap of her purse over her head. That was when Gabrielle made her move. Suddenly bucking and writhing, she managed to knock him off balance just enough to twist out from under him. He grabbed her with his right hand— an instinctive action, she guessed, judging by the expletive that came out of his mouth when his injured hand couldn't hold her. By the time he corrected his error and tried to anchor her with his left, she had the gun.

"Get up," she said, scooting farther away and aiming the muzzle at his chest. The hot ground had burned her back through the fabric of her shirt, and she'd taken a few cactus spines in her hand when she'd lunged for the gun, but adrenaline was pumping through her body by the gallon and she could hardly feel a thing as she forced her shaky legs to support her.

Her purse, and the water in it, lay between them. Fortunately, the cap was the screw type and had survived their little tussle.

She watched Tucker's eyes flick toward the jug as he got slowly to his feet.

"Take a short drink, then shove the water over here," she said.

"No problem." He shrugged, but his gaze was watchful, and Gabrielle didn't trust his nonchalance. He closed his eyes in apparent relief as he drank, then capped the jug. But instead of pushing it her way, as she'd told him, he settled it in her purse as though it was as precious as a newborn baby and slung the strap crosswise over his body. Because of his size, the bag hit him between the shoulder blades and looked funny resting so high—and being carried by someone so masculine—but Gabrielle knew from experience why he'd want the purse to tote the water.

"Give me the water and the rest of my stuff, or I'll shoot," she warned. "It's over. We're going back now."

He seemed to take her measure, then shook his head. "I don't think so, Hadley."

Gabrielle's heart started beating so loudly she had trouble hearing her own voice over the steady thrum in her ears. Sweat mixed with sunblock dripped into her eyes, stinging them, causing tears. She blinked rapidly to clear her vision and told herself to stay calm. She had him right where she wanted him; she just had to convince him she was in charge.

"Do as I say," she insisted. "I don't want to use this, but I will."

His gaze locked onto the gun. "Have you ever killed anything before? Any*one?*" he added softly.

"I've never had to. But I will."

"I don't think so."

"Oh, yeah?" She knew she needed absolute credibility now. Pointing to a prickly pear cactus sprawled to the left of him, she squeezed off a shot. The tip she'd been aiming at instantly disappeared, but the only acknowledgment she received from Tucker was a casual glance at the evidence of her marksmanship and a slight lift of his brows.

"So you've killed a cactus. Nice shootin', Tex, but I'm afraid that isn't going to change my mind. Whether or not you can hit me isn't the question. Not at this range, anyway. I'm more concerned with whether or not you *will.*"

"I will," she said, fighting to keep her voice steady.

"No, you won't."

Perspiration poured down Gabrielle's spine, beaded on her top lip, wetted the hair at her temples. "Are you willing to bet your life on that?"

"I guess I am," he said.

She told herself to aim for a foot and pull the trigger. A violent felon stood facing her, eyes sparking with challenge. Arizona State Law authorized deadly force in two instances: when human life was at stake and/or to prevent an escape. She was within her rights.

But he wasn't exactly attacking her, which made it feel unprovoked. Out here, even a small wound might kill him. She couldn't drag a two-hundred-pound person across the desert for three hours to the highway. Neither could she get help in time to save him if the bullet did a little more damage than intended.

She imagined the recoil of the gun traveling up her arm, pictured his blood spilling onto the hot, parched earth, and knew he was right. She couldn't do it. She'd never killed anything in her life, and she wasn't about to start now, regardless of who or what he was.

They'd reached a stalemate. He wasn't going to come with her; she wasn't going to shoot him. Now what?

"You're not thinking," she said. "You could easily die out here even if I don't shoot you."

"Maybe. But it won't be here and now." He squinted at the horizon. "It'll probably be out there somewhere. Tomorrow. Or maybe the next day."

At least he knew how precarious his situation was. Maybe she could reason with him. "That's exactly my point. You need water and medical treatment—"

He held up his broken hand. "And prison is just the place to get it, is that right?"

He had her there. But at least he'd stay *alive* in prison...probably. "This desert is over a hundred thousand square miles, Tucker. Regardless of what happened at Florence, your only chance for survival lies with me."

"Then I have no chance," he said, "because this is where we part company. Think of that baby waiting for you at home and take it slow on the way back. If you don't panic and work up too much of a sweat, you can make it.''

Work up too much of a sweat? Her hands were moist and clammy on the butt of the pistol, which made it difficult to retain a firm grip, and she couldn't blink fast enough to keep the sunblock and perspiration out of her eyes. ''I won't go back without you.''

''Yes, you will. There's nothing else you can do,'' he said, and started down the mountain as though she held nothing more dangerous than a Twinkie.

''Tucker!'' She fired the weapon into the air, expecting him to dart for cover. But he didn't. From what she could see, he didn't even flinch.

''Don't waste any more of that magazine,'' he called over his shoulder when the echo of the report died away. ''You might need a few bullets before you get back.''

She needed them now. Only she couldn't bring herself to use them. ''What am I going to need them for? We're completely alone out here, you and I, and you're leaving.''

''You never know who you might run into on the road.''

Gabrielle was pretty sure he was joking—an escaped convict telling her to be careful of whom she might meet—but she wasn't in the mood for humor. ''That's all you have to say? I come clear out here to save your lousy skin, and you're going to leave me on my own, without any water?''

''You're trying to take me back to prison so you don't lose your job. Am I supposed to feel indebted to you for that?''

Professional pride had figured into her initial motivation. She'd been angry that he'd taken advantage of her compassion and felt determined to bring him to justice. But it had been life-and-death considerations that had kept her trudging into the desert. "I have a baby at home, remember? Do you really think I'd be out here if my job was the only thing at stake?"

He shrugged. "Maybe you've got something to prove. In any case, let me give you a good piece of advice. Get going. There are coyotes and javelina and maybe even a few mountain lions out here, and none of them are too particular about what they eat if they're hungry enough. Once the sun starts to set, even the rattlesnakes will be out foraging for food. It isn't wise to waste much time getting back."

"You'll run out of water eventually. You know that, don't you?" she said, watching him take another drink and already longing for one herself.

No answer.

"If you come back with me, I'll put a few hundred dollars on your books so you can buy stuff from the prison store. That's a better offer than you're going to get from anyone else."

Nothing.

"If you wait for the police to hunt you down, you'll probably end up on death row."

He stopped halfway down the mountain and faced her, and she felt a brief flicker of hope—until she saw the sun glinting off his teeth and knew he was laughing at her. "Didn't anyone give you an aptitude test before hiring you as a prison guard?"

She let her breath go in a long sigh and put her Glock in its holster. "No."

"Well, they should have. I don't think you could shoot a rabid skunk," he said and left.

CHAPTER SIX

DIDN'T ANYONE GIVE YOU an aptitude test before hiring you as a prison guard?

She should have shot him, Gabrielle decided as she trudged wearily back the way she'd come. She would've been perfectly justified. But he wasn't likely to survive in the desert, anyway. And the highway hadn't seemed so far away then. As long as he was letting her go, she hadn't felt in imminent danger—until now.

Gabrielle doubted it had been much more than thirty minutes since she'd seen Tucker, but already it felt like days. The desert stretched in front of her in all directions, so much the same she could be traveling in circles and never know it. And the terrible thirst! Her tongue, thick and unwieldy, seemed foreign to her mouth.

If only for a small drink, just a sip. Then she could think straight again. Then she could find her way out of this hell of cactus and sand....

Shading her eyes, she squinted into the sky and cursed the blazing sun. Would it never go down? The heat was making her stumble and weave and feel as though she might throw up. She considered sitting for a few minutes—she couldn't seem to reach the other side of this oven-like valley—but there was no shade.

Without shade, the ground was too hot to touch for more than a couple of minutes.

Licking dry lips that were already beginning to crack, she thought of the small treasures Tucker had stolen from her when he'd taken her bag. At first she'd lamented the loss of her credit cards and driver's license, even thought she might miss, at least until payday, the thirty bucks she had in her wallet. But none of that meant anything to her anymore. At this point she longed only for her chapstick and sunblock—and water, of course. Nothing mattered more than water.

Gabrielle imagined coming face-to-face with Tucker again, the water jug between them, and thought she could very possibly shoot him now. That consoled her for a moment...until she tripped over a cactus she'd anticipated clearing and landed chest-first in the rocky, arid dirt.

"Ouch," she cried as several sharp spines stabbed through the fabric of her pants and entered the flesh of her leg. She scrambled off the plant and yanked the spines out one by one, but even after they were gone and the stinging had faded, she couldn't seem to gather the energy to stand. The ground below her felt as hot as the sun above, but even when her bottom began to burn, the pain wasn't enough to motivate her to stand.

If help doesn't arrive soon, I'm not going to make it.

It was the first time Gabrielle had allowed herself to really consider that fear. She hated giving in to it now, hated knowing discouragement would only weaken her. But at this point, the fact that she had little chance of ever seeing her baby again seemed so obviously the truth, she could no longer deny it.

David would take care of Allie; he'd never let anything happen to her. She'd been saying those words to herself over and over, only this time she followed them with a sincere prayer of thanksgiving for the man who'd been her best friend for nearly ten years. Then she pulled her knees to her chest and rested her head on them. She'd wait. Someone would come. Someone would come soon....

A rustling in the underbrush brought Gabrielle's head up. What was that? A lizard? A pack rat? Or...a *snake?* The image of a rattlesnake slithering up beside her finally gave Gabrielle the adrenaline jolt she needed to get back on her feet. She jumped up and stood teetering on shaky legs, wishing the ground would stop spinning so she could tell if there was, indeed, something poisonous in the vicinity. But she couldn't see any creatures near her, wasn't sure what had moved, and then the soreness in her leg from the cactus collision gave her an idea. Cacti stored water to survive their harsh surroundings. If she could cut into one and extract the moisture, she might make it to the road. She'd once heard that the Pima, who'd lived in the desert during the time of the Spanish explorers, got water that way. There were certainly plenty of barrel cacti around.

Except she didn't have a knife or anything sharp to cut into one. And she'd also read or heard somewhere that only one species of barrel cactus yielded potable water—the others were toxic. How would she tell the difference?

Did it matter? she asked herself, taking a hard look at reality. Either she found water and lived. Or she didn't find water, in which case she was going to die anyway.

Withdrawing her pistol, she began shooting at the

biggest barrel cactus she could find, but her aim was no longer true. She had to go right up next to it, just inches from the thick curved spines, to do any damage. Even then her Glock left nothing in its tough skin but small bullet holes surrounded by gunpowder residue. No water dripped out at all.

She picked up a rock with a sharp edge and tossed it from hand to hand until it cooled, then used it to chip away at the bullet-ridden cactus. The rock only made a few cuts and dents near the holes. Before long, she didn't have the energy to continue banging away at it.

"Damn!" she cried, finally dropping the rock as tears of frustration and hopelessness welled in her eyes. She was so hot. She'd never been so hot and miserable in all her life, and she knew it was going to get worse. A person could live in the desert without water for three days. But it wasn't really living. It was more like a slow, terrible death.

She stared at her Glock. Her second magazine was empty now. But she had one more in her belt. If help didn't come soon, maybe she wouldn't have to go the slow way.

TUCKER SHIFTED his position to avoid the rock that jutted into his left shoulder blade, and leaned his head back to rest against the wall of the cave. It was hot, even in the shade, but at least he didn't have to move in the open sun anymore. Now that he had water, he could be more cautious about his escape. He could sleep during the day, when the police would be out looking for him, and travel at night. Under cover of darkness, he could move faster and more freely. He wouldn't go through his water so quickly. He could double back toward the highway and follow it to civilization, where he was most likely to find help.

But the gunshots that had rung out, breaking the tomblike silence only moments before, bothered him. He knew it was Hadley—had to be her with that pistol she'd been carrying—though why she'd be emptying her gun, he had no idea. He'd counted a couple of separate shots and then ten more in rapid succession. Was it meant as some kind of signal? A smart way to lead the rescue party to her?

Or was it a cry for help? An act of desperation?

Opening one eye and then the other, he stared down at the purse at his side as though it had turned into one of the rattlesnakes for which he'd searched the cave so carefully before crawling inside. He hated that purse. It symbolized how far he'd fallen from the Little League dad he'd once been. He'd sponsored fundraisers for politicians and different charities; he'd been on the school board and driven a Porsche; he'd owned a half-million-dollar home and another few million dollar's worth of real estate. Never in his life had he dreamed he'd have reason to steal anything. But the fact that he hadn't thought twice about taking whatever was inside Hadley's purse, as well as the water, showed him he wasn't the man he used to be.

Why hadn't he dumped out the personal stuff and given it back to her? The pictures and money and whatever else she kept in that big bag? He'd considered it briefly, but another part of him had instantly rebelled. There might be something inside he would need— change for a pay phone, a few bucks for a meal, a credit card to rent a car. Why should he give away something he could use? What had clean living done for him in the past? Nothing. Andrea had failed him.

Truth and justice had failed him. Even the guards at Florence had failed him. He had no more faith in the system, no more belief that right would prevail. Survival of the fittest, that was what he believed in now. Taking what he needed was the only way back to his son.

Grabbing Hadley's purse with his good hand, he yanked out the water jug and poked through her sack lunch. A turkey sandwich, potato chips, a little bag of carrot sticks, a handful of cookies and a diet soda. He turned the purse upside down and dumped out everything else, let it all tumble onto the ground as though the bits and pieces of Hadley's life meant nothing to him: one pack of gum, a few gum wrappers, some loose crayons, a baby's pacifier in a plastic bag, a packet of Kleenex and another of Band-Aids, a box of diaper disposal bags, a tube of diaper rash ointment, a handful of small change, a book of matches, a wallet with a twenty and several ones, keys, sunblock, chapstick, some other glossy lip stuff and various items of make-up, a book of checks that gave her address as 618 Pueblo Street, Space 13, and birth-control pills.

Birth control pills. Tucker picked them up and turned them over in his hand, wondering about the father of Hadley's baby. He was a lucky son of a bitch. So why wasn't he taking better care of his wife, his family? The man had to be stupid not to care more about a woman like Hadley. She was so beautiful she could steal Tucker's breath at twenty yards, even when she was covered in dust and sweat and wearing that damn uniform. She had the kind of body that begged to be touched—soft and curvy in all the right places. And those eyes... Big and luminous, they revealed everything she was feeling. Tucker loved that. He was tired of coy and cynical, had lived with Andrea long enough to know he didn't appreciate secrets.

Hadley had more than looks. She had guts and compassion. Without any but the most nominal support from her fellow guards, she'd stopped the fight and come to his cell to treat his wounds. This morning, when she knew he was in pain, she'd defied Eckland by insisting he loosen the cuffs, which meant she'd have hell to pay later.

And he'd stolen the water along with her purse and left her to make it, if she could, on her own.

With a grimace, Tucker tossed the birth-control pills back inside her purse and started gathering up everything else. He didn't want to see this stuff. It made Officer Hadley too human, made her seem no different from the kind of person he'd once been. She was just living her life, trying to make ends meet while raising a kid. He might've had more money than she did, might have lived in a nicer home, known more prestige—but so what?

He thought of the way she'd felt beneath him when he'd tackled her, remembered the defiance in her face—admired it—then paused with a hand on her wallet. While taking stock of his current resources, he'd checked to see how much money she had in there, but he hadn't let himself pore through the pictures opposite her coin purse. He knew better than to do it now…except he couldn't help himself.

A baby stared back at him first, a chubby baby with a round head, fuzzy blond hair and a big gooey smile. Wearing a pink-and-white frilly dress, she had a matching bow stuck to her head, and resembled Hadley through the eyes. Next came a tall, lean man in a suit. Tucker didn't look very long at him; for some reason, he didn't really want to see him. And then he found what had to be a family photo. The man from the second picture stood next to Hadley, who held the baby in her arms.

The shot had obviously been taken with a regular camera and been cut down to fit the wallet, which meant it had special significance for Hadley, and it was no wonder. In it they were all smiling happily, but not for the camera—for each other. The man had his arm wrapped protectively around Hadley, grinning as though he was the happiest soul on earth. Hadley was wearing a tank top and shorts, which showed plenty of glowing, tanned skin, and was kissing the baby's head. The baby was jamming a chubby finger in her mouth.

Tucker couldn't quit staring at the three of them. He memorized the way the man's hand curled around Hadley's shoulder, studied the angle of his head as he leaned toward her, noted the pride on his face and wished…wished things were different. He belonged with Landon, even though there was no more Andrea, and Hadley belonged with this man and this child.

Would she make it?

So far, Tucker was innocent of murder. He'd never so much as struck Andrea. The night his wife disappeared, they'd had a particularly bad argument, and she'd tried to slug him. In the end, he'd stormed off but he'd left her very much alive. And that was how he'd left Officer Hadley—alive.

Only he wasn't sure she'd stay alive. And if she didn't, this baby would never see her mother again. Because of him.

Closing the wallet, he put it back in her purse and shoved the whole thing away.

Go to sleep. You didn't ask her to follow you out here. You didn't ask for any of this.

But he'd taken her water....

If she doesn't make it out on her own, help will find her in time. She'll be okay.

But he didn't know that, couldn't be sure. He thought of the entries in her check register listing small amounts for groceries and diapers. She was a mother, a woman. She was innocent—

He was innocent, too, dammit! Why'd she have to work at Florence? Why couldn't she be someone else? Hansen or Eckland? Someone who deserved to wander around the desert for a while?

Another gunshot sounded, and he froze. She was close. What was she doing with that damn pistol?

Angry that he could still care, Tucker finally slipped out of his cave and went to look for her. It was crazy, he knew, and risked everything he'd gained in the last few hours. If he went back to prison he'd probably die before he hit forty. And yet, he had to answer to himself at some point. Evidently that hadn't changed—or at least not enough.

"THAT SMELLS like my sunblock," Gabrielle mumbled, thinking she had to be hallucinating when the aroma of coconut registered in her brain. She opened her eyes to see Randall Tucker bending over her.

"That's because it *is* your sunblock," he said.

"Oh, well, we wouldn't want you to get burned." She closed her eyes, knowing that when she opened them again, he'd be gone—*wham, zap,* vanished into thin air—along with the water jug he was getting out of her purse. But then a man-size hand lifted her head, and he told her to open her mouth, and it all felt very real.

"Here you go. Drink a little. It'll help."

The water was hot, almost as hot as the ground and his body, but all her previous hallucinations had ended with her sucking in nothing but air. This time she felt the liquid roll down her throat and hit her stomach and once she'd gulped enough, she grabbed hold of his wrist to make sure he wasn't going anywhere. "It *is* you," she cried.

"How many other men do you know running around this desert carrying a purse?" he asked.

Her thoughts seemed to whirl around in her head, making her chase them. "At least you're not wearing my makeup," she said. A silly remark, but it was the first thing she could come up with.

"I took a few birth-control pills, though. Hope you don't mind." He capped the water and helped her to sit up.

Again it took her a few seconds to respond. "That's okay. I've missed a few days so I have some to spare," she finally said, even though she hadn't taken the Pill in a couple of months. Since her divorce, she'd only dated a few times and certainly hadn't come close to making love with anyone.

"Why'd you come back?" she asked.

He scowled, and when he spoke his voice was much gruffer than it had been only moments before. "I didn't, or not very far, anyway. You've been going in circles and I just happened to see you."

"And you thought you'd give me a drink?"

"Since I have so much."

"Right."

"Can you get up?"

"What?"

"Get up."

The command seemed to grow loud, then soft, then loud again and made no sense to Gabrielle. When she didn't move, he grabbed her by the shirtfront and hauled her to her feet.

"Is that my Chap Stick, too?" she asked, grabbing onto him so she wouldn't fall while staring at the shine on his lips. He felt good, so solid and alive.

He pried her fingers away as though he'd rather not be touched, retrieved the Chap Stick from her purse and applied it liberally to her mouth. Then he took out her sunblock and smoothed it on her face.

"There you go," he said, holding the water to her lips and allowing her to drink freely again. "You're all set."

"I feel a little better already," she admitted. "Thank you. I really can't thank you enough. I thought—"

He raised a hand. "I don't want to hear what you thought. And I don't want your thanks. I don't want to know anything more about you. Here's your baby's pacifier and your diaper rash ointment and your wallet." Keeping only the water, he settled her purse over her shoulder and pointed her toward a mountain range that looked exactly like the one she'd emerged from not long ago.

"Just start walking. The highway's over there. If you keep on a more or less straight course through those mountains, you'll eventually find it. Okay? And it might be a good idea to fire that gun every once in a while. That way, if they're looking for you, they'll know where to go. Good luck."

"Good luck?" she echoed.

"Yeah, good luck. Get going. You should be fine now."

She didn't feel fine. She felt numb, unable to process words as easily as she normally did. "You're leaving me again?"

He scowled. "What did you expect? An escort?"

She wasn't sure that she'd expected anything. She just couldn't bear to see him walk away from her right now, not when she was feeling so weak. She wouldn't make it out, wouldn't see Allie or David again, would never be able to confront Naomi or meet her sister.

"Don't look at me like that," he snapped.

She blinked and nodded obediently, feeling the inevitability of soldiering on alone. It wasn't over. She wasn't done yet.

Some of the discouragement she felt must have communicated itself to him, because he suddenly pulled her back and shoved the water jug into her purse. "Take the damn water, too," he said. "Just get out of here."

The water nearly toppled her, though it couldn't have weighed all that much. He seemed to notice her unsteadiness and his expression darkened, but Gabrielle took a deep breath and told herself to forget him. She didn't need him. She didn't need anyone. She'd come this far on her own, hadn't she? She'd been alone since she was three years old....

She turned away and started walking, but when she lifted her eyes to the sky, something in the distance made her wonder if she was seeing things. A dark cloud seemed to be moving her way. Only it didn't come slowly, as clouds usually did. It rushed toward her, filling the sky, blocking out the sun, eating up the horizon. "What's *that?*" she breathed.

Tucker must've heard her, or maybe he'd already

spotted it himself. When she glanced over her shoulder, she found him staring in the same direction, a mixture of surprise and disbelief on his face. "Oh, no," he said. "Not now."

CHAPTER SEVEN

THE NEXT THING Gabrielle knew, she was running. Tucker had taken hold of her hand and was fairly dragging her behind him, carrying the purse and the water on his shoulder and heading in the opposite direction. She didn't feel strong enough to wrench away or to cry out. Somehow she didn't even want to. He seemed to know what he was doing, moved with a strength of purpose she lacked, and she was glad enough to let him pull her along.

"Is that what I think it is?" she gasped, her lungs burning, as they finally reached the mountains.

"It's a monsoon," he said.

The tempestuous monsoons had always appealed to Gabrielle. She liked the way they came up so suddenly, raising the humidity and blackening the sky. They were atmospheric and exciting; they threw everything into chaos. But she'd always witnessed such storms from behind the safety of her front windows in suburbia, U.S.A., surrounded by buildings and concrete and trees and grass. Now there was nothing to hold down the dust, nothing to block the sudden wind. The gathering storm wasn't like anything Gabrielle had ever seen.

"Where are we going?" she cried as the wind began to claw at her clothes.

"We need to get higher. It doesn't rain often in the desert but a large storm can be violent and this one doesn't look good," he shouted. "If it comes down as fast as I've seen in the past, we might find ourselves in the middle of a flash flood. More people drown in deserts than die of thirst."

Gabrielle had a hard time believing so much rain could come out of nowhere, even though she'd seen it before. But that wasn't why she slowed. Her legs felt as if they were inflexible wooden poles. She wanted to stop her rapid flight and simply hunker down, but he didn't give her the opportunity. Wrapping an arm around her waist, he practically hoisted her up the mountain, prodding her and pushing her with his good hand when she faltered.

It wasn't long before Gabrielle thought she couldn't go any farther. The sun had already leeched all the energy from her body, leaving nothing for the wind and the rain. Now she felt cold and tired. She knew it was because she hadn't completely re-hydrated, but water became a secondary concern as the dust whipped around them, blinding them, stinging their cheeks.

"I have to stop," she said, squinting to see Tucker in front of her.

"No, just keep moving."

The wind tore the sound of his voice away almost the second he uttered the words. A rolling boom crashed overhead. Rain started to fall in drops that felt like small pebbles and lightning streaked across the sky.

Fleetingly, Gabrielle wondered whether desert snakes came out during a storm and thought maybe she should warn Tucker about the possibility. But there seemed to be little point. They could barely see where they were going and would just have to take their chances.

"I can't go on," she said when she'd given everything she had. Wet to the skin, she was shivering from the sudden drop in temperature, although the air was still relatively warm.

Tucker didn't answer. Neither did he let her go. He kept climbing and yanking her along with him. Just when her knees buckled and she thought he'd have to carry her—or leave her behind—he reached the crest of a low rise. Saying something she couldn't hear above the rain and wind, he ducked inside a small opening in some rocks and pulled her in after him.

Gabrielle collapsed on the ground and gasped for breath, wondering if she'd ever have the strength to move again. Goose bumps raised her skin even as the sunburn on her face radiated heat. The combined extremes created maximum misery. In the back of her mind, she couldn't help fearing what the storm might mean for her survival—and for Tucker's. Surely a rescue party wouldn't scour the desert for either of them in this weather. Were they on their own? And if so, for how long?

She felt Tucker's eyes on her and met his gaze, but he looked as worn out as she felt and neither of them spoke. He dug the lunch out of her purse and offered her half the sandwich, but she waved it away. She couldn't eat. She needed to sleep. Her body wanted to shut down, forget, heal, recover…

She propped herself against the wall of the cave and let her eyelids droop.

A moment later Tucker nudged her. "Drink some more," he insisted. "You need it."

She nodded and swallowed, then curled up on the ground and fell almost instantly asleep.

IT WAS PITCH-BLACK when Gabrielle opened her eyes. For a few minutes she didn't know where she was. The air was damp, close, and every muscle in her body complained when she tried to move. So she lay still, listening to her own heartbeat. Something had happened. Something bad. And even though she hesitated to drag whatever it was out of her memory, she had to know.

Florence…Eckland…the accident… Slowly the images paraded through her mind, and by the time she remembered the blistering desert and Tucker, she knew exactly where she was and what had happened. They'd holed up in a cave to escape the storm. She didn't know how long she'd slept, only that it was night. And she didn't know whether or not she was alone.

Fear of a new kind seeped into Gabrielle's consciousness as she realized that even if she could've found her way out of the desert before, she had no concept of where or how far they'd run once the monsoon hit. Her chances of reaching the highway now, or even knowing which way to travel, were next to nil. And, strain as she might, she couldn't see anything. There wasn't even a glimmer of moonlight to show her the entrance to the cave, and a soft patter told her why. Although the wind had died, it was still raining.

"Tucker?" she breathed, almost afraid to hear her own voice in case he didn't answer. Inching her hands over the cool ground, she searched for evidence of his presence. She feared she might find a rattlesnake instead, or nothing at all, but that didn't stop her panicked groping. She wanted Tucker to be there as desperately as she'd longed for water in the heat of the day.

Had he left her?

"Tucker?" she said again, her voice rising. This time she heard movement. As she homed in on the sound, her fingers quickly encountered his arm, firm and warm and covered with a sprinkling of soft hair.

"You're still here," she whispered, sagging in relief.

He grunted, obviously asleep and not quite willing to wake up.

Gabrielle took a deep, heartening breath and withdrew her hand, even though the warmth and comfort of his body tempted her to creep a little closer. Randall Tucker might be a stranger, an escaped convict, but in this place, in these circumstances, nothing that had happened before their trip to Alta Vista seemed to matter.

But Gabrielle didn't take him for the cuddly "let's share body heat" kind of guy. Curling up next to him might be like cuddling with a Gila monster, and she needed Tucker too badly to risk crossing any lines.

Instead she hugged her knees to her chest to ward off the cold and sat in the middle of the floor, wondering how long before morning. Then she thought of water. It might be cold now, but the temperature here fluctuated by as much as forty degrees in one day. Once the storm passed and the sun rose, the temperature would skyrocket again, and she and Tucker wouldn't make it very far without more water.

Groping through the darkness for the water jug, Gabrielle found it near her purse. She hefted it to judge its weight and was sadly disappointed to find it far too light. They had a cup or so left. That was all. Desert survivalists recommended something like one gallon per person per day. How could she get more? From the sound of it, the rain was coming down pretty heavily, but she had no way to collect the drops. The mouth of their jug was too small.

She did a quick mental inventory of the items in her purse and decided that one of the plastic bags she'd bought for diaper disposal away from home just might work as a funnel…if she could dig a hole deep enough to position the jug.

Pulling her purse along with her, she felt her way to the entrance of the cave and glanced out at the sky. She couldn't see much of a moon through the clouds overhead, but it was a little lighter in the open, which helped her establish the lay of the land and avoid any more cactus spines.

In a small clearing several feet beyond the entrance, she used a sharp rock to dig a hole and positioned the water jug inside. Then she used her car key to tear open the plastic bag so it would lie flat and poked a pea-size hole in the middle. Spreading the plastic over the hole in the ground, she anchored the edges in place with rocks, and placed a light pebble in the center to make the sides slant downward. She knew she'd have to un-plug the hole every so often to allow the water to drain into the jug. And she doubted the water she collected would be very sterile. But depending on their degree of desperation, it could very possibly save their lives.

By the time she'd finished, Gabrielle was soaked again. Raindrops dripped off her eyelashes and ran down her face, and her hair clung to her neck and back in stringy strands. But it was the dark that made her most uncomfortable. Now that she'd completed the task she'd set herself and no longer had something to concentrate on, the blackness seemed to press in on all sides, making her feel cut off from everything she'd known, making her wonder if her life would ever be the same.

Morning would come, and with it the hot sun. She knew that was the one thing that wouldn't change.

Crawling back into the cave, she listened carefully for Tucker's breathing. Once her eyes had adjusted to the lack of light outside and she'd gained her bearings, she'd actually been able to see fairly well. But the darkness in the cave was total; she couldn't see his form, and she couldn't hear anything. Using her hands, she located him again, just to be sure he hadn't moved since she'd been out. Then she lay down a couple of feet away and squeezed her eyes shut. All that digging had taken its toll. She hadn't felt very strong to begin with; now she was utterly spent. Yet she couldn't sleep. She was too wet, too chilled, too uncomfortable on the hard ground, and her strange surroundings made things even worse.

Think of David and Allie, she told herself. Everything at home was probably fine, which was what mattered most. And help would surely arrive in the morning.

But the promise of future relief couldn't warm her now.

Sitting up, she chafed her arms and eyed the darkness that enveloped Randall Tucker. He was sleeping so soundly. If she could only get warm, she'd be able to sleep, too.

Fortunately he was turned away from her. She inched close, being careful not to actually touch him. When he didn't stir, she allowed herself to press closer still. Soon, she could feel his back warming the front of her and gratefully curled her legs beneath his to take full advantage. She was so cold, so terribly cold. And Randall Tucker was so wonderfully warm....

THE ABSENCE OF NOISE finally woke Tucker. Prison was a constant cacophony of snoring, talking, groaning, grunting, cursing, murmuring, rattling, clattering, clanging, buzzing and screeching. Living in a cage was like living inside a large cement mixer that churned continually, but the world was silent now, peaceful. The air smelled clean, and although the ground was slightly harder than his bunk, something soft was pressed to his backside—something that felt familiar and made his heart leap into his throat.

Turning slowly, Tucker caught his breath. Sure enough, Officer Hadley had migrated across the few feet that had originally separated them and was clinging to him as if *he* were the man in that picture in her wallet.

He rolled onto his back. She burrowed closer, accepting without question the added comfort of resting her head on the relative softness of his shoulder. Her hand slid up his chest, and Tucker's stomach did a flip-flop. It had been so long....

She sighed in approval and seemed to fall into a deeper sleep. He lay still, unsure whether or not he welcomed this unexpected contact. She felt good. There was no denying that. The softness of her body molded perfectly against his side, and the solid weight of her halfway on top of him was a satisfying sensation. But the craving she evoked on another level made him hesitate between scooping her closer and shoving her away. He didn't need this. This made him weak, cost him focus, left him vulnerable. And he hadn't been vulnerable to anything or anyone since his son had been torn from him.

But when he breathed deeply he could still catch the subtle scent of her shampoo amid the dust and dirt.

Had he never gone to prison, he doubted he would've been able to appreciate such a simple thing. Whenever he'd pulled Andrea to him, or any woman before her, he'd either progressed toward lovemaking or continued to watch television or whatever movie they'd rented. Not since he was a teenager had he simply luxuriated in the initial contact between a man and a woman, in the scent of a woman's hair, and it amazed him now that he could take so much for granted.

Hadley stirred, and Tucker stiffened in preparation for the sudden rejection that would come the moment she opened her eyes and realized who it was that held her. Pride demanded he pull away first. He'd encountered enough scorn since Andrea's death and wasn't willing to take any more. But before he could dislodge his arm, he saw that she was already staring up at him.

She looked startled when she saw him, confirming the fact that she hadn't realized, until that moment, where she was. But she didn't immediately shrink away. She smiled. "Good morning."

Tucker hesitated, then scowled and yanked his arm out from beneath her so he could get up. Why did she have to constantly surprise him? Why did she always have to behave differently from what he anticipated? He was convicted of first-degree murder. She should look at him with the same repugnance he saw in the faces of the other guards, so he could hate her just as easily. Instead she made him feel as though she could slip beneath his defenses whenever she wanted, and he couldn't tolerate that. He knew she'd ultimately spit in his face. She had to. They were on opposite sides of the law.

"Where's the water?" he asked.

She shoved a hand through her tangled hair. "Outside."

"What's it doing there?" He ducked through the opening of the cave but couldn't see anything.

When she appeared and pointed it out to him, he blinked in surprise. Sometime during the night, she'd dug a hole. A puddle of water had collected on a piece of plastic over the jug. As he watched, Hadley removed the small rock in the center and let it drain through.

"Looks like a desert still," he said.

"I'm from Oregon. I've never heard of a desert still." She carefully removed the plastic, so the surrounding dirt wouldn't spill into their water, and lifted the jug out of the hole. "It was raining when I woke up, and I figured we should take advantage it."

"A desert still uses the sun to draw moisture right out of the ground, or whatever plants you toss inside, and it's perfectly sterile. With a piece of plastic and a jug, you can make water out of urine."

She made a face as she held the water up to the sun. "I was about to ask whether or not you thought this was safe to drink, but I guess I'll take my chances. At least I know it's rainwater. It's kind of murky, but we have almost a gallon. That should help."

"The still was good thinking," he said. He couldn't offer more praise than that. He was afraid it might elicit the same sleepy smile she'd given him in the cave, and that smile had shot straight to his groin. "You hungry?"

"I am. Is there anything left?"

"Half a sandwich and some carrots, couple of cookies."

"You didn't eat it last night?"

He'd wanted to. After going ten hours on nothing

but oatmeal, stopping at half a sandwich wasn't easy.
But he'd kept looking over at Hadley's sleeping form,
knowing she'd wake hungry, and had saved what he
could for her.

He ducked inside the cave, retrieved the food and
brought it out to her.

"What about you?" she asked, sitting on a flat rock
and starting right in.

Tucker shook his head. "I'm not hungry."

She raised her brows. "Really? Don't you want a
bite?"

The innocent look of expectation on her face, her
willingness to treat him as an equal despite their po-
sitions, reminded him how good she'd felt against him.
But he'd become a master at controlling his emotions—he'd had to, just to survive—and he refused to
crave what he couldn't have.

"No." Glancing away, he turned his attention to the
valley below and the reddish hue of sunrise. A man
didn't see a sight like that from inside the walls of a
prison. Other men, free men, saw it all the time, but if
they were the way he used to be, they didn't appreciate
it.

He took a deep breath and decided that even if the
police caught him and dragged him back to prison today, or tomorrow, or any day thereafter, seeing this
sunrise had made the whole escape worth attempting.

"You're smiling," she said, intruding on his
thoughts. "You don't do that very often."

He immediately sobered. "I haven't had much to
smile about. You just about done? We gotta get going."

They had one water jug between them. For both of
them to make it out of the desert, they had to stick

together. He thought she might question his use of the word "we" but she didn't.

"Where are we going?" she asked.

He propped his hands on his hips and studied her. "I'm not going back to prison, I'll tell you that. At least not willingly. But if you want to tag along until we reach someplace safe, that's fine. Just understand that I'll do whatever I have to in order to protect my freedom."

"Like you did yesterday?" She finished the last of the sandwich, wadded up the paper bag and shoved it into her purse.

"What do you mean?"

"You just *happened* to come across me and save my life, remember?"

"I don't know what you're getting at," he lied. And then she gave him that smile, the one that had the same effect as seeing the sun creep over the horizon. She cocked her head when she looked at him, and he could tell something was different—the utter lack of fear or caution in her eyes, perhaps. He wasn't sure, but he didn't like the change. Probably because he liked it too much.

"I think I'm on to you," she said.

"You don't know me. If I were you, I wouldn't take anything for granted." He put the water inside her purse, slung it on his back and started off, and it wasn't long before Hadley fell into step beside him.

It was early yet. As they walked, a jackrabbit darted through some bushes, a lizard scampered over nearby rocks and, a half hour or so later, a bird wheeled and circled overhead. Tucker remembered Hadley's gun.

Before the day was over, he might have to kill a rabbit or a bird for food, if he could. But despite a ravenous hunger, he felt strangely reluctant to do so. Life was too precious in the desert.

CHAPTER EIGHT

BY TEN O'CLOCK the ground had already soaked up most of the moisture from the storm and, other than the occasional shallow puddle, there was little improvement over the dry, sand-colored place the desert had been yesterday.

Gabrielle squinted over her shoulder at the miles they'd come, glanced up at the blazing sun, then trained her eyes on the miles ahead, and sighed. She was already starting to feel the heat. Perspiration made her sticky. She longed for an elastic to tie up her hair and some cool water that tasted better than what she'd salvaged from the monsoon.

"How much farther do you think it'll be before we find a house or a town or something?" she asked.

Tucker shrugged. She'd tried talking to him several times over the past couple hours, had asked him about his family, where he'd grown up, what he used to do for a living. He'd given her only short sketchy answers that kept his private life very much a mystery and never asked any questions of his own. Once in a while he'd stop, remove the jug from her purse and let her drink. Then he'd take a measured sip and start off again. But that was all the attention he gave her.

Maybe he was trying to play it smart. Blabbing the intimate details of his life to a corrections officer probably wasn't the wisest thing in the world. But she had no doubt the police already had the answers to the questions she'd asked. In a criminal investigation, it was standard procedure to document a suspect's background and upbringing. So what was the harm in talking to help pass the time? She was bored and more than a little curious about her companion.

Hansen and the others considered Tucker so terribly dangerous. She'd seen how he could fight, yet he didn't seem particularly violent to her. He seemed to have a conscience, which was something she hadn't expected, and it was making her wonder how he lived with himself after killing his wife—or whether he was even guilty.

She hated to believe they could put an innocent man behind bars. The weight of evidence had to be stacked against him, but she knew mistakes were made. She'd once heard a statistic that in the past twenty-five years, more than eighty men had been released from death row after proof of their innocence came to light. Despite all the fail-safes in the system, there was always a chance that Tucker was one of those....

She opened her mouth to ask about the murder, then firmly closed it again. What if he admitted to killing his wife? She doubted she could handle the gory details right now, when they were completely alone and had no alternative but to rely on each other.

"What?" he said.

She stared at the ground, being careful where she stepped. "Nothing."

"You thirsty?"

She *was* thirsty, but he'd given her a drink a few minutes earlier, so she said no.

"Then what is it? You keep looking at me as if you have something to say."

His face was slightly burned. A thick shadow of beard covered his jaw, making him look dark and rather swarthy. But his clear blue eyes contrasted with the black of his hair, eyelashes and whiskers and seemed anything but evil.

"Did you do it?" she asked at last.

He must have known from the tone of her voice what she meant, because he didn't ask her to clarify. He kept moving for several paces, long enough that Gabrielle assumed he wasn't going to answer her. Finally he said, "No."

She waited, expecting a long sob story of being wrongly accused. Most convicts claimed to be innocent and persecuted by the system. But that was all Tucker said.

HE'D BE RID OF HER SOON. Keeping that thought in mind, Tucker continued walking and refused to look at Hadley, refused to speak to her any more than was absolutely necessary. As soon as they reached the first hint of civilization, he'd dump her, be on his way and never see her again, he told himself. He doubted he'd ever forget her, but he wasn't willing to think about that, either.

His eyes on the horizon, he constantly scanned for any sign of human habitation, and felt a flicker of hope when he eventually caught sight of something that looked promising. Was it a building?

Hadley saw it at the same time. After she'd asked whether or not he'd murdered his wife she'd grown quiet. She'd thrown frequent covert glances at him that indicated she wasn't quite sure whether or not to believe him. But whatever was going on inside her head was clearly forgotten when she grabbed his arm and pointed. "Do you see that?"

He nodded.

"What do you think it is way out here in the middle of nowhere?"

Tucker didn't care *what* it was, as long as it could provide them with food, water and a phone, or any one of the three. "It's not a convenience store, I can tell you that."

"It looks like a house."

Wishful thinking at best, Tucker decided. At this distance he couldn't tell exactly what they'd found, but it didn't look like a house.

"Someone could live out here," she said. "The family I grew up with had relatives that lived off on their lonesome in a shack with a dirt floor and an outhouse and some pigs."

Tucker didn't see any pigs. He didn't see any animals at all—or any other sign of life. "And they did this in the desert?" he asked.

"Well, not the desert exactly, but it was kind of a dry wilderness area most of the year. They had to haul in their water using big metal jugs. That makes it similar."

Tucker knew she was scrambling to keep her hope alive. She had to realize that the likelihood of finding someone crazy enough to try living out here without irrigation, electricity or plumbing was next to nil. But she'd said something else that caught his attention. She'd talked about the family she'd grown up with as though it wasn't *her* family, which made him wonder what kind of childhood she'd had. He might have asked, but he was too focused on trying to remind himself that he didn't *want* to know her any better.

They were moving closer to the building. The white adobe walls standing resolutely against a pale blue sky were definitely manmade, but everything seemed so still, so quiet. For his own hope's sake, Tucker tried to blame the absence of movement or sound on the heat. But deep down, he knew better.

"Maybe it's a desert observatory or an outpost of some kind," Hadley said, but the look on her face revealed her crushing disappointment. He knew she saw what he saw—an old church in ruins. The chances of finding water or help at such a place weren't good, which meant they'd be traveling together a little longer.

Suddenly, Hadley asked for her purse. He gave it to her, and she hurried on ahead of him.

Tucker was glad to let her go. He'd noticed her blinking more rapidly and didn't want to see her cry any more than she wanted him to. But when he found her several minutes later, sitting in the shade of a wall that looked as though it had formed some sort of outer courtyard, she wasn't crying. She was staring, trance-like, at the family picture in her wallet.

He stood a few steps away, feeling awkward. He wanted to say something to ease her despair but didn't know what. He'd just checked the old well that had once supplied the church with water. It was only a few steps away, but the rope and bucket were long gone, and it was dry anyway. The underground aquifers had been so badly depleted by pumps and urbanization that a well had to be very deep and carefully placed to find water here. An old well, especially one this old, would never be deep enough. Tucker had tossed a pebble inside, just to be sure—and heard it thump on solid earth.

"Well's dry, isn't it?" she asked without meeting his eyes.

"Yes," he answered, knowing she must be wondering what insanity had possessed her to risk never seeing her family again by following an escaped convict into the desert. He wondered the same thing. Was she just doing her job when she'd made that fateful decision? Or had fear for his life really drawn her away from safety?

Evidently she didn't know that the life of a convict destined to spend the rest of his days behind bars wasn't worth such a sacrifice. At least his own life didn't mean that much to him anymore—not if he had to live in prison for a crime he didn't commit.

Regardless, the fact that she was here, staring dejectedly at everything she stood to lose, gnawed at his insides, made him angry. He didn't want to *feel* anything, least of all *her* pain. So where was her husband? Why hadn't he looked out for her? Protected her?

"Your husband's crazy. I hope you realize that," he said.

She didn't raise her eyes again, despite the edge in his voice. "I don't know what you're talking about."

"The man in that precious photograph of yours. He had no business letting you become a prison guard. He should've looked out for you better, should've—"

"Kept me safe? Like you kept your wife safe?" Her eyes sparkled with offense, the exact reaction he'd been hoping for. He was spoiling for a good argument to release some of his own frustration and disappointment. But somehow her words sucked the fight right out of him. A picture of Andrea as he'd once known her, laughing and carefree, as in love with him as he was with her, flashed in front of his eyes, and the old pain returned, along with regret and a terrible sense of failure. He might not have killed Andrea, but he hadn't kept her safe. Judging by the spatter in their garage, she'd died a bloody death, and now she was gone forever.

He wanted to tell Hadley that he'd *tried* to protect Andrea, tried to convince her to clean up her life. But even after he'd hired a private detective and gathered proof of the affairs and the drugs—the things she so consistently denied—he couldn't save Andrea from herself, not even for Landon.

But those were only excuses. Hadley was right. He'd failed Andrea and their son. He had no right to preach to anyone.

Reclaiming her purse, he left Hadley alone as he should have in the first place. They were low on water again. He needed to focus on what really mattered, needed to take advantage of the recent moisture from the storm and the sun's heat to build the still he'd mentioned to Hadley when she'd given him the idea that morning.

Finding a soft spot, he used a rock to dig with his left hand and quickly reached moist earth. He placed the water jug in the hole, as well as some chunks of cactus he managed to gouge out with the same rock, and covered the jug and cactus pieces with another of Hadley's plastic bags. Using dirt and rocks to seal the perimeter, he tried to make the still as airtight as possible, then found a small pebble to weigh down the middle, so the condensation underneath would run into the jug, just as the rainwater had slipped down the top side.

Hadley was sitting in the same place when he'd finished. He ignored her and entered the old church, which had enough of a roof left to provide a little shade. They'd get some sleep and wait until night to move on, he told himself, struggling to shove the messy emotions Hadley's words had evoked back into their tidy compartments in his head. She didn't know Andrea, didn't know how spoiled she could be, how determined to have her way.

In any case, what was done was done. He couldn't change the past. He could only do everything in his power to save his son from paying for it in the future.

AFTER TUCKER WENT INSIDE the church, Gabrielle closed her eyes and leaned her head against the wall. What had she done? The expression on his face when she'd said that about his wife...he'd looked as though she'd just laid him open.

But he'd asked for it! He'd insulted David and spouted off more of his sexist bullshit, and he had no right. David had always been supportive. Gabrielle couldn't allow him to be blamed for anything, especially when *she* was the one who'd screwed up their marriage. *She* was the one whose life felt like this ill-fated journey through the desert—as though she was stumbling around lost, forever searching for something she couldn't find.

She sighed hopelessly. None of this was supposed to happen. Being a corrections officer was just a job. But she couldn't imagine what she should have done differently. Should she have stayed out of it, like Officer Bell, and let Hansen have a free hand? Or let Tucker escape without at least trying to bring him back? He was her responsibility. What kind of person would she be if she shirked her responsibility in favor of her own selfish interests?

Sweat trickled from her temples. She swiped at it and opened her eyes. About three feet away, the shadow of the church wall met harsh sunlight—dark juxtaposed against light in a neat line on the ground. Too bad the shadows of a person's soul weren't so easily demarcated, she thought.

Standing, she brushed off her pants. They were too dirty to even bother, but it gave her a moment to gather her nerve. Then she stepped into the church. She had no idea whether Randall Tucker was innocent or not. But if he was, what she'd said was pretty hurtful, and he was human and as capable of sorrow and regret as she was.

The rectangular building was dark on one side, where what was left of the roof provided shelter from the sun. Rubble, mostly brush and dirt and sun-dried bricks from the crumbling walls, littered the open area. Tucker had cleared away a spot in the corner and was lying in the shade.

Gabrielle felt his eyes on her, knew he wasn't sleeping. "What were you making a few minutes ago? One of those desert stills you mentioned?" she asked, hoping to reestablish the tentative peace they'd known all morning by ignoring what had happened outside.

He took a few seconds to answer her, as though he didn't really want to. Finally he grunted and Hadley interpreted it as a positive response because going to so much trouble to dig a hole for any other reason made no sense.

"Do you really think it'll work?"

"I wouldn't have built it if I didn't."

"But how much water can we get from something like that? A few drops at most?"

"Even in the most arid conditions it's supposed to provide something like a pint a day. And we're lucky— it just rained."

Gabrielle took a deep breath and tried to think of some topic that might draw him out. "What kind of church do you think this used to be?"

Tucker didn't respond.

"Aren't you going to answer me?"

"I don't know anything about old churches," he said. His voice was full of irritation—obviously he wanted her to leave him alone—but Gabrielle wasn't satisfied. She needed to ease the sick feeling she'd gotten in her stomach when she'd looked into his eyes and realized she'd just added to whatever pain he carried around inside him. Other than that one monosyllabic answer when she'd asked about his wife, he hadn't proclaimed his innocence, hadn't explained what had landed him in prison. Tucker hadn't tried especially hard to convince her of anything. Yet something enticed her to believe in him on such a gut level she had a difficult time reasoning it away.

"I think it might be one of those mission churches," she went on. "You know, the ones the Jesuit missionaries built in the late sixteen hundreds."

Again he didn't answer.

"That would make it over three hundred years old. Amazing it's still standing, isn't it?"

No response.

Gabrielle considered leaving him to brood, or whatever he was doing, then tried once more to reach him. "I've seen a couple of other mission churches. There's one in Tumacacori, just south of Tucson, that's in pretty good condition, and another in Cocóspera, Sonora."

She walked around the building, pretending to be absorbed by the ruins. "When I was pregnant with Allie, David took me to see them. This whole area used to be the northwest border of New Spain. He said the desert on both sides of the Mexican border is—''

''Am I supposed to care about this?'' Tucker interrupted.

Gabrielle let her breath go and shook her head. What was the point in trying to befriend him? Of course he wouldn't care about anything she said. Why would he? They were both thirsty, hungry, tired and miserably hot.

Cursing whatever weakness had brought her into the church, she turned and headed for the door.

''David's your husband?'' he asked before she could reach it.

Pride tempted her to keep right on going, but she was too much of a peacemaker to reject what might be an offer to let bygones be bygones. ''Not anymore,'' she said, pausing at the entrance.

''If you love him so much, why'd you divorce him?''

She turned to face him. ''What makes you think *I* did the divorcing?''

''Instinct.'' He sat up. ''Am I right?''

Feeling defensive again, she tried to fan herself with one hand as she leaned against the lintel, but there was no relief from the heat. ''Maybe.''

''That kind of *maybe* is always a yes. Why did you leave him?''

Gabrielle preferred not to delve into such a personal subject. Tucker still seemed rather combative, and things with David were…complex. He was her ex and yet she loved him dearly. She loved him dearly, yet she'd never go back to him. How could she expect anyone to understand such conflicting emotions?

When she didn't reply, he scowled. "Oh, so we can talk about me, but your past is off limits?"

"We *haven't* talked about you," she pointed out. "You weren't interested in conversation, remember?"

He gazed at his injured hand and gingerly moved his fingers. "You asked me if I murdered my wife, and I answered you."

"Don't most people want to know the answer to that question? You could be dangerous."

"You're the one with the weapon."

"It certainly hasn't done me any good," she mumbled, and slid down the lintel to sit on the floor. With her finger, she drew designs in the hot dirt.

"That's because you're judging the situation from your own reality. If someone pulled a gun on you, you'd do what you were told. You still have a lot to lose. You don't know that some things are worse than death."

"Like living in prison?"

He sighed. "Like losing the life you knew, losing your child, because of a crime you didn't commit."

She wiped the dirt from her finger on her pants and undid the top button of her uniform. She'd kept as much of herself covered as possible to protect against burning, but now she felt as though her clothes were trapping the heat, roasting her.

"I don't *know* you're in that situation. I only have your word," she said, eager for any distraction.

"I haven't hurt you. I haven't even touched you. Doesn't that tell you anything?"

Gabrielle didn't want to think about what his behavior told her. He'd been heroic, all things considered. And now that she felt fairly confident that he wasn't going to hurt her, she hoped he *was* guilty of the crime for which he'd been imprisoned. There was solace in justice, rightness in appropriate consequences for misdeeds. But *injustice*...punishing a man for something he didn't do...

She couldn't imagine how that would scar a person. If she thought Tucker was innocent, believed it with all her heart, she wouldn't be able to face knowing what was going to happen to him when they caught him. Wouldn't be able to face knowing what he'd gone through already.

"I'm sorry I asked about your wife," she said.

He laughed softly. "You're finally figuring out that we're better off staying out of each other's lives."

"I figured that out a long time ago. I'm the one who could get fired for overfamiliarity with an inmate." She tried fanning herself again, but she was still in direct sunlight. It was useless. "And quit calling me Hadley."

"What do you want me to call you?"

She thought about hearing her first name on his lips. "Never mind. Hadley's fine."

He rested his elbow on one knee and let his injured hand dangle. "So why'd you leave David, Hadley?"

She looked up, surprised. "What about taking your own advice?"

"Sometimes I act against my better judgment. Are you going to tell me?"

She lifted her shoulders in a shrug. "I left him because he deserved more than I could give him," she said, distilling her problems with David into their simplest form.

"So you did it as a favor?"

His sarcasm bothered Gabrielle. "I just wasn't happy, okay?" she snapped.

He said nothing for a few seconds, then murmured, "Tell me why you weren't good for him."

She gave up trying to stir the air and went back to drawing in the dirt. "I just—" she created a smiley face, ruined it and drew a frown instead "—I just wanted to be friends. We work better that way."

"Does he agree?"

"I think so."

Tucker chuckled. "I'll bet."

"What's that supposed to mean?"

"It means I can't imagine him being happy about taking a step back."

"Why not? You don't know either of us. What makes you think he wanted anything different?"

He fixed her with an unswerving gaze. "Because I'd want something much different if I were him."

The gravity in his voice made Gabrielle forget about the dirt. All day she'd scarcely been able to get a word out of Tucker, but she had his attention now—so completely she felt swallowed up in it. "And what would that be?" she asked.

He raised his eyebrows appraisingly. "All of you or none at all."

All of her… A drop of perspiration ran between Gabrielle's breasts. She felt its slow descent as though it was Tucker's finger and could only imagine what giving all of herself to this man might be like. He wasn't easygoing or fun-loving, like David. He was hard-edged and angry most of the time and usually rather cynical. But there was at least a small chance that he had good reason for the chip on his shoulder, and she didn't doubt him when he said he didn't believe in doing things halfway. Being loved by him would, from every indication, be a passionate, all-consuming experience…a wonderful experience if he was as normal as she suspected.

Swallowing hard, she shoved a selfconscious hand through her snarled hair, knowing she must look terrible.

A flash of white teeth told her he'd noticed that she was suddenly aware of him sexually. His eyes held hers, as if he meant to assure her that he didn't care about a little unruly hair and dirt-streaked skin. Which only added to the tingling sensation that had started low in her belly.

"All or nothing could be interpreted in a lot of different ways. It could be scary if you're obsessive," she said. "Do you mean you'd never *let* a woman leave you?"

He made a sound of disgust and the intensity of the moment eased. "I'm not obsessive. My wife wasn't about to leave me, Hadley. She needed me to support her habits, and I—I was trying to work things out for our son's sake. I've never hurt a woman. I never would. But then you know that already, or you wouldn't still be sitting there."

She hadn't moved, but the ground and the sun were both too scorching to remain where she was for much longer. Or maybe it was the way Tucker had looked at her when he said "all of you or none at all." She seemed to be burning inside as well as out. "You told me not to take anything for granted. Maybe I should tell you the same thing," she said.

A faint smile softened his face. But then he shoved some nearby rubble farther away and stretched out again, and his expression hardened into the sober planes and angles more typical of him. "You'd better get out of the sun and go to sleep for a while. We'll start moving once we've collected some water and it cools off a little."

Gabrielle stood. Now that she was inside with him, outside seemed that much more barren and lonely. Fear of scorpions and snakes, of the unknown, made her reluctant to let him out of her sight. But after his reaction to finding her in his arms this morning, she doubted he'd be particularly open to sharing his shady corner. He obviously expected her to return to the courtyard.

"I—I'll be outside," she said.

Eyes closed, he looked as though he'd already fallen asleep.

"Unless you want me to stay in here with you," she added hopefully.

He glanced up and scowled, and Hadley got the impression he was about to refuse. But then he surprised her.

"Stay if you want," he grunted. "It's up to you."

CHAPTER NINE

TUCKER SLID OVER and braced himself for Hadley's close proximity. He didn't want to be tortured by the memory of how it felt to lose himself in the arms of a woman, by the promise of what it would feel like to lose himself in the arms of *this* woman. But desire for exactly the things he told himself he *didn't* want warred so powerfully with his self-control, he couldn't refuse her a place next to him.

When she sat, she left as much space between them as possible in the limited shade, but she was still far too close to allow Tucker to relax. The tension in his body notched up, and with it his irritability. He'd been wrong to succumb to the sweet appeal in her voice. He should have insisted she go outside so he could sleep.

"What I wouldn't do for a bath and a change of clothes," she muttered.

Her face was beautiful despite her lack of toiletries. He liked the way she smiled, the way she sometimes looked at him under her long lashes, as though trying to read him without letting him know it. It had to be the sexiest look he'd ever seen. But that was the problem.

"At least we both have long pants and long sleeves, or we'd be fried to a crisp," she went on, filling the silence with what sounded like more nervous chatter.

Tucker watched her blow into the opening of her

shirtfront and suddenly hit upon an idea he felt sure would make her withdraw. "Long pants and sleeves don't help much in the shade," he said.

She blew down her shirt again. "I guess we can't have our cake and eat it, too."

"Why not? If your uniform's bothering you, take it off."

Her eyes widened, riveted on his face. *"What?"*

He bit back a smile. "You're wearing underwear, aren't you?"

"Of course."

"Then take off your uniform—your shirt, anyway. You need to cool down or we're going to run into real problems with dehydration." To lend credence to his words, he unzipped his prison jumpsuit and shoved it off his arms, removed his T-shirt and tossed it aside. The air hit his naked, perspiring torso and helped cool him—a little. He leaned back in relief, thinking he'd been right to strip down, whether his ploy to scare Hadley off worked or not. What he'd said about dehydration was frighteningly true, and he felt better already.

After a moment he glanced at Hadley, expecting her to be wearing an affronted expression. But she didn't appear all that ruffled. She seemed to be considering his suggestion.

No, she'll never do it.

"You're a guy," she said, frowning. "You can take off your shirt in public."

"Public? This is about as private as you're going to get. I wish it was a damn sight less private, to be honest with you. But privacy doesn't have anything to do with why you're hesitating. You're still afraid that I'm dangerous, that a glimpse of your skin will make me lose control and try to rape you or something."

"No, I don't. I know that being convicted of murder doesn't automatically make you a rapist." She chewed her bottom lip. "On the other hand, I don't want to be stupid. Some guys have pretty violent sexual experiences in prison that can…you know, change them."

He grimaced. "If you're saying what I think you're saying, don't worry about it. Not everyone on the inside gets raped or turns bisexual." He lifted his injured hand. "Why do you think I got in so many fights?"

"Those guys tried to *rape* you?"

"They tried a lot of things. Anyway, two years of celibacy isn't enough to turn me into a predator."

Her eyes lowered briefly to his chest and arms before darting quickly away.

Any minute now, she'll head for the door, Tucker thought. *She's too aware of what I'm feeling not to bolt.*

"Okay," she said with a shrug, and Tucker felt as if someone had just slugged him in the breadbasket.

"What did you say?"

"I'm willing to trust almost anybody if it'll bring me some relief." Rocking up on to her knees, she set her gun aside, pulled her shirt out of her pants and began to unbutton it. Now that the decision had been made, she seemed not to give it a second thought. "A body's a body. I'm sure you've seen it all before."

He *had* seen it all before. But it'd been two years— two of the longest years of his life—and he hadn't seen *her.* Grabbing his T-shirt, Tucker rolled it up for a pillow and turned to face the wall. He wasn't going to look at Hadley. If she'd been driving him mad before, he could only imagine what she'd do to him now.

But then he heard her sigh in relief, heard her moving around, and couldn't help stealing a glimpse. Looking wasn't touching. Looking wouldn't hurt anyone.

The moment he saw her, he realized he'd made a grave mistake. He'd expected her to be wearing plain, functional underwear, but she had on a black lace bra that left little to the imagination. His clever attempt to frighten her off had backfired. The joke was on him, and his body's instant reaction let him know it.

With a curse, he rolled over again and presented her with his back. But it was too late. He'd already caught sight of the dark aureolas of her breasts—beautiful breasts that were neither too large nor too small—and his fingers ached to touch them.

She didn't say anything for a while and he wondered whether his negative reaction was making her consider putting her clothes back on. Or leaving. She did neither. She lay down a couple feet away and soon stopped moving.

Tucker blinked at the wall for several minutes, fighting the urge to turn and enjoy the view. He'd already seen her once. The sight was indelibly etched in his brain. So what difference would looking make now?

He eased himself over, but she'd obviously been anticipating such a move because he immediately came nose to nose with her I-caught-you expression.

"For all your pretended disinterest, you're full of shit," she said.

"I told you I didn't murder my wife. I never said I was a saint."

"Uh-huh."

Close, but not touching, they stared at each other without speaking for what seemed like an eternity. Then Tucker broke the silence. "Do you wear this kind of bra every day? Or did you have something special planned for David?''

"I haven't slept with David since the divorce," she said. "If I loved him in a romantic way, I would've stayed with him. I just wear a few pretty things because it helps."

"It helps to know you could cause a riot in that prison?"

She smiled. "Lacy panties, a little perfume, it all helps me remember I'm still a woman and in touch with what's beautiful and good."

"You're definitely in touch with what's beautiful," he said, letting his eyes sweep over her. "I don't think I've ever seen anything more beautiful in my life."

He hadn't meant to say it, at least with such yearning. He'd managed to ignore her all day, had almost believed he could remain indifferent. Now he sounded as emotionally starved as he felt, and that embarrassed him. But she seemed so calm and trusting, lying there without covering up or running away. And that trust felt fantastic, as though she'd somehow put him back in his old skin.

"What is it?" she murmured.

He forced back everything that was suddenly whirling around in his mind, begging for release, and shook his head. Too many emotions were surfacing, bearing down on him all at once. "Nothing. We'd better get some rest."

Closing his eyes, he waited for his pulse to even out and silently begged sleep to overtake him and numb the exquisite mixture of desire and regret, hope and hopelessness.

But Hadley didn't let him go to sleep. "What's wrong? You're hurting in some way, aren't you?"

He didn't answer. Damn her, why wouldn't she just go away?

"Tucker? If I touch you, you won't take it as a sexual advance, will you?"

"Don't touch me," he snapped. He knew any other woman would have given up on him, but not Hadley.

"We could die out here," she said. "Not much else matters when you think this might be all there is."

What could he say to that?

Moving closer, she tentatively ran a finger along his jaw.

He felt his muscles bunch in response, nearly pulled her to him. What was she doing? What was she trying to prove? He told himself to jerk away, to let her know he didn't need her pity or her comfort. But he couldn't. The softness of her body and her feminine scent immobilized him.

After a few minutes of lying perfectly still, she settled his head on her shoulder and kissed his brow, just like in his dream. She didn't speak, but she ran her fingers through his hair in a soothing gesture. And that was when he felt the dam inside him begin to crack.

He stiffened, started to roll away, but she held him where he was. "It's okay," she murmured, and although he feared what was happening, hated that he'd brought it on himself by allowing her to come so close, he needed what she was offering. Needed it so badly he couldn't move. Tears blurred his vision and eventually fell on the soft skin of the woman he both resented and longed to caress. He'd been falsely accused and imprisoned; he'd lost his wife and his son and he'd had to fight on an almost daily basis for the simple right to live. Yet he'd never broken down. Until now.

He clung to as much restraint as he could, tried to

choke back the tears. He despised weakness and swore he could withstand anything for Landon's sake. If Hadley had offered him, instead, a fight with five men, he felt he would've stood a chance.

But he had nothing left inside him powerful enough to overcome her tenderness.

HOT AND WET, Tucker's tears fell on Gabrielle's skin and seemed to sink into her heart. Never had she seen such a proud man cry; never would she have expected Randall Tucker capable of this kind of intense emotion. He'd suffered numerous injuries and shrugged them off. He'd sat in the back of a patrol car for three hours, riding in what could only have been excruciating pain, without murmuring a word. Unlike her, he hadn't complained of any discomfort in the desert. He'd brought her water, saved her from the storm, warmed her through the night. Tucker was just about the toughest man she'd ever met. But now Gabrielle knew there was more to him than toughness....

She stared at the ruined ceiling above and let her fingers continue to work their way through his hair, giving and taking what comfort she could in their closeness. It felt as if they were the only two people on earth. They had no guarantee of surviving; they had no guarantees at all. But they had each other. Somehow, despite everything, that brought peace.

Finally, Tucker's breathing relaxed and Gabrielle knew he slept. She curled more comfortably into his body and caressed the soft, smooth skin of his back. She wanted to sleep but couldn't. The sun was pushing the shade closer to their corner and seemed to be shedding that same brilliant light on the soul she'd found so shadowed just minutes before. Or maybe it was bringing light to the dark corners of her own soul. Either way, she believed Tucker was innocent. She knew, after this moment, that she'd always believe it.

TUCKER WOKE to the feeling of something wonderful against his face, something soft and full. Something perfect as a woman's—

He opened one eye and realized he'd done exactly what he was afraid he'd done—he'd buried his face in Hadley's breasts.

Lifting his head so he could use both eyes, he wondered if perhaps he'd forgotten something important. But he found her sleeping deeply, still wearing her pants and bra, which was a good sign. If he'd made love to her, she sure as hell wouldn't be wearing any clothes. It was too hot, and he wouldn't have wanted any barriers between them. He'd want free access to love her again and again and…

His body immediately hardened at the thought, but he was glad he hadn't crossed any lines. He didn't want to feel obligated to Hadley or to anyone else, didn't want to create expectations, carry or leave any emotional baggage. Fortunately the pillow she'd let him enjoy was just the overflow from her bra, and if he'd become a little emotional earlier and embarrassed himself…well, there was nothing he could do about that. Landon needed him. He'd have to ignore what had happened and move on, bury the memory along with all the other unpleasant events of the past two years.

But he had a hard time thinking of those moments with Hadley as unpleasant. She hadn't questioned him, hadn't demanded anything. She'd just held him, and somehow, her touch had reached deep inside him.…

I'm imagining things. Nothing's changed. He'd still go back to prison the second the police apprehended him—and Hadley would stand by and watch. All the evidence pointed to him as Andrea's murderer. What else could she do?

Frowning, he allowed himself one more head-to-toe perusal of her, lying there so vulnerable and trusting, and nearly placed his lips over one perfect nipple. If they were going to die, he'd rather die right here in a glorious celebration of having lived, provided he could convince Hadley to share his view. He had no desire to touch her unless she welcomed it, but the way she'd behaved earlier, her daring in pulling him to her in the first place, led him to believe she might not be opposed to taking what joy they could find. Except he wasn't sure exactly what her relationship with her ex-husband was like. She claimed she didn't love him romantically, but she'd sure grown defensive of him in a hurry.

In any case, he had more important things to worry about than making love. If he was ever going to find his son, he needed to get moving.

Forcing himself to stand and withdraw from temptation, he pulled on his T-shirt and went outside to check on his still, which was working far better than he'd expected, thanks to the rain. He hated to disturb it, but he was parched, and hunger was quickly becoming a secondary concern. They'd be able to travel farther and faster on a full stomach, he decided, and went back into the church to retrieve the gun Hadley had set aside when she'd removed her shirt. He'd never been much of a hunter, but the lives that were quickly becoming most precious to him were his and Hadley's, and he knew he'd do what was necessary to survive.

SHE WAS ALONE! Hadley gazed around the church, hoping to see Tucker somewhere, anywhere, to hear him outside, perhaps. But there was no sound except the soft cooing of a dove from the rafters, which made her feel more forlorn than if there'd been nothing.

Sitting up so fast her head swam, she blinked away the dizziness and scanned the empty church. He was gone. And so was her gun.

"Tucker? Where are you?" she cried.

Alarmed, the bird flapped its wings and flew off, startling her as badly as she'd startled it. But what frightened her more was the fact that Tucker didn't answer. Only her voice bounced back at her from the three-hundred-year-old walls.

Getting to her feet, she tied her shirt around her waist—it was late afternoon but still too hot to bear putting it back on—and went to the door. He could be relieving himself behind a cactus somewhere out of earshot, she told herself, and decided to take the opportunity to do the same.

When she'd finished, she hurried into the open and turned in a circle, gazing in all directions. But she couldn't see anything remotely human.

Then she remembered the still.

She found the spot where Tucker had been doing his digging and her hope faltered. The still had been dismantled; the water was gone.

What now? she wondered. He'd taken everything, even her purse and her pictures of Allie.

Her first impulse was to hurry after him. At the very least, she had a few things to say about emotional maturity and human kindness. But her watch indicated that she'd slept for more than three hours. She had no way of knowing when Tucker had left. By this time, he could be anywhere.

She glanced disconsolately at the well then forced herself to leave it behind and start walking. The sun was setting. It looked like a huge fireball melting into the earth, but soon darkness would fall. The air would cool to a comfortable seventy degrees and, away from the city, the stars would appear brighter than any she'd ever seen. Along with the moon, they'd light her way. Then she'd have approximately twelve hours to find help or—

Gunshots rang out, and she froze. One…two…three rounds…a pause…then several more. Turning toward the sound, she stared into the distance, listening as the reports faded away. Tucker! She jogged in the direction she'd heard the shots, feeling a relief so profound she thought she might cry, and soon saw Tucker coming toward her.

Lifting something, he yelled, "I got one! Let's eat!"

IMMEDIATELY feeling selfconscious, Gabrielle pulled her shirt back on and buttoned it as she stared at the dead jackrabbit in Tucker's grip. "How did you manage to shoot that with your left hand?" she asked.

"My karate training probably helped. When you fight, it's best to be able to use both hands. Anyway, I missed a few times, and it took me a lot longer than I figured it would, but I managed."

"How are we going to skin it?" She was famished. The half sandwich she'd eaten at dawn hadn't lasted more than a couple of hours. But she'd never so much as plucked a chicken, and found it hard to equate this poor animal with food.

"A sharp rock and your keys, I guess. I'm new at this myself."

"And then?"

"Then we try starting a fire."

"Great. That should be easy. Except we don't have any matches or a flint-steel set or even a magnifying glass."

"There's some matches in your purse."

"No, there's—" Gabrielle suddenly remembered. "Oh, I picked them up for Allie's birthday. I must've stuck them in my purse and forgotten."

"Fortunately for us," he said. "Why don't you gather some wood while I see about skinning this?"

She looked around, feeling skeptical. "We're not exactly in a woodsy area."

"Not for an Oregonian, perhaps, but there's plenty of wood here. If you can't find enough scraps in the church, we can always dig up the taproots of a mesquite bush. Next to ironwood, mesquite is the best firewood in the desert. It burns slowly and is smokeless." He yanked on a nearby bush and pulled off a pod. "And if we want to add a side dish to our meal, we could always eat these."

"What are they?"

"Mesquite pods. The Papago ate them all the time. They made tea and syrup from them, and ground them into meal."

"Roasted rabbit and mesquite pods. Sounds almost gourmet."

"I aim to please, ma'am." His smile made Gabrielle's breath catch. It was sexy and endearing. Her eyes automatically dropped to his lips as she remembered what it had felt like to hold him, to caress him.

She wondered what kissing such an intense man might be like....

"I owe you an apology," she said, pulling her gaze back up to his eyes.

His brows lifted. "For what?"

"I thought you'd left me."

He studied her for a moment, then sighed and shook his head. "Believe me, if I could have left you, I would've done it by now."

She felt her lips curve into an answering smile. "Having a heart can get in the way, can't it?"

"You don't know me—"

She raised a hand. "And I shouldn't take anything for granted. You've put me on notice already."

"I've been in prison for two years, Hadley—"

"Gabrielle."

"What?"

"My name's Gabrielle."

"Like I was saying, *Hadley*. No one does hard time and comes out soft and sweet. For your own sake, you need to remember that. Now gather the wood. It's getting late," he said, and stalked off.

CHAPTER TEN

TUCKER BREATHED DEEPLY to savor the sweet, woodsy aroma of roasting rabbit and burning mesquite and closed his eyes. Nothing had ever smelled so good. After an entire day of going without, the promise of food made his mouth water and his stomach growl, but he felt strangely content with the anticipation. The bars of the prison were gone. The stench was gone. The terrible noise and taunting faces were all gone. Here, it was absolutely peaceful. He knew he'd eat soon, but he felt even better knowing Hadley would have food to fill her belly, too. Why providing for her was so important to him, he wasn't sure. It felt so similar to the impulse that made him want to look out for Landon, or for Andrea when she'd been alive, he didn't want to think about it.

It's just a male trait, he told himself, *some genetic leftover from caveman times.*

He opened his eyes to see Hadley standing across from him, staring into the flames while holding the opposite end of the stick he'd used to skewer the meat. They'd hardly spoken since they'd started roasting the rabbit. The comforting crackle of the burning wood, the smell of the cooking meat, and the unparalleled brilliance of the stars overhead evoked a certain serenity. But for Tucker, Hadley was very much part of the magic of the night. Her long blond hair fell to her shoulders, thick and inviting despite the tangles. Her face, flushed from the heat of the flames, glowed with perspiration. She looked sensual, earthy. He yearned to feel her moist skin sliding against his own. Would she close her eyes and part her lips if he were to—

Clearing his throat, he yanked his thoughts to safety and broke the silence to keep his mind from drifting. "The meat should be done soon."

She nodded but didn't answer. When silence fell again, he tried to think of something to say that would actually result in a lasting conversation. Something to distract them both. The mirage-like image of her, shimmering in front of him in the heat of the flames, appealed to him far too much.

"Have you done a lot of traveling in Arizona?" he asked.

She shoved her hair away from her face. "Just the usual tourist stuff—the Grand Canyon, Sonora, Old Tucson. I've only lived here about six years, and Allie's taken up almost two of those. She's not really old enough to travel."

He thought about the cute baby he'd seen in her pictures, knew Hadley had to be missing her, and decided not to let his thoughts wander in that direction, either. "Arizona's got a lot of variety," he said. "Everything from snowcapped peaks to this."

"At this point, I'm wondering why everyone doesn't live near those snowcapped peaks."

"Actually there's more plant and animal life in the desert than in the mountains."

"Really?"

Tucker knew she probably didn't give a damn, and neither did he, but he didn't want to talk about anything more personal. Otherwise he'd end up asking all the questions that were crowding to the forefront of his mind—what David was like, whether she'd ever go back to him, how she'd met him in the first place and why he couldn't make her happy.

"I haven't seen much life here," she said.

"Most animals only come out at dusk and dawn or at night. Some hibernate entirely during hot weather. Others remain dormant until it rains."

"How does an animal remain dormant until it rains? It can go almost a whole year without raining."

"Desert toads stay deep underground in moist soil until the summer rains fill the ponds. Then they emerge…and mate."

She caught his eye and quickly looked away. "Were you a biology teacher in your former life?"

He frowned, shaking his head. "No, I've just had a lot of time on my hands."

"So you studied the desert?"

"Seemed like a good idea, considering I was being held in a cage in the middle of one of the largest deserts in North America."

She shoved a strand of hair out of her face. "You did this in case you could escape?"

"I did it to pass the time. Inmates are allowed five books a week, remember? But I admit I hoped the knowledge would come in handy someday."

She fell silent. He thought he was going to have to search for another neutral topic or go back to thinking about touching her, but then she piped up on her own. Her topic was hardly neutral, though. "Do you miss your wife, Tucker?"

"Have I told you about the kangaroo rat?" he asked, focusing on the roasting rabbit as though it required a lot of concentration to turn the spit. "They can make their own water from the digestion of dry seeds. They won't drink even if water's available to them."

"Is that a yes?"

He met her eyes. "There're a lot of unusual plants in the desert, too. Organ Pipe cacti grow only in one small section of the Sonoran Desert."

She crossed her arms. "Fine. If you don't want to talk to me, then don't."

He noticed the stiffening of her spine and nearly smiled. "I thought I *was* talking to you."

"You've opened your mouth more in the past fifteen minutes than in the entire time I've known you, but you've never said less."

Scowling, he went back to watching the rabbit cook. "There's nothing wrong with discussing things that are easily forgotten."

"What is it you're afraid you'll remember?" she countered.

You. He stared at her for a moment, then cursed. "All right. I miss my wife," he said, "but if I was being honest, I'd have to tell you that I miss my son a lot more. I loved my wife when I married her, but I'm not too sure I liked the person she became."

She seemed to consider this. "Okay. So where's your son?"

"In foster care."

"Don't you have parents or other family who can take him in?"

He studied the stars overhead. "My parents wanted to, but they're too old, and my mother has multiple sclerosis. They were old when they had me. My brother would probably take him, but he's single and not the most responsible guy in the world. Even though he's two years older than me, he isn't ready for an eight-year-old child—or any child, for that matter.''

''What about Andrea's family?''

''Andrea never got along with her family. Her parents split when she was little and both of them remarried spouses with children. Now her father lives in California and her mother's divorced her second husband and moved back east. She once offered to take Landon, but I didn't want him so far away.'' He leaned closer to make sure the rabbit was done and motioned for her to lift her end of the spit. ''Let's eat.''

They settled beside each other so they could share the food and stay close to the fire. They didn't need the heat, but gazing into the leaping flames with the starry night as a backdrop was soothing, almost mesmerizing. The desert no longer seemed vast or lonely; it seemed intimate. And even though the mesquite pods Gabrielle had collected tasted terrible, the rabbit was sweet and tender. Tucker watched Hadley enjoy her food, and once again struggled with the desire to possess her in some way—physically, emotionally...

Obviously he'd had too much sun.

''Does David live in Florence?'' he asked as he piled the bones from their feast next to the fire for coyotes or other animals to scavenge. He knew they should be leaving soon. Landon was constantly in the back of his mind. But a strange calmness had fallen over him, lessening the immediacy of his mission, as though he needed to take advantage of this moment because he might never get another like it.

''He lives in Phoenix.''

''What brought you to Florence, then? A new boyfriend?''

''No. I'm not married to David anymore, but...''

''Let me guess—you're still faithful to him.''

Tucker saw surprise flash through her eyes. ''How do you know that?'' she asked.

He groaned. ''God, that man must hate what he's lost. You're not even married and you're true to him.''

''David's not hating anything. He's fine. He's over me already,'' she said, but the false cheer in her voice told Tucker it was a lie.

''Are you trying to convince me? Or you?''

''I'm not trying to convince anyone,'' she said. ''It's the truth.''

''If it was, you'd let yourself move on.''

''I'll move on when the time is right. I just—'' she hesitated ''—have some things to do first.''

''Like?''

She took a drink of water and offered him one, but he'd had enough. He felt good, better than he had since before the fight. His hand didn't hurt unless he tried to use it, and his ribs seemed to be healing, too. ''Did you know the saguaro cactus can live to be two-hundred years old?'' she asked.

He chuckled and decided to stop probing. Thinking about David was driving him nuts. He envied him and yet they'd never met. Obviously, David couldn't be too perfect or Gabrielle wouldn't have divorced him. Even if he was, Tucker didn't want to know about it. Jealousy was one thing he couldn't afford.

''I knew that,'' he replied. ''Let's go.'' Standing, he held out his hand.

She hesitated as though she wasn't going to take it. But then she met his gaze, smiled and grabbed on, and it was all Tucker could do to let go of her once she was on her feet.

"WHAT ELSE do you know about the desert?" Gabrielle asked to keep her mind off the unseen animals and rodents that rustled in the bushes as they passed.

Tucker's profile looked pensive in the moonlight as he marched slightly ahead of her, but he allowed her to catch up with him when she spoke, and his answer was congenial enough. "I know that as inhospitable as this place seems, it's provided food for indigenous people for centuries."

"Food?" she echoed. "Certainly not through farming."

"The Indians farmed a little, before we dammed the rivers and diverted the waterways. But they also ate what grew naturally. Something like one-fifth of the desert's plants are edible."

She grimaced. "Like those tasty mesquite pods?"

"Not a big hit, huh?" he said, grinning broadly. "Well, there are others, the agave for one."

"The agave?" She circled a rock and nearly reached for his hand as they started up an incline. His fingers had felt so warm and secure when he'd helped her to her feet after they'd eaten. It seemed natural to hang on to him, especially now that it was getting a little chilly and the scurrying noises all around made her nervous.

"The Indians used the agave for a lot of things," he said. "Food and beverages, syrup, fiber, cordage, clothing, sandals, nets, soap, medicine, you name it."

"Sort of an all-purpose plant, hmm? Sounds yummy. I've always wanted to eat something that could be made into soap *or* cordage."

With a laugh, he said, "I hate to disappoint you, but there are edible and inedible kinds, and I don't know the difference."

An owl hooted in the distance, immediately followed by a coyote's mournful howl, and Gabrielle again felt the impulse to grab onto Tucker. "With such bounty, surely there's something else we can eat."

"You'd think so, considering there's supposed to be over five-hundred edible plants in the region. Unfortunately, I can't remember what they are and probably wouldn't know how to recognize them even if I did."

"A lot of help you are."

"That particular book wasn't the most entertaining I've ever read, and it's been a while. Anyway, it's different when you're looking at a picture, compared to the actual specimens."

"Don't you think you're a little unusual?" she asked. "Most guys in prison don't bother reading about desert plants. And the only pictures they look at are of scantily dressed women."

He cocked an eyebrow at her. "Still, I'm sure they'd agree a picture isn't quite the same as the real thing."

"I don't know. Some of those guys take their calendar models pretty seriously."

"They're just making do."

"You don't have any pictures up in your cell, except that one of the boy I'm guessing is your son."

"I have trouble buying into dreams anymore."

"You're too disillusioned?"

"I'm not very good at settling." He stepped over a saguaro carcass, then turned to help her. "I take it you aren't either."

"What do you mean by that?" she asked.

"What do you think?"

"You're talking about David again."

"Who else?"

Gabrielle felt the old defensiveness rise. "Any woman who hooked up with David wouldn't be settling. He has everything. He's handsome, driven, successful, kind—"

"Then why did you leave him?"

"It was my fault, not his," she said. "He just couldn't reach me, couldn't reach…" She let her words fall off because she wasn't sure what, exactly, she was going to say. If she knew what they'd been missing, she would've found some way to solve the problem. "Something," she finished lamely.

Tucker stopped and turned to face her. His head and broad shoulders eclipsed the moon and the stars, leaving her in what seemed like total darkness except for the gleam in his eyes. "What *something* is that?"

That flutter in her belly, the one she'd experienced in the church, returned, making her more aware of him than she'd ever been of any man. Fleetingly, she imagined him pressing her to the desert floor, his mouth moving over hers, his hands on her breasts. For a moment she was so overcome she couldn't speak. This near stranger had the power to excite her in a way David never could. But Tucker wasn't the right man. He was a convict caught in a terrible tragedy. He had too many problems, too much anger, and would only break her heart.

She told herself to back away, but the promise of later pain seemed insignificant compared to the here and now. His face was shuttered, revealing nothing of his thoughts or feelings—except desire. But desire was enough to keep her there.

Lifting his left hand, he trailed a finger lightly over the curve of her cheek. Gabrielle closed her eyes at the sensation his touch evoked, then felt his hand slip beneath the hair at the nape of her neck. He pulled her gently toward him, as though he wanted her to know exactly what he was about to do before he did it. It wasn't enough for him that she submit. He wanted her to *want* what was happening and to let him know it.

Part of her did want what he was offering, more than anything. The other part was too confused to be effective. So she shoved the decision away and refused to think about what she was doing. Tilting her head back in expectation, she gazed up at him, feeling as though she'd just jumped off a cliff and was now free-falling through space.

Would he catch her? He paused, waiting, and she feared he'd pull away. But he didn't. He settled his mouth over hers and slid his tongue along her bottom lip, tasting her in a sort of slow-moving kiss that resonated with awe and reverence. The sound he made in his throat confirmed that the kiss brought him as much pleasure as it brought her, and Gabrielle felt everything inside her melt. As the rapid beating of his heart thudded above her own, she could hardly tolerate the exquisite sensations tumbling through her.

"What was it David couldn't reach?" he murmured, lifting his head to stare down at her.

She felt as though she could drown in his eyes. "That," she wanted to say, but her loyalty to David wouldn't allow it, and she suspected Tucker already knew the answer, anyway.

"You're better off with him," he said curtly when she didn't speak. Then, his control back in place, he stalked off. But Gabrielle knew, whether she saw Randall Tucker again or not, that no kiss would ever compare.

THEY'D ONLY BEEN WALKING a few hours when Gabrielle's legs began to feel as though they weighed a hundred pounds each. Unwilling to complain, she forced herself to go on, but she was no longer sure they were traveling in the right direction. If they were, they would've arrived somewhere by now—a gas station, a ranch, a town, *somewhere*—wouldn't they? They could just as easily be moving away from help as toward it, and she was dying to see her baby.

"Are you sure you know where we're going?" she finally asked.

Tucker didn't answer immediately. He hadn't spoken to her since their kiss, and she'd known instinctively to leave him alone. He seemed put out, as though *she'd* done something to *him* instead of the other way around, but she didn't care. She was angry herself this time—angry that he was angry, angry that he'd suffered so much pain, angry that she felt so drawn to him even though he was obviously wrong for her, angry that she'd gotten herself into this mess.

"I know where *I'm* going," he said.

"Where?"

"That's none of your business. I'm dropping you off at the earliest opportunity."

"As if I'd want to stay with you any longer," she retorted, but he didn't respond, and after another half hour or so of silence, she asked if they could stop and rest. What was the point of rushing when they could be moving further away from help instead of closer to it?

"We have to keep going," he said, his words clipped. "We can sleep in the morning."

"I didn't ask if I could sleep. I just need fifteen minutes to rest. My feet are killing me."

"Then stop and rest."

"And what will you do?"

No answer.

"Will you go on without me?"

"You can try to catch up once you're rested. I can't do any better than that."

"What?"

"I'm not going to let you get in the way anymore."

His words stung, especially after the tenderness of his kiss. How could he snap back and forth so easily between an absolute ogre and someone she could almost fall in love with? "Fine," she said. "If you can keep going, so can I."

He said nothing. He kept up the same pace, giving Gabrielle no choice but to gather her remaining strength and march on. "I don't know what you're trying to prove," she said at last.

Silence.

"Are you afraid kissing me has compromised your hard-ass image?"

No response.

"Well, don't worry about that. I know you're a jerk, okay? And that kiss meant nothing to me. It was the worst kiss I've ever had. I wouldn't kiss you again if you were the last man on earth."

He kept walking.

"Tucker, you bastard!" She picked up a rock and hurled it at him. He glanced back in time to dodge it and, the second she scooped up another, he caught her arm before she could throw.

"Drop it," he said, his grip like a vise.

She let the rock fall, but the desire to pierce his hard exterior only grew stronger. "I should've let you come out here alone without water or anything else!'' she said.

He didn't ease his hold on her arm. "That's *exactly* what you should have done."

"I should've let you die a miserable death."

"I don't need you to save me," he said, glaring down at her. "I don't even want you here."

She tilted up her chin in defiance. "Oh, yeah? Well, you might not want me *here*, but you want me, all right."

"No, I don't," he growled.

"Yes, you do. You'd never admit it, but your body gives you away and so does your kiss." Raising up on her toes, she boldly licked his lip in the same slow-moving manner he'd licked hers earlier, wanting to taunt him, to fight with him, to incite him in spite of all the reasons she should do her best to keep the peace.

Even though she'd expected some type of response, the quickness of his movement surprised her. Crushing her to him, he covered her mouth in another kiss, only this one was nothing like the first. This was rough and hungry and demanding, but somewhere in the deep recesses of Gabrielle's mind it was also gratifying.

"What do you want to hear?" he said as he pressed himself against her. "That I've never wanted a woman more? That I want to make love to you until I can no longer move? That I dream about you, crave you? Is that what you want to hear?"

"Yes," she breathed.

He pulled back, looking stunned, but only for a moment. Then his hands were yanking on her clothes, finding their way to her breasts, and he was kissing her again, as greedily as though that simple response had sapped all restraint.

Quickly ridding her of her shirt and bra, he stared down at her bare breasts. When he spoke, his voice came as a harsh whisper. "This is a dream I can believe in." His mouth closed over one nipple, and Gabrielle moaned and arched into him, so caught up in the moment that she didn't hear the distant beating of helicopter blades until he froze. Then she knew something was wrong. The steady *thump, thump, thump* entered her consciousness. But not until she saw a spotlight sweeping the ground about half a mile away did she realize what it meant.

"Oh, God," Tucker said, then he grabbed her clothes and her hand and began to run, pulling her along behind him.

CHAPTER ELEVEN

"LET GO OF ME!" Gabrielle cried, digging in her heels and trying to release her arm. She had no idea what had happened when she was in Tucker's embrace only moments before, what had possessed her to provoke him as she had. But the confusion and frustration she'd felt, even the anger and the passion, were quickly replaced by sheer desperation. She had to flag down the rescuers in that helicopter. If they didn't find her, they'd keep going and she might never see Allie again.

"Let go of me!"

Tucker said nothing. Neither did he relinquish his hold on her wrist. He kept dragging her behind him until the distant thump of the blades beating the air turned into a loud *swoop, swoop, swoop.* The helicopter was drawing close. Gabrielle's lungs burned by the time it was above them, but Tucker forced her to keep going, dodging this way and that to stay out of the light.

"I'm here! I'm right here!" she shouted, waving her free arm at the sky. But the light hadn't found them yet, and she knew the men in the helicopter couldn't hear her above the engine and the prop.

She began clawing and swinging at Tucker, doing everything in her power to break free, but nothing seemed to affect him. He was too bent on escape and only tightened his grip until it hurt.

"You can run if you want to," she told him, "but I'm not going to die in the desert." She tried to bite him, but he jerked their clasped hands away from her mouth and shoved her down onto the ground. Quickly rolling her beneath the ledge of a small rock outcropping, he used his own body to pen her in out of sight.

The helicopter hovered not far away. Gabrielle could hear it taunting her with every turn of the prop. *Swoop…Swoop…*

Tears of frustration sprang to her eyes. "I'm here!" she yelled until she was hoarse. But she couldn't overpower Tucker. He was too strong, too heavy. She wrestled with him anyway, but he had her pinned down so she could barely move, and she knew that the helicopter would soon pass them by. Maybe then the rescuers would give up. Maybe they would assume them both dead, go home to their own families and never come back.…

Gabrielle reached for her pistol. She didn't want to shoot Tucker. She didn't want to shoot anyone. But she was going to return to Allie, regardless of what she had to do to get there.

Pressing the muzzle of the gun against his chest, she tried to lower the pitch of her voice to just this side of hysterical so he'd know she meant business. "I'm going home. Let me out, or I'll shoot."

He stilled, and she knew instinctively that he believed her. "If they find you, they'll find me," he said.

Gabrielle was crying now and couldn't keep her voice steady, but she didn't care. "I'll shoot you, Tucker." She gulped a breath of air. "I'll shoot."

"I'm not going back, Gabrielle."

It was the only time he'd ever used her first name. He'd spoken it as though she meant something to him, but Gabrielle was too frantic to let anything so subtle make a difference. She had to get to Allie, couldn't risk losing her daughter. Allie was all she had. "I want my baby. She needs her mother."

"You'll see her soon," he said. "But I can't let you go until we reach a town or some other neutral ground. If the police find either of us right now, I won't stand a chance."

On some level, his words made sense. Except they might not reach a town before they ran out of water. They could die within a few miles of where they were now. "We're lost," she said.

"We'll find something," he assured her, but his answer wasn't specific enough to counteract the appeal of help so close by. When? When would they find a town?

As the helicopter passed and the noise of the rotors began to dim, Gabrielle's panic suddenly spiked. Her hand was sweating on the butt of the gun, and she felt dizzy, ill. "I have to get out! I have to go with them now!" she cried.

"I can't let you!" he said again.

Before she even knew she was going to do it, she pulled the trigger with one hand and tried to shove Tucker's body out of the way with the other so she could get out before it was too late. But the gun only clicked. There was no report, no recoil. It was empty.

Gabrielle heard Tucker's quick intake of breath, felt his eyes bore holes through the darkness, and couldn't believe she'd just tried to shoot him. She loved him. No, she hated him. She loved him *and* she hated him. God, what had he done to her?

Shaking and crying, she dropped the gun and buried her face in his neck, but he didn't respond. As soon as the helicopter was gone, he scooted out from beneath the ledge and silently handed over her shirt and bra. Then he turned his back on her and strode away.

HE WAS REALLY going to leave her this time. Gabrielle could tell by the set of his shoulders, the finality of his walk. Over the past two days he'd let his defenses slip just enough to show her he was still human, that as much as he tried to deny it, he still had the hopes and dreams most men possess.

And she'd just thrown his trust back in his face.

"Tucker?" she called as he disappeared into the darkness. But she knew he wouldn't respond.

She stared after him, letting tears roll down her cheeks and drip off her chin. Whatever emotion he might have felt toward her had disappeared in that moment. She'd seen it in his eyes. They'd gone empty and cold in the space of a heartbeat. Somehow, seeing that—and knowing what she'd done to him—felt as if she'd just plunged a knife between her own ribs.

But doing anything less would have compromised Allie, David, her colleagues at the prison, herself.

"I had no choice! You would've done the same thing," she called. Only an owl called back.

"HERE, HAVE A DRINK."

Someone nudged his shoulder and Tucker blinked, momentarily blinded by the sun until Gabrielle moved to block the glare. Evidently he'd slept for some time. His nice shady spot was now in direct sunlight—and he wasn't rid of her yet. God, what did it take?

"What are you doing here?" he asked. "I thought we parted ways."

"You left the water behind."

"You think I don't know that? How'd you find me?"

"I followed you."

"You were exhausted."

"I was also determined."

"You should've stayed where you were and made a still," he said.

She held out the almost-empty jug. "Once you stopped to rest, I tried to make a still, but this is all I got. I broke it down when I began to worry that you'd gone without water for too long."

She reached out to press a finger to his cheek, then frowned when he ducked away from her touch. "You're getting burned pretty badly. You need more sunblock," she said.

"I don't want you looking out for me," he snapped. "I don't need anything from you."

"Are you going to have a drink or not?"

He considered the water; he almost refused but ultimately sacrificed some of his pride to his terrible thirst, then gave her back the jug. "Thanks for the drink. Now take your water and get out of here."

She accepted the jug, but stood right where she was, hands propped on her hips. "What you did to me was just as bad, you know. You kept me from reaching safety. Out here, that's almost the same as pulling the trigger."

He squinted up at her. "You think I'm blaming you for what happened?"

"Aren't you?"

"No. I turned on you. You turned on me. We're enemies. That's how it's supposed to be."

"But I didn't really mean to hurt you. You know that, don't you? I just…" She shoved a hand through her hair and seemed to search for the right words. "I panicked, I guess. All I could see was—"

"It doesn't matter," he said, cutting her off before her soulful eyes could weaken his resolve. "Considering the situation, we shouldn't be traveling together."

"We've come this far," she said.

"That doesn't mean anything."

"I think it does."

They stared at each other, locked in some sort of psychological standoff.

"Hate me if you want," she said finally. "But get up and get moving. We need to find some shade."

Tucker considered her as she turned and started walking. The fatigue in her movements told him she was close to exhaustion. Tired as she'd been last night, it was a wonder she'd made it this far. "Haven't you slept?" he asked.

She shrugged. "I dozed off a little after I built the still."

He scanned the flat monotonous desert, softening despite the fact that they should part company. If he hadn't been around when that helicopter came by, she would've been free to flag it down. She'd already be on her way home to Allie and David instead of facing endless miles of walking, unknown hours of hunger and thirst, almost unbearable heat and the distinct possibility that things wouldn't end well. Didn't she understand that?

"Over there," she said. "We're going to have to walk a ways, but there's a cluster of paloverde trees that should provide some shade where we can rest."

"Can you make it?" he asked.

She nodded, giving him another glimpse of her backbone. After two days of peeling back the emotional layers that made Gabrielle Hadley who she was, he'd finally reached the core—and she was far tougher than he'd imagined.

"Where's the still?" he asked.

She led him to the hole she'd dug.

It was no wonder she hadn't come up with much water. Whatever stick or rock she'd been using to dig with wasn't big enough to be very effective and had obviously caused a lot of work without much reward. The hole wasn't even deep enough to sink the jug, so her still wasn't going to do them any good. But he was amazed and impressed that she'd had the willpower and presence of mind to attempt its construction after everything they'd been through.

He glanced at her hands, noted the broken nails and dirt and blisters, and felt something very close to admiration.

She grabbed the plastic she'd used for the still cover, shoved it into her purse, along with the empty water jug, and started out. Tucker caught up with her long enough to take the purse so she wouldn't have the added weight of it, but then let her move on ahead of him. They'd withdrawn from each other completely, and he knew they were better off that way. What good would it do to plunge back into that same sweet torture he'd known last night, when she'd clung to him as he'd scrambled to rid them of their clothing? What good would it do to allow himself to touch and taste and feel her? He'd instantly want to pull closer and closer, to bury himself inside her until he no longer knew where his body stopped and hers began—only to have her torn away from him in the end. Either they were going to live, which meant they had to go their separate ways, or they were going to die. There was no in-between.

He walked slowly, watching her plod stubbornly on despite her exhaustion, and wanted to make love to her, anyway. But the memory of loving Gabrielle Hadley was one form of torture he would not give fate to use against him. Neither would he leave her with the shame of it. As things stood, she'd be able to go back to work at the prison, hold her head high among the other guards and tell them she did her damnedest to bring him in.

And—he thought of that surreal moment when she'd fired the gun—it would be true.

GABRIELLE couldn't believe her eyes. She blinked several times, wiped the sweat off her brow and squinted to see if the vision in front of her would vanish.

It didn't. They'd found an old weatherbeaten house, a row of single-room adobe huts, two mobile homes with junk-filled yards, several cars and a tractor. Best of all, they'd found someone driving an old pickup between several long rows of buildings made mostly of corrugated metal. A cinder-block building painted the same blue as the house sat in the center of everything, angled slightly away from them, with a sign painted along one side that read, Bountiful Harvest Egg Ranch.

They'd found an egg ranch. They'd found life!

She started to run, but her legs had no strength left in them. She fell almost immediately. Tucker came up from behind and hauled her to her feet. Then he pulled her into the trees. She tried to run again before realizing he still held her and wasn't letting go.

"Not so fast," he growled. "What are you going to do?"

What did he think? She was going to drink water

until she couldn't drink any more. She was going to rush back to her daughter and hold Allie close until the need to feel her baby against her lessened to something tolerable. Then she was going to eat and sleep and forget, in that order. But when she saw the intensity on Tucker's face, she knew it wouldn't be that easy, even though he'd promised to let her go once they reached "neutral" ground.

"What are *you* going to do?" she asked warily, knowing that her earlier panic wouldn't help her now. Tucker couldn't trust her; he'd know better than to let her go running into this little settlement wearing a Department of Corrections uniform and pointing a finger at him.

He stared straight ahead at the rooster tail of dust created by the moving truck. "I'm going to do you a favor." Forcing her down onto the dirt in the cover of the trees, he rolled her onto her stomach and started twisting her arms behind her back.

"No, stop," she cried as the tiny rocks bit through the fabric of her clothes. "Don't do this. Please! Tucker! We'll figure something out. I'll give you a few minutes' lead time or…or…" She couldn't think or talk fast enough to stop him. He was pressing her down with one knee while removing his T-shirt.

"I'll scream! I can't let you leave me here," she told him. "I could die, Tucker. What if they don't find me until it's too late? Tucker!"

"They'll find you. I'll make sure of it," he said. "This is for your own good. It's best for both of us."

"*Both* of us?" She screamed even though she doubted anyone could hear her, considering that it was a mile or so to the egg ranch and the truck had already disappeared from view. She hoped there were other men, in the long metal chicken coops perhaps, who might react to her screams. But Tucker silenced her in a matter of seconds by pressing her face into the dirt, where she dared not breathe for fear of suffocating.

The truck motor suddenly coughed, sputtered and died, but no one came running. Only the sound of ripping fabric broke the deathly silence as Tucker tore his T-shirt into strips. He gagged her with one strip, then hoisted her into an upright position and used the others to tie her to a tree.

"Sorry about the gag," he said, double-checking the security of his knots. "I'll make sure someone finds you before dark."

Dark! It was only midmorning. Dark seemed like eons away, and she wanted out of here *now*. She wanted Allie....

Humiliation and fury welled up inside Gabrielle. She longed to get her hands on Tucker one last time, to physically vent her powerful rage with her fists, her legs, anything she could use to hurt or maim him. He made her crazy. She spent half her time wanting to make love with him and the other half wanting to kill him.

But then his fingertips gently brushed her cheek, and confusion clouded her anger. "Gabrielle, in another time, another place, I could have..." Suddenly he fell silent and dropped his hand. "Never mind."

The implacable mask he'd worn since the helicopter incident last night fell into place again as he stood and squinted toward the egg ranch. Retrieving her purse, he began riffling through it.

"I'm taking your money," he announced, his tone matter-of-fact, as though it hadn't been filled with regret, even tenderness, just a few seconds before. "I'll mail it back to you later."

He tossed her wallet, now empty of thirty-five dollars, next to the water jug and her purse.

Gabrielle didn't respond. She could barely breathe because of the gag and the emotions pounding through her. She stared up at him, feeling an odd, panicky aggression borne more of helplessness and fear than that initial surge of anger.

He moved cautiously away from her, then paused. Gabrielle felt a spark of hope as he returned, but he didn't even look at her. Picking up her wallet, he flipped through her pictures.

What was he doing? What could he possibly want with—

He stopped at the photo of her and David and Allie and gazed at it for several seconds before sliding it out of its plastic sheath. Promptly tearing David away, he let her ex-husband's likeness flutter to the ground.

"What are you doing?" she tried to ask.

If he understood her groans, he offered no explanation. "I'll make sure someone finds you as soon as I'm away from here," he said. Then he tucked the torn picture in his good hand, along with the money.

Sparing her one final glance, he slipped out between the trees in the direction of the stark, lonely place someone much more optimistic than her had dubbed the Bountiful Harvest Egg Ranch.

CALM DOWN, BREATHE. *Gabrielle closed her eyes and stopped struggling. Tucker wouldn't strand her out here for long, she told herself. He knew how hungry and thirsty she was, how desperately she longed to see*

Allie. He wouldn't save her in the desert, feed her and bring her with him all this way to let her die now.

Except she'd tried to shoot him not twelve hours ago. Surely that would encourage little loyalty and less compassion in a man like him. And what if he got himself shot trying to steal food or clothes? Or trying to avoid capture? What if he got in a car chase and crashed before he could tell anyone about her? No one would know where she was. She'd sit out here and die a slow, agonizing death while David and Allie searched for her....

She angled her head to see the torn picture of David lying faceup on the ground next to her and experienced a twinge of guilt. Even now, she felt something for Randall Tucker she'd never felt for David. She cared for David, wanted him to be happy. But it was Randall Tucker who made her heart race.

I've finally lost my mind, she decided. It was David who'd stood by her through thick and thin, David who was the father of her baby. Tucker had just left her bound and gagged in the desert as though she didn't mean any more to him than a bag of rocks. And she preferred *him?*

No, her mind was playing tricks on her. She felt nothing for Tucker, she told herself, nothing. She was going to go home and love David the way he deserved to be loved. She was going to quit her job and move to Phoenix, forget about her birth mother and remarry David so they could raise their child together. The happily-ever-after that had eluded them the first time would come. She'd *make* it happen—for David and Allie, if not herself—because now she'd found what she'd been looking for and knew that finding it didn't matter. What she wanted was something, some*one,* she could never have.

Keeping her back firmly against the tree to relieve the pressure on her hands, Gabrielle stopped pulling at the knots binding her wrists, denied her panic and decided to think through her situation. Tucker hadn't really wanted to tie her up. If he had, her bonds would have been a lot tighter, and he would've used something much stronger than a cotton T-shirt. He was only trying to delay her freedom until he could reach a safe distance, which meant that if she was patient, she could probably release herself.

Following this logic, she plucked at the knots he'd made. But her wrists hurt too badly to work at such a difficult angle for very long, and she soon had to give up. She allowed herself another moment to rest, then started straining against the gag instead, using the trunk of the tree behind her to stretch the fabric until she felt some give. After several more minutes of concerted effort, she managed to roll the gag out of her mouth far enough to take a deep breath—and yell.

"Help me! Help!" she cried again and again until her throat was too sore and her mouth too dry to scream anymore. She thought no one had heard her and was trying again to free her hands when footsteps crunched on the rocky ground behind her. Peering through the trees, she saw two Hispanic men, one short and stocky and close to her own age, the other much younger, barely a man at all, approaching her dubiously. They each wore a hat, chinos and work boots covered in dust, and their bare torsos were streaked with sweat. Speaking in Spanish, they conversed back and forth, no doubt exclaiming at the odd occurrence of finding a woman tied to a tree with a T-shirt.

"What is this?" the younger man finally asked in heavily accented English.

Gabrielle wanted to tell them she had a baby at home who needed her. Even though she doubted they'd understand her, the words were on the tip of her tongue. But when she opened her mouth the only thing she could mutter was, "Water...*agua*."

CHAPTER TWELVE

CLUTCHING A GLASS of tepid water, Gabrielle sat at the kitchen table in the dilapidated cinder-block house. The Hispanic laborers who'd found her had brought her directly to a man who'd identified himself as Richard Griffin, the ranch manager. He'd invited her into his home, given her plenty of water, fed her scrambled eggs—from the chicken coops they'd passed outside, no doubt—and let her use the phone.

She'd spoken briefly with David and assured him she was okay. Then she'd turned the handset over to Mr. Griffin so he could give David directions on how to pick her up. They were just beyond the small town of Wellton, about twenty-five miles east of Yuma, Griffin explained. After he hung up with David, the manager took a series of business calls that tied him up for over an hour, which, for the most part, left Gabrielle waiting. Waiting to see Allie. Feeling oddly reluctant to see David. And wondering what had happened to Tucker. Mr. Griffin hadn't volunteered any information about missing food or clothing, had said nothing about seeing a stranger wearing an orange jumpsuit. But she was afraid the Hispanic laborers who'd found her would knock at the door any moment with some discovery. A man Tucker's size couldn't simply disappear. He needed too many things to make good his escape.

For his sake, Gabrielle hoped he'd already found

what he needed and fled. Despite the fact that she'd gone after him with every intention of bringing him back, she wanted nothing more to do with the situation. If he was guilty, someone else could track him down and make him pay. If he wasn't...

God help him if he wasn't.

A swamp cooler rattled in the hallway just beyond the kitchen as the bearded, ruddy-faced Mr. Griffin finished another telephone conversation. "I'm sorry, Mr. Yang," he said, standing at the sink, his back to her. "I told you, the delivery truck's running a little late today. I just radioed the driver. He said he's almost there...."

Gabrielle took another sip from her glass, even though she was already so waterlogged she felt as though she might squish when she walked. What a relief to know she had water right here in her hands, that it was constantly available, that she would—she hoped—never have to go without again.

"Okay, I understand," he said into the phone. "By how much? No problem. I'll add it to the next order. That's for this Friday, right?"

This Friday... What day was it today? Somehow, the entire week had blurred together. The individual days didn't seem important now. Nothing seemed important except reuniting with Allie and getting some sleep.

And wishing Tucker safely away. But Gabrielle wasn't going to think of him. She wasn't ever going to think of him again. Then maybe she wouldn't have to decide whose side she was really on—Warden Crumb's and the system he represented? Or Tucker's?

Finally, Mr. Griffin hung up and turned to face her. "Sorry about that. You can use the phone again now, if you want to let anyone else know you're okay."

The only call she needed to make was to the prison, to give them an update on their escaped convict. They would expect her to contact them at the earliest opportunity. But she couldn't bring herself to do it. Not yet. She couldn't deal with all the questions, the pressure—the knowledge that calling would minimize Tucker's chances for escape.

Don't think about him, she reminded herself. *Don't choose.*

"I'll call the prison when I get home," she said. "I don't know anything that could help them, anyway. I'm sure they already have men on horses, with tracker dogs, searching the area."

"I haven't seen any," Mr. Griffin said, lifting the coffeepot in lieu of asking her if she wanted some.

Gabrielle shook her head. He poured himself a cup, carried it to the table and sat across from her. "Sorry about all the calls," he said. "It's been a busy morning."

"No problem."

"So what's the deal with this escaped convict? When did it happen? I haven't even heard about it."

Was the warden keeping it quiet, trying to reclaim his boy before anyone found out he'd gone missing? If he was, Crumb would be forced to appeal to the press if they didn't catch Tucker soon. Then Tucker's picture would be splashed across television sets throughout the state. "I'm surprised it hasn't been all over the news," she said.

"Maybe it has been. I'm a little behind on current events. I just returned from two weeks at Lake Powell. I go every summer."

"Sounds like fun. Did you go with family?"

"Just some friends," he said, but she knew her attempt to change the subject hadn't worked when he went right back to Tucker.

"So who is this guy who escaped?" he asked.

Gabrielle's grip tightened on her glass. She didn't want to talk about Tucker because then she *had* to think of him. "His name's Randall Tucker."

"And he's dangerous?"

Surely, Griffin would find it strange if she told him Tucker wouldn't hurt anyone. He was convicted of murder and sentenced to life in prison. There was probably an all-out manhunt going on to find him. "If a man's desperate enough, you can never tell," she said. Which was the truth. Look what she'd almost done. She could have killed Tucker in that moment of madness when she'd pulled the trigger.

"What'd he do?"

The constant pounding of a headache made it difficult for Gabrielle to be polite. Where was David? She wanted to go home, close the blinds and shut out the rest of the world until she could come to grips with everything that had happened to her. "They say he murdered his wife."

A light went on in Griffin's eyes. "Oh, I think I did hear something about that. A water-skier at Powell mentioned it. Beat her to death, right? Couple of years back? He's some kind of karate expert, if I remember right."

Gabrielle rubbed her temples, hoping to ease the pain. "That's what they say," she murmured.

He slung an arm over his chair back. "Sounds like a pretty bad dude. What made you go after him alone? Or did you have help?"

A glance at the clock over Griffin's head told her it'd been nearly two hours since she'd called David.

Surely she wouldn't have to wait much longer. "I'm sorry. I appreciate your kindness, but I'm not feeling well," she said, hoping to dodge any more questions. "I'm probably still a little dehydrated. Do you think maybe I could lie down on your couch for a while and wait for my ride?"

"Of course." His chair squeaked on the linoleum as he shoved it back. "I should've realized you wouldn't be feeling well. It's just such a fascinating story, you know? To be lost for...what did you say? Three days?"

She nodded.

"Three days, yet you came out alive. You're one lucky lady, you know that?"

Gabrielle felt grateful to be alive, but she wasn't sure she felt lucky. She smiled and stood, eager to escape Griffin's attention by lying down, when a staccato knock sounded at the door.

David. He'd arrived. The tension in Gabrielle's body eased a bit as she followed Griffin to the door. But it wasn't David. A small Hispanic woman wearing a colorful cotton skirt and sandals stood on the front step. The worry lines in her forehead alarmed Gabrielle.

The woman spoke in Spanish, the words *"donde"* and *"esposo"* standing out from among the rest. Her luminous dark eyes kept darting past Griffin to Gabrielle as she gestured wildly toward the far corner of the ranch.

Gabrielle didn't need to understand her to know something monumental had occurred. Tucker! Had they found him?

"What's wrong?" she asked, her stomach tightening.

"After you arrived, I had Manuel get a rifle and

search the property, just in case,'' Mr. Griffin said, his own face flushing with excitement. ''He's found someone hiding in the shed behind the processing plant.''

Suddenly, Gabrielle wondered whether or not she'd be able to remain standing. ''And?'' she managed to say.

''And what? Didn't you hear me? They have him cornered at the plant. We might have your man,'' he said happily. ''Let's go see.''

She sucked in air so she wouldn't pass out. ''Yeah, let's go see.''

THE MOMENT they stepped outside, the hot Arizona air hit Gabrielle like a blast from a raging furnace. Beads of sweat rolled down her back and itched her scalp, but the perspiration was caused as much by the panic racing through her blood as the heat. They'd found a man hiding on the ranch. What was she going to do? She couldn't watch them drag Tucker back to prison, knew his life wouldn't be worth anything if they did.

Don't let it be Tucker…don't let it be Tucker, she prayed as they walked. But she knew such prayers were futile. Who else could it be? What other stranger had reason to be lurking about such a barren place? Tucker must not have been able to get what he needed. He must've been waiting for dark.

Damn him! How could he have gotten himself caught after everything they'd been through?

Gabrielle knew her reaction was completely irrational, but she was incapable of stemming the tide of anger that lashed through her. Couldn't *anything* go right? She just wanted Tucker safely gone. She wanted him out of her life. If something bad happened to him, she didn't want to know about it because…

Because was one of those things she wouldn't think about.

Fortunately, Griffin and the woman continued to converse in Spanish and didn't seem to notice how reluctantly she followed them. She could hear the clucking of the hens and the whir of conveyor belts as they moved down the row of chicken houses toward the blue building she'd seen earlier. A rooster crowed not far away, even though it was well past noon. But all of that was merely background noise. She was frantically trying to decide what to do the moment she came face-to-face with Randall Tucker—under the watchful eye of Mr. Griffin.

"There they are." The ranch manager pointed as they rounded a corner and the blue building came into view.

Gabrielle saw one of the men who'd rescued her earlier, along with another Hispanic she hadn't met before. She could make out both men perfectly, could see the glimmer of sweat on their foreheads, the concentration on their dark faces. But they stood in the hot glare of the sun while the man they'd cornered crouched against the building, in the shadows.

Tucker was more difficult to see, but as she moved closer, there was no mistaking his identity. He no longer wore his orange prison jumpsuit but had on a pair of patched cutoffs, a button-up shirt with the sleeves torn out, and a pair of old athletic shoes, all of which looked significantly too small. Where he'd gotten these clothes and shoes, Gabrielle had no idea. Neither could she guess what he'd done with his jumpsuit.

The laborers acknowledged Mr. Griffin's approach by saying something to him in Spanish and motioning toward Tucker. The ranch manager answered, then looked to her. "Is this your man?" he asked, obviously expecting an affirmative answer.

Gabrielle gazed into the shocking blue of Randall Tucker's eyes and found them smoldering with resentment. He expected her to give him up, she realized. After what had happened with the helicopter, Gabrielle could understand why. But she couldn't do it. If she told them who he was, they'd continue to hold him at gunpoint until the police arrived, and he'd find himself back in prison by the end of the day, facing new charges. No one at the prison would care that he'd saved her life. No one would care that she thought he was innocent. They'd punish him—severely.

"Officer Hadley?" Griffin prodded when she hesitated.

The ramifications of what she was about to do flooded Gabrielle's mind. But there was justice, and then there was justice. Certainly she could hang her decision on a higher law. Was she really worried about justice, though? Gabrielle wasn't sure. The only thing she knew at this moment was that to betray him was unthinkable.

"No," she said. "That's not him."

Tucker stiffened and Griffin's eyes widened. "It's not?"

"No. My guy's wearing an orange jumpsuit."

"But he could've gotten these clothes anywhere. We have laborers who come and go all the time. They live in those huts at the back of the property and they…well, sometimes they have to leave in a hurry. We have no way of knowing if—"

"I've chased Randall Tucker through the desert for three days," she interrupted, infusing her voice with the proper amount of indignation. "I saw his face again when he tied me up just last night. Do you think I don't know what he looks like?''

Tucker's expression remained inscrutable as Griffin turned toward him. The ranch manager was obviously having difficulty reconciling the coincidence of finding him here, in the shed no less, the same day his men rescued a corrections officer who'd been bent on recovering an escaped convict. But as far as Griffin was concerned, she would have no reason to lie about that escaped convict's identity.

Fortunately, a man who hired illegal aliens wasn't typically anxious to call the police—unless he felt certain he had good reason.

"So what do you have to say?" Griffin asked Tucker. "Who are you and what are you doing here?"

Tucker's eyes settled on the barrel of the gun. "Name's Joe. I went hiking earlier this morning, got turned around and ran out of water. Then I came upon this place."

Griffin wiped the sweat off his brow. "Manuel said you were in the shed."

"I was hoping to find something to drink."

Griffin raised his brows. "There's nothing in there except egg crates," he said, but he must have been somewhat satisfied because he motioned for Manuel to put down the gun.

The older Hispanic obeyed, asking something in Spanish. Griffin answered, then smiled in a way that told Gabrielle she was right—he'd decided to give them the benefit of the doubt. "Sorry if we scared you," he said. "I guess there's been a bit of a mix-up. Can I give you a lift back to town?"

"That'd be great," Tucker said.

"I take it you live in Wellton?"

"Yeah."

"Well, we'll have you home in a few minutes." He shooed the Hispanic woman away, took the gun from Manuel and pointed the muzzle at the ground. "Let's go back to the house so I can get the keys to my truck."

As they walked over the parched earth, Gabrielle watched Tucker from the corner of her eye. His movements were deceptively relaxed. He spoke casually to Griffin, as though he was every bit the hiker he purported to be, but she couldn't affect the same calm. In her view, they couldn't move fast enough. She wanted Tucker to get away from the ranch as soon as possible—before someone stumbled upon his orange jumpsuit or figured out which hut he'd broken into.

Before they both got caught.

Forty yards had never seemed so long. When Gabrielle and Tucker were in the desert, the line between right and wrong had definitely blurred. She'd broken the first cardinal rule of being a good corrections officer: thou shalt not become too familiar with an inmate. But she hadn't done anything punishable by law. Until now. Lying about who Tucker was, helping him escape, moved her firmly across the line, and there was no going back.

At least she knew whose side she was on, she told herself. The decision pulling her completely into his camp had finally been made. But just as they reached the house, she saw David's Toyota Forerunner turn into the drive and was confused all over again. She had a child, a job, a life. And she'd just risked it all—for Tucker.

"I'LL WAIT HERE," Gabrielle heard Tucker say as Griffin ducked into the house to get his keys.

David parked and killed the engine and, although she was looking at David and not Tucker, she could feel the acuteness of Tucker's attention, knew he must recognize David from the picture he'd torn.

She hated having them together. Lying about Tucker betrayed David and everything he thought she was. Telling the truth betrayed Tucker and everything she *really* was.

"Gabby," David said, his voice filled with relief, his eyes only on her as he came around the car. "Thank God you're okay. I've been worried sick about you."

Gabrielle longed to throw herself into his arms. She would have three days before. But things had changed. David looked like the same old David. Just over six feet, two hundred and twenty pounds, he was a little heavier than Tucker and not nearly as sinewy. He had no reason to be. He didn't train with weights or fight with anyone. He lived a comfortable, moderately successful life and the only weapon he ever used was his smile. Gabrielle had always loved the way his eyes crinkled in the corners when his lips curved up, how the sun lightened his sandy-colored hair in summer and tanned his face.

But he felt like a stranger to her now. She could think only of putting her arms around Allie, whose fuzzy blond head barely crested the top of the back seat.

"Gabby?" he said when she didn't immediately respond.

"Thanks for coming," she said, and embraced him, but it wasn't the happy reunion it would've been had Tucker not been standing there. She was too conscious of Tucker, too afraid David might recognize him from some news report.

As soon as she thought she could disengage herself without making David feel slighted, she went to the Forerunner and unfastened her baby from the car seat.

"Allie..." Gabrielle hugged her daughter close, inhaling the scent of baby shampoo and reveling in the softness peculiar to young skin. She considered the satisfying sensation that passed through her in that moment far better than her first drink of water when she'd emerged from the desert. Allie was safe. They were together. Somehow, everything would be all right. "Momma's back now, baby," she murmured, kissing her head. "Momma's back."

"Who's this?" David asked.

Gabrielle glanced over her shoulder to see he'd finally noticed Tucker. This was the moment of truth. She didn't know how publicized Tucker's escape had been. If she told David she didn't know him, he might respond with, "Wait a second...didn't I see him on the news? Isn't this the guy you went after?"

"He's just some guy Mr. Griffin is going to take into town," she said, gambling. When David didn't respond the way she'd feared, she looked away, wishing it were true that she didn't know Tucker. If she didn't know him, she couldn't care about him. If she didn't care about him, she could go back to life as she'd known it and the relative ease of her old problems.

"So he works here?" David asked.

"I don't think so. He just needs a ride." Trying to conceal her nervousness, Gabrielle put Allie back in her car seat. Her daughter was far from happy at the prospect of being restricted again so soon, but they had to leave, to get away from the ranch before—

"Where you headin'?" David asked Tucker.

"Wellton," Tucker said, as though he'd known where he was all along.

"I just passed Wellton. It's only five miles away. Why don't we take you and save Mr. Griffin the trip?"

"I think it's already handled, David," Gabrielle said, hoping he'd drop it.

The slamming of the screen door interrupted their conversation, and Mr. Griffin appeared, keys in hand.

"We're driving straight through Wellton," David said to him. "You want us to give this guy a lift?"

"If you're sure you don't mind," Griffin said.

"No problem," David assured him. "Right, Gabby?"

Gabrielle muttered something she hoped was intelligible *and* polite and slid into the passenger seat. David thanked Mr. Griffin for taking care of her, then got behind the wheel. When Tucker strode across the drive and climbed into the back with Allie, Gabrielle felt his presence behind her like static electricity in the air.

The impulse to turn to see his reaction to Allie shot through Gabrielle, but at that moment, Manuel came into view. He immediately caught her attention because he was walking so purposefully toward the house, calling Mr. Griffin's name. Had he found Tucker's jumpsuit? Something else that would give them away? Her stomach tensed at the thought. "Let's go," she said.

David glanced up from inserting the key in the ignition. "That's what I'm doing, babe. Give me a second."

"I mean now. Right away. Hurry."

Manuel came closer. Griffin walked over to meet

him, and they bent their heads together in conversation. The next thirty seconds seemed to pass in slow motion as Gabrielle's headache escalated to migraine proportions.

Any minute, they'll turn and wave us back, she thought. *Or go after their guns.*

But Griffin only nodded. Then the two men walked off in the direction of the plant—and Gabrielle felt her whole body go limp with relief.

"I'm David Hadley," David was saying, oblivious to her terror as he looked into the rearview mirror at Tucker.

"Name's Joe," Tucker said.

Finally their tires crunched on gravel as David swung around and headed out of the ranch.

"I don't get out this way very often," David went on. "Things have sure changed. I guess there's a nice golf course in Wellton now, huh?"

"Yeah, it's beautiful," Tucker responded, even though Gabrielle doubted he knew anything about any golf course.

"You lived here long?" David asked.

"No."

Gabrielle's nails curled into her palms as she stared out the window, willing the miles to pass quickly. Now she'd not only lied about Tucker's identity, she'd allowed David to transport him.

David reached across and took her hand. "You'll have to forgive me if I'm not much for conversation," he told Tucker. "I'm a little preoccupied with getting Gabby back. She gave us quite a scare, disappearing for so long."

"That's what I heard," Tucker said.

The nails of Gabrielle's free hand bit deeper into her flesh.

"Are you sure you're okay, babe?" David asked, turning to her now that he'd done the polite thing by introducing himself and making Tucker feel welcome. He was so predictable, so...*nice*. Why hadn't nice been good enough for her? What was wrong with her?

"You seem upset. You're not hurt, are you?" he asked.

Gabrielle shook her head.

"What happened out there? Did you ever catch up with the guy who escaped?"

Instinctively she shifted more toward the window but forced herself to speak. She had to offer David some explanation. "Last night I, uh, came upon him and he...he tied me up because he was tired of me following him, and—"

"He *what?*" Concern changed the smile lines around David's mouth into more of a frown, and Gabrielle felt the Forerunner slow. "You didn't say anything about meeting up with him when I talked to you on the phone. I got the impression you'd gone into the desert after him and gotten lost before you ever found him."

"That's pretty much what happened," she said.

"Except you did find him."

"Briefly."

"And he tied you up."

"Yeah."

"He didn't—" his eyes flicked toward the rearview mirror and Tucker, then back to her as he lowered his voice "—*hurt* you, did he?"

Guilt shimmied down Gabrielle's spine. Judging by the inflection of David's voice, he was asking if Tucker had raped her. But if she and Tucker had made love, it would've been far from rape, and she hated even thinking that because she knew it would hurt David. "No," she said.

"You're sure? Maybe we should take you to the hospital, have you checked out—"

"He didn't rape me," she said a little too forcefully. "There isn't any evidence to gather, there are no wounds to treat. I just want to go home."

David scowled at her. "You're not really acting like yourself, Gabby."

"I'm sorry. I have a headache."

"Okay. We'll talk about it later." David's chest rose and fell as he sighed, then he let go of her and put both hands on the wheel.

They drove the next ten minutes in silence, except for Allie's coos and gurgles. Gabrielle would have turned and spoken to her daughter, but she didn't want to face Tucker. She wanted him gone—from her heart, from her mind, from her life—before he could change her any more.

"You can let me out here," Tucker said as soon as they reached the outskirts of Wellton. "I know you're in a hurry to get home."

"It's okay. We'll drop you by your house," David insisted, still trying to be polite.

"No, I'm going to grab a bite to eat here in town. Thanks for the ride."

"No problem."

David pulled to the side of the road, and Tucker got out. Gabrielle told herself not to look back at him, to start forgetting right now. But she looked anyway— and saw him standing at the curb watching her as David drove away. He didn't wave or acknowledge her in any way. He just stared after her, and she did the same until they were too far apart to see each other anymore.

CHAPTER THIRTEEN

GABRIELLE SLEPT the rest of the ride home. She slept the rest of the day. She slept well into the night. Then she got up and went into Allie's room to watch her baby sleep. Somehow, seeing her daughter curled up so peacefully in the safety of her crib comforted her, kept her from worrying about Tucker and wondering where he was, how he was getting by on only thirty-five dollars. Surely he had friends and family who would help him, she told herself. Surely he'd reach the boy who meant so much to him. She wondered what Landon was like—

"What are you doing awake?" a voice whispered.

Gabrielle glanced up to see David standing in the doorway wearing nothing but a pair of pajama bottoms, his hair rumpled from sleep.

"I just woke up and needed to see Allie," she murmured. "How'd you know I wasn't sleeping?"

"I peeked in to check on you and found your bed empty. Is anything wrong?"

"No." Gabrielle nodded toward Allie. "It's just good to be back, to be safe and to know she's safe, too. Thanks for looking after her."

He smiled. "Hey, she's my baby, too, remember?"

How could Gabrielle forget? That was part of the reason she felt so guilty for not being able to love David the way she should. The way she wanted to.

"Are you feeling good enough to come talk to me for a little bit?" he asked.

Gabrielle swallowed hard. She didn't want to talk about what she'd experienced. She wanted to file those thoughts and emotions in some section of her brain labeled Inexplicable Attraction. But she knew she still had a lot of explaining to do. To David. To the authorities.

"Sure." She kissed her fingertips and pressed them to Allie's round cheek, then slipped into the hall behind David.

When they entered the living room, she folded her legs beneath her on the couch and he took the chair closest to her.

"I called the prison as soon as we got home, like you said, and told them you're safe."

She nodded. She hadn't been able to make herself place that call, but she knew she'd lose her job if she didn't contact them. "Thanks. Were they upset that I didn't call myself?"

"Not under the circumstances," he said. "I told them you were sick. A Sergeant Hansen called me back a few minutes later. He and the warden are coming to visit at nine o'clock in the morning."

Gabrielle sighed in resignation. It was starting, and she'd never been a good liar. What if they saw through her? What if David already knew something was up? Yesterday, when Tucker had been in the Forerunner, her tension had been palpable. Had David felt it?

"Tomorrow's only Thursday," she said. "Maybe we can put Hansen off a little longer. I'm not quite myself yet."

David frowned. "You're kidding, right?"

"No. Why would I be kidding?"

"They want to catch this guy, Gabby. He's danger-ous. They only want a few minutes of your time to ask where you saw him last, where you think he might've gone, stuff like that. It shouldn't take too long or be too demanding."

"Okay." She knew he'd find it strange if she pushed the issue. It was tough to remember that everyone else thought Tucker a menace to society.

"You gonna be okay?" he asked, reaching over to squeeze her knee.

"Yeah."

Silence fell, except for the engine of a car outside her front window. Gabrielle watched the headlights slice through the darkness, knowing it was probably another officer coming home from the graveyard shift. Her trailer park was located across the street from the prison, and most of its occupants worked at Florence, Eyman or the federal facility just down the road.

David cleared his throat, catching her attention. "Was this experience enough to convince you?" he asked.

"Convince me of what?"

"That you have no business here."

"Here? At the prison, you mean?"

"In Florence."

She didn't say anything, but that didn't stop David from continuing.

"I want to take you home with me, Gabby. It's time we got back together. I've tried to be patient. I've given you space, but—"

Gabrielle shoved a hand through her hair. "David, I can't go into this now."

"I know you've been through a lot. And I'm not trying to add to your pain. I just want things to be right between us. We love each other, Gabby." He raised a hand before she could respond. "I know you want to qualify that, and say this is one kind of love and that's another. But we have Allie to think about. And our futures. You can always contact your mother from Phoenix, where I can look out for you. You don't have to do it from here."

Gabrielle remembered the promises she'd made herself in the desert, after Tucker had tied her up. She'd decided to remarry David and make him happy. So why did the very thought of sleeping with him again cause her whole being to rebel?

"David, please. Not now," she said.

He sighed. "Then when, Gabby? When are you going to be ready?"

"I don't know. I've told you to date, to meet other women—"

He shot out of his chair. "I don't want to date, damn it! You're the mother of my child. You're the one I love, Gabby!"

Gabrielle closed her eyes. "David, I'm sorry—"

He pinched the bridge of his nose, obviously struggling with his impatience. "I don't want you to be sorry. I just want you to think about coming back home, okay? Let's put all this behind us. We could go on a second honeymoon—"

"I can't bear the thought of leaving Allie for more than a few hours so soon after what's happened."

"Then we'll take her. It'll be the three of us. That's how it was meant to be, okay?"

She nodded but felt tears prick the backs of her eyes. "You deserve better than what I can give you, David."

"I don't want better. I just want you." He stood and kissed her forehead. For a moment Gabrielle feared he'd try to kiss her on the mouth. She knew she couldn't tolerate it, not after kissing Tucker. But he didn't. He lifted her chin and gave her a weary smile.

"Everything will be okay," he promised. "I'll do my best to make you happy, you know that."

FOR THE FIRST TIME since they'd reestablished their relationship after the divorce, Gabrielle didn't want David around. He watched her too closely, made her feel hemmed in when she couldn't afford his scrutiny. She had enough on her mind without having to pretend that nothing had changed, but he insisted on staying until she was back on her feet. Given what he'd said about her returning to Phoenix, she suspected he didn't plan on leaving Florence—at least for any length of time— without her. He was waiting for the fallout from Tucker's escape to settle down and work itself out. Then he thought he'd be able to talk her out of all the feelings and beliefs that had made her divorce him in the first place.

She stared at her reflection in the bathroom mirror, taking solace in the high-pitched whine of the blow-dryer because it cocooned her in noise and allowed her a few minutes of privacy to gather her thoughts before Warden Crumb and Sergeant Hansen arrived. They were going to be here any minute, and she still wasn't sure exactly what to say to them. She'd always been a strong proponent of law and order, of truth. How was she going to sit across from the men she worked for and perpetuate the lies she'd started at the Bountiful Harvest Egg Ranch? Especially, with David looking on? Surely her ex-husband would see through her even if Crumb and Hansen did not.

But she was in too deep to back out now.

"Gabby, they're here," David said, rapping on the bathroom door.

Gabrielle shut off the blow-dryer and set it on the counter. "I'll be right there."

She listened to his footsteps retreat, heard low voices coming from the living room, and knew she could no longer stay locked in the bathroom. Letting her hair fall loose around her shoulders, she buttoned the white cotton shirt she'd ironed for the occasion and removed a few specks of lint from her khaki pants. Then she slipped on her black sandals and belt, braced herself and unlocked the door.

"Would you like some coffee?" she heard David ask as she made her way down the hall. The warden accepted, but Sergeant Hansen refused.

"There's our new officer," Sergeant Hansen said when she appeared, but the insincerity of his smile was enough to remind Gabrielle how much she disliked him.

"Hello, Sergeant Hansen," she said, offering her hand.

"Glad to have you back safe," he said as they shook.

"I'm glad to be back." She turned to the Warden. "Warden Crumb." Crumb shook her hand before accepting his coffee from David. Then he sat forward on one end of the couch, as though conscious of not wrinkling his suit. Sergeant Hansen sat on the other. Gabrielle took the chair opposite both of them, her presence immediately attracting Allie's attention. The child had been standing by the coffee table, staring wide-eyed at the strangers who'd just infiltrated her world. When she toddled over to Gabrielle, David tried to scoop her up, but Gabrielle waved him away.

"She's fine," she said, and curled her arms protectively around her daughter. David hesitated only briefly before leaning against the kitchen doorway, where he kept a polite yet supportive distance.

"How are you doing, Officer Hadley?" the warden asked.

She remembered their meeting in his office, the way he'd hidden his real feelings by pretending to be so genteel. "Better, now that I've had some sleep," she said.

"You've been through quite an ordeal."

"The past few days certainly didn't work out the way I'd planned. How's Officer Eckland?"

"He's fine. He has a cast on his leg, of course," Crumb said. "But it'll heal."

"I'm glad."

"And the others? The people in the truck?"

"They're both fine."

"Good."

The warden cleared his throat, set his cup on the coffee table and leaned forward a little further. "You know, Gabrielle—you don't mind if I call you Gabrielle, do you?"

Gabrielle didn't mind his using her first name. His patronizing tone, however, grated on her nerves. "No," she said.

"Great." He rubbed his hands together. "You know, we understand that you're new at the prison. And with a thirty-percent vacancy rate, Lord knows we need good officers." He bestowed a benevolent smile on David this time, then quickly sobered. "But Officer Eckland has told us some things that we, quite frankly, find worrisome."

Gabrielle had been so preoccupied with the questions

she knew they'd ask about Tucker, this took her by surprise. "What things?" she asked.

Crumb and Hansen glanced at each other. "He said you caused the accident. He said you yanked on the wheel, trying to force him to pull over when he refused to stop and remove Randall Tucker's cuffs," Crumb said.

"Yanked on the wheel!" Gabrielle cried. "I never touched the wheel."

"But you did remove the inmate's cuffs, did you not?"

"After the accident, I did. I was afraid leaving them on would cause him to sustain further injury. His hand was broken before Eckland cuffed him, remember?"

"I remember you *thought* it was broken." Crumb took a sip of his coffee. "So after you removed the prisoner's handcuffs, what happened?"

Everything. Her whole world had changed. But Gabrielle couldn't say so. She stuck with the story she'd told David, that she started into the desert but got lost before she could find Tucker, that she didn't run into him until she came upon the egg ranch. She told them she last saw him when he'd tied her up, but she said he'd tied her up twelve hours earlier than he had, hoping the added hours would send them off-course long enough to give Tucker a small advantage.

"So you encountered him Tuesday evening?" Hansen asked, jumping into the conversation.

"Yes."

"What time was that?"

"I don't know. I'd managed to glean some water by making a desert still, but the heat was getting to me. I'm afraid I was pretty disoriented."

"Three days in the desert with little water and no food would disorient anyone," David said.

"Of course it would," the warden replied. His tone was congenial enough to let Gabrielle know he'd heard the defensive note in David's voice and was working to defuse it.

"Actually, I did have some food," Gabrielle admitted. "I...I had the lunch I'd packed, and Tuesday night I shot a rabbit and roasted it."

"You did?" Sergeant Hansen said.

She nodded.

"That's pretty resourceful. How'd you start the fire?"

"I had a book of matches in my purse, left over from my daughter's birthday."

"If you had matches, why didn't you light a fire to signal any rescuers who might be looking for you?" Hansen asked. "It might've helped us locate you."

For a moment Gabrielle's breath caught in her throat. Why did she have to volunteer more information than necessary? That was stupid, idiotic.... "I—I didn't think of that," she said. "I was traveling at night and trying to stay out of the heat during the day, so I wasn't in one spot for long. It never occurred to me to start a fire and stay put." Probably because she and Tucker weren't trying to attract anyone to *them*. They couldn't, without compromising his future. They were both scrambling to reach safety, but safety meant something different for Tucker than it did for Gabrielle.

"Not even when you were sleeping?"

"She just told you how disoriented she was," David said.

"I heard," Hansen replied, but his eyes didn't so much as flick David's way. They were boring holes in

Gabrielle. "So that must be why, when you ran into Tucker at the egg ranch, you didn't use your gun."

Gabrielle crossed her legs and folded her hands in her lap. "My gun was empty by then, Sergeant Hansen."

"From killing rabbits?"

"From shooting at rabbits, among other things. I'd also tried to shoot off part of a cactus to see if I could get some moisture from inside. I was pretty desperate most of the time. What I did might not have made sense. I realize that now."

"Since you were so disoriented, maybe it was better you didn't have a useable weapon when you found Tucker," the warden said. "If he'd been able to relieve you of your gun, you might not be here today."

The image of Tucker's head blocking the bright sun as he bent over her while she lay on the desert floor flashed through Gabrielle's mind, bringing defensive words to her tongue. But she said nothing. She couldn't have Hansen or the warden guessing how split her loyalties were. Especially when they already suspected her of being too sympathetic to Tucker because she'd tried to help with his injuries. *I remember you* thought *it was broken....*

"How do you think Tucker managed to survive?" Hansen asked. "He had no water, no gun, no food."

"He must've figured out a way to collect rainwater, too," she said. "Or something."

Or something. They'd collected rainwater together. They'd eaten together. They'd slept together. They'd almost made love.... The truth seemed to vibrate through Gabrielle, and her cheeks flushed hot, which made her discomfort that much more acute, because Hansen didn't seem to be missing a thing. Pressing his hands together in a prayerlike attitude and resting his chin on them, he pursed his lips. "I can't imagine how he could've done that. What would he have collected it in?"

"I don't know," she said. "I can't say what he did. Like I told you, I didn't run into him until I got to the egg ranch."

"And that's where he tied you up and left you. All night. Is that correct?"

"Until I was able to rid myself of the gag in my mouth and call for help. Some immigrant workers heard me and came to see what was going on sometime the following morning." For the first time since the incident, Gabrielle understood why Tucker had said he was doing her a favor by tying her up. He'd given her valuable proof.

"This was *Wednesday* morning?"

"Must've been."

"I see. Why didn't you call the prison as soon as you were rescued?"

"I did. I had David call as soon as we got home."

"But you didn't call from the egg ranch."

"I'd just spent three days lost in the desert! I wasn't thinking straight. And I had nothing to tell you, anyway. I didn't know where Tucker was."

"You were the last person to see him."

"He'd already been gone fifteen hours. Depending on whether or not he had outside help, he could be anywhere. I hardly thought I could add anything useful, and I was pretty sick, as you can probably imagine."

"It's not as though you were left in the dark," David said. "She asked me to call you."

Gabrielle felt more guilt than relief for David's help.

He was getting sucked in, too. She didn't want that. She didn't want to hurt him.

The clock on the wall seemed to tick more loudly than normal as the warden sipped his coffee. "Do you have any idea where Tucker might be heading?" he asked, obviously choosing to change course.

Gabrielle didn't doubt that Tucker was heading straight to his son, wherever that was. But she wasn't about to give him away. "Wouldn't most escaped convicts try to cross the border?"

The warden shrugged. "Maybe. But Tucker doesn't strike me as the usual convict."

Tucker wasn't usual in any way—at least she wasn't the only one who recognized that. "How do you think he's different?" she asked.

"He's arrogant. He may think he can outsmart us, but I promise you this, we'll catch him. And when we do—" he smiled "—he'll be sorry he ever put us to so much trouble."

A chill cascaded down Gabrielle's spine. That was exactly what she feared most for Tucker—Crumb and Hansen's retribution.

"Is there anything else you can think of that might help us?" Hansen asked.

Gabrielle shook her head. "Our contact was too brief. He snuck up on me from behind, tackled me and tied me up so I couldn't give him away at the ranch. He was looking for some lead time, I suppose. That's all."

"He didn't—" Hansen's gaze swept over her body before rising again to her face "—take advantage of you sexually, did he?"

Gabrielle got the impression Hansen was actually hoping to hear a positive answer. From the look of anticipation on his face, she suspected he'd delight in the thought that she'd been raped. Wouldn't that show her? Wouldn't that teach her for siding with an inmate? "No, Sergeant Hansen. He didn't rape me. He didn't hurt me at all."

"I wouldn't call leaving you in the desert to die being kind," Crumb put in.

"I didn't say he was kind, Warden Crumb."

"No, you didn't. But I'm not detecting a great deal of anger, either," Hansen said.

"That's not fair," David said. "How do you know what she feels?"

Hansen glanced at him but didn't deign to answer. His attitude told everyone in the room he thought David had no business even joining the conversation.

"I have nothing to be angry about," Gabrielle said. "I was trying to transport a prisoner who managed to escape. I went after him—"

"And nearly lost her life doing it," David added, his voice more emphatic.

"—and I wasn't able to recapture him," Gabrielle went on. "To me, there's nothing personal in that. I did what I could."

"It doesn't bother you that there's a man out there who may murder another innocent person tonight because you were worried about his cuffs being fastened too tight?" Hansen asked.

"I didn't cause the wreck," Gabrielle said. "Eckland did."

"The whole thing would never have happened if—"

"That's enough," David said. "I think it's time for the two of you to go. Gabby's told you everything she knows. She's been through too much already."

"I agree, Hansen," the warden said. "What's done is done. I suggest we put the past behind us and talk about the future. We can probably all benefit from that." He smiled at David, again trying to soothe him, before returning his focus to Gabrielle. "Are you planning on coming back to work, Officer Hadley?"

Gabrielle thought of the prison, of going back and facing Eckland, with his broken leg and accusing eyes. She thought of Officer Bell, who resented her for taking the stand she was too afraid to take, of Hansen, who could barely contain his resentment of her, of the catcalls and disrespect of the prisoners. Then she thought of returning to Phoenix and trying to build a life there. If she did, she'd eventually remarry David. She wasn't good at withholding, especially when she knew that her refusal hurt someone she cared about deeply.

"I haven't decided," she hedged.

"Well, we'd like you to be able to keep your job, if you want it," Warden Crumb said. "We got off to a rocky start, I'll grant you that, but I think it was more a big misunderstanding than anything else. Wouldn't you say?"

A *misunderstanding* that Tucker couldn't get the medical treatment he needed? That Hansen wouldn't break up the fight, even after the Border Brothers had gotten Tucker on the ground? What was there to misunderstand about that?

Gabrielle didn't answer, but he continued anyway.

"Considering what's happened, I think a move is in order. If you come back, I'm going to transfer you to Eyman Complex. You'll be working with a new bunch of officers there, and the facility is state of the art.

Serious incidents are rare, so we shouldn't have any more trouble.''

That was because Eyman Complex, located two miles from where she worked now, housed level five prisoners who were locked down twenty-four hours a day, seven days a week. They lived in cells by themselves and remained alone virtually all the time. They ate in their cells. They were let out to shower and exercise only three times a week. Their exercise consisted of an hour alone in a cement room the size of a racquetball court, with a handball if they wanted. Those who persisted in being difficult were strapped to gurneys whenever they were transported through the complex for visits with attorneys or for medical reasons.

Still, even in this restrictive environment, the inmates managed to fabricate knives, ropes—Gabrielle had heard that one guy had actually made a viable rope out of toilet paper—and blow darts, so it wasn't the safest place in the world. But the complex was new, as the warden had said, and offered electronic security the old Territorial prison complex couldn't compete with. It was cooler in summer, warmer in winter, and far quieter than central unit.

And Hansen wouldn't be there.

"That sounds good," Gabrielle said, thinking maybe she could get her life on track again, after all.

She could tell David wasn't pleased with her answer. "She's still recovering," he said. "Let's give her a few days to decide."

The warden deposited his cup on the coffee table and stood. "I understand. I won't expect you until next Wednesday. Call me if for any reason you won't be there."

Gabrielle nodded.

"And if you happen to think of something that might be helpful in apprehending Randall Tucker, let me know."

"I will."

He and Hansen moved to the door and Gabrielle followed to let them out.

"Get some rest," Crumb said.

"If you can sleep tonight," Hansen muttered as he passed her.

Crumb must have heard him because he scowled, but Hansen hardly looked repentant when he gave her a parting smirk. "We'll miss you at central."

"You know, now that I think about it, there *is* something that might help you find Tucker," Gabrielle said. Both men turned.

"What is it?" Crumb demanded, brows raised.

"When he was tying me up, he kept cursing his injured hand and blaming Sergeant Hansen for the pain, saying he'd be glad when he finally settled the score. But—" she frowned "—Tucker doesn't know where you live, does he, Sergeant Hansen?"

The blood drained from Hansen's face and Gabrielle knew he was remembering how well Tucker could fight, what Tucker might be able to do on an even playing field, when Hansen wasn't in possession of any weapons and Tucker wasn't cuffed or behind bars. He had to know how easy it would be for Tucker to find him, too.

"He wouldn't dare come near me," Hansen said, his voice full of bravado.

"You're right." Gabrielle shrugged. "He's probably too afraid." She smiled to keep up her veneer of civility, but they both knew Tucker felt no fear of Hansen, only contempt.

Hansen looked up and down the street before getting behind the wheel of the warden's government-issue van. His worry made Gabrielle feel better than she had since he and the warden had arrived. But her pleasure dissipated the moment David came up behind her.

"Do you think it was wise to taunt him that way?" he asked. "They were pretty nice about the accident. They could cause you a lot of trouble over that, you know, maybe even bring you up on criminal charges. I know you weren't at fault, but it's your word against Eckland's."

Gabrielle turned to face him. "They weren't being nice," she said.

"How do you know?"

"Because they just offered me a deal. Didn't you hear them?"

"I think you're reading things into the conversation, Gabby. I didn't hear any deal."

"Oh yeah? They let me know they had a different version of the accident, then they offered to sweep it under the rug along with everything else—*if* I keep my mouth shut about what happened to Tucker. They're just letting me stay on at the prison to sweeten the pie, and to stop anyone from asking questions as to why they'd fire me."

David rubbed his neck with one hand as though the tension was starting to get to him. "Come on, Gabby. They didn't even refer to the stuff that happened at the prison before Tucker was transferred."

"Yes, they did. The warden called it a big misunderstanding, remember?"

"Are you sure he meant what you think he meant?"

She watched the cloud of dust from the tires of the

warden's van settle, then sighed. "No, I'm not sure. Maybe you're right."

"Either way, why not take away their power? Come to Phoenix with me. You won't have to work unless you want to," he said.

Gabrielle closed the door, folded her arms and leaned dejectedly against it. "David, do you know what you're asking me to do?"

He stared at her for a few seconds and his voice dropped. "All I know is that I want you to love me the way I love you, Gabby."

Their eyes locked. "And what if I can't?" she asked softly, wishing she could dictate her emotions.

A muscle flexed in David's cheek. "He raped you, didn't he?"

Gabrielle blinked in surprise. "What?"

"What happened in the desert wasn't how you made it sound. Are you afraid to tell me because I didn't want you to come down here in the first place?"

"No, it's not that at all."

"Then what?"

She shook her head. "He didn't rape me," she said. But he'd done something almost as bad. He'd stolen her heart and her soul, and ruined her for David or any other man.

CHAPTER FOURTEEN

IT RAINED that night. Gabrielle lay in bed, listening to large, fat drops ringing like coins on the metal of her trailer. But she was remembering another storm, the one in the desert when she woke to find Tucker sleeping beside her in the cave. She relived the fear that had seized her at the thought of being alone in such a situation, the relief that had taken over at finding another human close by, and the comfort that Tucker had provided when she finally curled up next to him. He'd instinctively shifted to hold her while she slept, and the contact had kept the fear and discomfort at bay. At least for a little while.

Kicking off the covers, Gabrielle got out of bed, considered going down the hall to Allie's room, then decided against it. David slept in the room next to her own, and the hall floor creaked. She didn't want to wake him as she had before, didn't want to be confronted with any more questions or doubts or searching glances. Especially since he'd be leaving the next morning. He'd told her before bed that he needed to go home to take care of business for a few days. He was hoping to return to Florence by the following weekend, but Gabrielle wasn't sure she'd want to see him even then. She appreciated what a good father he was to Allie, but she was confused about her feelings right now. She needed some time alone, time to deal with what she'd been through and what she'd done.

Pulling back the drapes to gaze out at the stormy night, she pressed her forehead to the cool glass. There was little here in Florence. A main street with an old-fashioned grocery store, a small post office, a town hall that desperately needed refurbishing, several stores that had gone out of business and were sitting empty, a few buildings that dated back to silver-mining days and were boarded up—like the hotel—awaiting the funds to save them as historical landmarks. Florence boasted only one fast-food restaurant, no hospital, certainly no mall and no hotels to speak of. And yet this town held...something she needed. Her real mother. A means to support herself and Allie. Space to figure out what she wanted from life. Somehow, moving back to Phoenix smacked of giving up and settling. She couldn't do that. But how could she continue to hurt David?

Lightning stabbed across the sky, illuminating a car parked across the street from her house and yanking Gabrielle out of her thoughts. She doubted she would've noticed except that it was facing in the wrong direction and, when she looked closer, she saw the blurry image of someone's head and shoulders in the driver's seat. Whoever it was seemed to be staring at her house! Staring right at her!

She jumped back from the window and put a hand to her chest as if she could stop the sudden knocking of her heart against her ribs. Who was it? She tried telling herself it must be her neighbor coming home from work, but the digital alarm clock on her night-stand confirmed that graveyard didn't end for another two hours. Besides, the plain white sedan sitting across the street was not her neighbor's car.

Could it be Tucker?

She felt a strange quiver in her stomach, a mixture of fear, for his safety and hers, and a sudden aching desire. How many times had she wondered if he was okay? If she'd ever see him again?

She peeked around the edge of the window, but raindrops, flung against the trailer by the wind, pinged against the glass and rolled down the pane, distorting her view. Although the streetlight glowed eerily, it was nearly half a block away.

It had to be Tucker, she decided. Who else would it be? Florence was a community of corrections officers and other prison workers, and there was very little crime. She doubted her visitor was casing the place.

Tucker must need her. But what could she do for him? She doubted David would sympathize with or understand her feelings for Randall Tucker. He'd tell her to let the system handle the situation, that Tucker's problems weren't her problems.

On one level, Gabrielle knew he was right. But she cared too much about Tucker to divorce herself from responsibility where he was concerned.

She had to warn him of David's presence, send him away.

Wearing a muscle shirt and men's boxers, she slipped out of her room and tiptoed as quietly as possible down the hall. The floor creaked, as it always did, jangling her nerves. She caught her breath, listening for sounds of movement in David's room.

She heard nothing. *Thank goodness.*

Fearing Tucker might come to the door before she could stop him, she didn't pause long. She hurried on, moving more quickly once she reached the living room, being extra-cautious when she opened the door to brace for the wind and not let it tear the door out of her grasp and bang it against the side of the trailer.

Outdoors it was cool but certainly not cold, only wet and windy. Gabrielle could still feel residual heat emanating from the concrete sidewalks and blacktop of the roadway, leftovers of another one-hundred-and-ten-degree day. But the rain quickly doused her, chilling her as soon as she moved out from under the shelter of her carport and started across the street.

She was nearly at the white sedan when she slowed, suddenly hesitant and regretting her thoughtless haste. The person in the car wasn't getting out to meet her. Certainly Tucker would have seen her by now and made some move to—

The headlights flashed on. In the split second before they blinded her, she saw a face she recognized.

It wasn't Tucker's. It was Hansen's.

Gabrielle considered beating a quick retreat, then forced herself to continue around the car. She couldn't slink away because that wasn't something she'd do if everything she'd told Hansen and the warden had been the truth. She'd bang on his door and ask what the hell he was doing skulking around her place.

Her hair was plastered to her head and she was shivering, hugging her arms to her body for heat, by the time he rolled down his window.

"Nice outfit," he said, his eyes settling on the wet fabric covering her breasts. The scent of alcohol drifted from inside the car. Gabrielle stifled a grimace.

"You let Tucker see you like this out there in the desert?" he asked. "Or did you take it all off? Give him a real show and a free ride, too?"

"You've been drinking," she said.

He shrugged. "I'm entitled. It's Saturday night, and I'm off duty."

Gabrielle thought she could make a good case that he was too intoxicated to drive, but she had other things on her mind at the moment. "What are you doing here?"

"It's a public street."

"That's not an answer."

"You want an answer?" He slung an arm over the steering wheel and leaned closer, lowering his voice to a whisper. "I've been wondering what it is about you, Hadley."

"What do you mean?"

"Why would a sexy little thing like you prefer prison trash to a real man?"

"Are you using yourself as the example?"

She knew he'd caught the insult in her tone when his eyes turned hard. "I'm more of a man than you could handle, Hadley," he said. "If I ever f—"

"Go home," Gabrielle said, cutting him off and backing away before he could get too vulgar.

"Not until you tell me a few things."

She glanced across the street, wishing she hadn't been so quiet when she left the trailer. David would've been a welcome interruption about now. "Like what?"

"Like how Tucker survived in the desert long enough to tie you up at that ranch."

"I have no idea," she lied.

"And why the manager of the Bountiful Harvest said he found an orange jumpsuit in an egg cooler that had been locked from five o'clock the previous night to eight o'clock the morning you turned up?"

When Gabrielle didn't answer, he smiled. "I called you this morning. Your hubby, David—"

"My ex-husband."

"—told me where to find the ranch. He was very helpful. Even gave me directions."

"I would've done the same."

Hansen's chuckle was disbelieving. "I bet. You probably would've sent me to Tombstone."

"So you went out there today?" she asked, wondering what else Richard Griffin had told him.

"Yeah, I had a look around."

"Pretty industrious for your day off, wouldn't you say?"

"I'm going to get Tucker. I'm going to get that son of a bitch if it's the last thing I do. He won't make a fool out of me."

In Gabrielle's opinion, Hansen did a fine job making a fool out of himself. But he was just twisted enough to be dangerous, and she wasn't about to provoke him any further. "Maybe you're wasting your time," she said, trying to defuse his anger. "Maybe Tucker went back into the desert, tried to cross the border and never made it. He could be carrion right now and you're sitting out here in the middle of the night obsessing."

"You'd like me to believe he's dead, wouldn't you? Then maybe I'd give up."

"Why would I care?"

"I don't know." He studied her. "But you do."

"It's cold," she said. "I'm going inside."

She started to walk around his car. Moving much faster than she'd thought him capable of in his current state, he stepped out and caught her by the wrist before she could clear the headlights. "Griffin said some of his workers found a man hiding in his storage shed the same day they found you."

Fear ripped through Gabrielle, making her whole body tingle. "So?" she managed to say.

"He told me you had a look at him, said it wasn't Tucker."

"It wasn't. It was some hiker who'd gotten turned around and run out of water."

"He fit the description," Hansen pointed out.

"You don't think I know what Tucker looks like?"

"I don't think you want us to bring him in."

"Why?" Gabrielle yanked her hand free and pushed her dripping hair out of her face. "I went in to that desert after him."

"That's the part I don't understand," he said, squinting through the rain beading on his lashes. "If you caused that accident to help him escape, why'd you follow him into the damn desert? Did you plan to disappear together?"

"And abandon my baby? You're sick! I didn't cause the accident—Eckland did. I thought I was doing my job when I went after him."

"Maybe," he said. "Or maybe you were just trying to make it look good."

"I nearly died out there, you son of a—" She bit off her words, took a deep breath. Inciting Hansen wouldn't accomplish anything.

"Sometimes plans go awry," he said, her suffering in the desert obviously meaningless to him. "But I want you to know this much. If you're in this thing, Hadley, if you're dirty, I'm going to nail you to the wall. You got that?"

"I think you've been watching too many Clint Eastwood movies," she said.

He smiled. "We'll see."

Gabrielle didn't answer. She just watched, her heart in her throat, as he got back into his car and drove away.

BY THE FOLLOWING weekend, David had been gone a week, Tucker had been splashed all over the news, and Gabrielle had reported for work at Eyman Complex, Rynning Unit, on Wednesday as Warden Crumb had requested. She'd already worked three shifts there. She'd expected to hate her job, to find it difficult to go back into the same dark surroundings she'd left the day she was supposed to transfer Tucker to Yuma. But she found the new complex a completely different experience. A modern facility, it was much quieter than the old Territorial prison, and the deputy warden who ran Rynning Unit seemed like a man of integrity. He was strict with the inmates but fair at the same time, and the corrections officers under his watch worked hard to do a good job.

On her first day, Gabrielle had sensed some reticence among her co-workers and wondered if Hansen had passed the word that she was trouble. But by the end of her third shift, almost everyone had relaxed; without exception, they were as friendly with her as they were with each other. A group of officers, both women and men, had even asked her to go out for a drink with them tonight. She'd declined because Felicia had a date and couldn't baby-sit for her, and David had called to say he couldn't come until Sunday.

She would have taken them up on the offer otherwise. Now that she was physically recovered from her stint in the desert, she no longer wanted to sit at home. She hated the way the minutes dragged, hated the constant worry that she'd turn on the television to see the police taking Tucker into custody. And having Hansen park outside her place in the rain last Saturday certainly hadn't helped her state of mind. Just the memory of it was enough to give her the creeps, especially when she remembered how he'd looked at her breasts and asked why she preferred prison trash to a *real* man.

Shivering at the memory, and the heavily air-conditioned atmosphere of the Gas 'n Go service station, she tried to put it from her mind. She'd purchased gas a few minutes earlier and was standing in line to collect her change. But it was tough to concentrate on anything that didn't revolve around the events of the past few weeks. Her only solace was that the police hadn't caught Tucker yet. Maybe they never would, she thought, her natural optimism starting to buoy her now that everything seemed to be returning to normal. Maybe he'd be able to build a new life in Mexico or—

The person in front of her shifted, giving Gabrielle her first unobstructed view of the newspaper bins. There, on the front page, was another picture of Tucker. He'd been in the papers several times over the past ten days—generally the same photo—so seeing him again didn't surprise her. It was the headline that grabbed her by the throat: Florence Escapee Thought To Have Kidnapped Son.

Oh, my God, he managed it!

"Ma'am?"

Gabrielle blinked and looked up at the skinny, red-headed clerk who was waiting with an impatient scowl.

"What can I get for you?" he asked.

For a second Gabrielle couldn't remember what she needed. Her mind was going a hundred miles a minute, considering every tangent she could possibly connect to this new piece of information. Tucker was still alive, still free, and he wasn't too far away. Security being what it was at airports, she doubted he'd try to hop a plane, which meant—

"Ma'am, I'm going to have to ask you to step aside if you're not ready. We have a line," the checker said.

Gabrielle quickly plopped the newspaper on the counter. "I'll take this."

"Seventy-five cents."

She began to dig through her purse, then remembered her change from the gas, the reason she'd come into the store in the first place. She told the cashier she'd used pump number five, mechanically held out her hand to receive her change and walked out, oblivious to everyone and everything around her as she read the opening paragraph of the article.

Phoenix, Arizona—Eight-year-old Landon Tucker was abducted from his home in Chandler late Wednesday night while his foster parents, Maureen and William Boyer, were sleeping, police spokeswoman Clara Cunningham told reporters this morning. Authorities believe his father, Randall Tucker, an escaped convict from the Arizona State Prison at Florence, Central Unit, to be responsible for the kidnapping. Tucker, serving a life sentence for beating his wife to death, escaped during a routine transfer to Yuma Prison on August 15th and fled into the Sonoran Desert where...

Gabrielle skipped the parts she'd read at least a dozen times and knew anyway and finished with the last paragraph.

...Investigators say Tucker used a crowbar to wedge open a window that might not have been tightly closed. Fingerprints matching the convict's were found on the window and a crowbar left in the yard. But police say no one in the area heard or saw anything unusual that night.

There is no indication of how Tucker is traveling or where he might be taking his son. His brother, who owns a karate school in Tempe, hasn't been available for questioning. Asked whether authorities fear for the child's safety, Cunningham said they have no record of Tucker injuring Landon in the past but police are concerned that the child is in the physical custody of a convicted murderer. Should anyone have information on the whereabouts of Randall or Landon Tucker, they are advised to contact police as soon as possible.

Tossing the newspaper onto the passenger seat of her Honda, Gabrielle forced herself to get behind the wheel, start the car and pull away from the gas pumps. She needed to get home. Felicia would be wondering where she was. But it was difficult to go home as though this were a night like any other. Tucker had reached Landon! She couldn't imagine how happy he must be to have his son with him again—after two long years. He'd beaten the odds and was still out there....

Gabrielle paused at the turnout, watched a tumbleweed blow into the street ahead of her and made a decision. If Tucker could do what he'd done to achieve what he wanted most, she was going to have the guts to do it, too.

THIS TIME Gabrielle didn't hesitate when she pulled up in front of her mother's house. She and Allie were getting out and walking to the door, regardless of the consequences, regardless of the hurt or the disappointment. Resolve couldn't stop her palms from sweating or slow her pulse, however. She was going to face her mother, the woman she'd dreamed about for more than two decades. And she was going to do it now.

Naomi Cutter's Toyota Camry sat in its usual place. Gabrielle shifted Allie on her hip and turned sideways to skirt the car as she approached the door. The blinds had been drawn. She hadn't been able to see what her mother and the man she lived with might be doing, but it was almost dinnertime, so she guessed they'd be preparing food or possibly eating already.

Once she hit the step, the notes of some Big Band music drifted to her through the door and she thought she heard a male voice announce "Jeopardy."

Throwing back her shoulders, Gabrielle stretched her neck, took one last look at Allie, who gave her a sweet, wet smile, and muttered, "Here goes, kid." Then she knocked.

"Can you get that, Hal?" someone called. "My hands are wet."

Gabrielle braced herself, wishing she could will away the butterflies in her stomach.

The door swung open to reveal the man she'd seen once or twice through the window. Only this time he was wearing a button-up shirt over his customary T-shirt, and his silver hair looked as though it had been combed neatly back. "Yes?" he said, the smell of grilled onions wafting through the opening as he blinked at her and then at Allie.

Gabrielle struggled to find her voice. "My name's

Gabrielle Hadley." She cleared her throat. "Is…is Naomi Cutter available?"

He glanced beyond her, toward the street. "You're not selling anything, are you?"

"No."

"And you're not one of those church people come 'round to distribute flyers?"

"No."

His gaze settled on Allie. "Just a minute."

The next few seconds seemed to extend through all eternity. Only the thought of Tucker sneaking into a stranger's house in the middle of the night to reclaim his son kept Gabrielle standing stubbornly where she was. She was going to do this. She owed it to herself. Not everything in life came easy. Sometimes one had to fight, take chances—

"Yes?"

Gabrielle swallowed hard as her mother's face, lined but still pleasant-looking, appeared in the doorway. Brown eyes bearing a touch of makeup regarded her curiously from beneath a head of neat brown hair threaded with gray, and Gabrielle couldn't help wondering if others would look at them both and say, "Gabrielle definitely has your eyes." She'd spent her whole life listening to the friends and acquaintances of the Pattersons exclaim about the similarities between Bev Patterson and the twins—"They're the spitting image of you, Bev." Whenever some kind but uninformed fool ventured to include her, Gabrielle had to launch into the awkward explanation that she really didn't belong at all.

This was her mother. She was also a stranger.

"My name's Gabrielle Hadley," she repeated. "Sometimes people call me Gabby for short." *You* used to once, remember? I do. I was only three and yet I've never forgotten that look you gave me when you dropped me off at that daycare and said, "Bye, Gabby. I'm sorry, baby. I love you."

In those days, Naomi was always saying she was sorry, so Gabrielle hadn't paid much attention. She'd waved and smiled and, in the innocence of childhood, let her mother go. But when evening came, her mother never arrived to pick her up. The new adults in her life, strangers all of them, started speaking in hushed tones and shuffling her from place to place. She slowly grew to understand what that final apology had meant, and her understanding brought rage and then bitterness.

It was bitterness that threatened to choke Gabrielle now. How could any mother do what Naomi had done?

As Allie kicked her chubby legs and gurgled, "Ma, ma, ma, ma," Gabrielle wondered why she felt such compulsion to approach this person who'd betrayed her so deeply. Gabrielle was now an adult with a child of her own. She should simply forget, move on—

"Never mind," she said. "I—I must have the wrong house." She whirled, thinking only of escape, when the sound of her name on her mother's lips froze her to the spot.

"Gabby? *My* Gabby?"

Gabrielle closed her eyes as something twisted painfully inside her. "No. I have the wrong house," she said, without looking back. She couldn't peer into that face again, couldn't deal with the emotions and memories tumbling down on her like water gushing through a broken dam. They threatened to sweep her away into a vortex of even greater bitterness. Gabrielle feared she'd never be able to pull herself free.

"Gabby, don't go," her mother said, following her

when she took a few more steps. "Please. The least we should do is talk now that you're here, don't you think?"

Talk? Now? It was too late.

"Please," her mother muttered again.

Gabrielle paused and slowly turned, telling herself she'd seek answers to the questions she'd been asking herself since forever, then leave here and be done with it. But when she faced her mother, she didn't feel like an adult anymore. She felt like the little girl who'd waited by the window night after night, refusing to believe that the one person who was supposed to love her had let her down so terribly. Somehow, the hurt didn't seem even one day old. Fresh and raw, it was so poignant Gabrielle couldn't stop tears from gathering in her eyes and spilling down her cheeks.

"How could you?" she murmured, her defenses falling away with the years.

Her mother looked stricken. She opened her mouth, but no words emerged. She blinked quickly, swallowed and finally began to speak. "If I explain what was happening in my life back then, it'll only seem as though I'm trying to excuse myself. And I already know there's no excuse for what I did. None I could give myself. None I could give you."

"I want to hear it anyway."

Gabrielle could feel the scrutiny of the man who'd answered the door, watching her from behind Naomi. He seemed to want to say something, the way he hovered there, but he maintained his silence.

"Come in and sit down," her mother pleaded.

Gabrielle hesitated.

"Just for a few minutes."

Allie, tired of being held, began to push and kick to

be let down, but Gabrielle only clung to her that much tighter. *The past can't hurt me now. It's over,* she told herself, dashing a hand across her damp cheeks. But she knew, deep inside, that the past was far from over, or she wouldn't be here.

She followed Naomi Cutter into the Spanish-style house she'd seen from the outside at least three previous times, and took a seat on a comfortable-looking brown sofa in the living room with the big window. A shampoo commercial blared on a small television, but the man who'd answered the door retrieved the remote from the recliner nearby and flipped off the volume.

"This is Hal, my husband," Naomi explained.

Gabrielle summoned a polite nod, wondering how Naomi might introduce her—"This is the child I abandoned..."—and whether the young woman she'd seen at the house before was Hal's daughter as well as Naomi's.

"Can I get you something to drink?"

Gabrielle shook her head. "No."

Naomi's eyes moved to Allie. If Gabrielle wasn't mistaken, she saw sadness there. "Is this your daughter?"

"Yes. Her name's Allie."

"You can put her down, you know. There's nothing that'll hurt her in here."

Gabrielle allowed Allie to squirm to the ground, then cringed when she crawled right for Naomi and tried to pull herself to her feet using the hem of Naomi's dress. "Come here, Allie," Gabrielle said, and snatched her away.

"Tell her, Naomi," Hal said suddenly, speaking for the first time.

"It won't do any good," her mother said. "There's

nothing that can fix what I've done. Nothing can take back—''

"Tell her anyway." His words were gruff yet surprisingly tender.

Gabrielle felt nervous energy pour through her body. What was it her mother had to say? That she'd lost her job twenty-five years ago and had no way to support a child? That she couldn't deal with the emotional demands of motherhood? *What?*

"I'm sorry, Gabby. I was confused and stupid and so wrong. I've spent half my life wishing I could go back—'' She paused to gain control of herself, and Gabrielle realized Naomi was wrestling with her own emotions, just as she was. "I have no excuse to offer you, no reason good enough for what I did. But if it makes you feel any better, I'm paying for it. I've paid every day of my life since…'' Gabrielle heard the quaver in her voice "…I walked away from that day-care center. Sometimes it'll hit me out of nowhere. I'll see a child about the age you were when…when I last saw you…and then I can't breathe for the terrible longing inside me.''

"Why'd you do it?" Gabrielle asked. "Was I such a difficult child?"

Naomi braced herself with a hand on the back of the recliner, as though the intensity of her feelings was robbing her of strength. "No, you weren't difficult, Gabby. You were a good girl, a beautiful child. It was just that, well, your father had run out on us—I didn't even know where he was—and I wasn't making my rent each month. My mother, my only living parent, died shortly after you were born, so I had no help. I was working hard as a secretary for an elementary school and doing my best, but you weren't old enough to go to school, and your day care was expensive. There just wasn't enough money to go around. I was getting behind and more and more depressed. Then I met this man, a teacher, who—'' she sighed ''—who I thought was the man of my dreams. Except that he didn't want anything to do with you. At first I thought he'd change his mind, but the one time I brought him to the house, he would hardly look at you. Do you remember that?''

''No...''

''Then he started paying attention to one of the other teachers at the school where I worked,'' she continued, ''a single woman with no children who was younger than me, and I started to panic, to feel like I was losing him. I was so afraid of being alone, forever fighting a battle I couldn't win. And then...''

Hal moved close and put a reassuring arm around her as her tears dripped off her chin and fell to the floor.

''And then he asked me to marry him,'' she said.

''Did you?'' Gabrielle asked, but she could already guess the answer.

Shame made Naomi look far older than she had only moments ago. ''Yes, but the price of his love was far too high.''

''So it wasn't my fault,'' Gabrielle said. ''I did nothing wrong.''

''It wasn't your fault,'' her mother admitted. ''I'm the only one to blame.''

''I've told her to contact you,'' Hal put in. ''But she's never felt worthy of even apologizing to you. I can't tell you how often she's mentioned you, though, how often she's cried in the night. The past has been like an open wound that just won't heal, and I knew it wouldn't until she talked to you. So whether you can forgive her or not—and I'm not going to tell you you should. No one has that right because only you know what you've been through and what your heart can bear, young lady. But I'm glad you've come. Naomi has made her mistakes. She was right when she said there's no justifying what she did. But she's also paid for her actions with the worst kind of regret. When I started teaching at the same school, she was an abused wife, hanging on to the man she just told you about. I think she stayed with him to punish herself, but I couldn't stand to see it go on any longer. I helped her get away from him. Then I changed schools, but we met up again at an Honors Band concert a few years later. We started to date and fell in love. The rest is history. That was twelve years ago.''

As Hal spoke, Gabrielle realized she'd misjudged this stranger she'd seen through the window. She'd assumed from his appearance that he sat around and drank beer all day. But she could tell by his demeanor that he wasn't slovenly or abusive and that he cared about Naomi. Maybe he was the first man ever to do so.

''So the two of you don't have children together?'' Gabrielle said, remembering the slim blonde her mother had called ''honey.''

''No,'' Hal said. ''I'm a widower with five children from my first marriage. Naomi has two by her first husband—a daughter who's about five years younger than you, and a son who's going to the University of Arizona.''

She had a brother as well as a sister. The news took a moment to sink in.

''Are you married?'' Hal asked.

"Divorced."

"You and Allie live alone?"

Hugging her daughter a little closer, Gabrielle kissed her head. "Yeah, it's just the two of us. My ex-husband lives in Phoenix and comes to visit us often, though. He's a great guy."

"Where do you live?" Naomi asked.

Gabrielle forced her eyes to turn to her mother, even though it was difficult to face her without feeling a remnant of the pain and resentment she'd known for so long. "Across from the prison."

"Here? In Florence?" her mother cried.

"I'm a corrections officer at Eyman."

"Then you're in the area. You'll have to meet Lindy. She'll be so thrilled. I know how you must feel about me, and I don't blame you, Gabby." She dried her eyes, her voice more vigorous now that they'd moved on to a new subject. "But you'd love Lindy. And I know she'd love you. Will you come back? Will you let me have your phone number?"

There was still so much to forgive. Gabrielle wasn't sure she was equal to the task, but the terrible weight of the memories she'd been carrying already seemed a little lighter, and she knew she wanted to try.

"Sure," she said, and Hal gave her a smile that promised he'd do everything he could to make things easier for her. Although Gabrielle wasn't convinced she could ever have a relationship with her mother, she began to wonder if maybe, just maybe, she'd found a friend in Hal.

CHAPTER FIFTEEN

"YOU WON'T BELIEVE IT, David," Gabrielle gushed the second her ex-husband picked up his cell phone. "I did it! I approached my mother."

A pause. "You're kidding," he said, obviously surprised by her announcement.

"No. I just got back a few minutes ago."

"What made you finally approach her?"

Gabrielle thought of Tucker and Landon. "I don't know," she lied. "You were right. I needed to get it over with."

"And? How was she?"

"She was—" Gabrielle sat on the couch and kicked off her shoes, trying to find the right word. "Nice," she finished lamely, because she was unable to distill her mother's behavior into anything more descriptive. A harsher word wouldn't have been fair. A kinder word would have indicated Gabrielle was ready to forgive her, and she wasn't sure she was.

David called her on it right away. "Nice? That's all you can say?"

Allie shoved another cookie into her mouth and toddled around the coffee table to try to shove one in Gabrielle's. Gabrielle managed to interest her in smashing it against some blocks she'd left out earlier. She'd have to wash the blocks and the table later, but she was willing to do the extra work to buy some time now. "She was glad I came."

"So she wants to get to know you?"

For some reason he didn't sound as pleased as Gabrielle had expected him to. "I think so. She's pretty contrite about what she did, although she hasn't said much about any kind of future relationship. But she looked at Allie with such…longing. I got the impression she wanted to hold her. And this is the most exciting part—"

David covered the phone and spoke to someone else.

"David?"

"I'm here."

"Where's here?"

"The office."

"But it's nearly eight o'clock."

"Shauna and I are trying to catch up on a few things."

"Shauna?"

"She's the gal I told you about, the one who's been drumming up new business. She's sort of doubling as my assistant."

"Oh. How old is she?"

"About your age."

"Married?"

"No."

"Attractive?" she asked.

"Fairly, yeah."

Gabrielle tried that information on for size, wishing she felt a twinge of jealousy, but she didn't. She hoped only for David's happiness. "I'm glad you've found someone to help out. You really needed some backup."

"I was afraid you'd say that."

"What?"

He sighed. "Nothing. What did you want to tell me? Something exciting about your mother."

He didn't make it sound too exciting. "She wants to introduce me to my sister."

"That's good."

David was altogether too reserved, as though he was holding back. "What's going on? Are you okay?" she asked, frowning.

"Fine. Just tired and a little frustrated. I'm pretty behind here at work."

"It's my fault for keeping you in Florence so long. I'm sorry."

"It was my decision to stay. I didn't bring this up to make you feel responsible. Besides, I really enjoyed the time with Allie."

Normally he would have said "with you and Allie." Gabrielle heard a phone ringing in the background and another voice saying he had a call. "Do you have to go?" she asked.

"No, I'll call whoever it is back." Briefly he covered the phone again, then returned to their conversation. "Did your mother say what was going on in her life that she'd abandon her own child?"

Gabrielle explained the whole visit, down to the goodbyes she, Naomi and Hal had exchanged at the door, when her mother had gone into her pantry and brought out a jar of pickle relish, some strawberry preserves and a loaf of homemade bread she insisted Gabrielle take home with her.

"I just finished a piece of toast from the loaf she gave me. Isn't that weird?" she asked. "Yesterday I hadn't spoken to her in twenty-five years, and today I'm eating her bread."

David didn't comment. "When do you meet your sister?"

"They're going to call her, see when she can come down. She just passed the bar exam to become an attorney."

"Where does she live?"

"In Mesa. Her name's Lindy. Isn't that a pretty name?"

"I hope they're not setting you up for a fall, Gabby."

"Setting me up for a fall?"

"I don't want you to be disappointed if…if they don't ultimately embrace you as family."

Gabrielle didn't really expect them to embrace her as family. She was taking one day at a time, and this day she was proud of herself. The only person disappointing her right now was David. Why wasn't he more excited? She'd finally done what he'd been telling her she needed to do ever since the investigator had located her mother. She'd expected him to be happier about it. "Are you going to tell me what's wrong?" she asked.

"There's nothing wrong."

Gabrielle picked up the remote and snapped on the television. "Okay, I'd better go," she said, hoping to get off the phone before he completely destroyed her euphoria.

"Wait, I want to talk to you about something else."

"What's that?"

"Sergeant Hansen called me today."

"He what?" She snapped off the television.

"You heard me."

"What did he want with you?"

"He asked me some very strange questions."

Gabrielle's muscles went taut, and the last vestiges of her good mood slipped away. "Like…"

"Like whether or not you and Tucker knew each other before you moved to Florence."

Gabrielle jumped to her feet, startling Allie so badly she nearly fell over. "That's crazy! Of course we didn't know each other. What did you tell him?"

"The truth. That you wouldn't have had any opportunity to know Tucker until you moved to Florence with the grand aspiration of becoming a corrections officer."

The grand aspiration of becoming a corrections officer.… Gabrielle hated it when David got sarcastic. He was generally supportive and upbeat, which led her straight back to the feeling that something was wrong. "Let's have it," she said. "What's going on with you?"

"You're the one who's been acting strange, Gabby. I was so afraid I'd lost you when you didn't come home after going into the desert. And then, when you survived, I thought we'd been granted a second chance to make things right between us. I thought I'd be able to reach you, that you'd realize our family is the most important thing in this world. Instead, you throw up defenses that haven't been there in months. It's like you went into the desert as one person—the Gabby I used to know—and came out another."

Part of what David said was true. Their family *was* the most precious thing in the world. So why was she the weak link? The guilt caused by her shortcomings weighed heavily on Gabrielle, yet she still faced the same problem. She couldn't go back to David because she wasn't in love with him. "I'm the same person, David—"

"You're not acting like it. You've been almost… secretive. And then I get this call from Hansen who tells me…"

"What?" she prompted when he seemed to lose steam.

"Who tells me he thinks you have some kind of romantic interest in the convict you went after, that the fight you mentioned breaking up wasn't anything more than a little scuffle between inmates, a scuffle Hansen couldn't have stopped any sooner than he did."

"That's a lie!" Gabrielle said, equally enraged at Hansen for trying to turn David against her and at David for allowing him to succeed. "You know how I met Tucker. You know everything that happened at the prison that day. I told you when you called me that night."

"But do I know everything that happened *after-ward?*"

Gabrielle pressed a fist to her forehead. Her movements were odd enough to be noticed by Allie, who knocked her blocks onto the floor in her hurry to come over and pat Gabrielle. "Ma, ma, ma," she said, but the world outside Gabrielle's head seemed to exist in another dimension. She could barely feel her daughter's hand.

"I went into the desert to keep Tucker from dying of dehydration," she said. "I was trying to save a man's life. It's that simple. I'll admit it was an issue of professional pride at first, but that wasn't enough to keep me following him for more than a few hours, not in that heat."

"So you're saying there's nothing to what Hansen is intimating. You were just being a good Samaritan."

Gabrielle couldn't claim that, not after everything

she'd done. "Hansen is trying to discredit me for obvious reasons," she said instead.

"I wouldn't have believed him, Gabby, not in a million years. You've never given me any reason to distrust you in the past. But today, in the paper, there's a picture of Randall Tucker."

"There's been a dozen pictures," she said tentatively.

"I know. But after Hansen's call, I really looked at this one. And I have to admit there's a resemblance to that hiker I met at the egg ranch."

Oh, God, what did she say now? "That picture probably resembles a thousand different men, David. It's so distorted, how can you tell anything from that?"

"I can't, but add that to what Hansen's been saying and the fact that you've changed, and…I don't know what to think anymore."

"You're worrying about nothing, David. I'm never going to see Tucker again, anyway. Right?"

The ensuing silence lasted so long, Gabrielle wished she could bite off her tongue for saying what she'd just said. Her conscience was getting the best of her, trying to come out with the truth. Only she couldn't tell the truth. She had to put what had happened and how she *felt* about it behind her, for everyone's sake.

"I wish that had been a denial," he said softly.

"David, I don't know what you want me to say. If you want me to tell you I admire Tucker, okay, I do. He's so different from what Hansen makes him out to be. I know you'd like him, too, if only—"

"He's a freakin' murderer! God, Gabby, would you listen to yourself? No wonder Hansen thinks what he does."

Gabrielle thought of those tender moments in the

church when she'd tried to comfort Tucker and he'd fought her, at first, then ended up crying like a brokenhearted little boy. Those tears had been sincere, evidence of pain far deeper than most men ever experience. But she had no way of convincing others, no way to prove that Tucker wasn't what Hansen said he was. David, especially, wouldn't be happy to hear she believed in Tucker's innocence, not because of any solid proof but because her intuition told her so.

"I think I'd better go," she said.

"Wait. That was him, wasn't it? The hiker was Randall Tucker."

"No. I'll talk to you tomorrow, okay?" She hung up before things could get any worse and sat staring down at Allie, almost oblivious to the fact that her daughter had just smeared the gooey cookie she still clutched on Gabrielle's leg.

"Your dad's my best friend," Gabrielle told her above the chug of the swamp cooler. "He always will be."

If only that was enough.

GABRIELLE FINISHED bathing Allie, rocked her to sleep and placed her gently in her crib. Then she looked around, wondering what to do next. She'd been having trouble sleeping lately and didn't want to go to bed. Neither did she want to turn on the television. She was afraid she'd see something about Tucker that would upset her, some interview of Crumb giving his opinion on the terrible danger Landon was in. Or worse—Tucker's capture.

She thought of her conversation with David. The phone had rung several times since she'd hung up with him, but she hadn't answered it. She didn't want to talk to David again, any more than she wanted to risk trying to sleep or watch TV. He knew she'd let Tucker go that day at the egg ranch. She doubted he'd do anything with the information; he was too loyal, and it was now in the past. But she didn't want to deal with any more probing questions, didn't want to try to explain her emotions. They were too complex, and what she felt didn't matter anyway, because Tucker couldn't be part of her life.

So she started cleaning. After she'd finished the two bathrooms, she washed down the cupboards in the kitchen, scrubbed the fridge and organized the closet in the hall. By the time she'd rearranged the clothes in her drawers, she thought she might be tired enough to fall into a dreamless sleep. But on her way to bed she couldn't help pausing when she saw the newspaper article she'd read earlier laying on her bedroom dresser. Carrying it with her, she propped up a few pillows and sank down to look at the face of the man she couldn't forget, the face David had recognized.

Tucker's eyes stared back at her, hard and unyielding, from what must have been his mug shot. She'd seen him look better, even unshowered and unshaved, which worked to their advantage. Anyone trying to identify him from this photo would have a difficult time. David hadn't even made the connection at first. But it was him. She could tell by the slight flare of his nostrils, the heart-shaped arch on his top lip, his high forehead.

Closing her eyes, she remembered how his hands had felt on her body, the passion he'd incited in her when she'd realized that his need was as raw and powerful as her own. Her pulse quickened now, just imagining it. She wanted Randall Tucker more than any man she'd ever known. She loved him. But she had to forget him. They didn't have a chance....

Gabrielle tossed the newspaper aside, then pulled off the tank top and cutoffs she'd been wearing, turned off the light and climbed into bed dressed only in her panties. She'd never been much for nightgowns—she hated the way they twisted around her legs during the night—and with David gone and the weather so oppressive, there seemed little point in wearing anything.

Her sheets felt cool against her skin and smelled of fabric softener, but she still found it impossible to relax, to get comfortable. All evening, she'd purposely tried not to think about Hansen and what he'd told David. She'd tried to focus on the memory of seeing her mother and the hope of soon meeting her sister. But now David's voice seemed to intrude on the silence, and Hansen's face, the bleary-eyed way he'd looked last week when he'd parked in front of her house, wouldn't disappear from her mind.

That was him, wasn't it? The hiker was Randall Tucker.... He tells me he thinks you have some kind of romantic interest in the convict.... You've been almost...secretive.... I don't know what to think anymore.

Well, that made two of them. She'd known David for ten years and had never been able to conjure up the kind of desire she'd felt for Tucker after only three days. Why? Why couldn't she fall in love with the person she was *supposed* to be in love with?

The answer never came, but she must have drifted into a restless sleep. When she woke again, it was nearly three o'clock. She squinted at the glowing numerals of her alarm clock, wondering what had awak-

ened her. Then she heard something that made her
blood curdle. Footsteps. In the hall.

Remembering her last confrontation with Hansen,
she slipped out of bed, pulling the sheet with her for
cover. Surely he wouldn't have broken into her home.
Surely he wouldn't take his vendetta against her that
far....

But she wasn't completely convinced. Part of her
believed Hansen would do whatever he thought he
could get away with. *Why would a sexy little thing like
you prefer prison trash to a real man?* he'd asked. Did
he plan to show her what his version of a real man was
like?

Whoever had entered her house was moving too cautiously to be David. After their earlier conversation, she
wouldn't put it past her ex-husband to show up unex-
pectedly. He had a key and usually just let himself in.
But he knew his way around the trailer. He had no
reason to move so slowly.

She could hear breathing now. The sound sent panic
ripping through her. Someone stood right outside her
door, and Allie was at the other end of the trailer. How
was she going to grab her baby and get them both out
safely?

Heart pounding, Gabrielle glanced around her room,
looking for a weapon. The handgun she'd bought for
target practice was on the top shelf of a kitchen cupboard, which made it pretty inaccessible. She didn't
have time to decide on an alternative before the door
clicked and started to open.

Instinctively, she grabbed the lamp to use as a club.
She hadn't even raised it over her head, however, when
she recognized the person stepping through the doorway. It was Tucker. He hadn't shaved for a few days—

she could tell even in the dark—but he'd had his hair cropped short and his hand was in a cast.

Gabrielle didn't move or speak. She wasn't sure she could.

His eyes found her immediately. He straightened, waiting for her reaction.

"How'd you get in?" she asked in a shaking voice.

"The lock on the back door wasn't up to much," he said.

The entire *door* wasn't up to much. But she'd never imagined anyone wanting to break into a mobile home that looked as though it housed so few valuables. Especially in Florence, where the risk of running into a corrections officer was far greater than that of surprising a little old lady.

"What are you doing here?" Because of the dark, her sleeping baby and an irrational fear that Hansen, wherever he was, might overhear her, she kept her voice to a whisper.

Tucker didn't answer. He just stared at her, and Gabrielle felt a rush of poignant longing. She wanted to cross the room and throw herself into his arms, to feel his mouth crush hers, to let her hands wander over his body to assure herself that he was still whole and unhurt.

But she wasn't sure how he'd react. He'd done nothing to encourage her.

"Tucker?"

"I had no choice," he said.

Not the most romantic answer. Thank goodness she hadn't thrown herself at him. "How did you get here?"

"I drove."

"Tell me your car's not out front." She moved to peek through the blinds on her window, fearing she

might see Hansen parked at the curb, jotting down the
license plate number of Tucker's vehicle.

"I'm not an idiot, Gabrielle."

She liked the sound of her name on his lips, but she
wasn't sure exactly why he'd finally decided to use it.
"I didn't say you were," she said, but she checked the
street, anyway. He didn't know Hansen was wise to
them. He didn't know that David had made the connection, too.

Everything looked just as it did every other night.
Still, the memory of her sergeant's visit left a lump of
fear in Gabrielle's stomach, and seeing the empty street
did little to relieve it. What if he came back? Found
Tucker in her house?

"It isn't safe here," she said.

Tucker's palm rasped over his whiskers as he
stroked his chin. It wasn't difficult to tell he was exhausted. Gabrielle wondered how long he'd been up,
what he'd had to do to survive, and if he'd had anything to eat. "Do you want me to go?" he asked.

"No! Yes. Wait…" She rubbed her left temple. "I
don't know. What do you need?"

"A safe place for Landon while I check out a few
things."

He wanted Landon to stay with *her?* There had to
be a better place.

"But the prison's only a stone's throw away!" She
peered out the window again. Nothing had changed—
the street was still empty of unwanted visitors—but
that didn't mean it would stay that way.

"I know where I am," he said softly. His eyes
dipped to the cleavage revealed by the sheet she'd
wrapped around her, and Gabrielle's knees went weak.
But it was the somber note in his voice that really got

to her. Tucker was a man who'd stopped trusting, a man who believed he could rely only on himself, and yet he'd come to her for help. How could she turn him away?

"You should be heading to Mexico or somewhere," she said.

"Maybe." He shrugged. "*Probably.* But—"

"What?"

"I owe it to myself to answer the questions that keep nagging me. To clear my name."

"You're too stubborn for your own good," she said. "David recognized you from that picture in the paper today."

"I knew he'd figure it out eventually. Can you trust him not to say anything?"

"I can trust *him,* but Hansen's a different story, and he's been acting strange. He—" She almost said he suspected the truth about her feelings for Tucker, but caught herself just in time. Tucker already had enough to deal with. Caring for someone besides Landon was the last thing he needed at the moment. She didn't want to declare herself in the face of all that.

"What?" he prompted.

"He went to the egg ranch and Griffin told him all about the mysterious hiker that I claimed wasn't you."

"How does he know it *was* me?" Once again, his gaze flicked over the parts of her body revealed by the sheet, and Gabrielle remembered the first time she'd seen him. How striking she'd found him, how intimidating. He'd frightened her. Now, one glance from him still made her heart race, but for entirely different reasons.

"He doesn't know for sure, of course," she said,

pulling the sheet up a few inches. "But the coincidence is definitely bothering him."

He scowled. "He's just looking for a scapegoat."

"I'm sure he is. But he makes me nervous all the same."

It was Tucker who was making her nervous now. Nervous and aroused....

He joined her at the window, his close proximity heightening her awareness of him and the fact that nothing besides a loosely draped sheet concealed her body from his view. He was wearing a T-shirt that stretched taut over his pectoral muscles and revealed the muscular contours of his arms, faded blue jeans that accentuated his long legs and a pair of sports sandals. It was the first time she'd seen him in regular clothes, she realized, barring those ill-fitting odds and ends he'd mustered from the egg ranch. And all she could think about was taking them off....

"How's your hand?" she asked.

He lifted his cast and wriggled his fingers. "Better."

"How did you get it set?"

"Showed up at a med center and told them I broke it in a karate match."

"They could tell it wasn't a fresh break, couldn't they?"

"That doesn't necessarily mean anything. I said I'd been living with it for several days, hoping it wasn't actually broken."

"And they didn't recognize you from the news? What did they say?"

"Nothing. I gave them a false name, paid cash and they fixed it."

"I'm glad you finally got it taken care of."

He turned to look at her. The closed blinds made it

difficult to ascertain his expression. "Why'd you lie for me out at that egg ranch?" he asked.

Gabrielle felt a flutter in her stomach. She'd lied because she loved him. She also believed he was innocent. She hoped that belief in his innocence was why she'd done what she'd done, but there was no way to be sure. "Can't you guess?" she asked.

"If I had to guess, I'd say you know I didn't kill my wife."

She cleared her throat. "Yes."

"That's it? That's the only reason?"

"Maybe not the only reason," she said, twisting her fingers in the hem of the sheet.

"Then what?" He stepped even closer, until the front of his chest nearly brushed her own. "I tied you up, Gabrielle. I left you. You had every right to tell them who I was."

"I—I didn't want to."

"Why?"

"I couldn't see you go back to prison."

She wondered if he'd press her with another "why?" but he didn't. He lifted his good hand and, for a moment, Gabrielle thought he was going to touch her. She wanted him to so badly, she nearly closed her eyes and swayed toward him.

But then he took a deep breath and shoved his hand into his pocket instead. "I'm sorry," he said. "I shouldn't have come here."

He whirled to go but didn't get as far as the door before Gabrielle called him back. Now that he was actually leaving, panic that she'd never see him again suddenly blotted out everything else.

"Tucker—"

He turned.

"You need some rest," she said. "At least stay the night. Hansen can't come into my home without a search warrant, and he has to have a reason in order to get one. We'll be okay until morning. Then we can figure out something else, okay?"

"No, this was a mistake." He opened her door.

She spoke quickly, before he could pass into the hall. "I'm sure Landon could use a good night's sleep. Stay for his sake, if not your own." She could see him waver as soon as she mentioned his son. "Being on the run can't be easy for him. Let the poor kid come in and sleep, okay?"

No response.

"Where is he?"

"I had to leave him in the car until…"

His voice fell off, but Gabrielle understood what that "until" meant—until he could see if it was safe, of course. Thank goodness David hadn't been able to make it back this weekend, or he would've been sleeping in the other room.

David would think she'd lost her mind for what she was about to do. Maybe she had. But if she couldn't have Randall Tucker for a lifetime she wasn't going to waste this one night.

"Bring him in," she said, "I'll make you both something to eat."

LANDON'S SOLID WEIGHT felt good in Tucker's arms. His boy had grown a lot taller in two years, although he didn't seem to have gained much weight. He had spindly arms and legs that promised a lot more length as the years passed, a few missing teeth and eyes like saucers—as blue as Tucker's own—beneath a shock of brown hair that never wanted to stay down.

And growing a little older certainly hadn't made him any less inquisitive. Tucker couldn't help smiling as he remembered all the questions his son had bombarded him with over the past two days. "Where are we going, Daddy?... What are we going to do now?... Can we go to McDonald's?... What would happen if I could play basketball like Chris Webber?... What would happen if we put water in the gas tank instead of gas?... Are there animals on Mars?... Am I ever going back to the Boyers'?" That was the only question that had given Tucker significant pause. He'd asked Landon if he *wanted* to go back, while trying not to give away how much the answer meant to him.

Fortunately his son hadn't hesitated. "Nah, I want to stay with you," he'd said, his voice full of conviction.

Adjusting for his cast, Tucker bent his head to breathe in the subtle scent of childhood that still clung to Landon, the smell he'd missed most while in prison, and carried his sleeping son in through the back door of Gabrielle's trailer. He shouldn't have come here. He'd known it the moment he'd seen Gabrielle wearing nothing but that sheet. He was in danger of complicating his life even more, but with his brother out of town, he didn't have a lot of options. Gabrielle was like a homing beacon to him, promising safe harbor. And after so many days on the run, he was too tired to resist.

He'd never experienced such exhaustion. Just lifting his young son and putting one foot in front of the other required a concerted effort. Probably because he hadn't given himself time to recover from living on so little food and water in the desert. He'd spent most of the last ten days walking, hitching rides, taking buses and secretly meeting with his former secretary, a friend of the family, a college buddy—anyone he could trust to help him. He hadn't eaten regular meals or slept more than two hours at a time. Once he reclaimed his son, he'd managed to borrow enough money from Robert, the man who used to be his business partner to buy a cheap compact car from a cheesy, two-bit lot. He and Landon had been living out of that car for the past two days, but whenever he found some out-of-the-way place to pull off the road and rest, he couldn't close his eyes for more than a few minutes for fear someone would come upon them and turn him in.

The clank of pans told Tucker that Gabrielle was in the kitchen. He hesitated in the hall, amazed that such a simple sound could ease the anxiety curling through his blood. It was so domestic, so normal....

So out of reach. He'd been robbed of the simplest, purest things. The unfairness of it made him clench his jaw as he carried Landon toward the kitchen.

As soon as they entered, his son buried his face in Tucker's chest to avoid the light. Gabrielle, hearing his step, looked up.

"Oh, he's asleep?"

Tucker nodded.

"Do you think we should wake him? Have him eat?"

"It's probably more important that he sleep. I bought him a burger earlier."

"Okay. Let's put him to bed in the room next to mine."

Gabrielle led the way and turned down the bed. Tucker deposited Landon on the sheets, removed his blue jean shorts and sandals so he could sleep more comfortably and covered him.

"We home, Dad?" Landon muttered sleepily.

Tucker felt a twinge of embarrassment. He'd always prided himself on his ability to take care of the people he loved, hated the fact that he couldn't provide a safe, stable environment for his son.

He promised himself he'd fix that. He'd clear his name and then, finally, the nightmare would be over. If only he could find out what had happened to Andrea....

"No, not home, exactly," he said. "We're at a friend's house."

"Oh." It was easy to tell that Landon was too tired to worry about details, or he would've demanded to know which friend, who Gabrielle was, how long they were staying and what they were doing here. Instead he mumbled, "See you in the morning, Dad."

"Okay, buddy. Sleep tight."

Landon's eyelids started to close. "Dad?" he said, momentarily rousing himself.

"Yeah?"

"Think we can play some ball tomorrow?"

Tucker smiled. "Maybe not tomorrow, but soon," he said.

His son nodded and let his eyes drift all the way shut.

"Soon," Tucker repeated, watching him snuggle deeper into the covers. He smoothed Landon's hair off his forehead and, for a moment, the bitterness that so often plagued him disappeared. He could hardly believe he had his son with him and knew, when he finally gave in to the weariness pressing upon him and slept, he'd probably wake fearing it wasn't true. During all those months in prison he would've given anything for the chance to help Landon with his homework, coach his baseball team, or make sure he ate all his peas at dinner—any of the simple fatherly things he missed so terribly. And here he was.

Maybe God hadn't forgotten him after all.

"I can see why you risked what you did," Gabrielle said from the doorway.

Struggling against the conflicting emotions inside him, Tucker glanced up. "Have you ever loved someone so much it hurts?" he asked.

A curious expression crossed her face. "Right now I love two people that much," she said, then hurried down the hall.

Tucker stared after her. David and Allie?

CHAPTER SIXTEEN

TUCKER COULDN'T TAKE his eyes off Gabrielle's breasts. He hadn't come to her house with any lascivious intent. He'd been searching only for sanctuary. But then he'd seen her with that sheet wrapped around her and nothing but bare skin beneath, and his body had immediately reminded him that it had been two long years since he'd appeased his sexual appetites.

She was dressed now in a yellow tank top and a pair of cutoffs, but she still wasn't wearing a bra and the change hardly made the situation any easier on him. Every time she moved, her full breasts swayed gently, reminding him of that brief moment in the desert when he'd cupped them in his palms and tasted her sweetness. The memory caused every muscle in his body to tense. Like that sunrise he'd witnessed on the first morning of his freedom, he found Gabrielle's body breathtaking, almost sacred, certainly nothing to be taken for granted. He wanted to caress her, to excite her in small degrees and work up from there until...

She turned to ask him how he liked his eggs, and he immediately yanked his attention to the glass of water she'd given him.

"Over easy is fine," he muttered.

She went back to cooking, and he let his eyes return to her, admiring the tone of her legs, the perfect curve of her buttocks....

"Orange or apple juice?" she asked, catching him looking at her again.

He dragged his gaze up to meet her eyes. "Pardon?"

"What would you like to drink?"

"Coffee's fine," he said, even though he'd basically lived on coffee and caffeine-laden soft drinks for the past few days and felt as though they'd burn a hole through his stomach.

"When's the last time you had something solid to eat?"

Tucker couldn't remember. He'd used the pay phone when he'd stopped to buy Landon a Happy Meal and had accidentally left his own sack of food in the booth. When he realized what he'd done, he'd driven too far to go back and hadn't wanted to risk stopping again. "I don't know."

"You don't know?" She seemed genuinely distraught. "You've got to eat, or you'll never get through this."

Why did she care whether he survived? She might believe he was innocent of Andrea's murder, but he was just some poor sucker she'd met in prison. She'd already done far more for him than simple compassion would dictate. She should have demanded he get out of her house; instead she was standing at the stove making him breakfast as though he wasn't an escaped convict who'd just broken into her trailer!

"Why do you keep helping me?" he asked suddenly.

"Aren't you hungry?" She turned again, surprise apparent on her face.

"That's not what I meant. You shouldn't have let me in."

"I didn't let you in."

"You shouldn't have let me stay."

"Why not?"

Because she got to him, that was why. Her beauty tied his stomach in knots, and her goodness and idealism attracted his beleaguered soul, like a beacon giving light to the darkness. He knew how jaded and bitter he'd become. The comparison between them showed him more than he wanted to see, made him resent her at the same time he was tempted to love her. Maybe part of her appeal lay in the hope that he could reclaim the innocence of his former self by possessing her in some way. "I could be dangerous," he said.

She folded her arms across her flat stomach. "You could've murdered me while we were in the desert. Then you wouldn't have had to dispose of my body."

"I'm not talking about murder."

"Then what are you talking about?"

"Maybe I want more than you're willing to give me."

She put his food on a plate and brought it to the table, coming so close as she set it in front of him that her left breast nearly grazed his cheek.

Tucker leaned away quickly to avoid contact, but she only grinned and reached across him to get the salt-shaker. "Your eggs might need a little more seasoning," she said, and this time as she moved, her breast did touch him. It brushed his arm, sending a jolt of pure testosterone through his veins.

He held himself perfectly still until he could regain control. "Don't provoke me, Gabrielle," he warned, his voice as menacing as possible. "You might get more than you're asking for."

"Would that be so bad?" she said.

"I'm not the man I once was," he tried to explain.

"Then maybe we should find out who you are now." Her hands settled on his shoulders and began to knead his tired muscles, and her touch went to his head like half a bottle of tequila. He said nothing as her fingers eased the tension in his back; he wasn't sure he could speak. But then she shifted, and his peripheral vision told him he had only to turn his head to take her nipple into his mouth....

With a groan, he shoved her away. "Don't."

She stared at him for several seconds without moving. "What's wrong?"

"Nothing."

"You don't want me?"

"No," he snapped. "I'm not interested."

"That's funny. You sure *look* interested." She arched an eyebrow as she eyed his lap.

"Don't push it, Gabrielle."

"Why?"

Because he wanted her *too* badly. Because he feared the messy emotions she inspired. Absolute control was the only thing powerful enough to see him through the nightmare that had become his life. If he lowered his defenses now, he might simply come apart in her arms. "Believe me, you don't know what you're asking for."

"I think I do." Stepping forward, she placed a sweet kiss on his temple. He closed his eyes against the lonely ache the tenderness of that simple action engendered.

"I know you've been to hell and back, Tucker," she whispered. "I'm guessing any real intimacy at this point scares you to death. But I'm not going to hurt you. I just want to make love with you, to feel you naked against me, moving inside me. I want to touch you and be touched by you and forget that anything else even exists.''

Her words turned his heart into a jackhammer, the pounding so loud it seemed to echo in his ears. But he refused to allow himself to respond as he wanted to. ''What? Are you one of those women who get off on having sex with the worst of the worst?'' he asked, striving to drive a wedge between them.

His words succeeded in surprising her, and she stepped back. A small voice in Tucker's head told him he was crazy to throw away what she'd just offered him. The other part understood that if he made love to her, it would be almost impossible to get up and walk away in the morning, knowing she'd probably go on to marry someone else. He had nothing to offer her, wasn't sure he ever would, and there wasn't a damn thing he could do about it. She deserved more. Shutting her out was the kindest thing he could do.

''I think you know better,'' she said.

''I don't know anything. I'm only after a meal and a good night's sleep,'' he said. ''That's all.''

The look on her face tested the limits of his will-power. He could barely keep from reaching out and pulling her into his arms. He longed to assure her that she hadn't misread the signs his body was sending her, that he did want her. So badly... But such an admittance would only weaken his defenses, and he was determined not to destroy her life.

''Fine,'' she said quietly. She got him some blankets from the closet at the end of the hall, walked into the living room and made him a bed on the couch.

TUCKER WAS DEAD TIRED and still he couldn't sleep. He couldn't sleep, and yet he couldn't go down the hall to join Gabrielle. He was pacing a hole in the carpet in front of the sofa, torn between the belief that he'd done the right thing and the temptation to forget about the right thing altogether.

He'd been insane to come here, he decided. And yet he couldn't imagine being anywhere else. He'd scarcely been able to think of anything or anyone besides Gabrielle since he watched her drive away with David after they'd emerged from the desert.

David... The thought of Gabrielle's ex-husband and the close relationship that still existed between them bothered Tucker as though he had some stake in the situation, something to lose. But of course he didn't....

A noise at the back of the trailer brought Tucker to a standstill. Suddenly alert, he listened for the sound to be repeated, then heaved a sigh of relief when he recognized a baby's soft gurgle. It was nothing to worry about. Allie was awake; that was all.

Tucker wondered if Gabrielle could hear her daughter. He guessed she couldn't when the door to her bedroom remained firmly closed. If he waited long enough, he was sure Allie would begin to cry and Gabrielle would come for her. But there seemed little point in waking Gabrielle when he was already awake.

Hesitating for only a moment, he strode to the baby's bedroom. He'd seen Allie in the car the same day he'd met David, but he'd been beyond thirst and hunger then and living on nerves. He'd hardly given the child a glance. But what he remembered was a chubby baby with a pink, bowlike mouth and blond flyaway hair, and that was exactly what he found. Sitting in her crib, chewing on a couple of fingers, Allie gave him her full attention the moment he stepped into the room. Evidently she'd been waiting for someone to come. She probably couldn't remember him from their brief encounter, but that didn't seem to matter. She immediately grabbed the slats of her crib, pulled herself to her feet and gave him a gap-toothed grin so full of trust he couldn't help returning it.

"Da...da...da..." She stomped her feet and held out her arms to him, as though morning had arrived and she was ready to be set free for the day.

"Oh, no, you don't," Tucker said. He'd been through this with Landon. If he took her out of her crib, she'd never go back to sleep.

"Are you hungry, babe?" He looked through her bedding and found an empty milk bottle. Holding it, he started to leave, but she began to cry the second he moved toward the door.

"Shh, don't cry, Allie. I'll be right back, okay? Look, I'm going to fix you another bottle."

"Ba...ba...ba," she replied. He'd gained her approval there, but the quiver of her lip and the tears glistening in her eyes indicated she'd only cry again if he left her.

He gauged his chances of preparing the bottle and returning before she awakened the whole house, and didn't deem them very good. Not only that, if Gabrielle came out of her bedroom now, he wouldn't be able to let her return alone. Not a second time. And not if she was still wearing that T-shirt and those damn shorts....

He considered the alternative. Maybe Allie wasn't like Landon. Maybe she'd go back to sleep even if he got her out for a few minutes. Or maybe it wasn't even a bottle she wanted. She could be wet.

Her smile reappeared the instant he moved toward her again, and he laughed softly at how easily she'd manipulated him. "Come on," he said. "Let's change your diaper. Then we'll make that bottle I promised you.''

Allie was definitely as soft as she looked, and she smelled of baby shampoo and baby powder. Tucker decided he liked those scents almost as much as the little-boy smells that clung to Landon. His son was now eight years old, but Tucker remembered his diapering days well. That was before Andrea had gotten so caught up in the lifestyle she'd been living at the end, before he realized his marriage would probably end in divorce.

A changing table took up part of one wall. Allie waited patiently while Tucker laid her down and used the supply of paper diapers on the shelf beneath to change her. The receptacle next to the changing table made a small clang when he disposed of the wet diaper, but the rest of the house remained quiet.

So far, so good. Except that Gabrielle's daughter didn't seem sleepy at all. She clapped her hands and squirmed for him to pick her up before he could get her pajamas back in place.

''Just a minute, babe. I'm a little rusty and this cast isn't helping much,'' he told her, struggling to manage the snaps on her Winnie the Pooh one-piece.

She jammed one fist in her mouth as he carried her from the room, and he wondered what Hansen and the others would think if they could see him now. No doubt they expected him to be on the run, heading for the border or hiding in Phoenix or some other place big enough to get lost in a crowd. Instead he was right across the street from the prison, getting a fresh bottle for Gabrielle's baby.

His smile disappeared as the irony of it gave way to an awareness of everyone's horrified reaction. No one would believe a baby to be safe around him. According to the papers, the police feared for his own son's well-being. Because of that one bogus trial, that one dreadful travesty of justice, everyone assumed the worst, even though he'd never hurt a woman or a child in his life and never would.

Now, a man was a different story. Tucker thought if he ever got his hands on Hansen, he'd hurt him pretty badly. That was where he'd changed. He'd learned hate, and he'd begun to crave vengeance.

Allie tried to share her wet fist with him. As he moved her hand away, he purposely turned his mind from those dark thoughts to the beautiful baby in his arms. Gabrielle was lucky. She'd soon forget about him, marry again, have more children, live a normal life.

He wanted those things for her, even though he wasn't the one who could give them to her. He wanted those things badly enough to sleep on the couch.

GABRIELLE WOKE with a start. Her heart hammered in competition with the chug of the swamp cooler, and the morning sun glared harshly through her blinds, yet it was only six o'clock.

"Jeez, how could it be so hot already?" she muttered.

Damp with sweat, she rolled over and stared at her closed door as everything that had happened the night before came tumbling back to her. Deep down, she'd believed Tucker would eventually join her. She knew she couldn't have imagined the way his eyes had devoured her, the hunger she saw in them. Nearly every time she looked at him, she'd caught him staring at her. But he'd remained on the couch—unless he'd already slipped out of her trailer as quietly as he'd slipped in.

Or maybe the whole encounter had been a dream.

She kicked away the sheet and sat up, putting a hand to her head. Too little sleep and too much stress had combined to give her a terrible headache.

At least she wouldn't feel guilty when she called in sick, she thought. She was supposed to report to Eyman Complex in just a few hours, but she couldn't go anywhere if Tucker left Landon with her.

Standing, she shoved a hand through her hair and shuffled toward the hall. She needed to find out if Tucker was still around. And she wanted to check on Allie. Last night had seemed so long it was almost surreal. It felt like days since she'd seen her daughter.

She glanced in to Landon's room, just to be certain he wasn't a figment of her imagination, and discovered him sleeping peacefully, which answered one question.

When she reached the kitchen, she saw the frying pan she'd used to make Tucker's eggs in the dish drainer. In the living room, she found the T-shirt he'd been wearing tossed onto her vinyl recliner and his sandals at the foot of her couch—all further proof that she hadn't dreamed a thing. Not that she needed incidental proof anymore. Tucker was still there, big as life, sleeping on her couch. And Allie was with him.

Gabrielle's heart melted at the sight of the man she loved holding her baby. He'd seemed so hardened in prison, so powerful and dangerous. But he looked almost boyish now, with his hair mussed and his face softened in sleep. Allie lay on her belly, her cheek to his bare chest, sleeping comfortably if appearances were anything to judge by, and Gabrielle was so moved by the sight she went for her camera. She knew it was stupid to want to preserve this moment. A photograph would only prove her guilty of aiding and abetting his escape. But she had to have something to hold on to because she couldn't hold on to him.

The flash woke Tucker. His blue eyes opened and focused on her immediately. Then his brows gathered in a scowl. "Give me that," he whispered, trying not to wake Allie, who stirred anyway.

"No," Gabrielle said.

"You can't have a picture of me sleeping in your house, Gabby. You shouldn't have a photograph of me at all."

He'd torn David out of one of her pictures and then taken the photo with him. "You have a picture of me."

Allie raised her head and grinned sleepily at Gabrielle. Gabrielle lifted her baby into her arms and kissed her soft cheek, trying not to let her eyes linger on Tucker's broad chest. He'd rebuffed her once. She had no intention of asking for a second rejection.

"That's different," he said, the muscles in his arm bunching as he leaned up on one elbow. "That's an old picture, and it doesn't prove anything except that we crossed paths, which Hansen and the others already know."

"So? You have to leave me with something," she said. "I can't go through everything we've been through and walk away empty-handed."

He seemed to consider her answer. Surprisingly he dropped the subject. "I've got to go. Can I use your shower?"

The thought of all six-foot-something of him naked in her shower made Gabrielle's cheeks flush. "Of course. I'll get you a towel."

She turned and headed down the hall and could hear

him following barefoot behind her. "Do you need me to wash some clothes for you while you're gone?" she asked.

They'd entered her bedroom, and he didn't answer. He glanced around, taking in the worn and dated furnishings.

For the first time, Gabrielle wished she'd tried harder to make this place a home. "I'm only staying here temporarily until I can afford something better," she explained.

He rested one shoulder against the wall and folded his arms. "David seemed like a successful guy. Why did you leave him for this? For working in a damn prison?"

Gabrielle folded her arms, too. "You know why. I already told you."

"You also said you love him."

"I said I didn't love him in the right way."

"So? What does that really mean? Maybe I've never loved anyone in the *right* way."

"You said it last night, Tucker. The right way is loving so much it sometimes hurts. It's loving another person so much you'd sooner stop breathing than stop loving them."

"Why can't you love David like that?"

Gabrielle didn't know why. She'd always liked him, admired him. But it was as if her soul was holding out, secretly yearning for the one man who could complete her. And now she'd found him. She knew she couldn't have him, but there was still no chance for her and David. Not after loving Tucker, not after proving to herself that the emotional depths she'd imagined were not only real but possible—even for her. "There's no explanation for some things, Tucker." She frowned. "Why are you pushing me toward David?"

He ran a finger lightly down her cheek, his touch filling Gabrielle with the same longing she'd felt last night—to be significant to him in the most fundamental way, to join with him and share her body, her heart, her life. "Because I want you safe. Even from me."

Meeting the icy blue of his eyes, she covered his hand with her own and nestled her cheek against his palm. "I'm not afraid of you, Tucker. I'm in love with you."

The look on his face told her how unexpected her words were. She watched as several emotions gripped him—first and foremost, an obvious desire to believe her. For a brief moment she felt his fingers tighten as though he'd give in and pull her toward him. But then the opposing emotion—"I can't get hurt if I don't let myself need anyone"—seemed to win out, and he moved away.

"I'm sorry, Gabby. I can't allow myself to care about you," he said. "I can't even stay more than a couple of days. Don't sell yourself so short."

Taking the towel she handed him, he stepped into the bathroom and closed the door, and Gabrielle let her breath go in a long sigh. So much for avoiding rejection a second time.

CHAPTER SEVENTEEN

GABRIELLE STARED across the kitchen table at Landon. He stared right back at her.

Tucker had gone into his son's room just an hour earlier to explain that he'd be gone for a while, but Landon was obviously not happy about being left behind. He was so unhappy, in fact, that he'd apparently decided he wouldn't speak—to Gabrielle or to Allie. His silence didn't bother Allie. She kept bringing him her toys and dropping them at his feet or patting him joyfully on the leg, thrilled by the mere presence of another child.

Gabrielle wasn't quite so pleased. How was she supposed to get through a whole day of this silent animosity?

She glanced at Landon's barely touched plate, considered coaxing him to eat more, then decided not to waste her breath. Going by his attitude, if he thought she wanted him to eat, he'd refuse. If he thought she *didn't* want him to eat, she might have half a chance of getting some food down him.

"Are you finished?" she asked as cheerfully as possible. "Because I'd like that egg if you're not going to eat it."

He looked at her with those eyes that were so much like his father's—confident bordering on arrogant, complex, deep—and neither shoved his plate away nor ate his egg. He mutilated it until even a dog would refuse it.

"Thanks," she said, not bothering to hide her sarcasm as she carried his plate to the sink.

"When's my father coming back?" he asked, repeating the only words he would utter.

"I don't know," she answered truthfully. "But you and I have a decision to make. We can be miserable the whole time he's gone, or we can relax and make the best of a bad situation."

"He *is* coming back, isn't he?" he asked.

Ah, new words. *That* was progress. But Gabrielle couldn't answer even this simple question with any more certainty than she had the first one. "I know he'd walk through fire to get to you. Does that help?"

Landon didn't answer, but the guarded expression on his face softened Gabrielle's heart. The poor kid had been through a lot. He'd lost both parents at the age of six and had probably been trying to make sense of his world ever since. But then he opened his mouth again, and some of her sympathy faded.

"What are you and that stupid baby to my dad?"

Maybe the silent treatment wasn't so bad, Gabrielle thought. "Allie is not a stupid baby, Landon, and I'd appreciate it if you'd remember your manners while you're here. Your father and I are friends."

"Are you his new wife?"

Gabrielle cleared her throat and busied herself with washing up. "No."

"Then why am I here?"

"Because your father needed someone to watch you for a while, and I'm trying to help him out. Only you're not making it very easy."

"I don't like it here," he said.

"That's obvious."

"I want to go home."

Gabrielle finished filling the sink with hot soapy water and turned to face him. "Where's home, Landon?" she asked softly.

His face fell and he began to kick the leg of his chair. "It's with my father."

"Then you're in the right place, because this is where he's coming back for you."

He lapsed into silence again, and Gabrielle's sympathy returned full force as she watched him struggle against tears.

"It's okay to cry, Landon," she said. "We all cry now and then. I know you're unhappy and that you miss your dad a lot, but—"

"Shut up! I'm not crying. Only sissies cry," he shouted, and ran down the hall to the bedroom he'd slept in.

Gabrielle felt completely out of her element. How could she help the poor kid? He was so much like his father—too stubborn and proud for his own good.

The slamming of the door scared Allie. Puckering her lower lip, she looked to her mother in bewilderment, then broke into a howl. Gabrielle wasn't far from tears herself. To top it all off, the telephone rang. Gabrielle eyed it nervously, wishing she didn't need to answer. She'd called in sick. It could be someone from the prison. Or it might be Felicia. Her baby-sitter had still been asleep when she'd called to let her know she didn't need her today. Gabrielle had left a message with her mother.

Resolutely she picked up the phone. "Gabby? Is it you?" the caller asked.

"Yeah, it's me," she said, sweeping Allie into her arms and trying to comfort her so she could hear.

"It's...it's Naomi. I...I got hold of Lindy this morning, and, well, we were hoping you'd be able to join us for dinner at my place tomorrow night. My son, Conrad, might be able to make it, too. He has some commitments, but he's going to try and reschedule."

Her mother seemed to be talking too fast, as though she was afraid Gabrielle would refuse, given half a chance. Gabrielle knew she *should* refuse; she had too much to deal with right now, and most of it was criminal. She was baby-sitting a kidnapped boy for an escaped convict, and she was letting that escaped convict sleep at her place. But she could detect the hope in her mother's voice and, much as she thought Naomi deserved it, she couldn't disappoint her. Especially since she was dying to meet her siblings. "Okay. Is there anything you'd like me to bring?"

"No, just yourself and an appetite. Hal's planning to grill steaks. I'll make some salads. You're not a vegetarian, are you?"

"No."

"Fine. We'll stick with that menu."

"Sounds good."

"Is six o'clock okay?"

"Six works."

"Great."

Gabrielle's call-waiting beeped, and she felt the same unease she'd experienced earlier. Who would it be this time? David? Hansen? Anyone else she didn't want to talk to? "I'll see you tomorrow—" She hesitated, not knowing what to call Naomi, and was rescued from the awkwardness of the moment by her mother's smooth interruption.

"Hal and I can't wait."

Twisting her fingers through the phone cord, Gabrielle said goodbye and switched lines. "Hello?"

"Gabrielle?"

It was Tucker. She could tell by the immediate tingle that swept through her body—followed by fear. Had something happened to him? Was he calling to say he was in trouble? "Is everything okay?" she asked.

"Yeah, fine."

Traffic whizzed and rumbled in the background and she guessed he was using a pay phone.

"How's Landon?" he asked.

"He's…" She wondered how much to tell Tucker. His son was miserable, but she didn't want to make Tucker's burden any heavier. Surely she could figure out some way to reach an eight-year-old boy, keep him happy for the day. "He's doing great," she lied. "I'm thinking about taking him and Allie to the community pool in Chandler."

"Why Chandler?"

"Because I just called in sick. I'd rather not be spotted in Florence."

"That would be a problem."

"Do you want to talk to Landon?"

"No, I said my goodbyes this morning. If he's doing that well, I'll just see him tonight."

Gabrielle waited for him to give his reason for calling, but he said nothing further. "Are you worried I won't take care of him or something?" she asked.

"No."

"Then what? Why'd you call so soon?"

A long pause. "I just wanted to tell you I'm thinking of you," he said.

Gabrielle caught her breath in surprise. "What does that mean?" she asked, but he'd already hung up.

TUCKER TURNED HIS FACE away and moved to the side as a Mexican woman who'd come up behind him while he was talking to Gabrielle used the pay phone. He doubted she'd recognize him, or call the police even if she did. He suspected she didn't speak English. But he saw no point in taking chances.

Keeping his face averted, he leaned against the hood of his old Datsun while listening to her rapid Spanish and wondered what had possessed him to call Gabby. He needed to distance himself from her emotionally and to concentrate on salvaging what was left of his life, not negate everything he'd established last night by eroding his own resistance.

The woman abruptly ended her call and hurried into the gas station without sparing him a glance. He moved back into the booth. Ever since his escape, his brother, Tom, had been out of town—on a Caribbean cruise according to some woman who had identified herself as his housekeeper. He was supposed to get back yesterday, and Tucker had hoped he'd be able to reach him this morning. His brother hadn't written or visited for over a year, but Tucker had no doubt Tom would help him.

Since high school, Tucker had taken care of his big brother, bailed him out of scrapes with the law, included him in real estate transactions that made them both good money. Tucker had brought Tom in on the biggest opportunity of his career, the one he'd been working on when he'd gone to prison, with the understanding that Tom would help his partner Robert finish the deal, then split his share of the profits with Tucker.

Tucker hadn't seen a dime yet, but turning raw land into finished lots often took several years. He didn't expect to see any money for another twelve months or so. But things had to be going well for his brother, judging by the fact that he now had a house big enough to require domestic help.

The persistent ringing on the other end of the line made Tucker curse. *Come on, dammit. Somebody pick up.*

The morning was only a few hours old, yet the sun beat down on his back, making him damp with perspiration. As he gazed off into the distance, the Superstition Mountains looked hazy. It was going to be another scorcher. Too bad his little car had no air conditioning.

Nine rings...ten... Tucker was about to hang up when the housekeeper he'd spoken to earlier finally answered.

"Tucker residence," she said with a heavy Spanish accent.

Tucker gripped the handset more tightly. "Is Tom there?"

"I'm afraid he's still sleeping. He and his wife got in very late last night."

Wife? His brother had married and never told him? Tucker still received weekly letters from his mother, but she'd never mentioned it, either.

"Can I take a message?" the housekeeper asked.

"No, I need to talk to Tom. Tell him it's urgent."

"I'm sorry, he got in very late last night."

"I understand that. Just tell him his brother is on the phone. He'll take the call, okay?"

A pause. "One moment," she said with a deep sigh.

He heard some shuffling and then a *thump* that told him she'd set the phone down.

While he waited, Tucker stared absently at a sea of saguaros jutting up from the Superstition Mountains into the pale blue sky. Apache Junction. There was a stark beauty about this lonely little outpost, but it had a melancholy feeling, too.

"Come on, Tom. It's me," Tucker muttered, growing impatient.

After another few minutes, the housekeeper returned. "I'm sorry. Mr. Tucker says he'll have to call you back. Can I get your number?"

Tucker stared at the pay phone with its metal face glinting in the sun, feeling as though someone had just landed him a good right hook to the chin. *Call him back?* "He can't call me back, dammit. I'm in trouble and I need his help. Go get him!"

"I'm sorry. He's given me strict instructions that he and his wife are not to be disturbed. But thank you for calling," she said, and hung up.

Shocked and enraged, Tucker whirled toward his car. Then he jammed a hand through his hair and pivoted back to the pay phone. There had to be some sort of misunderstanding. Maybe the housekeeper had garbled his message or Tom didn't understand his situation. Maybe Tom had been gone so long he'd missed all the news reports.

Tucker fed the phone another few coins and called his brother again, but the housekeeper only reaffirmed what she'd said earlier. When the dial tone buzzed in his ear a second time, he pinched the bridge of his nose and wondered what he was going to do now. He had some money of his own in a savings account at a local bank, what little he hadn't spent on his defense. But he dared not access it, since the police could trace the transaction and pinpoint his whereabouts. He needed some cash, he needed a place to hide, and he needed both right away.

Glancing over his shoulder to make sure his lingering at the phone wasn't raising any suspicion, he dialed another number. He'd purposely not contacted his parents since his escape. He hadn't wanted to drag them into the line of fire. He knew they'd be worried but letting them worry was better than giving the police any reason to harass them. However, Tom had left him no choice. He had to find out what was going on before his luck ran out.

"Hello?"

In prison, he'd been allowed two five-minute calls each week to anyone on his "ten" list; he'd generally used them to phone Landon. He'd spoken to his mother a handful of times, but Dee Tucker sounded older now, frailer than he remembered.

"Hi, Mom. It's me."

"Randall! Are you okay?" she asked. "We've been worried sick about you."

"I'm fine, considering the situation," he said.

"And Landon?"

"He's good. He's with me."

"You shouldn't have taken him, Randall. You've got to turn yourself in. The police have been coming by here and calling us all the time, asking if we've heard from you. They've been saying terrible, frightening things."

His mother's voice broke, which made Tucker's stomach tense. God, he hated the shame and unhappiness his imprisonment had caused everyone he knew—

his family, his in-laws, his employees and friends, his business partner, his young son.

"They say you could get the death penalty for this," she went on. "You've got to turn yourself in right away, before it goes any farther. I couldn't bear it if they—"

Tucker squeezed his eyes shut and interrupted before she could say what it was she couldn't bear. "I'm not turning myself in, Mom. It's too late for that."

"Then what? What are you going to do? What *can* you do?"

"I'm going to figure out a way to get my life back."

"How?"

"I don't know," he admitted. "But the truth is out there somewhere. I thought I'd start by trying to trace Andrea's movements during her last few days. The police spent all their time and resources trying to pin her death on me. They never bothered to look for other suspects. Maybe I'll hire another private detective."

"You tried that once."

"I'm thinking about doing it again. There's got to be *someone* who can help me find the truth."

"How are you going to avoid being picked up by the police?" she asked.

"I was hoping Tom would help me out with that. I thought maybe he could find someone willing to rent me a place. But he wouldn't accept my call this morning. You have any idea why?"

"Tom..." She sighed. "Between what's happened to you and the way he's been acting, I don't know what to think."

"What do you mean?"

"Sometimes I worry that he's never going to grow up. He did well on that last land deal of yours, the one you were working on when you were arrested, remember?''

The one he was supposed to split with me? "I remember.''

"Well, he hasn't been up to much since he cashed out of that.''

Tucker's blood ran cold. "He cashed out? Why didn't he see it through?''

"I don't think your partner wanted to continue working with him. Much as we love Tom, he isn't like you. He doesn't have the same mind, the same work ethic. Robert offered to buy him out over a year ago.''

"Why didn't you tell me?'' Tucker asked. His parents didn't know the specifics of the arrangement he'd made with Tom, so they wouldn't realize that Tom had cheated him. Still, his coming into a lot of cash would be significant news, considering his brother's history of going from one job to the next.

"I knew it would only upset you to see your work wasted that way. Developing that land was your dream, and Robert offered Tom far less than he would've received in the end.''

Tucker had met Robert in college when they were both business majors. While they were too different to spend much time together socially, they'd clicked on a professional level. During their senior year, they'd started buying duplexes around A.S.U., which they'd rented to other students. They'd sold when property values went up and rolled their profits into other investment properties, each one bigger and better than the last until they became one of the most successful young real estate companies in Tempe.

A no-nonsense achiever who rarely let anyone or anything stand in his way, Robert had been a fair part-

ner and, in certain ways, a friend. When Tucker was
first arrested, Robert had fronted thousands for his defense and had worked hard to liquidate some of their
joint assets so Tucker could continue to pay for rep-
resentation. Robert had also carried the brunt of the
workload through the months that Tucker was awaiting
trial. Of course, at the time, he and Tucker had both
firmly believed that after Tucker was acquitted, they'd
be able to get back to business as usual—back to the
high life, back to making money, back to being on a
roll. Then Tucker was sent to prison instead of being
acquitted, and Robert did the only thing that was prac-
tical: he moved on without him. He'd visited Tucker
once in prison, and Tucker had called him a few times.
But after the first month or two, they'd rarely communicated. There hadn't been anything to say. Still,
Robert had been kind enough to lend Tucker the money
for the car, and Tucker knew he could count on him
not to call the police.

"So Tom took the money and ran." No wonder his
brother wouldn't accept his call. Tom hadn't passed on
Tucker's share, hadn't even let him know that he'd
cashed out.

"What?"

"Nothing. Does he still own the karate school?"

"Yes, but he's too busy buying big houses and fancy
cars and going on exotic vacations to run it. He's
turned the school over to his manager for the most part,
but I doubt it's still making a profit. I went by not long
ago. There were only three students in the class I interrupted."

His brother's betrayal cut like glass. He knew Tom
probably saw little point in giving him his share of
anything when he was in prison for the rest of his life

and couldn't spend it. But Tucker had wanted that money for Landon, for his son's college education. Throughout the past two years, it was the one thing Tucker had believed he could give Landon.

"His housekeeper said he's married," Tucker said.

"I wrote you about that, but it happened so recently you probably never received my letter. They eloped to Vegas just a couple of weeks ago. I don't think they knew each other more than a month before they decided to get married. She's a stripper from a local girlie show and likes to spend money as much as Tom does. It won't last."

Tucker heard his father's voice in the background, first asking who it was, then demanding to speak to him.

"Your father wants to talk to you," his mother said.

A car pulled up behind Tucker, and he shifted to keep his back toward the driver. "Tell him I'll call again in a few minutes."

He hung up, then waited in his car until the person who'd parked behind him had used the phone. When he dialed again, his father answered immediately.

"Son, how are you?"

He'd been better before he realized what his brother had done, but he didn't mention that. "Hangin' in there. You?"

"Ornery as ever. And still working to get you out of this mess. I won't give up, you know."

His father always said that. His efforts hadn't made any difference so far, but the fact that he stuck by Tucker so devoutly felt good. "There's nothing you can do, Dad. Just take care of Mom. How's she doing, anyway?"

"Oh, she has her bad days, but she's holding up."

Then his father covered the phone and asked Dee to step out of the room for a few minutes so they could speak privately. Tucker fell silent, wondering what his father had to say that his mother couldn't hear. "What's going on?" he asked.

"I found something last week."

"What's that?"

"I was in the attic, trying to set a few mousetraps, and came across a shoebox shoved way out in the rafters."

"What was in it?"

"An old warrant for Tom's arrest—I guess he didn't pay a speeding ticket or something—and some letters from a woman he used to date. None of that stuff looked like it was very important, but then I found an envelope with some pictures I think you should see. Any chance you can meet me somewhere?"

Tucker straightened. "We'd better not meet. You could be followed. Why don't you put them in a manila envelope addressed to John Adams. Take the envelope to Fiesta Mall and leave it at 'will call' at Nordstrom. I'll pick it up later, okay?"

"I'd like to see you."

"I'd like to see you, too. But it isn't wise, not right now."

"Okay."

"What are the pictures of, Dad?" Tucker asked. He could hear his mother again, saying something to his father, so if she'd ever left the room, she hadn't stayed out long.

His father paused. "I'd rather not say right now. Tom's been out of town, so I haven't been able to ask where he got them. But I'll call him right now. Just be prepared—they're not pretty."

CHAPTER EIGHTEEN

"LANDON?" Gabrielle knocked on the door of her spare bedroom, hoping to elicit a response from the miserable little boy.

He didn't answer.

"Landon?" She cracked open the door and peeked inside. He was lying on the bed, facing away from her, where he'd stayed for the past thirty minutes. She'd been trying to allow him time to deal with his emotions, but she didn't want to let things go on for too long.

"I talked to your dad a little while ago," she said, moving into the room.

Mention of Tucker made Landon turn toward her. She could tell from his red, puffy eyes that he'd been crying. "He's not coming back, right?" he said, his voice sullen.

"Wrong. He'll be back tonight." Gabrielle said those words with such confidence, they were almost a promise—and she knew it. But the uncertainty in Landon's eyes haunted her. She knew he was begging for something to cling to, something he could count on. And she couldn't stop herself from doing everything in her power to give him that much. She understood too well what it felt like to be cast adrift. "He just wanted to know what we're having for supper."

"Really?"

"Yeah."

Silence, then, "What are we having?"

"I don't know. I'm thinking frog legs sound good."

He made a face. "Ick."

"No? Well, there's always chicken gizzards."

"Chicken *what?*"

"Gizzards. You know, those slimy things from inside a chicken?"

"They sound gross."

She pretended consternation. "Boy, are you picky. Okay, we'll have cow's tongue, then."

"No, way! My dad would never eat that," he added quickly.

Gabrielle smiled. "But a brave boy like you would, I'll bet."

She sensed that her praise tempted him to agree, but ultimately he shook his head. "Nah, I wouldn't eat anything my dad wouldn't eat."

"Then what does your dad like?"

"Pizza," he answered immediately.

Gabrielle was willing to bet Tucker wasn't the only one who liked pizza. "Does he?"

Allie had heard their voices and left the toys she'd been playing with in the kitchen to work her way down the hall. She rounded the corner to see them both in the room and instantly broke into a big smile at her accomplishment.

"See that?" Gabrielle asked. "Allie likes pizza, too. What kind do you think we should order?"

"Cheese is always good," Landon said.

"Everyone likes cheese," Gabrielle agreed.

"But maybe we'd better add some of the big-people stuff for my dad."

"You mean like onions and olives?"

He nodded solemnly.

"Sounds like a good idea." Gabrielle pulled Landon's discarded shoe away from Allie, who'd latched onto it as though she was about to eat it for lunch. "Now that we know what we're going to have for dinner, maybe we should go make something for dessert, hmm?"

Landon's face brightened. "Isn't it too early for dessert?"

"It's too early to *eat* dessert. But it'll take a while to make something really good, and a little sample here and there won't hurt anything. I'm thinking we should mix up a batch of my super-duper, double-delicious, chocolate-fudge brownies with lots of thick frosting. Or maybe some soft and gooey chocolate-chip cookies." She tried to think of something else that might interest an eight-year-old. "We could shape them into giant hearts," she suggested. "Your dad would probably like a cookie as big as his plate, don't you think?"

"Yeah!" Landon sat up. "I saw one of those once. It had writing on it with blue and white frosting."

"We could whip up some frosting and write on ours, too. I have some of those fancy decorator tips. I used them when I made Allie's birthday cake."

He glanced at Allie, a hint of his old animosity returning. "How old is she?"

"Just one."

"She's kinda chubby."

"Yeah. Lots of babies are."

He seemed to consider this. "And she doesn't have very many teeth."

"Not yet."

"How does she eat?"

"She sort of gums her food until it falls apart."

He wrinkled his nose. "That's pretty gross. Can she talk?"

"She says a few words. Mama, dada, kitty."

"I bet she can't say my name."

"We could try and teach her while we bake."

"Okay!"

The eagerness in his voice gave Gabrielle hope. "So what should we write on your dad's giant cookie?"

Landon screwed up his mouth as he thought. "Welcome home," he volunteered, and any reserve Gabrielle had felt toward this little boy melted instantly. He missed his father so terribly. No wonder he'd been angry about being left behind.

"Perfect," she said. "But we'd better get going because we don't want to be baking cookies this afternoon."

"Why not?" he asked, scooting to the edge of the bed.

"I thought we could go swimming when it gets really hot." She hesitated as though she felt some doubt. "That is, if you know how to swim."

"I know how to swim," he quickly assured her. "I love to swim."

He was close enough that Allie could reach him now, and she happily patted his leg. Gabrielle thought he might lapse into a scowl or push her little hand away, but he didn't. "Does Allie know how to swim?" he asked, watching her.

"Not yet," Gabrielle said. "But she has a life jacket and we can keep an eye on her, don't you think?"

"Oh, yeah. That's easy."

"Great. So what are we waiting for?" Gabrielle headed toward the kitchen, hoping Landon would follow, and she wasn't disappointed.

"Come on, Baby," she heard him say to Allie. "Hey, can you say my name? Lan—don. L..a..n..d..o..n," he repeated stretching it out.

"Na, na," Allie responded.

"No, Landon," he corrected, and Gabrielle chuckled under her breath. She'd made progress with Tucker's son, made him happy for the moment. But all the cookies and pizza in the world weren't going to compensate him if his father didn't return tonight.

There wasn't anything that could compensate her, either.

TUCKER SAT on a green wooden picnic table in the corner of the park, shielded from the hot glare of the afternoon sun by the dappled shade of a paloverde. He was alone. It was midafternoon on a Saturday, but no one else was fool-hardy enough to abandon air conditioning for one-hundred-and-thirteen-degree weather. Located on a small corner lot tucked into a lower-middle-class neighborhood on the outskirts of Chandler, this park had only three swings, a slide that looked hot enough to scorch and nothing else except some bermuda grass, the only grass hearty enough to withstand the Arizona heat.

He'd expected a manila envelope to be waiting for him at Nordstrom and had found a small box instead. His father had enclosed a couple of thousand dollars in cash, which would definitely help, and his mother had made him a lunch that included several of her home-made chocolate-chip cookies. He ate one now as he considered opening the third item in the box—an envelope that would no doubt contain the photographs his father had mentioned on the phone.

Tucker had no idea who or what they were all about,

and was curious to find out. Yet he felt a strange reluctance. What other surprises awaited him? What other setbacks? Never in a million years would he have guessed the twists and turns his life would take in recent years. He'd been raised by good parents, known love. He'd done well in school, excelled in sports and done exceptionally well in his short professional career. Being convicted of a crime was something that happened to other men, *guilty* men.

Yet, here he was, hiding from the law. And he'd have to keep hiding unless he found something that would give the police reason to reexamine the circumstances surrounding his wife's murder.

His father's note said Tom had found the pictures shoved beneath a mattress at the cabin he and Robert used to own. They'd lent it to him one weekend before Andrea disappeared. "He hid them in the attic because he didn't want you hurt," his father wrote, which didn't bode well.

Taking a deep breath, he tore the seal and withdrew a stack of Polaroid snapshots. It was Christmas, just three months before Andrea died. Tucker recognized the dress his wife was wearing, the new coat he'd bought Landon. They'd decided to spend the holidays at their cabin with friends who lived next door to them in the valley—Sean and Sydney Marshall, and their two young daughters. Tucker had hoped that inviting the Marshalls might help keep the peace in his own family long enough that he could reestablish some common ground with Andrea.

But the whole vacation had been a disaster. Andrea had remained aloof and uncommunicative for the better part of the first day and then provoked an argument that night about selling their house and building some-

thing larger. Tucker saw no point in a bigger home
when they practically lived in a mausoleum already.
He wanted to stay in a neighborhood that was family-
friendly, where Landon could pal around with the kids
on his block, not reside behind a ten-foot gate with
guard dogs and security. Tucker wanted to add to their
family, too, which entered the argument several times.

As usual Andrea refused. She claimed she wouldn't
have another child until he gave up his ''little girlfriends.'' Only he'd never had any girlfriends. Andrea
was the one who'd been unfaithful to him. And these
pictures were proof.

He wiped the sweat from his forehead with the back
of his hand and shuffled quickly through the stack. The
first few were shots of both families at dinner, opening
presents, playing in the snow. Those toward the bottom
showed Sean Marshall in various stages of undress and
obvious sexual arousal. One depicted Andrea, completely nude, wantonly posing for the camera. Although
Sean wasn't in this particular picture, Tucker knew he
was behind the lens. Andrea was lying on his discarded
pants.

The Marshalls had split up the following summer.
Tucker hadn't given their divorce much thought because he'd been behind bars by then, neck-deep in his
own trouble. But now he knew why two people who'd
once seemed happy together, much happier than he and
Andrea, had ended up with a broken marriage. The sad
thing was, he knew Andrea had never really cared for
Sean.

The private investigator he'd hired prior to Andrea's
death had provided proof of affairs with at least two
other men during that same period, both of whom
worked out at the gym where she did aerobics. Sean

looked like George from "Seinfeld" and simply wasn't her type. Andrea had often told Tucker she couldn't imagine what Sydney ever saw in her couch potato of a husband. Knowing Andrea, she'd come on to Sean just to see if she could tempt him away from his marriage vows, to prove that she was just as irresistible as she'd always been.

But having sex with Sean at the cabin... That was pretty daring, even for Andrea. Tucker knew he and Sydney must have been somewhere nearby. Had this happened when they were outside building a snowman with the kids, or running to the grocery store? Sydney had needed syrup for the waffles she wanted to make for breakfast, and Tucker had offered to drive her, since he had a four-wheel drive and was more familiar with the area. They'd taken the children to let them choose treats and to give them a break from the confined space, but Andrea and Sean had stayed behind. Andrea had said she needed to shower; Sean had been reading the paper. Tucker had never considered they might have an affair. He'd never sensed any threat coming from that direction. But by then he'd been so disappointed in Andrea, he hadn't really cared.

He didn't care now. He felt sort of sorry for Sean, which was probably a pretty strange reaction under the circumstances. But his neighbor had lost a good wife for a quick, meaningless fling with Andrea.

"Dumb bastard," Tucker muttered. He shoved the pictures back into the envelope and stood as the wave of sadness quickly disappeared in favor of new hope. It had been so long since he'd had good news, so long since he'd had any reason to believe he'd ever find Andrea's murderer. The two men she'd been seeing from the gym had had sound alibis; Tucker's investi-

gator had confirmed them. But no one had paid much
attention to where Sean Marshall was that night. The
police had checked with all the neighbors, of course,
to record what they'd seen or heard while the crime
was taking place.

If Tucker remembered right, Sean said he'd gotten
home late and heard nothing. But he typically left work
at five o'clock and his whereabouts hadn't been veri-
fied by anyone. Maybe he was home the whole time
and had cornered Andrea in the garage after she and
Tucker had had their argument and Tucker stormed off.
Who could say? Sean certainly didn't strike Tucker as
the kind of man who would harm a woman, let alone
beat Andrea to death. He couldn't see his neighbor losing his temper to such a degree. Neither could he picture Sean dragging off her body and hiding it so well
no one would ever find it. Sean Marshall had always
been soft, easygoing and only moderately driven, even
in his work as an accountant.

But Lord knew, Andrea had a way of bringing out
the worst in a man.

THE HUSHED QUIET felt odd as Tucker let himself into
Sean Marshall's backyard from the alley behind and
stood gazing over the fence at the house he used to
own. A little more than two years ago, the Marshall
girls would've been splashing in his and Andrea's pool
along with Landon, while Sydney and Andrea watched
from chaises along the side. Tucker had often arrived
home from work to find both women slathered in sun-
tan lotion and nursing glasses of iced tea, laughing as
they swapped stories about anything from an unfriendly
grocery checker to a new stair-stepper at the gym. He
would tease them about working too hard; they'd beg

him to stay home for a few days and see what being a mother was really like. Then he'd go inside and change clothes while they got up and dried off the kids. Sometimes Sydney and the girls would stay for dinner and Sean would join them. Tucker would throw steaks or burgers on the barbecue, the women would make salads, Jell-O, maybe corn on the cob, the kids would break out the cookies and soda. Those were good times…really good.

Awash with bittersweet memories, Tucker closed his eyes. He could almost hear Andrea's laugh. Full-bodied and warm, it was infectious. She'd thrived on company, on attention; had always welcomed a party. But toward the end, she hadn't been interested in their usual friends and hadn't laughed much at all.

What they'd once shared as husband and wife no longer seemed relevant to this strange, quiet place that looked so much the same yet felt so different.

Tucker sighed and scanned the yard he used to mow once a week. He'd sold that yard, and the house that went with it, while he was awaiting trial eighteen months ago. He hadn't wanted to bring Landon back to the place where Andrea had died, hadn't wanted to see it again himself. Yet he felt a sort of morbid fascination with it now, probably because of the way life had gone on without him. On the heels of their tragedy, new people had moved into their home and, to these newcomers, his loss meant nothing. They were busy living, working and raising children of their own. Someone still trimmed the bushes; someone still mowed the lawn. The house and yard looked just as good now as when he'd lived there.

He couldn't say the same about Sean's place. Turning, Tucker surveyed the mess. Instead of the cut green grass and flowers that had once flourished, weeds choked most of the landscape. Trash littered the patio, mostly Coke cans and cigarette butts, though to Tucker's knowledge Sean had never smoked. The Marshalls had owned a dog when Tucker lived next door, but there wasn't any sign of Jasper now. Only a small inflatable wading pool, punctured and filthy, reminded him of the children who'd once played with his son. If not for the fact that the new phone book still listed Sean at this address, Tucker might have thought he'd moved.

After crossing through the weeds of Sean's backyard, Tucker pressed his nose to the glass of the kitchen window. Inside looked no better than out. Dishes were piled high on the counters, encrusted with food, and the furniture Sydney had so lovingly purchased was mostly gone. The house appeared empty, hollow, much older than Tucker remembered. Gone was the expensive leather couch he'd helped the Marshalls unload that last Christmas. In its place sat a beige cloth sofa that had probably been bought secondhand, and a cheap side chair. Of the original furniture, only Sean's recliner remained, and the television.

Evidently, Tucker's old neighbor had lost more than his wife and children in the divorce. He'd lost his whole way of life.

Tucker waited and watched for a few minutes, but there was no movement in the house and no sound. Sean was obviously gone. Now was the perfect time to go inside and take a look around, but the back door was locked. If Sean's behavior had stayed true to form, Tucker knew there'd be a spare key in the planter off the front porch, but he wasn't very keen on going where the neighbors might see him. He considered breaking a window instead, then changed his mind and slipped through the side yard. Quiet as it was this afternoon, he doubted he'd run into anybody.

The front yard was some improvement over the back. An attempt had been made to mow the grass, but big brown spots testified to a serious sprinkler problem, and the flowers that had once graced the redwood planters were all dead. Only their stiff, dried carcasses remained—another relic of better days.

Tucker ignored the dead flowers and the steady hum of electricity shooting through the wires along the street and began searching the planter for a key, which he found almost immediately.

"Maybe some things haven't changed," he muttered, remembering the many times he'd used the Marshall's spare key to water plants or take mail inside when they were out of town.

As he unlocked the door and let himself in, it occurred to him that what he was doing was illegal. He was breaking the law again—but he didn't care. He wasn't returning to custody, not if he could help it. Still, the irony of going to prison an innocent man and coming out a criminal didn't escape him.

The house smelled of eggs and old tennis shoes, but the air-conditioning provided a welcome respite from the heat and Tucker breathed a sigh of relief to think he was now inside, where there was much less chance of being seen. He locked the front door and, on a whim, pocketed the key. Then he ignored the kitchen and living room and went straight to the bedrooms. He wasn't sure what he was looking for. The police had never located Andrea's body. Tucker was sure her remains could have exonerated him at one time, but after two years, he knew chances were slim they'd ever be found—or that there'd be anything left in the way of evidence even if they were.

In any case, he wasn't going to find Andrea's body in Sean's house. He was more hopeful he'd find a letter, additional photos or an article of clothing that might link Sean to the night of the murder. He was searching for a needle in the proverbial haystack, but he had to start somewhere.

Two of the four bedrooms were empty. The bedroom closest to the master looked as though it had been converted into an office. An old wooden desk sat in the middle of the floor, buried beneath loose papers and surrounded by boxes of files. The closet stocked reams of paper, printer cartridges, phone books, mailing labels and containers of storage disks—nothing exciting, nothing that linked Sean to the murder.

He moved to the master bedroom and began to sort through Sean's bureau. The top drawer was filled with junk: keys, new shoelaces, a sewing kit, random buttons, a small screwdriver, some old bills, receipts and wadded-up letters. Tucker flattened out the letters, but none of them were written in Andrea's hand. Only one of them was signed but, judging by the content, they were all from Sydney.

Dear Sean,
Why won't you return my calls? I'm still the mother of your children, you know. What about *them?* They ask about you all the time, cry for their daddy. I've told them you're busy, that you need to figure out a few things. But you really need to start coming around more. I know you blame me for everything, but you're the one who's to blame, Sean. You know that, don't you? Any-

way, it's okay. I'm ready to forgive you. We can still work things out. We just need to forget the past and move on. We were both acting crazy, but that's all over now, right?

Call me.

Sydney

Dear Sean,

I waited up for you last night, but you never came. What's going on that you can't even keep a dinner date with me? I need you, babe. What about Courtney and Darci? They don't understand why their world's suddenly been turned upside down, and I can't keep it together for them. Not by myself.

Never mind. Forget about last night. I'm ready to start with a clean slate. Our anniversary is this weekend. Maybe we can go out to dinner at the Point, like we used to. Remember how much fun we used to have? Let's put the past behind us, Sean, please.

No signature.

Sean,

How long are you going to give me the cold shoulder? I don't deserve this! I went a little crazy for a while, that's all. But I was just so jealous. Can't you understand that? We need to move on, okay? Surely you're tired of living alone. Or are you not alone anymore? Is that what's going on?

Again, no signature.

Tucker frowned as he stuffed the letters back in Sean's top drawer. He'd assumed Sydney had discovered Sean's infidelity and left him, but these letters sounded as though it was Sean who'd broken up the marriage, Sean who was reluctant to get back together. Why? Sydney was an attractive woman. She was outgoing and ambitious. Why would Sean prefer the life he was currently living to the life he'd had before, when he'd seemed so happy?

Maybe he hadn't been as happy as he seemed, Tucker decided. So much that happened during a divorce defied understanding. Emotions swung in a wide arc, and the very person who filed for divorce was often the one who begged for reconciliation. The only way to know what had happened would be to ask Sean, and Tucker planned to do exactly that.

He spent another forty minutes searching the house without any success. Except for a few cans of soup, the cupboards were bare. There were more dirty clothes in the laundry room than clean ones in the bedroom. The refrigerator held nothing but a six-pack of beer and a bottle of ketchup. A filled ashtray could be found in almost every room. Sean might not have smoked before, but he certainly did now.

There was no evidence of a girlfriend. Tucker found no feminine articles in the whole place. No messages jotted on scraps of paper or left on the answering machine. No letters besides those from his ex-wife. No photos of Sean with anyone but his daughters. To all appearances, Sean was living a very staid, boring life. Only the heavy smoking indicated that it was a neurotic one, as well. Why? What had happened to the easygoing guy Tucker had known?

Maybe he'd been foolish enough to fall in love with Andrea and was still pining for her.

Tucker mulled over that possibility, then discarded it. He'd been around them enough to know that neither one had felt more than a passing sexual interest for the other. What had happened at the cabin was about lust and risk, not love, or Tucker would have known about it before now.

He opened the door heading into the garage to see what he might find there, but the gears of the garage door-opener suddenly sprang to life, sounding raucous and loud in the silence, and he jumped back. Sean was home. Now maybe he'd get his answers. Either that, or Sean would attempt to call the police. Tucker had no idea how his old neighbor might react to seeing him, but he thought it was worth his time to find out.

He waited in the living room, thumbing through the Polaroids his father had found.

When Sean came in, Tucker saw a man whose skin was sallow, as though his health wasn't quite what it should be. Sean had gained some weight—soft weight that suggested he was eating too much junk and not enough vegetables—and his widow's peak was more pronounced than ever. In short, he looked almost ten years older.

"Hi, Sean," Tucker said.

Sean's head jerked up from the document he'd been reading on his way into the house, and he flushed. "W-what are you doing here, Randy?" he asked. "I thought—" he swallowed "—I mean, I heard about your escape, but I never thought you'd show up here. Not in a million years."

"Why not? We're friends, aren't we, Sean? I always believed we were friends, anyway." Tucker began to look through the Polaroids again, making it a point to stop at the one that most compromised Sean. "I came because I had a few things to ask you. You got a minute, old friend?''

Small beads of perspiration began to pop out on Sean's forehead. His eyes cut to the counter, where a pack of cigarettes lay next to the phone. ''I—I'm supposed to be somewhere, actually. Why? What do you want? What are those?''

''You don't remember?''

''Remember what?'' he said, but his voice rose at least an octave, and he glanced at his cigarettes again.

''These are pictures of when we all went up to the cabin for Christmas a couple of years ago. I assume this is you, although, from this angle, it's a bit difficult to tell.'' Tucker flashed him a picture of his penis. ''What do you think?''

Sean blanched, went to the counter and lit up a cigarette.

''I don't remember you being a smoker,'' Tucker said.

''I wasn't,'' Sean replied.

''What's changed?''

''Everything.''

''You're going to give yourself lung cancer.''

''The sooner the better.''

Tucker dropped his gaze to the pictures. ''You know, I knew my wife was messing around on me, but I never would've guessed she was doing it with you.''

Sean blew out a stream of smoke, looking awkward and self-conscious. ''Yeah, well, I told her taking those pictures was a stupid idea. But you know how she was. She had to have things her way, and she liked living on the edge. I think she wanted to hold them over my head. Or maybe she wanted some sort of proof for you.''

"For me?"

A scowl wrinkled his eyebrows as he regarded his cigarette. "She hated it that she couldn't rattle your cage, hated that you loved Landon more than her. I think what she did was to try and get under your skin. She wanted to bring you down to her level. Like the rest of us, she got damn tired of being inferior to you."

Sean's candor surprised Tucker. He hadn't cared about winning any popularity contests. He'd been too engrossed in his work to spend much time cultivating relationships beyond his immediate family. But he'd always considered Sean and the other guys in the neighborhood his friends. If they'd felt inferior, he hadn't realized it. "You want to explain that?"

"You were the guy with everything, Randy—the nicest house, the most beautiful wife, the fastest car, season tickets to the Suns. You worked out and ate healthy, which made the rest of us look bad by comparison. We couldn't even call you stingy. If any of our kids were doing any fund-raising, we'd send them over to your place, and you'd order up a whole bunch of Girl Scout cookies or whatever it was, as if fifty bucks meant about as much to you as three." Sean took a long drag on his cigarette. "Sometimes lesser mortals get jealous of that crap. It's not complicated."

"I ordered too many Girl Scout cookies? That's why you felt it was okay to screw my wife?" Tucker asked.

Sean swiped at his shiny forehead. "I knew it wasn't okay, Randy. I regret it to this day, if you want the truth. If not for that…oh, well." He waved a hand through the air as if he could erase his words. "Anyway, there was a time when I fancied myself in love with Andrea. She was so beautiful…" He sighed. "I even told her once that I loved her."

"Did she love you back?" Tucker asked.

Sean emitted a self-deprecating laugh. "Are you kidding? She scoffed at me, wanted to know how I thought I could compete with you. She said she'd never love anyone but you."

"Lucky me," Tucker said.

Sean studied him for a moment. "Yeah, lucky you."

Moving to the counter, Tucker spread the pictures out in front of Sean. "So why didn't you destroy these?"

"I didn't know what she'd done with them. I had no idea where to even look."

"And it never crossed your mind to come clean, to tell the truth?"

"Why would it? It wouldn't have helped you. The police were insisting you killed her in a jealous rage. What I had to say would only have put another nail in your coffin."

"Except I didn't kill her, in a jealous rage or otherwise," Tucker said.

"I know."

That surprised Tucker. He waited, hoping Sean would elaborate, but he didn't.

"How do you know?" he pressed.

"I just believe you, okay? That's all. I believe you." Sean would no longer meet his eyes. He busied himself looking for an ashtray and settled for a bowl of dried oatmeal that had been left on the kitchen counter for days if not weeks.

"You know something about Andrea's murder," Tucker said.

"That's bullshit." Sean's agitation grew. "What would I know?"

"Did you see anything that night? Hear anything?"

"I already told the police I got home from work late."

"You never used to get home from work late. At five o'clock every night, you called it quits. You inherited too much from mommy and daddy to worry about mortgage payments. And you weren't ambitious enough to stay any later."

Sean flicked some more ashes into the oatmeal. "Yeah, well, thanks for the compliment, but that doesn't change anything. That night I wasn't around. But I should have been."

"Why's that?"

"Maybe I would've heard something. Maybe I could've stopped it."

"Maybe you were the one who did it."

Sean shook his head. "Oh, no, you don't. You're not going to pin her murder on me. Why would I hurt Andrea?"

"You tell me. Did she threaten to tell Sydney? Make you jealous with another guy? Wound your ego? What?"

"You've got it all wrong," Sean said, still shaking his head. "I told Sydney myself."

"When?"

He shrugged and stubbed out his cigarette. "I don't know exactly."

"Before or after Andrea's death?"

"Before."

"Is that why your wife left you? Because of the affair?"

"That certainly started the whole thing."

"So where is Sydney these days?"

Sean shoved the bowl of oatmeal and ashes away

from him. "She took the girls and the dog, and they live in a rental house in Gilbert."

"Why the divorce?" Tucker asked, scooping up the pictures. Sean's eyes followed his hands, as though he longed to wrestle the pictures away and destroy them, but he made no move. "What happened between you?"

His old neighbor didn't answer. He stared out the window, into the backyard. "Do you remember when we were planning to put in a pool, one like yours and Andrea's?" he asked. "The four of us drew up all kinds of plans, one with a Jacuzzi, one with a waterfall, one with natural landscaping. Sydney and the girls were so excited about that damn pool...."

"What happened between you and Sydney?" Tucker asked again, refusing to be sidetracked.

Sean met his gaze, looking disillusioned and miserable. "I should have put in the pool," he said.

CHAPTER NINETEEN

TUCKER SUSPECTED Sean hadn't been completely truthful with him. He knew more about Andrea's death than he was willing to say. Too much had changed in his life starting at exactly that point, and none of it for the good. Yet Tucker couldn't believe Sean had actually killed her. There was no violence in him, even now. Surely Tucker would have seen some glimpse of capability or culpability—something. So what was the real story? And how did Tucker get to it? He wasn't a cop; he wasn't a private investigator. He was just a real estate investor who'd been sent to prison for a crime he didn't commit. Was he crazy to think he could unravel this thing on his own?

Probably. He yawned and rubbed his palm across the stubble on his chin as he signaled and moved into the fast lane of Eastbound 60. No, not probably—absolutely. He was in over his head. His name and face had been gracing the front page of every newspaper in the area for over a week. Sooner or later, someone was going to recognize him and turn him in, which meant he had only so much time to figure out who'd killed Andrea two years ago—and why.

But what did he have to go on so far? Except for proof of another of Andrea's affairs, he had nothing more than he'd had two years ago—a dead wife but no trace of a body and tons of circumstantial evidence stacked up against him. Just like before, he had only unsatisfactory answers in response to key questions. For example, everyone wanted to know why he'd waited so long to call the police when Andrea went missing. But Tucker had simply assumed she'd left on another partying binge. He hadn't wanted to find her badly enough to look for her, let alone call the police. He'd assumed she'd come home eventually. She always did. And their problems would be waiting for them.

Tucker checked his speed, realized he was doing seventy and eased off the gas. During the days following her disappearance, he was so preoccupied with work and taking care of Landon that he'd somehow missed the blood spatter in the garage. But how many people routinely examined their garages for blood? He couldn't understand why no one would credit him with having the good sense to clean up the mess if he was going to murder someone. Why would he leave blood on the floor of his own garage for the police to discover almost a week later?

The questions and inconsistencies in his case went around and around in his head. Where were the answers? He was exhausted and desperate and no closer to the truth, despite the unsettling pictures of Sean and Andrea.

He was stupid to stick around Florence, hoping to dig up something he'd probably never find. He needed to flee to Mexico, to get out of town. He had some money. He spoke a little Spanish. He could cross the border and rent a cheap motel in Nogales, where no one was likely to ask questions or to bother him. There, he could build a new life with Landon, figure out some way to earn a living. Nogales might not be heaven, but he'd be a whole lot safer there than in the States. And he'd have his son.

Except Landon wasn't the only person who'd come to mean something to him. As much as he'd fought the softening of his heart, he also cared about Gabrielle. Just the thought of her kicked his pulse up a notch. He knew he should get out of her trailer and leave her to enjoy her life. She was so much better off without him. To do anything else was selfish and foolhardy, but he couldn't walk away from her. Not again. She was brave enough to jump into that fight, stubborn enough to follow him into the desert, compassionate enough to risk her own well-being to give him a place to stay, and beautiful enough to fill him with longing. She was more than he'd ever hoped to find in a woman.

He glanced in his rearview mirror to see what was coming from behind, caught his reflection and frowned. If he stayed in Arizona, he'd spend the rest of his life looking over his shoulder, wondering what was going to happen next. But if he ran, he'd be giving up to the cruel fate that had already taken so much. He'd be letting go of the one thing he wanted most....

He wasn't going anywhere, he decided, at least not without Gabrielle. Neither did he plan to spend another night sleeping on the couch.

LANDON TURNED the cookie he'd made for his father a little to the left so that when Tucker finally arrived, it would be presented from its best side.

"I should've let you write the words," he said skeptically.

"Why?" Gabrielle asked. "You did a beautiful job."

"The first two letters are just a blob of frosting.

Looks like it says, 'Come home' instead of 'Welcome home.'"

Gabrielle considered the cookie. Landon was right. It did look like it said 'Come home.' But those words held more significance, anyway. They were both praying for that very thing, that Tucker would come home, and that he'd do it soon. "It won't matter once he eats it," she said.

Allie pulled herself up from the floor using Gabrielle's leg and demanded another taste of frosting. Gabrielle squeezed a dab onto her finger from the decorator bag Landon had just used and slipped it in her baby's mouth. Allie rewarded her by clapping her hands in approval.

"Do you think baking is for sissies?" Landon asked suddenly.

"Of course not," Gabrielle said. "Some of the best chefs in the world are men."

"Really?"

"Sure. Do you like to cook?"

He shrugged. "I like to make cookies."

"Well, that's a little different. I don't know very many kids who *don't* like to make cookies. I think it has something to do with sampling the dough." She grinned and wiped a smudge of frosting from his chin, and he surprised her by not flinching or moving out of her reach. He'd been skittish with her at first, reluctant to let her get too close. But they'd had a good day, overall, and she was making progress with him. They'd baked and swum and played with Allie. They'd even stopped by the drugstore before leaving Chandler and purchased a ball, a bat and a glove. Since Tucker couldn't play with Landon, Gabrielle had stopped at a park on the other side of town and done her best to fill in. She knew she was running a risk that someone from the prison might see her, but no one seemed to notice them.

"You're not so bad," Landon had told her when she managed to catch a fly ball he hit right at her head. He might've been the coach of the Diamondbacks for the way that grudging bit of praise had felt to Gabrielle.

"When do you think he'll be here?" Landon asked, his eyes again flicking toward the clock.

Gabrielle knew "he" was Tucker, of course, even though Landon hadn't mentioned him by name. She'd been stalling him with, "Anytime now" for the past two hours. She'd made the mistake of setting Landon's expectations too high. All that talk about what they were having for dinner had started the "When's he going to be here?" countdown too soon.

"It's like I was telling you before," she answered. "Your father's staying here is a secret. He has to wait until it gets dark so no one'll see him come in, but then he'll be hungry and want the dinner we saved for him."

"And my cookie. He'll want to eat that."

"And your cookie."

The smile that had claimed his lips quickly faded. "It's already kind of dark," he said, sounding worried.

"It won't be completely dark for another half hour or so. Your father's probably just playing it safe. I'd say we can expect him sometime after nine o'clock."

"What if he doesn't come?" Landon said. "Are you going to take me back to the Boyers'?"

Gabrielle extricated herself from Allie and feigned interest in cleaning up the mess they'd made. "Would you like to go back to the Boyers if you can't be with your father?" she asked, hoping she sounded as though that wasn't really a possibility.

He chewed his lip. Gabrielle ducked her head to get a better look at the expression in his eyes, which were shaded by his bangs. "Maybe I could stay here with you," he said somberly. "You know, to help with Allie. I could watch her when you take her swimming and stuff."

Gabrielle felt a tug at her heart. "That would be wonderful," she said, but she fought the warm feeling that made her want to pull him to her. She didn't *want* to love this child, to love yet another part of Tucker. Because of the situation and Tucker's own resistance, she couldn't expect the four of them ever to become a family.

The telephone rang, and Landon looked up at her expectantly. "Maybe that's my dad," he said. "Maybe he's calling to say he's on his way."

"Maybe." She wiped her hands on a dish towel and picked up the phone. "Hello?"

"Finally you answer," David said. "What's going on with you? I've been trying to reach you since last night."

Gabrielle glanced at Landon, feeling guilty and anxious. What she was doing for him and his father felt right when she was by herself, but the minute she heard David's voice, she began to question the wisdom of her actions. She shook her head to let Landon know it wasn't Tucker, watched with a frown as his discouragement edged a little closer, then turned her attention back to David because she had to handle her conversation with him first. "Is there some sort of emergency?" she asked.

"No emergency. I just…I just felt bad about our conversation last night and wanted to make sure everything's okay."

"It's fine."

"Really? When I couldn't raise anyone at the trailer for so long, I finally phoned the prison. They said you'd called in sick. I was so worried I was just getting ready to drive down there."

"Oh, there's no reason to do that," she said. Had she given away how desperately she didn't want him to come by speaking too fast? She took a deep breath, trying to rein in her galloping pulse. "I felt a little nauseous this morning, and thought I might be getting the flu. But it went away after a few hours."

"And then you left the house?"

"Yeah, I took Allie swimming."

"Where'd you go swimming?"

"In Chandler."

"Chandler! You drove halfway here and didn't come to see me?"

Damn. She'd been so thrown by David calling the prison, she'd said the first thing that came into her head. Why couldn't she have told him she went grocery shopping or something? "You're so behind with your work, I thought we'd better not interrupt," she said lamely.

A pause. "I put in a lot of hours this weekend. I'm actually doing better."

"That's good."

"I thought maybe you were with your mother."

"I'm going over there tomorrow to meet Lindy."

"You want me to come down and go with you? I'd like to meet everyone."

Gabrielle's eyes strayed to Landon. She had no idea how long Tucker planned to leave him with her, but now was not a good time for David to visit. She opened her mouth to say something to discourage him, but then she heard the back door open and Landon went charging down the hall, crying, "Dad!"

"Is someone there?" David asked.

Gabrielle bit her lip. She had the same impulse as Landon, to throw herself in Tucker's arms, but she waved them both to silence the moment they appeared in the kitchen. "It's just the television," she said, feeling lower than dirt for lying to him again. They'd always been honest with each other, supportive. No wonder he thought something was up. She was breaking every rule they'd ever established between them. But she couldn't think of any other way to handle the situation.

"Oh." Another pause. "So you're okay?"

"Yeah, I'm great."

"Good. Listen, I'm sorry we've been having such a rough time lately. Whatever happened in the desert, at that egg ranch, it doesn't matter now. It's in the past. I know what you went through was pretty hard, and no one would be thinking straight after something like that."

He was letting her off so easy. His kindness turned Gabrielle's guilt into a physical cramp. "Thanks for understanding," she said.

"Do you want me to come down tomorrow?"

"I don't think so. It's going to be awkward enough. I'll introduce you next time."

She hated the pause that met her rejection. "Okay," he said at last.

"Thanks for calling."

"Yeah, sure."

Gabrielle closed her eyes as she hung up the phone. What was wrong with her? She was rejecting the father of her child in favor of an escaped convict with a chip on his shoulder the size of Montana, an escaped convict who probably felt very little for her in return.

I just called to tell you I'm thinking of you....

It doesn't mean anything, she told herself.

"Who was that?" Tucker asked.

"David."

He narrowed his eyes. "I don't like that guy."

Gabrielle sank onto the couch and pulled Allie into her lap. "He's not too thrilled with you, either."

She expected him to pursue the subject, but he only shrugged. "Did you and Landon do okay together?" he asked. His eyes drifted down her body, then climbed back up, and the resulting hot flash made her wonder if the swamp cooler had broken down. Tucker was different tonight. Instead of scowling all the time and avoiding her gaze, he was watching her as if…as if he couldn't take his eyes off her. She thought of his earlier phone call. *I just called to tell you I'm thinking of you....*

"Is it hot in here to you?" she asked.

He grinned, but then Landon stole his attention with the presentation of his cookie. "See what we have for you? It's cool, isn't it, Dad?"

"It looks great."

Landon beamed at Gabrielle. "We made it together. We got pizza, too."

Tucker squeezed his son's shoulder and ate some of the cookie, making a big deal over how good it was. But his gaze eventually returned to Gabrielle. "Sounds like you two did pretty well today."

If he only knew how badly they'd started off, Gabrielle thought, but she nodded as though it had been easy.

"You were talking on the phone about something being awkward," he went on. "What?"

"Awkward? Oh, I'm going to meet my sister for the first time tomorrow."

He hooked a thumb in one pocket. "What's that all about?"

She told him about her mother, the day-care center where she was abandoned and the family who'd raised her. She also mentioned her plans to have dinner with her mother, sister and brother tomorrow night.

"I wondered what your childhood was like," Tucker said. "You once mentioned something about the family you grew up with as though you didn't quite belong to them."

He remembered? He certainly hadn't acted as though he was paying any particular attention when they were marching through the desert.

"What does it mean to be abandoned?" Landon asked apprehensively.

Gabrielle knew that with what he'd experienced, he could identify with her pain more than most children and spoke quickly to spare him any concern. "You've been through something very much like what happened to me, but it's over and you don't have to worry about it anymore," Gabrielle said. "It won't happen again."

"Because I can always stay here, right?" he said.

Hearing this, Tucker raised an eyebrow at her, but Gabrielle didn't have it in her to deny Landon. "You can always stay here," she repeated, and she meant every word.

For the first time since she'd met him, Tucker dropped the prickly facade that hid the man he really was. A vulnerable expression flitted across his face. He masked it immediately, but she'd seen enough to make her want to hold him close. Although he tried to hide it, he had a soft heart beneath his tough exterior. The way he treated Landon proved it; the way he was staring at her right now seemed to prove it, too. He wanted something. If she was reading him correctly, he wanted *her*.

"Do we get to go with you and meet your sister?" Landon asked, oblivious to the emotion of the moment.

"Are you still going to be here?" she asked. She held her breath as she looked to Tucker for the answer.

He crossed one leg over the other and leaned against the counter. "Do you want us to stay, Gabby?"

She wasn't sure how to answer. She wanted him to stay for the rest of his life. But she didn't want him caught and dragged back to prison, and she knew her trailer wasn't the best place to hide. She had both Hansen and David to consider. Even if they weren't such a serious concern, there were too many corrections officers living in her trailer park; she couldn't expect Tucker's presence to go unnoticed for long. "I don't want anything to happen to you," she said.

"That's not what I asked."

Suddenly feeling self-conscious, she gave Allie her Tickle Me Elmo doll and got up to warm Tucker's pizza. She had to pass him to get to the food in the refrigerator, and then the plates in the cupboard and finally the microwave, but he stayed right where he was, leaning against the cupboard with his hands in his pockets. She could feel the heat radiating from his body as she reached around him, could smell the subtle scent of soap that clung to his skin and remembered curling up with him in the cave that first night and feeling safe in spite of everything....

Clearing her throat, she tried to distract herself. "We

ordered pepperoni and mushroom. Landon said you'd like that kind. We can add a few onions or green peppers, if you want. We weren't really sure how hungry you'd be. We thought maybe you'd eat somewhere else before coming home. I mean coming here,'' she amended.

"I'm hungry," he said simply.

"Great." She piled four slices on a plate and put them in the microwave as Allie crawled into the kitchen. Rocking back, her daughter plopped on her diapered behind and considered the three people in her kitchen. Gabrielle fully expected her to crawl over and demand to be held, or to insist on more of Landon's attention—she already worshiped him—but she surprised Gabrielle by reaching for Tucker.

The pizza was already in the microwave, so Gabrielle moved to pick her up, assuming Tucker wouldn't want to be bothered with a baby. But he gently pushed her aside and lifted Allie into his arms.

"What did you do today?" Gabrielle asked him as Allie kicked her feet and patted his face in obvious pleasure.

He playfully bit the chubby fingers she kept trying to stick in his mouth, and she laughed and repeated the game. He had to pull her hands away to be able to speak. "I tried to get hold of my brother, but he wouldn't accept my call."

"Why not?"

"Long story."

"And?"

"And I visited an old—" he hesitated and shot a glance at Landon "—neighbor."

"Who?" Landon asked.

"Do you remember the Marshalls?"

"Yeah."

"I saw Sean today."

Landon's expression turned into a glower. "Mrs. Marshall brought the girls to visit me at the Boyers' once."

"Really?" Tucker sat at the table with Allie as Gabrielle took his plate from the microwave. "Wasn't it good to see the girls again?"

"No." He scuffed one toe against the other.

"Why not?" Tucker asked.

"Because Mrs. Marshall kept saying things about Mom that I didn't want to hear."

Tucker froze, his first bite of pizza halfway to his mouth. "Like what?"

"Like she's sorry for me and all that, but some people get exactly what they deserve."

CHAPTER TWENTY

EXACTLY WHAT *they deserve*. Sydney's words cycled through Tucker's mind as he sat on the couch, the television droning in the background. Landon was sleeping in the spare room. Gabrielle was putting her daughter to bed. And he was trying to imagine why Sydney would've said what she did. He kept telling himself it meant nothing, that he shouldn't get his hopes up, but he couldn't imagine anyone with any compassion saying such a thing to a kid who'd just lost his mother. Sydney had always treated Landon like family. What had she been thinking?

Tucker had tried calling Sean, but he wasn't home. If he had to live in that depressing house, in the echo of a past marriage, he wouldn't stick around much, either, Tucker reflected. But he hoped Sean would return home soon. He wanted to ask exactly where Sydney was and how he could get hold of her. Maybe she knew something Sean didn't. Or maybe she knew the same thing he knew and would be more willing to talk.

Gabrielle came in, looking beautiful but tired with wisps of hair falling out of her ponytail. She was wearing a simple white top that contrasted nicely with her lightly tanned skin, and a pair of loose-fitting Abercrombie shorts that, when she bent over to pick up a toy Allie had tossed on the ground, allowed him a glimpse of her bikini underwear. The pink color matched the fingernail polish on her fingers and toes, but she wasn't wearing any other makeup, or none that Tucker could see. She looked sexy as hell—very natural and earthy, as she had when they were in the desert eating rabbit from their makeshift spit. He imagined her beneath him, wrapping her legs around his waist as she pulled him inside her....

He was staring at her and could hardly swallow, let alone tear his gaze away. He wanted her. He wanted her right now.

She gave him a self-conscious smile that told him she sensed his interest. "Well, I guess the kids are down for the night." She toyed with a pair of glass poodles on a side table as though she didn't know what to say next, and came up with, "Can I get you a glass of wine or something?"

"No."

"Would you like to watch a movie before bed?"

"No."

She clasped her hands together. "Are you ready for me to make up your bed on the couch, then?"

"No."

Her brows arched in surprise. "That doesn't leave many options—"

"Except one," he broke in. "Come here."

Her eyes widened slightly and her chest expanded as she took a deep breath. He had the impression that she wasn't sure whether to trust the change in him, and he couldn't blame her. He knew he was probably making a mistake. He had no way of predicting his future, but their chances of being together were terrible. Loving her would only give him something else to lose, something else to crave when he had to move on. But he already craved her. She was in his blood. He might escape the police, but he'd never escape her.

"What are you suggesting?" She inched toward him.

Standing, he reached out with one hand. "Let's go to bed."

She hesitated for only a moment before stepping into the circle of his arms. Then she pressed her body fully against him and lifted her face to his, watching him from beneath her thick lashes. "Are you sure?" she breathed.

"Only of this," he said, and groaned as he let go of everything that had held him back. Crushing her to him, he lowered his mouth to hers.

GABRIELLE CLOSED her eyes as Tucker's lips moved over hers, tasting her, savoring her, exciting her. She opened her mouth to his tongue and felt a thrill go through her as he slid it into her mouth. Letting her hands delve into his hair, she weaved her fingers through the short, silky locks, reveling in the wonderful feeling of being completely caught up in the man she loved. She was holding Tucker, kissing him with absolute abandon, and it felt...perfect. She moaned to let him know she liked what he was doing.

His good hand traveled slowly up her spine, strong and sure as his fingers massaged her tired muscles. Her breasts tingled, wanting his attention.

"I've never craved a woman like I crave you," he murmured into her mouth. Then his lips moved along her jaw, beneath her earlobe, and down her neck. She shivered against him as his fingers slipped beneath her shirt and began to caress the sensitive skin of her midriff.

"I'm in love with you, Tucker," she said. Her guard was completely down. She couldn't have held those words back for anything.

He grew still, except for his heart, which was beating so rapidly she could feel it, too. "You can't love me, Gabrielle," he said. "I have nothing to give you. After tonight, you have to find someone else, someone who can be everything you deserve."

Gabrielle didn't know what to say. There would never be anyone else. She knew that. But she knew how important it was for him to believe he wasn't doing anything that would irreparably change her life. He had to feel as though he could walk away and never look back, as though his leaving wasn't going to hurt her. So she said nothing. Taking his hand, she guided it to her breasts, feeling her whole body tighten when his fingers lightly grazed her nipple.

"You feel so good," he muttered, his voice throaty, his eyes half-lidded.

"Are you still having second thoughts?" she asked, sliding her hands beneath his T-shirt to feel the smooth skin of his stomach and chest.

He sighed and pressed his forehead to hers, allowing her to touch him while his fingers continued to tease her. "No. I'm not that unselfish."

She laughed. "At your age, two years is a long time to go without sex."

"After this, the last two years aren't going to be half as difficult as the next two," he said. "But I'm going to love you anyway."

"Let's go to my room where we can lock the door, then."

He cupped the fullness of her breast. "Tell me you

have birth control,'' he said. ''I don't want to leave any surprises behind.''

''I'm on the Pill, remember?''

''I got the impression you haven't been very diligent about taking them.''

''I have since I met you.''

He gave her a cocky grin, glanced toward the kitchen to make sure they were still alone, and slid his hand down her shorts.

His fingers worked their way inside the leg of her panties, and Gabrielle gasped. ''I see you haven't forgotten anything,'' she said, her nerves humming.

He nuzzled her neck as his fingers found the most sensitive part of her. ''That's the problem, I have a long memory.''

Gabrielle closed her eyes and let her head fall back, no longer able to think clearly for the pleasure coursing through her. ''We might not have forever, Tucker. But we have tonight.''

''Then we'd better make the most of it,'' he said and, just as he brought her to the brink of climax, stopped long enough to pull her down the hall.

''TELL ME WHAT HAPPENED the day your wife died,'' Gabrielle said. She was resting comfortably in the crook of Tucker's arm, still damp with sweat from making love.

He lightly caressed her bare back. ''Why do you want to talk about that?''

''Because I don't want the mystery of it standing between us. I want to know what you know. Maybe I can see something you've missed.''

''Me *and* my wonderful defense team?'' he asked, mixing sarcasm with skepticism.

"At least I'll be able to start coming up with my own theories as to what really happened."

He kissed her forehead. "You're grasping at straws."

"Humor me."

Using the hand that was in a cast, he propped up his pillow and began to play with a lock of her hair. "We had an argument, which wasn't in the least unusual."

"Did your arguments ever get violent?"

"Not really. She tried to hit me a few times. I held her arms but never struck her."

"What was your argument about the day she died?"

He released her hair in favor of her breast. "Are you *sure* you want to go into this? Isn't there something more pleasant we could be doing?"

She covered his hand with her own, delighting in the intimacy of having nothing to hide from him. "I want to know. I want to feel like an insider in your life, okay? Come on. What was the fight about?"

He gave up trying to distract her and kissed her fingers instead. "Peggy."

"Who's Peggy?"

"She was my nineteen-year-old secretary at the real-estate office. Andrea thought I was sleeping with her."

"Were you?" Gabrielle said, pulling her hand away.

"Relax." He nipped softly at her shoulder. "I wasn't sleeping with anyone, not even Andrea most of the time."

Gabrielle softened, but only marginally. "Then why was she accusing you?"

"I think she wanted me to be having an affair."

"What? No wife wants her husband to—"

"Andrea did," Tucker said. "Then she could blame

me for our marriage falling apart and have a good excuse for her own actions.''

Gabrielle considered this as she stroked the light dusting of hair on his chest. She couldn't get enough of touching him. ''Hansen once told me you hired a private detective who caught her cheating on you.''

He chuckled but there was no humor in it. ''I did, but that wasn't all she was doing. She was taking drugs, staying out all night.''

Gabrielle couldn't imagine why any woman would turn to drugs and having affairs if she was married to a man like Tucker. She herself had never felt more satisfied. When she was with him, the terrible feeling of displacement she'd known since she was a child disappeared. ''What kind of drugs?''

''Mostly Ecstasy, I think. Who knows?''

''Who was she sleeping with?''

''Not a regular boyfriend or anything. Just some guys from the gym where she worked out, people she partied with. I knew I couldn't convince her to go into rehab unless I could get her to admit she had a problem. So I hired a private investigator to help me get the facts. I thought if she was faced with proof, she'd have to quit with all the denials.''

On impulse, Gabrielle pressed her lips to his warm neck, hating the pain and anger he must have experienced. ''I'm sorry.''

''By then it didn't hurt me. I just wanted to get her straightened out for Landon's sake.''

''But that's why you were always arguing, because of the drugs and the other men? Is that what you argued about the day she died?''

He gazed beyond her, out of the window. The moonlight drifting through the cracks in the blinds illumi-

nated his stark profile. As reserved and unapproachable
as he could sometimes be, Gabrielle had to admit she
found him beautiful. Irresistible.

"That day she was supposed to meet me at home
after work so I could take her to a psychologist,"
Tucker said. "I thought maybe counseling would help
our marriage, help her overcome her drug habit. But
when I got home, she wasn't there."

"Where was she?"

"At the gym, working out. So that's where I went."

"What did you do when you found her?"

"I lost my temper and demanded she come home
with me. It was a stupid move, because the whole aerobics class heard me, and they all testified against me
later. But I was so tired of how conscious she'd become
of her body and her almost insatiable desire for male
attention. It all seemed so shallow and pointless when
she had a little boy who needed her to be a real mom."

Gabrielle pulled the sheet over them both as the
swamp cooler kicked on, pumping a cool breeze
through the vent in her room. "Did she go home with
you?" she asked, snuggling close again. She loved
Tucker's body, loved being able to entwine her legs
with his.

"At my insistence, but she was furious that I'd
caused a scene. When we got home, she stormed inside, changed her clothes and said she was going out
again. It was almost time for me to pick up Landon
from his friend Matt's house. He'd stayed at school late
to rehearse his class play, and Matt's mother had taken
him home because I thought Andrea and I were going
to be at the counselor's. Landon and Matt were supposed to perform the play that night. I told Andrea she
needed to go with us, and she responded by telling me

I was dad enough to handle the job. She had no interest in watching a bunch of fidgeting kids forget their lines.''

"But one of those kids belonged to her!" Gabrielle said in surprise.

He sighed. "She wasn't thinking straight. Toward the end, she never was. She'd say and do anything she could to hurt me. She even used Landon."

"Why?"

"I don't know. My neighbor said it was because I cared more about Landon than I did about her."

"So did she go to the play?"

"No. I followed her out to the garage, where we argued some more. Then I had to leave to pick up Landon. I told her if she cared about her son, she'd be home when we got back. But when we returned, her car was gone. I assumed she'd gone out with her friends." He leaned on his elbow to look down at her. "I never saw her again."

Gabrielle held his whisker-roughened jaw. "So how did they convict you?" she asked.

He rolled onto his back and stared at the ceiling. "God, you want to hear about that, too?"

"Why not?"

"Because it was a damn circus act."

"Why?"

He scowled. "The prosecution brought tons of witnesses to testify about our rocky relationship—people from the aerobics class, neighbors who overheard our arguments, teachers who knew we were having a tough time. Then they brought in people who'd seen me fight at my brother's karate school—some I'd beaten in various kickboxing matches—who testified to the damage I was capable of causing with no weapon but my hands and feet. The D.A. made a big deal out of the fact that I'd hired a private investigator and knew about Andrea's extramarital affairs and—"

"And so you became the violent, jealous husband. You had a motive and the weapon."

"It didn't help that only a few months earlier we'd purchased big life-insurance policies."

"Why'd you do that?"

"My older brother had just hired on with a financial planning firm. To support him, we let him do a financial plan for us, and it called for bigger policies."

"No good deed goes unpunished."

"Exactly. Even something as innocuous as that came back to bite me."

Suddenly, an idea occurred to Gabrielle, and she sat up. "Wait, did anyone hear your argument in the garage the day Andrea died?"

"Two different neighbors," Tucker told her, "one across the street, and one who was just getting out of his car two doors down."

"Good!"

"Good?"

"Yeah, you wouldn't have had an opportunity to kill Andrea and dispose of her body between the time the neighbors heard you arguing and the time you returned with Landon, right?"

"Wrong. When I got to Matt's house, his mother told me his father had taken them out for pizza and had just called to say they were running late. She asked me in, but I was still angry with Andrea. I went for a drive instead, trying to cool down and decide what I should do about her."

"You were all alone?"

"For close to an hour. I gave Matt's mother my cell

phone number, but she didn't call for almost forty minutes. Landon and Matt were late for the play, and plenty of people remembered that, too.''

The excitement Gabrielle had felt died quickly. ''That gave you the motive, the weapon *and* the opportunity.''

''Now you're thinking like the D.A.''

''So…do you have any idea what might've happened to Andrea? Know anyone else who might've been just as frustrated as you were?''

Tucker scratched his chest. His body was still tense enough to let Gabrielle know he didn't like pursuing this subject, but she'd been honest with him in her desire to know. It was one thing to have blind faith in his innocence. It was another to hear his version of the events.

''They found her car in Saguaro Lake three days after she disappeared. Because it was February and the weather was still cold, there hadn't been a lot of activity out there.''

''There wasn't any fiber evidence or anything inside it?''

His laugh was more sincere this time. ''You've been watching too many of those true crime shows.''

''They always find fiber evidence.''

''If there was any evidence that pointed to someone besides me, the police covered it up.''

''What about your defense team? Weren't your lawyers able to come up with anything?''

''There was no body. My attorney kept saying they couldn't convict me without a body. Without a body, they couldn't even prove there'd been a murder.'' He rubbed a hand over his face. ''So much for that theory.''

Gabrielle bit her lip. "So where *is* the body?"

"That's the million-dollar question."

"Couldn't your private detective tell you anything?"

"I'd fired him a couple of months before Christmas. I had plenty of proof to convince Andrea that she couldn't lie to me anymore, and I didn't feel I needed him. She wasn't killed until February."

"She could've killed herself. Did they drag the lake?"

"The only evidence in the car was the heavy rock on the gas pedal. Someone ditched it after the fact."

"Well, her murderer could've been one of the men she was seeing, right?"

"The two men I knew she'd been with had alibis, and my lawyer really didn't want to focus on the extramarital affairs. She said it would only make me look more guilty."

It was getting late, but Gabrielle didn't want to sleep. She wanted to solve this so their problems could disappear. Covering a yawn, she said, "Wasn't there anyone else who looked even a *little* suspicious?"

"Not until recently."

"What does that mean?"

"Remember that neighbor I mentioned?"

She nodded.

"I just found out he and Andrea had an affair a couple of months before she died."

Gabrielle's fatigue instantly fell away. She rose onto one elbow. "Where was he during the time she was supposedly murdered?"

"He claims he was at work."

"Can he prove it?"

"That's what I need to find out."

"Wouldn't the police have checked?"

"They don't investigate everyone the victim knew. In a case such as ours, the husband's usually the killer, and the police had a ton of circumstantial evidence pointing to me. I'm sure they figured there wasn't any need to waste man-hours searching for other suspects. Nothing that raised any questions ever came to light. Why muddy the waters? They believed they already had their perpetrator, so they turned me over to the D.A., who worked her ass off to get me convicted. Case closed. The police and the district attorney looked good to the media, the citizens of Phoenix could sleep better at night, and I went to jail."

Gabrielle considered the scenario. What had happened to Tucker seemed grossly unfair, yet she could see how easily the police could be persuaded that they already had their man. "But it *wasn't* you. Do you think this neighbor might have done it? Does he seem like a man who's capable of something like that? Do you have any idea where he might have hidden Andrea's body?"

Tucker's lengthy pause made Gabrielle wonder about his thoughts. "Which question do you want me to answer?"

She slugged him playfully. "All of them."

"Sean doesn't strike me as the type, so don't get your hopes up."

"But where would—"

He silenced her with a kiss.

"What—"

"Shh," he said, kissing her once, twice, three more times.

She stubbornly tried to talk again, but he only used the parting of her lips to deepen his last kiss.

"Wait," she muttered. "I'm not satisfied yet."

He pulled his head back and grinned at her. "Neither am I. And it's my turn."

A NOISE WOKE Tucker out of the deepest sleep he'd known since his escape. Still filled with the lazy contentment of having made love to Gabrielle several times, his mind and body rebelled at the prospect of returning to complete awareness. But warning bells were ringing in his head, telling him he had to focus. Why, he didn't know, until he lay blinking at the ceiling and realized the noise that had finally penetrated his sleep was a series of footsteps.

Someone was moving around in the trailer.

Angling his head toward the door, he tensed to listen. Was it Landon? It certainly couldn't be Allie walking down the hall.

He slipped his arm out from beneath Gabrielle and eased out of bed. He was just reaching for his jeans when someone tried to open the door. Fortunately, he'd locked it to keep Landon from walking in on them. But the rattle was enough to wake Gabrielle.

"Where are you going?" she mumbled, blinking sleepily at him. "It can't be morning yet."

Another man's voice intruded before he could answer. "Gabby?"

Gabrielle sat bolt upright, her hair tumbling wildly around her face. "Oh no, it's David," she whispered, turning panic-filled eyes on Tucker.

"Tell him you've got company," he told her.

"I can't tell him that!" she said, scrambling out of bed.

"Why not? You're divorced." He thrust one leg into his pants, then the other. "You have the right to see other men."

"But he wouldn't—" She raked her fingers through her hair, looking miserable. "He'd be hurt."

The door handle jiggled again. "Gabrielle? What's going on? There's a little boy sleeping in my room."

Tucker grimaced. "*His* room?"

Gabrielle was too busy pulling on a robe to bother responding to his comment. "I'm coming, David. Just a minute," she said.

Then Landon's voice rose from behind the door. "Who are you? Where's my daddy? Is he gone? Did you take him away?"

Gabrielle cast Tucker another worried glance as he quickly buttoned his jeans. "Landon, he's still here, baby," she said, tightening her robe. "Don't you worry about anything, okay? I told you that you don't have to worry."

"Okay." The relief evident in his son's voice made Tucker feel slightly better, until he heard small feet pattering down the hall toward the kitchen. Tucker didn't have to see what was happening to know Landon was going to the couch in search of him.

"Shit," he muttered, heading for the door. His flight or fight instinct was kicking in pretty heavily, but he wouldn't run without Landon, and he certainly didn't want to hurt David. He knew Gabrielle cared about her ex a great deal; he wanted to leave what was said up to her, if possible.

"Gabby? Tell me this kid isn't who I think it is," David persisted, his voice now leery.

Tucker reached the door at the same time as Gabrielle and paused. "What are you going to do?" he asked softly.

She stopped him from turning the knob. "It'll be all right. David's always been a good friend to me. He's guessed some of the truth already. I'm going to tell him the rest and ask him to trust that I know what I'm doing.''

''That's taking a hell of a chance,'' Tucker said.

''You don't know David. He's more generous and kind than most people. He won't let me down.''

''Gabby! Open the door!''

Tucker frowned irritably. ''What the hell is he doing, showing up in the middle of the night, anyway?''

''He's been worried about me.''

''I'll bet,'' Tucker said, but he moved aside so she could unlock the door.

By the time he was facing David, Landon was running toward them, complaining that his father *was* gone. When he spotted Tucker, he quickly dashed a hand across his face to wipe away tears. ''There you are,'' he said, a sulky note in his voice.

Tucker pulled his son against him and ignored David's hostile glare. For Gabrielle's sake, he really didn't want this to erupt into an ugly scene. What they'd shared last night had been too good to let end this way.

''What are *you* doing here?'' David said to him. ''Don't you know what this could do to Gabby's life?''

Gabrielle quickly interceded. ''David, let me explain.''

Her ex whirled to face her. ''How could you, Gabby? I've given you the benefit of every doubt, taken this whole thing on faith, and now I find this son of a—''

''David, be careful what you say. Tucker's son is here,'' Gabrielle interrupted.

''His son! That child's been kidnapped!''

''He belongs with his father,'' she said.

''Are you crazy? This guy's been convicted of—''

He gestured at Landon, who was watching him with wide eyes, then at Tucker, who let him know with a glance that he might have himself on a leash, but it wasn't a very long one.

"Like hell he belongs with his father," David finished. "And what do you think you're doing, sheltering them? Are you trying to flush your life down the toilet? What about Allie, for God's sake?"

Tucker's jaw tensed. He'd been patient with David's intrusion so far, but he felt too protective of Gabrielle to allow David to rail at her, too protective of Landon to allow him to overhear the things David had to say. "Watch it," he warned.

Gabrielle laid a placating hand on Tucker's arm. "He doesn't understand," she said.

"I know," he responded, "but I'm not going to let him—"

"Why don't you put Landon back to bed and give us a few minutes, okay?" Gabrielle murmured.

Tucker glared at David. He was reluctant to go anywhere, to back down from the confrontation at this point, but the pleading in Gabrielle's eyes finally penetrated his anger. Taking Landon with him, he left the two of them alone. But their voices came to him in harsh whispers, carrying all the way from the living room and making it impossible for him to relax.

"Dad, who is that guy?" Landon asked, climbing back into bed.

Tucker lay down beside him. "No one to worry about."

"What's he doing here?"

"He's Allie's father. He probably just came for a visit."

"Why's he so mad?"

"Like everyone else, he thinks I hurt your mother. He's afraid I might hurt Gabby."

"But you didn't hurt Mom! I know that. I know you'd never hurt anyone."

Tucker managed a smile despite the heated argument taking place outside the room. "I love you, buddy. No matter what happens, always remember that, okay?"

"Okay."

Landon rested his head on Tucker's shoulder for another few minutes, then slid away. "You can go out and talk to them now, if you want," he said. "I'm okay."

Tucker shook his head in surprise and ruffled his son's hair. "You're growing up fast, you know that?"

Landon's smile was so wide Tucker could make it out even in the dark. "Yeah, and when I do, I'm going to be just like you."

Just like him. Landon had unwittingly given him yet another reason to hold on to his temper. Taking a calming breath, Tucker kissed his son's forehead, returned to Gabrielle's room for his shirt and pulled it on over his head. As he headed toward the living room, he wasn't surprised to hear Allie's coos mingling with the voices of her parents.

"…I can't help it, David. I'm in love with him," Gabrielle was saying. "I know you don't want to hear that, but it's the truth. I've always been honest with you before. I have to be honest with you now."

"Honest? You're saying you were honest with me when you told me he was a stranger? When you let me give him a ride?"

"What else could I do?"

"Are you kidding?"

"David—"

"He shouldn't be here, Gabby. Why would you want to involve yourself with a man like Randall Tucker?"

"I didn't choose to get involved with him. I sort of...I don't know, I got attached by accident, I guess. But I'm involved now, and there's no going back."

"That's not true. It's not too late."

"I believe in him. I know he didn't kill his wife. He could never hurt anyone who—"

"From what Hansen says, he's hurt lots of people."

"You can't listen to Hansen. He twists everything."

"*He* twists everything? He's not the one who told me he didn't know Tucker."

"Oh, come on, David—"

"No, *you* come on. Your feelings have made you blind. And now you're risking your future. God, what's it going to take to get you to understand what's happening here? He's using you, Gabby. He's using you for a quick piece of ass and a roof over his head. He's—"

"What?" Tucker interrupted, unable to bite his tongue any longer. "What other vile things could I be doing?"

Gabrielle and David fell silent the moment he entered the room, but Allie squealed and demanded David put her down so she could make her way over to him.

"I don't know." David was breathing hard from his anger. "Why don't you tell me?"

"You seem pretty sure of what you're saying," Tucker said. "Sounds like you have me all figured out." He scooped the insistent Allie into his arms so she'd quit squealing for his attention, but the look on David's face the moment he touched her caused most of Tucker's anger to dissipate. More than anything else, more than his concern for Gabrielle's future, what David felt was jealousy. It was as simple as that. He felt as though Tucker had stolen his wife and possibly his daughter.

With two quick strides, Tucker handed Allie back to him. "I'm not here to hurt anyone," he said evenly.

"Tell him he has to go, Gabby," David said.

Gabrielle shook her head. "David—"

"It's him or me," he insisted.

"No!" Gabrielle waved for Tucker to remain right where he was. "Don't make me choose," she pleaded with David.

"I've been patient long enough," David said. "He leaves or I do. And if I go, this time it'll be for good. I'll pick up Allie every weekend but I'll have nothing to do with you."

"Don't say that! After everything we've been through... David, we're too close for that."

"Close? In what way? You threw away our marriage. And I don't want to be friends, dammit! You know that."

Silence.

"Tell him to go!"

"I won't," she said. "I don't want him to leave. Ever," she added softly.

David winced. "And me?"

"I love you—"

"But—"

"Not like I love him." A tear slipped down her cheek. "I'm so sorry, David."

There was heartbreak in her voice, real sincerity in her words. But it wasn't enough, and Tucker understood completely. What she was offering David sounded very much like a consolation prize. It would never have been enough for him, either.

"That's it, then, isn't it?" David said. "I'll pick her up this weekend. Have her bags packed." Passing Allie to Gabrielle, he gave Tucker one last contemptuous look before he strode out and slammed the door.

CHAPTER TWENTY-ONE

"HE'S GOING to go to the police," Tucker said softly. "You realize that, don't you?"

Gabrielle wiped her eyes and turned to face him. They were still in the living room, where they'd stood in silence for long moments after David's departure. "He won't go to the police. I know David. He's not a vengeful person. You're fine here."

"Jealousy does strange things to a man, Gabby."

"Maybe to a regular man. But David's different. We care about each other. We care about Allie. He knows I wouldn't stand by you without reason."

"You heard what he said. He thinks you're confused, misguided. If they catch me here, you could be in serious trouble. I have to go."

"Where?" she asked.

"I don't know. Mexico, I guess."

"I'll go with you."

"You can't. What about Allie? What kind of life would that be for her?"

Gabrielle closed her eyes. He was right, of course. Allie's welfare had to come first but, God, it was tearing her apart to think he had to leave already, that this might truly be goodbye. "Will you ever come back?"

"I shouldn't. You'd be better off without me."

Fresh tears filled her eyes. "Can't you stay another hour or two, at least? I can't say goodbye so soon.

Besides—'' she took a shuddering breath ''—Landon's sleeping.''

''I doubt he's asleep, Gabby. And for his sake, I can't trust David as much as you do.''

''I know,'' she said.

Tucker came up behind her, put his arms around her and pulled her against him. He felt so solid, so wonderfully real. And yet she knew that soon, this night would seem like little more than a dream.

''This was the best night of my life,'' he murmured in her hair. ''I knew before I made love to you that I shouldn't, that the risks were too great. But—''

''But what?'' she prompted.

''It was worth it to me,'' he said softly.

His words were tender, but there was finality in the way he said them that confirmed what Gabrielle already knew—he was leaving. There wasn't anything she could do to make him stay. She'd be a fool to really try because she'd only put them all in danger. ''If you ever need anything—''

''No, don't. I won't have you holding on, waiting for me,'' he said briskly. ''Live your life without regrets, love again, marry again. That's what I want for you, Gabby. Go forward and don't look back.''

Gabrielle knew she'd never love anyone the way she loved him; she couldn't even imagine marrying another man. But she wasn't going to make his leaving any harder on him. Swallowing the lump in her throat, she nodded. ''Sure,'' she said as bravely as she could manage. ''I'll be fine.''

He kissed her neck, pressed his cheek against hers, then quickly released her.

''Tucker?''

He turned as he reached the hall, on his way to collect Landon.

"Be happy."

DAVID FELT SICK to his stomach. As dawn began to tinge the east a delicate pink, he sat in his Toyota Forerunner watching Tucker's beat-up old Datsun motor down the street ahead of him, wondering what he should do. He'd been following Tucker for over thirty minutes. Either he had to let him go, or he had to place the call he'd been dreading.

The light turned red, catching them both at an intersection in Casa Grande, twenty-five miles west of Florence.

David closed his eyes and momentarily rested his head on the steering wheel. He couldn't let Tucker go. Tucker was a convicted murderer. David had a responsibility to himself, to Gabrielle and Allie, and to the community. Maybe Tucker hadn't hurt Gabby or Allie yet, but he could. Besides, David had already spoken with Sergeant Hansen a couple of times and, although he found him abrasive and didn't especially care for him, he sympathized with his tough-on-crime stance. David, too, was tired of all the headlines and news reports of violence. Bad guys always seemed to get away with their misdeeds, while victim after victim continued to suffer. He had a chance, right now, to make a difference. If he made the call, the police would descend on Tucker in a matter of minutes and take him back to prison, and Gabrielle and Allie and everyone else would be safe.

That was what he had to do, he decided. This went beyond his or Gabrielle's personal feelings or background or future. Gabrielle thought she was in love with Tucker, but that wasn't the issue here.

Picking up his cell phone, David dialed the prison. Not only did he owe it to Allie and Gabrielle and the community at large to do his duty as a good citizen, he owed it to the little boy in Tucker's car. He might be Tucker's son, but the courts had decided Tucker didn't deserve the right to raise him. Who was David to condone the escape or the kidnapping? Who was Gabrielle, for that matter? Tucker had received his due process.

"Arizona State Prison, Florence," a woman's voice answered.

The light turned green. David gave his car some gas and rolled through the intersection, keeping an eye on the Datsun up ahead. "Sergeant Hansen, please."

"I have him on the schedule for the day, but I'm not sure if he's in yet. Hold on a second, and I'll check."

He tapped the steering wheel while he waited. Gabrielle didn't mean what she'd said at the trailer, he decided. She had too soft a heart and had just gotten in over her head. She'd realize, once Tucker was back behind bars, that David had been right all along. She'd know his calling Hansen was for her own good.

"Sergeant Hansen here."

David had halfway expected a reprieve, but now that he had Hansen on the line, he took a deep breath and identified himself. He loved Gabrielle—enough to do what was best for her in spite of everything she'd said and done.

"WHY ARE YOU FROWNING, Dad?"

Tucker glanced in the rearview mirror at his son and tried to smile. In the interests of safety, Landon was riding in the back seat, next to the duffel bag that held the sum total of their belongings. "I'm just thinking."

"About what?"

"Nothing important," Tucker said, but he was thinking about something—or rather, someone—pretty important to him. Gabrielle. After last night, after the physical and emotional intimacy they'd shared, living without her seemed almost pointless. If not for Landon, he doubted he would have bothered to run. Even so, he was having a hard time putting any energy or focus into it. He didn't want to be a fugitive; he didn't want to leave his country. He wanted to marry Gabrielle and raise a family like the free man he should be. Rationally he knew that was an impossible dream, but there had to be a part of him, deep down, that still believed in truth and justice. Otherwise, he'd be able to reconcile himself to living in a foreign land.

"Can we stop for a burger?" Landon asked.

Tucker turned down the radio he'd been using, ineffectively, to distract himself from his thoughts. "Can't you eat something that Gabrielle sent?"

"I don't like egg salad sandwiches. And you said I couldn't have any of the treats until after lunch."

"Well, we'll find a place to eat when we get a little farther down the road. For now, eat some of the carrots, okay?"

"All right," Landon said, and grudgingly rummaged through the paper sack that contained the food.

"Is your seatbelt on tight?" Tucker asked after a few minutes.

"You always ask that," Landon mumbled, but Tucker could hear him moving in the seat and knew he was double-checking.

"It's important."

"Why?"

Because Tucker was beginning to feel a little uneasy. His mind had been so consumed by Gabrielle, he hadn't paid much attention to what was going on around him. But for the last few miles, he'd noticed a white SUV that looked suspiciously like the Toyota Forerunner David had been driving the day he'd given him a ride to Wellton.

He checked his mirrors every few seconds, trying to see if it really was David, but when he slowed to close the distance and get a better look, the SUV hung back. Which only made him more suspicious. What was David trying to do? Tucker had expected him to call the police, but he hadn't expected David to follow him.

"Why, Dad?" Landon repeated.

"What?" Tucker said, still staring into his rearview mirror at the road behind him.

"Why do I have to wear my seat belt all the time?"

"Better safe than sorry," he said, thinking he should've taken that same advice last night instead of staying with Gabrielle. He missed her already. He could still smell her subtle scent on his clothes, and he kept replaying every moment of their time together. He'd left his heart behind with her, and without it, he wasn't so confident he'd make it to the border.

DAVID SAW THE RED LIGHTS flashing on the police car coming up behind him, doing at least ninety, and knew Hansen had called out the cavalry. In a few minutes, it would all be over.

"I did the right thing," he said out loud, but he still wasn't sure. Tucker's muscle tone and the hard edge to his eyes certainly made him appear capable of violence. But if he was so violent, why hadn't he tried to keep David from walking out of Gabrielle's trailer last night? He would have been wise to do so, looking at the situation from a self-preservation standpoint. For a karate expert, it wouldn't even have been difficult. David had no training, hadn't been in a fistfight since grade school.

But he didn't want to think about that. It eroded his confidence in what he'd done. He tried to turn his thoughts back to the good of the community, the good of taking one more criminal off the streets. But a vision of Tucker handing his baby back to him intruded, and he wondered if Tucker had been trying to tell him something with that one small act—that he wasn't trying to take anything that didn't belong to him already. That he had no intention of hurting anyone.

He pictured Gabrielle's face, pleading with him to understand, and remembered her saying, ''I love him, David.''

Shaking of his head, David floored his SUV and easily closed the distance between him and Tucker. Tucker had picked up speed. He was trying to run, but he obviously wasn't making a mad dash for freedom. David knew it was because he had his son in the car. Surely that indicated something about the kind of man he was. A truly violent criminal wouldn't care about the child in his car. A truly violent criminal would care more about himself than the safety of others....

The police were nearly upon them. David could hear the sirens, and he knew Tucker could, too. He tried to conjure up some enthusiasm for what was about to happen but the sense of satisfaction he'd felt when he first hung up with Hansen slowly drained out of him. He'd always trusted Gabrielle's opinions before. Why was he second-guessing her on this? He didn't know

Tucker; he didn't want to know him. He just wanted Tucker out of his life—and Gabby's. Which said much more than he wanted it to.

With a sigh, David raked a hand over his face, feeling the roughness of his unshaved chin. He shouldn't be here, shouldn't be doing this. He should be home showering so he could head into the office and finish catching up on everything he'd missed during the past few weeks. He should be home, going through the motions of moving on with his life. Regardless of how little he wanted to face it, his marriage to Gabrielle was over for good. The real question wasn't whether he loved her enough to do what was best for her. The real question, at least for him, was whether or not he loved her enough to let her go.

"Shit," he said and, instead of pulling over to let the police car pass, he slammed on his brakes and angled his SUV to block the road.

THE CALL, when it came, caught Gabrielle cleaning up after breakfast. Allie was playing at her feet, tossing utensils from the kitchen drawers onto the floor. Gabrielle didn't bother to stop her, even though the clanging made her nerves raw. Right now, it was more important for Allie's attention to remain focused on other things. Right now, Gabrielle needed a chance to cope with the fact that Tucker and Landon were gone, David was angry with her, and she was going to be seeing her real mother in just a few hours—at a time when she already felt emotionally exhausted.

Maybe she should call and tell Naomi she couldn't make it, she thought. She wanted to meet her siblings, but not today. Today was one of the worst days of her life. She wasn't herself, and doubted she could deal with anything stressful on the heels of this morning. But what if Lindy had canceled something important to be present? What if Naomi had already gone to a great deal of work?

The phone interrupted her deliberations. Tucker hadn't promised her any future contact. He'd told her to forget about him. But she couldn't help feeling a stab of hope that he might be trying to reach her. Flicking the soap from her hands, she reached for a paper towel and started for the living room just as the answering machine came on.

"This is Gabrielle. Please leave your name and number, and I'll get back to you as soon as possible."

Knowing Tucker would hang up rather than leave a message, she reached for the handset, then stopped abruptly when she heard Sergeant Hansen's voice.

"Hadley, are you there? If so, I suggest you pick up."

She did nothing.

"Hadley, I have David here with me. And he's in some trouble."

David? Gabrielle's mouth went dry. How could David possibly be in trouble? Tucker had thought he would go to the police, but she couldn't understand how that could get *David* in trouble.

"Gabby? Pick up. I need to talk to you."

It was David this time. Gabrielle's hand suddenly felt clumsy, but she forced it to work well enough to bring the phone to her ear.

"David, what's going on?" she asked, fear pouring through her veins. "Are you okay?"

"I'm fine."

She wanted to ask him if Tucker was okay, too, but with Hansen so close, she didn't dare. "What's going on?'' she said again. ''What kind of trouble are you in?''

''I called the police and followed Tucker, just like you told me to, but I'm afraid they didn't get him, and now they're trying to blame me.''

She gripped the phone a little tighter. ''I don't understand.''

He went on as though she'd asked him something else. ''I don't know what happened, exactly. I'm guessing my tire must've hit the soft shoulder, because just as the police were coming up behind me, something spun me across the road. Next thing I knew, the police car rammed into my back rear panel, and that hung things up pretty good.''

''You were in a wreck? Were you hurt?'' Gabrielle asked anxiously.

''No. Fortunately, no one was hurt, but Tucker got away. And now Sergeant Hansen thinks we're somehow in league with the escaped convict we just tried to help him catch. He wants to ask you a few questions, okay?''

Gabrielle didn't know how to answer him. In the end, she didn't have to, because Hansen came back on the line. ''What the hell kind of game are you two playing?'' he demanded.

''I don't know what you're talking about,'' she said.

''David called me this morning, said Tucker showed up at your place, trying to overpower you and escape with some money and food.''

''That's true,'' she said, knowing that all she could do at this point was trust David.

''So what happened?''

Oh, boy... Taking a shaky breath, she curled her free hand into a fist, hoping she could safely navigate her way through this. "Um…David showed up just in time to scare Tucker off," she said, praying that her story matched David's.

"So why didn't you call in?" Hansen asked.

"I had to stay with my baby daughter. David was the one who was following Tucker. Didn't he tell you where you could find him?"

"He told me all right. I dispatched a couple of cars, but then your ex-husband got in the way and let Tucker escape again."

Gabrielle took solace from the fact that Tucker was still free—and wondered what on earth had happened. David was an excellent driver, certainly not the type to make such a stupid mistake. "I'm sure it was just a simple accident," she said, even though she wasn't sure of any such thing.

"So how'd Tucker know where you live?"

"It wouldn't be hard to figure out in a town this size. Anyway, he probably assumed I live alone and thought I'd be an easy mark."

"Tell me something."

"What?"

"Why is it that, with Tucker, all roads seem to lead back to you?"

"It's just a coincidence," she said.

"You know what, Hadley?"

"What?"

"I don't believe in coincidence," he said. Then a dial tone suddenly hummed in Gabrielle's ear, and she sagged onto the couch.

DAVID ARRIVED at the trailer less than an hour after Gabrielle had hung up with Hansen. By then, Allie was down for a nap and Gabrielle was pacing the floor, still wondering what had happened this morning. And worrying what Hansen was going to do about it.

When she saw her ex-husband, she wasn't sure how to greet him. The past few weeks hadn't been easy on their relationship. They'd parted on bad terms this morning, something terrible had happened afterward, and now...and now they were entering brand-new territory.

He walked into the trailer, looking tired.

"You okay?" Gabrielle asked, perching on the arm of the couch as she watched him.

He nodded. "Where's Allie?"

"Napping. What happened this morning?"

With a long sigh, he sat in the chair opposite her. "I realized something."

"What's that?"

"That I love you more than I thought."

He wasn't making a play for her. Gabrielle could tell by the tone of his voice that a significant change had taken place. "You want to explain that?" she asked.

He shook his head, glanced around the trailer as though he might never see it again, and stood. "No. I'm going back to Phoenix, Gabby, where I belong. Can I have Allie next Saturday?"

"Of course." Gabrielle stood, too. "You have partial custody."

"Good. I'll send my child support this week."

He started for the door. She caught him by the arm before he could step outside. "Aren't you going to tell me what happened with Tucker and Hansen?"

"Can't you guess?"

"You called the police after you left here."

The look on his face told her she was right.

"So what changed your mind?" she asked. "Why'd you let him go?"

"I didn't want to send a man to prison because of my own jealousy. And I finally realized I'd already lost you, anyway."

She brushed a lock of hair off his forehead. "You haven't lost anything, David. You're still my dearest friend. You always will be."

He smiled, and it was the old smile, the one Gabrielle had long admired. "I hope Tucker's able to clear his name. Maybe then the two of you can be together. At least part of me hopes that," he amended.

Gabrielle felt profound gratitude for having known David, for his friendship and longtime support. "David?"

"Hmm?"

"Thanks." Standing on tiptoe, she gave him a kiss on the cheek.

"For what?"

"For being you. And for helping Tucker. I'm glad you weren't hurt pulling that little stunt."

"So am I."

"Any chance I could tag along with you and Allie this Saturday?"

"I don't think so," he said. "I thought I'd take Allie and the new woman in my office on a picnic. Shauna's been hinting she'd like that," he added with a grin. "It might be a little tough to explain why I'm bringing my ex-wife along."

She laughed. "I could tell her what a good guy she'd be getting if she was ever lucky enough to land you."

He held up a hand. "Let's give her a chance to figure out that kind of stuff for herself, okay? It might be a while before I'm ready for anything serious."

"I understand. Call when you have a little time to spare, then, and we'll catch a movie or something."

"Sure." He stared down at her for several seconds. "Goodbye, Gabby," he said, and Gabrielle knew from the way he said it that he was saying goodbye to their past.

CHAPTER TWENTY-TWO

TODAY WAS A DAY for change. Gabrielle knew that already. David had finally understood that she wasn't coming back to him; he was finally moving on. Thinking about all the adjustments that would be necessary in their relationship made her feel strangely bereft, even though she was determined to help him stay the course. With time, he'd find a wife, and Gabrielle would embrace her, too, if she was open to the friendship.

But it wasn't just David. Her life was changing in other ways. Last night she'd made love with the only man to whom she'd ever been able to commit her whole heart. Today she'd lost him. Now, as she stood on the curb of her mother's house holding Allie and gazing at all the cars jamming the drive, she wondered how the people she was about to meet might affect her future. Was she doing the right thing by coming here— and today of all days?

She didn't know, but she couldn't cancel on such late notice. Good manners wouldn't allow it. More than that, Naomi Cutter still intrigued her. Despite her conflicted feelings about the past, Gabrielle wasn't ready to walk away.

Shifting Allie to her other hip, she adjusted the flowers and wine she was also carrying, and approached the house.

She didn't even have to knock before Hal threw open the front door. "Come on in," he said exuberantly, taking the flowers and the wine and waving her inside as though they knew each other well. "Everyone's excited to meet you."

His welcome bolstered her. Squaring her shoulders, she stepped inside to face a roomful of people. Lindy was leaning against the wall, smiling expectantly. A lanky young man of about twenty lounged on a chair placed in front of the television, loosely holding a remote in one hand, which he immediately used to silence whatever program he was watching. Her brother? A middle-aged couple sat together on the couch. They clasped hands as soon as they saw her, as though enthralled by the moment.

Her mother came from the kitchen wearing an apron.

"Here she is," Naomi said. Her voice sounded as upbeat and happy as Hal's, but Gabrielle could tell she was far more nervous. "Hello, Gabrielle. I'm so glad you could make it."

Gabrielle's smile shook, and she wished she had more emotional reserves for this encounter. "Hello."

"Everyone, this is Naomi's oldest daughter, Gabrielle Hadley," Hal announced.

"Or Gabby for short," Gabrielle interjected, feeling self-conscious with so many new people. "And this is Allie, my baby." She turned so everyone could get a better view of Allie.

"She's darling," Lindy said to no one in particular.

"Gabby, this is your sister, Lindy," Hal said.

Lindy was wearing a sundress and sandals and wore her straw-blond hair pulled back from her face. When she smiled, a dimple winked in one cheek, and Gabrielle could easily imagine a great number of men falling at her feet.

Stepping forward, she reached out to shake Gabrielle's hand. "It's a pleasure to meet you," she said. Her words were formal, but they were sincere, and her grip was warm and sure.

"It's nice to meet you, too," Gabrielle responded.

"And this is your brother, Conrad," Hal went on.

Instead of getting up to shake her hand, Conrad smiled and waved. His actions were deceptively casual, though. As soon as he thought she wasn't looking, he regarded her from beneath his gold lashes. But there was nothing unfriendly or standoffish about him. Gabrielle felt his curiosity more than anything else.

"And these two people," Hal announced, turning to the couple on the sofa as though he'd saved the best for last, "are your aunt Margaret and uncle Peter."

Peter helped Margaret to her feet and they both came forward and embraced her.

"You won't remember them," Hal was saying. "Peter wasn't in the picture when you were little. Margaret's your mother's only sibling, and she was just going to college when you were born."

"So you live in the area, too?" Gabrielle asked as they released her.

"We're snowbirds," Margaret answered. "We live in Utah during the summer and Sun City during the winter. We just drove down to stay with your mother for a few days so we wouldn't miss meeting you."

"How nice of you."

"Oh, we wouldn't have missed it for the world," she said, a twinkle in her eye. "Naomi was so excited when she called."

Gabrielle glanced fleetingly at her mother, who gave

her a tentative smile. Gabrielle's worst fear had once been that Naomi would reject her again, that her mother wouldn't want to be found. But Naomi had called Margaret and Pete and, with hardly any notice, had them drive all the way from Utah just to meet her.

Yes, this was a day for change.

"Hey, Allie," Hal said, taking her from Gabrielle's arms now that he'd deposited the wine and flowers on the coffee table. "Wait till you see the new doll Grandpa and Grandma bought for you."

Grandpa and Grandma. Gabrielle liked the sound of that, but she caught her breath when Hal immediately handed Allie to Naomi. Gabrielle wasn't sure she was ready to share her daughter with her mother. She still wasn't sure she could forgive the past—until she saw Naomi close her eyes and hold Allie to her chest with the same kind of relief Gabrielle had known the day she came out of the desert. Tears began to slip down Naomi's face, and a lump the size of a baseball rose in Gabrielle's throat at the sight.

"Gabrielle, come sit down and tell me a little about yourself," Lindy said. "I've always wanted a sister."

Gabrielle blinked rapidly and felt a smile finally come to her rescue.

It was definitely a time for change, and some of those changes were going to be good.

TUCKER CALLED SEAN at work. It had been so long since he'd dialed his neighbor at the accountancy firm that he'd had to rely on directory information for the number. But he had a receptionist from Broadstone and Brinkerhoff, Public Accountants, on the line now. Fortunately, Landon was inside the Quick Mart, shopping for candy, while Tucker stood at the edge of the property, using the pay phone.

"I'm afraid Mr. Marshall is on another line," the receptionist coolly informed him.

Tucker leaned outside the booth so he could keep an eye on his son through the store window and maintain a clear view of the road behind him. Now that the police knew the make and model of his car, and that he was still in the area, thanks to David, he'd lost his advantage. And he was tired. He'd risked renting a cheap motel room on the outskirts of Tucson last night so Landon would have a bed, a television and a bath. But every noise in the place had awakened him—the showers in the neighboring rooms, the cars coming and going in the lot, the dispensing of goodies from the vending machine just down the hall. He woke several times, wondering if the police were at the door. Then he had difficulty sleeping after each interruption, because he'd start thinking about Gabrielle and how it had felt to take her in his arms. He'd remember her smile, the passion in her eyes when she gazed up at him. He'd hear her say, "I'm in love with you...." and at some point he'd have to face that it didn't make a damn bit of difference whether she loved him or not. He couldn't have Gabrielle no matter how badly he wanted her.

"Tell him it's his old neighbor," Tucker said into the phone. "If he's still too busy, tell him it's no problem. I'll just drop by his place later."

Evidently, Sean understood the implied threat better than his receptionist did. Maybe he'd checked to find his spare key missing. In any case, he picked up only a few seconds later. "What do you want?" he asked, his voice a desperate half whisper. "Why are you harassing me? I could go to the police, you know."

"But you haven't."

"Yeah, well, it's not too late."

"If you were going to the police, you would've done it by now. You don't want to talk to them. Why is that?"

"Hey, what can I say? I'm an old friend—"

"You screwed my wife, Sean. You know something about her death and instead of coming forward, you let me go to prison. That hardly makes you my friend."

Silence. "Poor Andrea," he said at last.

"What happened to her?" Tucker asked.

"I don't know."

"I think you know something. And I'm going to find out what it is. I'm sending the pictures of you and Andrea to a private investigator, who's going to take a closer look at where you were the night Andrea was killed. While he's at it, maybe I'll have him look at every other detail of your life, too. You won't be able to take a piss without checking over your shoulder."

"I didn't hurt her," Sean said.

"Then who did?"

"When I found her in the garage, she was already dead. I thought Sydney had freaked out and killed her in a jealous rage. If you'd heard the way she talked about Andrea after she—"

Every muscle in Tucker's body bunched. "You found Andrea in the garage?" he repeated slowly.

"I can't talk about this here," he said.

"Then meet me later."

Sean sighed. "This is never going to go away, is it?"

"Just tell me the truth," Tucker said. "Then it'll go away for both of us."

"If it was that simple, I would've said something long ago. Come by the house tonight," he said, and hung up.

TUCKER KNEW when he went to Sean Marshall's that night that he could be walking into a trap. Sean could have the police waiting for him, or some other surprise planned. But now that he was so close to finding out something about Andrea's murder, he had to take the chance. The only thing he regretted was the fact that he'd had to bring Landon along. He wanted to spare his son as much unpleasantness as possible, especially when it concerned Andrea. Considering the circumstances, however, he didn't have a safe place to leave him.

Landon stood next to him at the door, somber and remote, as though visiting the old neighborhood had cast the same pall on him as it did on Tucker.

"You okay, pal?" Tucker asked.

Landon nodded just as Sean opened the door wearing a black T-shirt with a motorcycle on it, a pair of khaki shorts and leather sandals.

"What's he doing here?" he asked, scowling at Landon.

Tucker placed a reassuring hand on his son's shoulder. "He goes where I go."

Sean opened his mouth to say something else, but Landon cut him off with a polite, "Hello, Mr. Marshall," which seemed to remind Sean of his manners.

"Hi, Landon," he said grudgingly, then pushed the door open wider and waved them both inside. "Sydney's here."

"Is there a reason?" Tucker asked.

"You'll see. Come in."

Tucker followed him into the kitchen, where Sydney was sitting at the table, staring off into space. Dressed in a pair of ankle-length slacks and a sleeveless blouse, she had her arms folded and was leaning back with her legs stretched out. When they came in, she stood and smiled hesitantly. "Hi, Randy."

Tucker nodded at her, noting the subtle changes in her appearance—the extra lines around the eyes, the new hairstyle, which was much shorter in length and darker in color than the way she used to wear it. Unlike Sean, Sydney had lost weight. Gone were the extra pounds she'd gained with her pregnancies. She looked good. "How are you?"

"I'm sure we've all been better, right?" She embraced him before turning to Landon. "Hi, Landon. Bet it's great to see your dad, huh?"

"Yeah," Landon said.

"Any chance you could put in a movie or something for Landon while we talk?" Tucker asked.

Sydney glanced at Sean. "That's probably a good idea. Come on, big guy, let's go see what we can find." She led Landon into the living room and didn't return for several minutes.

Meanwhile, Tucker leaned against the counter and tried to read Sean's expression. What was going on? It didn't appear that his old friend had betrayed him to the police. So what did he have to say about Andrea's death?

The blare of the television reached the kitchen just as Sydney walked back in. "God, Sean. You don't have anything here anymore," she said. "The poor kid's watching a tape of an old basketball game you recorded."

"We don't need long," Sean said.

"For what?" Tucker asked.

"For this." Sean pulled a piece of paper out of his pocket and handed it to Tucker.

Tucker slowly unfolded it to find a crude, hand-drawn map. He raised a questioning eyebrow at Sean.

"That's where you'll find Andrea's remains," Sean explained.

Tucker sucked in a quick breath and told himself not to overreact. "What are you talking about? How do you know?" he demanded.

"Because I buried her."

Nothing could have held Tucker back in that moment. Moving before he even knew what he was going to do, he grabbed Sean by the shirtfront and pinned him against the counter. "You son of a bitch! You knew where she was all this time and didn't say anything? You let me go to prison, let Landon lose his father—"

"Randy, wait," Sydney interrupted, putting a beseeching hand on his arm. "You have every right to be angry, but this isn't going to help. There's more."

Emotion was pouring through Tucker like a river. Logic told him he'd be smarter to let go of Sean and hear the rest of what he and Sydney had to say, to hear it all. Vengeance told him it was time to exact the retribution he'd craved for the past two years. This man had slept with his wife. Tucker could forgive that. But Sean had also caused Landon to be taken away from him and *that* Tucker could not forgive.

"Talk fast," he snarled.

"Let go of him first," Sydney said.

Logic or emotion? Tucker stared into Sean's eyes, wavering. In his former life, he'd learned to solve problems with his mind. In prison he'd learned to solve things with his fists. Now using his fists came more naturally to him. But Sydney was whispering that Landon was in the other room, and the thought of his son ultimately cut through the anger shrouding Tucker's brain.

"Tell me everything you know or so help me I'll beat it out of you," Tucker growled, and he meant every word. He was finished paying for another man's crime.

The second Tucker released him, Sean shuffled to the far end of the kitchen. "I didn't kill her," he said. "I had nothing to do with her death."

"Then why did you bury her?"

"I told you. I thought Sydney killed her. Once Sydney found out what went on at the cabin, she hated Andrea. She hated her for the affair, of course, but it was more than that."

"She took Sean even though she didn't want him," Sydney said.

"She often talked about wanting to kill Andrea," Sean went on. "She said she didn't deserve to live, that she couldn't bear to look at her anymore, and...and other stuff."

Tucker looked at Sydney.

"I didn't kill her," Sydney said. "But I'd be a liar if I told you I thought she got anything more than she deserved." Her voice, even now, was vehement.

"When I came home that night, Sydney was gone," Sean continued, the words coming faster now. "I knew my mother had picked up the girls from school and was keeping them for the weekend. She could tell we were having marital problems and wanted us to have some time alone to work things out. Sydney was supposed to be waiting for me so I could take her to dinner, but she wasn't here, and there was no note or anything. So I got a little nervous, wondering if she and Andrea had gotten into it, and went over to your place looking for her.''

''And?'' Tucker said coldly.

''When I couldn't find anyone inside the house, I went to the garage to see if the cars were gone. I found Andrea lying on the floor. She'd been beaten pretty badly.'' He grimaced and his skin turned a pallid gray. ''She was already dead.''

''You didn't think to call an ambulance?'' Tucker asked. ''The police?''

''And have Sydney go to jail because I was too weak to rebuff Andrea at the cabin? I couldn't do that. I thought what had happened was my fault. So I tried to protect my family by getting rid of Andrea's body.''

Tucker stared down at the map he still held in one hand. ''You buried her in the desert not far from Coolidge.''

Sean nodded.

''And where was Sydney?''

''I was just getting in my car to go to the grocery store when I heard you and Andrea arguing,'' Sydney answered, taking over. ''When you left, I tried to follow you. I wanted to tell you about the affair. I thought she should lose you, that a woman like her didn't deserve a man like you. I hoped Sean and Andrea's affair would be the final straw, and your leaving her would be my revenge. But you were driving fast, and I lost you in traffic. I drove around for a while, hoping to find you, but I never did. I even stopped at the coffee shop there on Broadway where the four of us used to hang out after the movies and had some iced tea while I watched the road. I knew you'd probably come back that way, but I had no luck. By the time I got home, there was no one at either house, and I couldn't reach Sean, even on his cell.''

"So who killed her?'' Tucker asked.

Sydney and Sean exchanged a guarded look. "We don't know for sure,'' Sydney finally said.

"But you have your suspicions.''

"At first we thought it was you,'' Sean said. "Sydney saw you leave and followed you, but that didn't mean you didn't kill Andrea before you left.''

"That argument you had with Andrea was pretty heated,'' Sydney concurred.

Tucker split his gaze between them. "What changed your minds?''

"I saw your brother pulling away from your house just as I was getting home to meet Sydney,'' Sean said.

His *brother?* Tom had never mentioned coming to the house that day....

Sean was still talking, explaining what he'd seen and what he'd surmised from it, and Tucker forced himself to pay attention. "When I found Andrea, I assumed Tom had knocked at the door, couldn't rouse anybody and left. I thought we'd been lucky, that if he'd found Andrea, Sydney would be going to jail for sure. But then he did something that's always made me wonder....''

Tucker could hardly speak for the sick feeling inside him. "What was that?''

"He came over just after you were arrested and said he had the photographs of me and Andrea. He said if I told anyone about seeing his car at your place the day she was killed, he'd take the photographs to the police. Then it would be anybody's guess as to who'd wind up going to jail for murder."

"You'd disposed of the body and you sank Andrea's car in the lake. You had no alibi and were at the scene of the crime."

Sean nodded. "Exactly. I was afraid there'd be some sort of evidence in the car linking me to the murder."

Tucker didn't know what to believe. He had only Sean and Sydney's word that what they were telling him was the truth. Maybe they were making some last-minute attempt to shield themselves. Or maybe they were trying to implicate his brother to confuse the issue. Tom had always been a screw-up, had frequently landed himself in trouble. But he wouldn't have hurt Andrea. He'd have had no reason to hurt her. And he wouldn't let Tucker go to prison for something he didn't do...*would he?*

AFTER LEAVING the Marshalls, Tucker drove straight to his parents' house. He'd assumed the police would be keeping an eye on their place, knew he was increasing his chances of being picked up. But he was beyond caring about this possibility or that. He needed someone trustworthy to watch Landon, and he needed it right away. Because he was going to his brother's house.

From the moment his parents opened their door, they were warm and supportive. In deference to Landon, they didn't ask a lot of questions. Tucker knew they had no idea that Tom was involved. They believed Tom had stumbled onto the pictures, then hidden them to keep Tucker from being hurt, and Tucker didn't want to tell them anything different. Not until he'd had a chance to talk to his brother. Just now, he wasn't sure he believed it himself.

His parents immediately made Landon feel welcome, gave Tucker Tom's address and let him go. To Tucker's surprise, he drove in and out of the neighborhood as if he was any other law-abiding citizen and not an escaped convict. He didn't see one cop.

Tom was now living in Scottsdale on Camelback Mountain, one of the most prestigious areas in the valley. Tucker was shocked at how much he'd come up in the world—and that he'd used his own brother to do it.

The night was cooler than the past few weeks had been. Already Tucker could smell a touch of autumn in the air. It certainly wasn't the turning of the seasons one would experience in most of the rest of the country; the change was far more subtle. But after living in Arizona his whole life, Tucker could tell when autumn was on its way, and he couldn't wait. The heat this summer had been almost unbearable.

The other cars on the road, the streetlights, the storefronts and pedestrians flew past in a blur as Tucker sped through Tempe. Scottsdale was only fifteen or twenty minutes away from where his parents lived in Mesa. He'd be there shortly.

The winding road that led to Tom's sprawling mansion was darker than the wide busy streets of the city. Tucker slowed as he crawled up the mountain, checking numbers on mailboxes as he passed. Finally he came upon the address his parents had given him for Tom and turned in to find a two-story Mediterranean-style house. The place was well lit, and several cars clogged the drive, all of them new or nearly new, and very expensive.

Tucker pulled his rattletrap Datsun in behind a shiny new Jaguar and cut the engine. His hair was windblown from traveling with his windows down, and his back was sweaty. Having gone several days without shaving, he could imagine how unkempt he was going to appear to the people in his brother's house, but he didn't care. He'd never been so angry or so determined in his life.

Slamming out of his car, he stalked up the drive and banged on the door.

A Mexican woman answered his knock. Dressed in a floral dress, she was small-boned with brown, wrinkled skin and black eyes that shone brightly in the porch light. Tucker guessed she was the housekeeper he'd spoken to on the telephone.

"I'm afraid Mr. and Mrs. Tucker are entertaining tonight," she explained in her thick Spanish accent, stepping into the opening of the door to block his entry. "You'll have to come back tomorrow."

Tucker wedged his foot in the door before she could close it. "You haven't even asked who I am," he said.

"I don't have to. I can tell you're not part of the party."

"Or Tom told you I might stop by," he said.

"Mr. Tucker is busy at the moment."

"I'm afraid he's not busy enough. I'm going to talk to him whether he wants to see me or not, so if you don't want a scene, I suggest you go get him."

She surprised him by meeting this statement with steely defiance. "Mr. Tucker won't appreciate the interruption."

"Tell Mr. Tucker I don't give a damn whether he appreciates it or not."

Her mouth flattened into a short straight line as she

glared up at him. "If you'll excuse me, I'll tell Mr. Tucker you're here."

"You do that," Tucker said.

Tom came to the door only moments later. Standing six foot flat, he was husky but well-built and looked spit-polished in a black suit and tie. His hair wasn't nearly as dark as Tucker's, and his eyes were more of a murky hazel than blue, but Tucker had heard others comment about their looks often enough to know they resembled each other a great deal.

"Randy, are you crazy?" Tom immediately demanded. "The police are scouring every corner of this city! You think they don't know where I live? That they won't check here? That's why I couldn't take your call the other day, man. I think they have my phones tapped."

"That sounds a little paranoid, even to me," Tucker said dryly.

"Hey, anything to protect my baby brother." To Tucker, Tom's smile appeared insincere. When had his brother become such a bastard?

Tucker stepped back to make a show of examining the house. "Nice place you got here. Were you protecting me when you spent my money to buy it?"

"Hey, that's not fair," his brother said. "I'm gonna give you your money. Don't worry about that."

"When, Tom? Now?" Tucker asked.

"Well, not now exactly." He smiled again, but his hands were fidgeting. "I've invested it, you know," he said, loosening his tie. "But it'll make a nice return. I promise you that. You'll get your money, and then some."

"You don't make money by throwing parties and taking cruises," Tucker said. "You gotta work if you want to earn a profit, Tom. But then, work's never been very high on your list of priorities, has it?''

Tom laughed as he shoved his hands into his pockets, but Tucker could see he was working hard to keep up his congenial veneer. ''There you go again, little brother,'' he said. ''I just got married. A man's allowed to celebrate, isn't he?''

Propping his hand against the house, Tucker leaned close. ''That depends on whether he's doing it on his own dime. But we can argue about the money later. I'm here about something else.''

''What's that?'' Tom yanked on his tie, seemed surprised to find that he'd already untied it, and proceeded to unbutton the collar of his starched blue shirt. ''If you need a few bucks to get you through, you know I'm your man. I have some cash here. Just give me a second and I'll run up and grab it so you can be on your way.''

''I'm not going anywhere,'' Tucker said.

Finally, Tom's smile faltered. ''What do you mean? The police could show up any minute.''

''Then maybe you'd better invite me in.''

Tom glanced over his shoulder. Tucker could hear voices, laughter, the clink of silverware coming from inside the house. ''It's not really a good time, Randy. We're having a few friends over, and—''

''And?'' Tucker lifted a challenging brow. ''Don't you want to introduce me to your wife?''

''Someone might recognize you. Tomorrow would be better. Let me get you that money—''

''I didn't come for money.'' Tucker watched Tom intently, still hoping the Marshalls were wrong. He didn't want to believe that his own brother could destroy his family, seemingly without conscience. He didn't want his parents to have to face it, either. "I know, Tom," he said evenly. "I know what you did to Andrea."

Tom's expression didn't change. "What are you talking about?"

Tucker felt a burst of hope—until he realized his brother's expression *had* changed, ever so slightly. There was a hostile gleam in Tom's eyes that Tucker had glimpsed before whenever he'd caught Tom in a lie.

"You know exactly what I'm talking about," Tucker said. "The only thing I don't understand is why. Why would you hurt her, Tom?"

His brother didn't answer right away but all pretense finally left his face. Stepping outside, he closed the door behind him. "I didn't mean to, Randy," he said, his voice low, his eyes watchful. "I just went over to talk to her. But she was such a bitch—"

"For the most part, she always liked you."

He chuckled without mirth. "She didn't like me anymore. She figured out I never bought that piece of land in Gilbert you gave me the hundred thousand for. She ran into Harvey Wells, the owner, and he told her the deal had fallen through. I'd gone through most of the money by then, but I was planning on paying it back, Randy, I really was. Only she wouldn't give me any time. She was gonna go straight to you. She was so angry, and I was so angry, and—"

Tom held his hands out in front of him as though they were foreign objects. "I didn't mean to kill her. I swear, Randy. You've gotta believe me. She just made me so—" he doubled his fist and gritted his teeth "—so damn angry. When you and Robert lent me the cabin for that ski trip I took in January, I found some pictures hidden under the mattress. They were of her and that fat S.O.B. who lived next door to you, getting nasty, and I thought I had her then. But she still wouldn't cut me any slack. She said it didn't matter if I showed them to you, that you already knew and didn't care. Nothing I said made any difference. She was pissed about the money and determined to ruin my life. She said you'd never be able to trust me again, never include me in anything. She said she was gonna see to it that I went to jail for fraud.''

"So you left her lying on the garage floor."

He jammed a hand through his carefully combed hair, mussing it. "I flipped out, man. I didn't know what I was doing. I didn't mean to hit her so hard, but she fought me, and...and she kept screaming what a loser I was, that I'd never measure up to you, that I was going to jail. I went a little crazy, and then I panicked and ran. Later, when the body never turned up, I realized I had a chance.''

"And when they blamed what you'd done on me?" Tucker asked dully.

Tom's gaze fell to the ground, but when he spoke, his nostrils flared with passion. "You'd always had everything. Mom and Dad preferred you, you got all the girls, won all the awards, beat me at every sport. It's not easy having your little brother steal everything, even the praise of your parents. I was tired of playing second fiddle, Randy. I figured it was my turn. Luck had given me a break.''

Tucker rubbed his chest against the crushing disappointment. "Well, Tom, I guess your turn's over, huh?''

Tom's eyes darted up. "You're free," he said, nervously licking his lips. "Just get the hell out of town.

I'll give you whatever money I've got, okay? Then we can both be free. No one has to know.''

"What about Landon?"

"Take him with you. You have him, right? The kidnapping was in all the papers. We heard about it as soon as we got back."

"You think I'm going to have Landon live a life with me on the run when I can give him better?" Tucker asked.

"But what about me, man? I'm your brother. You can't hang me out to dry."

Tucker thought of all the days he'd spent in prison. He thought of the foul odors, the fights, the abuse he'd taken from the guards, the resulting bitterness. The system had failed him, but his own brother had failed him more. "Sean Marshall knows where Andrea's body is," he responded. "He's finally coming forward. The police will soon be examining her remains for clues and evidence."

"So? It's been two years. There'll be nothing to prove I killed her," Tom insisted.

Tucker felt no satisfaction at seeing the panic in his brother's eyes—he felt sick. "You never know," he said. "If I were you, I'd pack up and start running."

He left his brother standing on the steps and headed for his car. After he started the engine, he glanced back at the door to find Tom gone. But Tucker still heard his brother's words. *There'll be nothing to prove I killed her.*

Lifting his shirt, he pulled off the voice-activated recorder he'd taped onto his back before dropping Landon at his parents. "Yes there will, Tom," he said softly, staring down at it. "There'll be this."

GABRIELLE RETURNED LATE, long after Allie should have been in bed. She'd been visiting Lindy at her condo in Chandler. They'd gone to dinner at a nice Mexican restaurant and enjoyed a couple of margaritas while they spent time getting to know each other, talking about their childhoods, Naomi, what they wanted out of life. Gabrielle had only known Lindy for a few days, but she loved her already. Her sister had a quirky, almost irreverent sense of humor and a way of putting things in perspective that made Gabrielle smile.

Just after ten o'clock, Gabrielle had convinced her sister to drive over to David's. They hadn't given him any warning. Gabrielle had been slightly afraid he might refuse and she really wanted to see him. They ended up dragging him out of bed, but Gabrielle was glad they'd visited. It was good to be with David, good to know he was still her friend. And Lindy was more than happy to meet him. She thought he was extremely handsome.

Gabrielle was thinking about the possibility of the two of them getting together as she unbuckled Allie from her car seat and carried her inside. Dropping her keys and purse on the coffee table, she carried her sleeping daughter down the hall to her room.

It wasn't until she was on her way back that she began to notice that her house wasn't quite the way she'd left it. An open duffel bag filled with little boy clothes and a few bigger T-shirts rested on the sofa and there was a set of keys she didn't recognize on the kitchen counter.

What was going on? Gabrielle's heart started to pound as she examined the keys. Leaning over the sink, she gazed out the kitchen window to see a beat-up old Datsun parked across the street. Had it been there when she'd driven up? She couldn't remember. She'd been too engrossed in thinking about Lindy and David.

Walking quietly down the hall, Gabrielle paused at the door of her extra bedroom. She was almost afraid to look inside. Would she find an eight-year-old with unruly dark hair and startling blue eyes? And, if so, would she find his father in the house, as well?

Hope stole her breath as she stepped into David's old room. Sure enough, a small lump in the center of the bed told her *someone* was sleeping there. When she moved a little closer, she could tell for sure; it was Landon. Which meant…

Gabrielle hurried into her own room, where she found her comforter tossed carelessly onto a chair. The blinds were drawn, but just enough light glimmered through for her to be able to see the profile of the man she loved, sleeping in her bed. He was here. For whatever reason, Tucker had come back to her.

Kneeling at the side of the bed, she ran a hand through the hair that had fallen across his forehead. "Tucker?"

He stirred.

"Tucker, what are you doing here?" she whispered, so glad to see him she felt suspended in time and space.

His eyes opened. When he saw her and had a chance to wake up, his mouth slanted in a grin. "Isn't this where I belong?"

"This is where *I* want you," she said, "but what about Hansen? And the police? What if—"

"Shh." He raised his hand and rubbed his knuckles across her cheek. "You don't have to worry about that anymore."

"What do you mean?"

"It's over," he said. "The police know I'm innocent. Everyone knows I'm innocent."

"But how?"

"Can I explain in the morning? Right now I just want to feel you against me."

Gabrielle hesitated because she could hardly believe it was true. "Just tell me if this means we're going to be together."

"Forever," he said.

His one-word answer was enough. He'd never promised her anything before. She knew that if he said it, she could rely on it like the sun coming up in the morning. Stripping off her clothes, she climbed into bed with him, and he immediately pulled her into his arms. "I love you, Gabrielle," he said. "I'm going to love you for a lifetime."

EPILOGUE

IT WAS FOUR DAYS LATER that Warden Crumb and Sergeant Hansen came to visit. As soon as a copy of the tape and the facts about Andrea's murder trickled down to them, Gabrielle knew they'd appear. They had too much to lose not to try to cover their tracks somehow. Now that Tucker had been proven innocent, he had sudden credibility, and his story would be worth quite a bit to the press.

But Crumb and Hansen came sooner than she'd expected. And as luck would have it, they arrived while Tucker was gone. He'd gotten up early and taken Allie and Landon to his parents' house. Dee was going to baby-sit while he met with Robert, his old partner, about managing some of his real-estate projects. From what Robert had said, he was still doing quite well and could use the help. Tucker was hoping to arrange something with a good salary until he could get back into the investment side of the business. He could sue Tom for whatever money he had left, of course, but Gabrielle agreed there was probably little point. Tom now had a wife, who might or might not be entitled to a share of everything, depending on how the courts viewed the situation, and the two of them had spent most of Tucker's money, anyway. They had a huge mortgage on their house and very little equity. It would probably go back to the bank through foreclosure within the year, and what Tom hadn't spent he would need for attorney's fees.

Gabrielle doubted Tucker would sue his brother even if there'd been a chance of recovering anything, and she didn't blame him. They could make it without the leftovers of Tucker's former life. They'd start over together and build from there.

She just wished they could start right away. But she'd stayed behind in Florence because she was still finishing up her last two weeks at the prison. She'd given her notice as soon as she knew Tucker would be part of her life. He'd wanted her to simply walk out— he couldn't tolerate any thought of the prison, let alone the fact that she was working there. Only she respected the Deputy Warden at Rynning Unit too much to leave without giving him proper notice, especially when she knew how desperately they needed good corrections officers.

She had just seven shifts left. Then she and Tucker and the kids were planning to move into a rental house in Tempe or Mesa, somewhere close to his parents and David and Lindy, until they could afford to purchase a home of their own. There, Landon would start school. He'd be a couple of weeks behind the other kids, but Gabrielle felt confident she could tutor him if he needed help catching up. He was such a bright boy and so happy to have his father back in his life, she thought he'd do just fine.

Having changed out of her uniform into a pair of shorts and a scoop-neck T-shirt, Gabrielle was thumbing through a new cookbook she'd bought the day before when the doorbell sounded. She wanted to make something special for dinner, something Landon would like as much as Tucker, and was hoping Tucker and the kids would be home soon. She missed them already.

"Hello, Warden Crumb, Sergeant Hansen," she said when she opened the door to see them standing on her stoop.

It was September now, but the weather was still hot. A bead of sweat ran down Hansen's ruddy face. The warden looked perfectly comfortable, even in his suit. She wondered if Crumb ever perspired.

"Do you have a minute, Officer Hadley?" Crumb asked.

"Of course." She held the door wide and gestured them both inside. "Would you like to sit down?"

They were silent as they passed her, eventually settling into the same seats they'd taken the last time. It would have been polite for Gabrielle to offer them something to drink, but she didn't want them to stay that long. After the way they'd treated Tucker, after the things Hansen had said to her, she could barely tolerate having them in the house. But she thought it was time they understood how completely the situation had reversed itself.

"What can I do for you?" she asked, letting them take the lead.

"We just stopped by to see if you'd heard the news," the warden said.

"The news?"

"They've called off the search for Randall Tucker. Apparently the police have uncovered some evidence that proves his brother's the person who killed Andrea Tucker. Just this morning, a judge signed the order making him a free man."

"I heard. They picked up his brother at the airport late last night, didn't they?" Gabrielle knew they had, because he'd called his parents right after he was arrested. The Tuckers had little sympathy for him, however. They'd been staunch supporters of Randall, but only because they believed he was innocent. To them, right was right and wrong was wrong, and anyone who crossed the line deserved to be punished. Even their son.

"I think so," the warden said. For the first time since she'd known him, she sensed his confidence wavering. "How did you hear that?"

"I have a friend who was involved with the whole thing."

"Oh."

They probably assumed her friend was someone on the police force. She wondered what they'd say if they knew Tucker was living in her house, that she was going to become Mrs. Randall Tucker in just a few weeks. "But surely you didn't come out on such a hot afternoon just to tell me that."

Crumb stared down at the floor and then at her. "Not exactly. Deputy Warden Wiseman said you gave him your notice."

"I did."

"Before you leave the prison, we wanted to make sure we've cleared up any past misunderstandings." He leaned forward and loosely clasped his hands between his knees. "Tucker was convicted through no fault of ours, of course, but the backlash from having imprisoned an innocent man can be pretty great. Depending on what he tells the press and others about his stay with us, this turn of events could rock the whole institution. I wouldn't want any innocent people to lose their jobs." His smile reminded her of an overeager salesman. "I'm sure you don't, either."

"No, I wouldn't want that," she said. "But I don't remember any misunderstandings, Warden Crumb."

He waved a hand. "You know, all that stuff about Tucker and the fighting."

"Are you referring to the time the Border Brothers attacked him, and Sergeant Hansen and the others refused to intervene? Is that what you're talking about?"

Hansen blanched and glanced nervously at Crumb. "Like I've told you before, you've got it all wrong, Officer Hadley. I was just about to break up the fight when you jumped in with your baton." Hansen seemed tractable and definitely scared. He certainly wasn't the same man who'd threatened her job the day she broke up the fight or sat outside her house in the rain or promised a fitting retribution for Tucker's escape.

"I'm sorry but I don't remember it that way, Sergeant Hansen," she said. "Neither does Tucker, I'm sure."

"That's just it," the warden said, his smile growing strained. "Tucker will probably try to stir up trouble, but if we all stick together, I'm sure we can quell any sensational reports of mistreatment and—"

"The only person I'm sticking with, on this or anything else, is my husband," Gabrielle interrupted.

A startled silence fell over the room. "Your husband?" Hansen echoed. "Did you and David get back together?"

Gabrielle heard a car pull up outside and stood to look through the window. Sure enough, Tucker was home. She could see Landon getting out of the back seat of her Honda, which they'd taken because it had air-conditioning. Tucker was helping Allie out of her car seat, but she knew he'd spotted the warden's van when he scowled in that direction. "No, but he's home now. You can meet him, if you like."

Crumb and Hansen rose expectantly. Gabrielle moved to open the door, but Tucker came in before she could reach it. As he stood just inside the doorway, Hansen's jaw tightened and Crumb's eyes grew wide.

"Hi, honey. Looks like we have company." Tucker sat Allie on the floor and strode over to kiss her.

"Warden Crumb and Sergeant Hansen are here to see what you're planning to tell the press about your stay in their prison," she said, wrapping her arms around his waist and leaning against him.

She'd thought Warden Crumb never perspired, but he was sweating now. She watched him mop a handkerchief across his damp brow.

"That's easy," Tucker said. "I'm going to tell the truth. I know that's probably a novel concept, especially to Sergeant Hansen, but there it is."

Landon came barreling in before anyone could respond. "Grandma said she'd buy me and Allie a guinea pig if it's okay with you," he cried the moment he saw Gabrielle. He pulled up short when he realized they weren't alone. "Who are these guys?"

"These men work at the prison," Gabrielle said. "But something tells me they won't be there much longer."

"You think you're pretty smart, don't you?" Hansen said, his solicitous facade instantly crumbling. "But I was on to you all along. I knew you two had something going. I knew you were helping him."

"What I remember," Gabrielle said, "is you threatening my job and harassing me. I remember you specifically telling me that a member of the 'fairer sex' had reason to worry in your prison unless she minded her own business.''

Crumb looked as though he wanted to choke Hansen, but Gabrielle felt no sympathy for him. He'd stood behind his nephew. Instead of rooting out the problem, he'd tried to cover it up. "Let's go," he said. "There's nothing more we can do here."

"I hope you two are finally happy," Hansen muttered sarcastically as they left.

Gabrielle smiled up at Tucker. "I think we're going to be," she said. "I definitely think we're going to be."

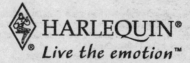

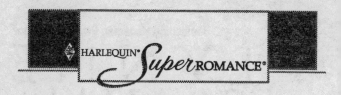
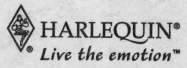